Praise for *The Over*

"Peter Beagle deserves a seat at the table with the great masters of fantasy. If you had any doubts, *The Overneath* will dispel them."
—Christopher Moore, author of *Lamb* and *The Serpent of Venice*

"These stories open a wider window on the work of a master storyteller. We all have something to learn—about writing, about humanity, about hope—from Peter Beagle."
—Seanan McGuire author of *Rosemary and Rue*

"*The Overneath* is Beagle at his very best."
—Brian Evenson, author of *Martyr*

★"Beagle's latest collection of short stories includes 13 fantasy gems and features many previously uncollected and never-before-published works. Highlights include a couple of stories about one of Beagle's most beloved characters, Schmendrick the Magician from his iconic novel *The Last Unicorn* (1968). A coming-of-age tale of sorts, 'The Green-Eyed Boy' offers a glimpse into the bumbling magician's inauspicious beginnings, when the wizard Nikos took him in as an apprentice. Nikos sees potential in the shy boy but soon realizes his student's unparalleled ineptitude could have deadly consequences. In the never-before-published 'Schmendrick Alone,' the magician, newly released from his service to Nikos, attempts to heroically defend a young woman from an unwanted suitor—with disastrous results. 'My Son Heydari and the Karkadann' is another remarkable story, chronicling a young Persian man's attempt to nurse a dangerous mythological beast back to health; as is 'Kaskia,' a poignant love story about a lonely man who buys a strange laptop that allows him to video chat with a beautiful alien. 'The Queen Who Could Not Walk' is set in a world where the rulers must, at some point in their reign, exchange their bejeweled crowns for a beggar's bowl and live out their lives in poverty. The story follows a crippled queen-turned-beggar who has her life saved by the unlikeliest of people. Two aspects of this collection stand out: the impressive diversity of stories (from interdimensional trips with novelist Avram Davidson in 'The Way It Works Out and All' to the supernatural horrors in a fish tank in 'The Very Nasty Aquarium') and the philosophical and thematic profundity of each story. Even in the most whimsical of tales, there are kernels of wisdom to be found. A masterful collection from a short story master—a must-read for Beagle fans."

—*Kirkus*, starred review

"Peter S. Beagle is writing some of the most exciting short form fantasy today."

—Jo Walton, author of *Among Others* and the Thessaly series

"What is truly beautiful about this book is that Beagle's writing lets you believe, if only for a little while, that magic, mythos and wonder are real. As you enter his world you become part of it and for that time the impossible is achievable."

—*Artistic Bent*

"Peter S. Beagle just has an incredible skill for putting together both short and full length stories. I have been in love with *The Last Unicorn* my whole life and I continue to adore every single thing Peter writes. *The Overneath* is no different. A fantasy lover's heaven from start to finish."

—*Life Has a Funny Way of Sneaking Up on You*

Praise for Peter S. Beagle

"One of my favorite writers."
—Madeleine L'Engle, author of *A Wrinkle in Time*

"Peter S. Beagle illuminates with his own particular magic such commonplace matters as ghosts, unicorns, and werewolves. For years a loving readership has consulted him as an expert on those hearts' reasons that reason does not know."
—Ursula K. Le Guin, author of *A Wizard of Earthsea* and *The Left Hand of Darkness*

"The only contemporary to remind one of Tolkien."
—*Booklist*

"Peter S. Beagle is (in no particular order) a wonderful writer, a fine human being, and a bandit prince out to steal readers' hearts."
—Tad Williams, author of *Tailchaser's Song*

"It's a fully rounded region, this other world of Peter Beagle's imagination."
—*Kirkus*

"[Beagle] has been compared, not unreasonably, with Lewis Carroll and J. R. R. Tolkien, but he stands squarely and triumphantly on his own feet."
—*Saturday Review*

Also By Peter S. Beagle

Fiction
A Fine and Private Place (1960)
The Last Unicorn (1968)
Lila the Werewolf (1969)
The Folk of the Air (1986)
The Innkeeper's Song (1993)
The Unicorn Sonata (1996)
Tamsin (1999)
A Dance for Emilia (2000)
The Last Unicorn: The Lost Version (2007)
Strange Roads (with Lisa Snellings Clark, 2008)
Return (2010)
Summerlong (2016)
In Calabria (2017)

Short story collections
Giant Bones (1997)
The Rhinoceros Who Quoted Nietzsche and Other Odd Acquaintances (1997)
The Line Between (2006)
Your Friendly Neighborhood Magician: Songs and Early Poems (2006)
We Never Talk About My Brother (2009)
Mirror Kingdoms: The Best of Peter S. Beagle (2010)
Sleight of Hand (2011)

Nonfiction
I See By My Outfit: Cross-Country by Scooter, an Adventure (1965)
The California Feeling (with Michael Bry, 1969)
The Lady and Her Tiger (with Pat Derby, 1976)
The Garden of Earthly Delights (1982)
In the Presence of Elephants (1995)

As editor
Peter S. Beagle's Immortal Unicorn (with Janet Berliner, 1995)
The Secret History of Fantasy (2010)
The Urban Fantasy Anthology (with Joe R. Lansdale, 2011)
The New Voices of Fantasy (with Jacob Weisman, 2017)

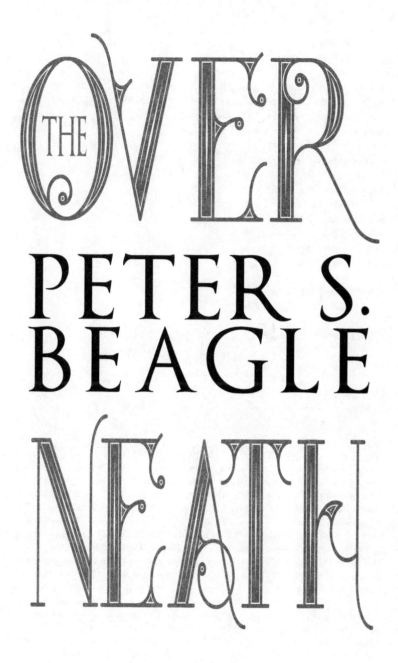

THE OVER

PETER S. BEAGLE

NEATH

TACHYON | SAN FRANCISCO

Interior and cover design by Elizabeth Story

Tachyon Publications LLC
1459 18th Street #139
San Francisco, CA 94107
415.285.5615
www.tachyonpublications.com
tachyon@tachyonpublications.com

Series Editor: Jacob Weisman
Project Editor: Rachel Fagundes

ISBN 13: 978-1-61696-269-2

Printed in the United States by Worzalla

First Edition: 2017
9 8 7 6 5 4 3 2 1

"The Green-Eyed Boy" © 2016 by Peter S. Beagle. First appeared in *The Magazine of Fantasy & Science Fiction*, September–October 2016. | "The Story of Kao Yu" © 2016 by Peter S. Beagle. First appearance in print. Originally published as a *Tor.com* Kindle Original. | "My Son Heydari and the Karkadann" © 2017 by Peter S. Beagle. First appearance in print. Originally published as a Humble Bundle e-book exclusive, 3/8/17. | "The Queen Who Could Not Walk" © 2013 by Peter S. Beagle. First appeared in *Weird Tales*, Summer 2013. | "Trinity County, CA : You'll Want to Come Again and We'll Be Glad to See You!" © 2001 by Peter S. Beagle. First appeared in *Orson Scott Card's Intergalactic Medicine Show* #18, August 2010. | "The Way It Works Out and All" © 2011 by Peter S. Beagle. First appeared in *The Magazine of Fantasy & Science Fiction*, July–August 2011. | "Kaskia" © 2010 by Peter S. Beagle. First appeared in *Songs of Love and Death: Tales of Star-Crossed Love*, edited by Gardner Dozois and George R. R. Martin (Simon & Schuster: New York). | "Schmendrick Alone" © 2017 by Peter S. Beagle. First publication. | "Great-Grandmother in the Cellar" © 2012 by Peter S. Beagle. First appeared in *Under My Hat: Tales from the Cauldron*, edited by Jonathan Strahan (Random House: New York). | "Underbridge" © 2011 by Peter S. Beagle. First appeared in *Naked City: Tales of Urban Fantasy*, edited by Ellen Datlow (St. Martin's Press: New York). | "The Very Nasty Aquarium" © 2016 by Peter S. Beagle. First publication. | "Music, When Soft Voices Die" © 2011 by Peter S. Beagle. First appeared in *Ghosts by Gaslight*, edited by Jack Dann and Nick Gevers (HarperCollins: New York). | "Olfert Dapper's Day" © First appeared in *The Magazine of Fantasy & Science Fiction*, March–April 2016.

For Jake,
Phil,
And Marty,

The Gunhill Road Geezer Gang,

Still here,
Still here.

TABLE OF CONTENTS

THE GREEN-EYED BOY

Schmendrick the Magician—"last of the red-hot swamis"—is generally considered the most beloved character in all of my fiction. (My own soft spot is reserved for Lalkhamsinkhamsolal, the heroine of The Innkeeper's Song, but that's a personal matter . . .) Over some fifty years, I've been asked so often to provide him with a pre–Last Unicorn history that I realized that I knew nothing about his background, except that he had studied with the great wizard Nikos (yes, definitely named for Kazantzakis!), who both blessed and cursed Schmendrick with immortality, decreeing that he must "travel the world round, eternally incompetent, until such time as you come to your full power and know who you are. Don't thank me—I tremble at your doom." This story is told from Nikos's point of view, recounting his first encounter with a 12-year-old Schmendrick, utterly out of place in his birth family—except for a sympathetic sister-in-law— and perhaps even under the tutelage of a master, however kindly. This, then, is the true beginning of the green-eyed boy's long, long journey to his destiny.

❈

No, his father brought him to me; that story about him wandering out of the woods to my door is just that—a foolish tale that no mere fact seems capable of putting to rest. He came draggling behind the old man: a tall, extremely thin boy with a perfectly unremarkable face surrounding a remarkable nose—someone else's nose, it looked like, borrowed for the occasion—and the most striking pair of green eyes I'd ever seen. Not your shifty, undependable run-of-the-mill blue-green or gray-green: this pair were green as the deep spring forests, green as the icy, shallow tides of the northern land where I was born. I don't know where he got them—though I make my own guesses—but no one in his family ever had eyes like those. I know, because I asked him.

"You're Nikos?" the father asked me straightaway. Not a *by your leave*, not a *give you good day*; no smallest attempt at courtesy or good manners. It was a gruff voice, sounding unused, as though without practice at casual conversation—or, indeed, any sort of talking, come to that. "Nikos the wizard?"

"That is my name," I answered him. It isn't, but it's the one I've employed so long that it's an effort to remember my real name. I've known some wizards actually to cast spells of forgetfulness on themselves in order to achieve the same effect. "What may I do for you, good man?"

"Prentice." He reached back without looking, grabbed a handful of the boy and dragged him forward. "Useless for my trade—I'm a cooper—useless for any of his uncles', so finally figured he might as well go for a wizard. Nothing left after that but a highwayman, and the booby'd never even learn to yell, '*Stand and deliver!*' What's your prentice fee, sir? Busy man."

All this while, the boy hadn't said a word, nor ever looked directly at me. Nor at his father, for that matter, nor at his shoes. He stood round-shouldered, slouching, those green eyes very far away, seemingly fixed on something no one else could see. Lord knows, that stare may just as easily—and more often— be the mark of a simpleton, a natural . . . but there's something else it can signify, and it roused the curiosity that has so often been my bane. I said, "What are you called, boy?"

He flushed, hesitated, mumbled—looked sideways at his father, as though he was well in the habit of being interrupted, having his sentences finished for him. He was not disappointed: his father broke in to growl the name, which was that of an ancient hero, best remembered for slaying a many-headed sea monster, but dying himself in the battle. "Wife gave him that one. I warned her—told her it'd be like naming a turnspit dog Pegasus—but did she listen? You call him whatever you like."

"Sir, I very rarely accept *students*," I stressed the last word, which I have always preferred to *prentice*. I said, "Magic is something that can be taught, yes, but I am not a magician. I am a wizard, and being a wizard is *not* something that can be taught. Do you understand the difference?"

I was *not* speaking to the father at that moment, but to the son, and to the green eyes that lifted to meet mine for the first time. *Who are you?* I thought, *who lives behind that look of vacant desperation?* and in that moment I determined to receive him as a student, as much as a challenge to myself as for any vision of his potential gifts. *Who is in there?*

The father left as soon as we had come to an agreement, genuinely annoyed that I had shown no interest in the fee he had offered, essentially for taking the boy off his hands. "But then you lose nothing by sending him home!" I swore to him—had I not been a wizard, he would have had me put it in writing—that I would not visit his son on him before the period of his indenture was expired; and with that he had to be content. He left, not with an embrace, however rough, of my novice, but with a cuff on the side of his head and a warning to "behave and work hard, or the magician'll turn you into something awful. Your mam sends love."

After he was gone, the boy and I stood looking at each other for what I remember as perhaps a month and a half, though it obviously could not have been nearly that long. I said, "I know your name now, but that was not what I asked you for. What are you called?"

"Schmendrick," came the answer, clearly and bitterly now. "Everyone calls me Schmendrick."

"That is not a name," I said. I was genuinely shocked, which does not happen often. "That is a word, a very old one. Do you know what it means?"

"The boy who is sent to do a man's job." The green eyes were focused on me now, seeing me as another in a long line of mockers and persecutors. "The person utterly out of his depth, far beyond his pitiful capacities." He did not raise his voice, but the self-contempt in his tone rattled my elderly bones. "Call me Schmendrick, master. I might not answer to another."

And so we began.

Yes, I will wait while you set down what I have told you thus far. I am interested in your desire to write of his early years, and—I must tell you—both annoyed and amused that you should have sought me out. No wizard ever truly retires; but with time, we go deeper into the woods, as you might say, and many things matter less to us than they did. Yet I remain fond of that strange boy, and I will tell you what I can. It should be known, I suppose.

All I did, that first day, and for several days thereafter, was to feed him. You tell me that he is still lean today; you should have seen him then. I cannot say fairly whether his parents starved him—all I know is that he went through my supplies like a forest fire. Past a certain age—as I certainly was then—wizards tend to become less and less interested in what most people would call food, but what would you? The boy had trouble thinking about anything *but* food, and I was forced to make various arrangements with my farmer neighbors. What? Yes, of course I could have whistled up this or that meal for him out of the ethereal, but he would have wakened hungry that same night, I promise you. In a way, that by itself was his first lesson: that magic never yet fed anyone properly. That is not what magic is for.

"I took you in because I smelled power around you," I told him, "the way one smells lightning before a storm. Power can neither be taught nor counterfeited, but it means absolutely nothing without skill, patient training, and humility—and of these, the greatest by far is humility. Are you ready to work with me to discover such magic as you may—or may not—have within you? Because otherwise you may as well go home. I am sure you may yet overtake your father on the road."

The look that came into those green eyes at that moment was a wonder to see. He shook his head, and though he hardly spoke at all during those early days, he said, "I will stay. I will do my best for you."

"No," I said. "Not for me—I am too old to be either pleased or offended by such things. And not for your father, either, but for yourself. Give yourself that much, young . . . Schmendrick. Give yourself that much."

I have never had a student who worked as hard as that scrawny, green-eyed boy. Nor have I ever, to this day, known any young wizard as spectacularly incompetent as he. Oh, he has never made a secret of it—I know that—but unless you were present at the time, you can have no notion . . . goodness, even he rarely speaks of that moment when, attempting once more to float a rusty old horseshoe in the air, there was suddenly an entire *horse*, bellowing in panic, coming straight at my head! I made the poor thing vanish, certainly; but that was a good deal easier than calming Schmendrick, assuring him that both I and the horse were undamaged, and then persuading him that this was actually a good sign, an indication of his born, bone-deep connection to the world beyond the world we know—the world on the other side of the mirror. Oh, I do remember his terror, both of his failings . . . and of his skills.

"The whole secret of magic," I told him over and over, "is that nothing is *fixed*, nothing is forever; that *everything*, from the house I built, to that willow tree I planted, to that mountain you can see from my front door . . . all of it yearns to be something else. This is the true fluid of the world—as for the universe, I cannot honestly say, though I have my suspicions. But here, where you and I are, a wizard is merely one with a certain gift for tapping into those wordless cellular desires of a kitchen table to be a meadow. Do you see, boy—Schmendrick? Do you see?"

"Yes," he said, very softly. "Yes, Master Nikos. I do."

And he *did* see, that's the point I'm making. It's not that he didn't grasp what I was trying to teach him—I never had another student who could go as straight and swiftly to the heart of my lesson as he; there was no comparison. The problem was the connection—or lack of it—between his understanding and his ability. Magic isn't all gestures and spells, fiery powders, chanted words, bargains with unpleasant beings . . . but there's that in it too, and that's where my poor Schmendrick almost invariably lost his way. Right gesture, scrambled spell . . . perfect pronunciation of the wrong words . . . summoning of demon, flawless—dismissal of demon, not so good. And then there was that embarrassing business with the mermaids . . . but that was as much my fault as the boy's. I thank God, and a few other people, every night, remembering that one.

The power itself was never in question; but there comes a moment when a responsible wizard has to consider the danger of having such wild, uncontrollable power loose in the world in the hands of a young man with family problems. Schmendrick, legendary as he is today, won't remember me attending the annual conventions of the Council of Mages while he was with me—because I didn't go. I didn't dare. The least of the wizards present at that gathering would have taken one look at him, or even at me alone, and . . . and—I don't know what. Recognized what he was, and how untrainable he was, and ordered him *abolished*, as we say? It could have happened. I won't say that the great mages are cruel, or unreasonable, but realistic? Yes, you could definitely pronounce them *realistic*. Besides, my dues to the Council were not in the best shape—as they are not today, thinking about it—and I did think it best to take no chances on having the subject come up at one festive dinner or another. Legendary I may officially be now, but I wasn't then, and you can't be too careful.

Mind you, the boy was a delight to have around the house, whatever you may have heard. Yes, he did ask me any number of times why I wouldn't simply snap my fingers and have the dishes wash themselves, the carpets shake themselves out and present themselves meekly for beating. But I explained to him, any number of times, that magic is not *permission*. That everything in this world *costs*, most especially including the gift residing somewhere in between his liver and lights and his soul. That part, alas, he failed to comprehend until it was—for a single moment—too late.

Our daily routine, during the time he lived with me, was as ordinary and matter-of-fact as any shepherd's or beekeeper's. Schmendrick rose early, at five or so, to do such minimal chores as I needed done, while I woke an hour or so afterward to tend to breakfast. As I've said, cooking is its own particular magic, and as high as my green-eyed boy may have risen, I'll wager that he still can't produce a morning meal whose aroma would lure a corpse from its own wake. Some of us can do it; some of us might just as well get busy rescuing princesses from dire fortresses. Two different things.

After breakfast, lessons would begin. Language first: a wizard can never know too many languages, even—especially—if no one in the world speaks them anymore. Schmendrick turned out to have a natural ear for accents, and an easy sense that language is not simply made up of words, and that spells and enchantments derive a great deal of their power from well-placed silences. I also schooled him rigorously in the history of every charm he learned, as well as every possible variant of that charm; and I gave him the run of my library and my *grimoire*, as I have done with no one else, before or since. Most nights, he was still reading—and writing, and practicing—when I went to bed.

And yet . . . and yet . . . for all his application, all his earnest, patient, uncomplaining study, always that missed connection. He himself makes a joke of it today, speaking of his years when happiness was a successful card trick, pride a magical escape from ropes or chains that a child could have managed. But he was performing these pitiful tricks for me—perhaps humiliated more when he succeeded than when he failed—and it is hard to say which of us was the most embarrassed. I know—I would have known even if he had not told me—that he woke each day certain that it would be the one on which I made a gracious, kindly little speech and sent him home. And I did have my moments, more than he knows . . .

There was, for instance, the awkward business with my familiar weasels. Not all wizards have familiars—though all witches do, of necessity—but my pair, Helen and Penelope, have been good companions to me for much of my life, as they are still. Schmendrick was quite fond of them himself, and it was surely out of kindness and consideration that he determined to provide my two sister spinsters with a virile young mate. The creature was, of course, a soulless shadow—I teach no one to create life, or near-life, and almost never do it myself—but it was substantial enough to cause all manner of discord between my normally devoted friends. They racketed all over the house day and night, snapping and clawing at each other, in pursuit of that lustful phantom. It was a week before I was able to exorcise the thing; longer until Helen and Penelope returned to anything like their normal relationship. I am afraid that I was somewhat short with the boy for some days afterward.

But that was all a minor annoyance, compared with the disaster—there really is no other word for it—of the Bloody Whacking Great Blizzard, as my neighbors still call it, all these years later. Snow is rare in this part of the country, and nobody regrets it except children pining for sleds and snowmen. And, to be fair, Schmendrick was never attempting to bring snow, but only practicing an exercise I had given him, one intended to clear a field behind my house of rocks and tree stumps—a chore I had been putting off for a good year. It is not a particularly difficult or complex charm, or I would never have left such a neophyte alone with it; but poor Schmendrick was struggling merely to gain the spell's attention—magic is always a two-way exchange—and he may have unconsciously altered the pitch of his voice, or possibly said a dangerous word or two that he may have heard me utter when a spell of mine is making difficulties. I have aggravating, frustrating days too; but it is different when *I* use those words. Though no less dangerous.

Whatever he said, or didn't say, is unimportant; what matters is the immediate result. Out of a clear, windless autumn sky, snow began to fall.

They were big, wet flakes, the kind that stick, and pile up, and last. They kept falling for eight days, never once halting. I did what I could to keep my neighbors' fields and pastures from freezing, their livestock from being buried, and the roofs of their homes and barns from collapsing under the weight of so much snow. But weather is lord even of the most powerful wizards: we may manage to direct a storm from *here* to *there*, or even, under the right conditions, to create one—briefly—but none of us ever imagines that we control it. The greatest wizards are the greatest realists, always.

When the snow finally stopped, leaving land and people alike white and silent, speaking in pale whispers, Schmendrick, saying nothing of his decision, packed his few belongings, petted Helen and Penelope farewell, and then came to me to bid me goodbye as well. "I thank you more than I can say for all your benevolence and patience," he told me, his gaze steady, his voice trembling only slightly. "My father would tell you it was more than I deserve, and he would have been quite right. But however much I may have cost you in time and wasted effort, I am grateful. I will never forget you."

I knew better than to protest, or to order him to stay. I asked, "Where are you bound, then? Not home, surely."

Schmendrick actually smiled a little. "No, I think not. I had thought of making for the coast and signing aboard a fishing smack, or a lugger. Perhaps I am meant to be a sailor, after all."

"Mmm," I said. "There are sailors, you know, who can prison the winds in patterns of knotted string, like cat's-cradles, and free them as necessary. They are much in demand aboard ship, such men."

The green eyes widened. "Really? Could you teach me such a skill?"

I shrugged. "Not while you are on the road, pack on your back and a song on your lips. I have my limits."

I doubt Schmendrick even noticed that he had set his pack down. He said, "Perhaps I could learn at least that much. I have certainly proved that I am no fit pupil for a master like yourself, but *that* trick, if I put forth a great effort—"

"It is not a trick," I said sharply. "Nothing I teach is a *trick*—perhaps it is your failure to understand that that causes you to fail in everything else. Go, put your things away, and see what is left of yesterday's potato stew. And remember, next time I will simply let you leave. Go, boy!"

He never spoke of leaving again. Even when he did part from me, in the end, we spoke as though we would be seeing each other the next day. As for tying up the four winds in a bit of string, he learned that in good time. I have never heard that he has ever used the skill, but I am sure that he still could if he wanted to.

The snow took a long time melting, and I saw no reason to hurry it along. We spent much of that fall and winter, he and I, sitting face to face, knee to knee, in my small kitchen and smaller study, going over and over, not merely the technique of this or that spell, but its history, its philosophy, its reason for existing at all. "Spells do not come into being merely to alter reality," I repeated constantly. "Spells have a relationship with reality, and if you fail to understand this, your spells will fail you in turn, generally when you need them most. Pay attention!"

Ridiculous, and unfair, of me to keep saying that, because Schmendrick *always* paid attention. Wake him in the middle of the night, and he could have recited the day's lessons word for word—not parrot-fashion, either, but with all the understanding any teacher could have desired. *But . . .*

. . . but ask him to *perform* the spell in question, so that both act and result settled properly into place, lining up together like the pins and cylinder of a lock, and he was a doomed man, a lost soul. The situation was worsened by that maddeningly real—if wild—talent of his, which would at times enable him to carry off a worthless parlor trick with something like flair, and at other times turn on him cruelly and leave him looking like the vacant fool his father took him for. And now and then, to my shame, so did I.

Neither his father nor his mother ever came to visit him while he was with me. Nor did either of his two brothers, who were being trained to take over the cooperage and had no more time for their strange, green-eyed brother than they had ever had. Only the younger one's wife, a small, dark woman whose name was Sardana, came unannounced one wintry afternoon, to learn whether he was happy and being treated well. It was brave of her, for she was plainly terrified of me; but I gave her tea and biscuits, and Helen and Penelope sat up on her lap and begged politely for crumbs, and in time she grew somewhat less fearful. A nice girl, with a tender air.

"He isn't like the rest of them," she whispered. "He isn't like anybody."

"A lonely place, that," I said. "Has he always not been like anybody?"

"As long as I have known him—since I came over the mountain to marry his brother Patros. I was a stranger, and far from home, and he was the one who was good to me." She leaned her head into her hands, studying me thoughtfully. "Do you think Schmendrick could ever become a great wizard, like you?"

I sighed; it had been a hard day, and Schmendrick's anxious clumsiness particularly tiring and depressing. "To tell you the truth, Sardana, I don't know. There is magic in your brother-in-law somewhere, and there are moments when I am certain I feel it ready and eager to leap up into his hands, to do with as he will. But then it is gone again, underground, not likely to surface again for weeks at a time. Often I feel that I am doing him no kindness by pushing him as I am, to teach it—this thing in him—to come out into the light without fear. But perhaps it knows what is best, for both itself and him; perhaps it serves him better than I ever can. In that case, the best thing I can do for him—"

But Sardana was shaking her head firmly. She said, "You must give him the chance. You must give him every chance, and then one beyond it. No matter what he says, there is nothing he wants more than to be what you are. He cannot *not* be a wizard, do you understand, Mr. Nikos? As I know it was for you, so it must be true for him—it *must*." She leaned close to me, her clasped hands squeezing each other white. "Please, do you understand me?"

Her concern for Schmendrick touched me; her passion for his fulfillment almost overwhelmed me. I looked into her eyes and said only, "Why?"

She understood what I was asking. She flushed and looked down, shaking her head in a different way now. "No, no, it is nothing like that, as sweet as he is. My marriage to his brother was a matter of business, yes, on both sides, but we both keep our word. But Schmendrick . . . Schmendrick is alone in the world, and you are all he has, truly. You *must* not abandon him— you must not let him abandon himself. Please, Mr. Nikos!"

I nodded and patted her hand—what else was there to do? She would have made her farewells then and started for home; but it being already twilight, I urged her to stay for dinner and the night. She agreed, after some hesitation, and I sent her to inform Schmendrick that he was excused his evening chores, while I set about cooking, directing Helen and Penelope to help me prepare the meal. As I have said, no one was ever fed by magic—not properly—but weasels have a natural knack for presentation, and those two could always be relied on to set a beautiful table. It was a splendid feast, if I do say so myself.

As I recall, I carried most of the conversation during that dinner, Sardana still being shy with me, and Schmendrick . . . Schmendrick was far too occupied stealing glances at his sister-in-law. For all her loving behavior toward him, there was a difference between his attitude and hers, and I could only hope that he understood the difference as well as she seemed to. I encouraged him to show off for her by clearing away the dishes magically: a bit risky, but not profoundly so, since he usually managed the spell four out of five times, as he did now. Sardana was much impressed.

She went to bed early, being fatigued—I have guest rooms as I need them—and I fully expected Schmendrick to excuse himself and follow after to sleep across her doorsill. But instead he pursued me into the anarchy I persist in calling my study, saying, "She is so *good*. Don't you think she is *good*?"

"Indeed," I answered him dryly, not wishing to add fuel to his infatuation. "Unquestionably. Now, if you'll excuse me." But the boy would not be dismissed so easily.

"I want to do something for her," he announced. "She will be gone from here tomorrow, and who knows whether I will ever see her again? Please, advise me, I beg you—what might I do, if I were a real wizard, to ensure that she sleeps sweetly and wakes joyously? I thought of filling her room with flowers, or having a dozen nightingales perch at her window, but I don't know. What do you think?"

The appeal in his eyes touched me more than the absurdity of his request irritated me, and I answered, "You think too grandly, as boys will. *One* flower, *one* singing bird, would be far more meaningful to any sensible person wishing for a good night's sleep than a room smothered with scent and deafening with birdsong. Besides, you are not courting her—she is *family*, married to your brother. One flower and a nice note will suffice. Go away now, I feel an important nap coming on," for, like most old people, wizards or no, I sleep in bits and pieces. "And you have two new spells to practice—three, if you bother me any further. Go."

Of course, it was all to impress Sardana—why else do boys do things? She had been so genuinely, sweetly astounded by his trick with the dishes; why not present her with an even grander performance to take home to her lout of a husband, as well as the rest of the family he had somehow been delivered to in error? Oh, I could follow his reasoning a day later, after the fact, as I could have my own—indeed, it *was* my own at one time, in all its pride and loneliness and idiocy. But it had been so long, you see.

And of all spells to choose, *that one.* I would never have taught it to him; he found it in an old journal, foolishly left unsecured. It involves, in a way, the summoning, not of a person in the body, nor exactly in the spirit; it is a love spell which calls directly upon the heart of the desired one, leaving reason, morality, responsibility, and shame completely—*completely*—out of the picture. And whatever centuries of poems, songs, and iconic representations of the heart may have told you, the heart of a human being is not always, or even that often, a compassionate, comforting, nurturing organ. The human heart disregards everything except what it wants, which is madness. People make jokes about the weakness and selfishness of the flesh, but I will bank on it every time against the heart's hungers, and I know what I am saying. The human heart is a killer.

Nine out of ten times, then? Ninety-nine out of a hundred? Fair enough.

I actually fell asleep in my study that night, snoring in my beloved ruin of an armchair—drooling, too, more than likely—with my feet up and a dusty, fragile copy of Rashadi's *The Lost Runes of Am-Nemil* on my lap. I was awakened by a scream overhead from the room I had invented for Sardana; it was followed almost immediately by thundering footsteps on the stairs, as Schmendrick went charging to her rescue. I started to growl something dismissive, something like, "Ah, what now, gods deliver us all?" but I broke it off in a hurry, because of what I heard, and what I smelled. In the end, there's nothing wiser than the nose for dealing with bad magic.

Sardana was crouched on the high bed in her nightgown, surrounded by uncounted perfect miniatures of Schmendrick, none of them more than six inches high. They were chattering and baying her name, tugging at the bedclothes and trying to climb up to her. I can't guess how many there were, but their eyes were wild and white, and their little teeth were bared, and I think they might well have devoured her if they could have reached her, eaten her up with love. They smelled of burning refuse.

Schmendrick was there with his back to the bed, flailing wildly, left and right, at his tiny mimics with Sardana's pillow, knocking them off the counterpane like bugs. But they were indeed as persistent as ants or roaches: they kept scrambling back to their feet and springing for a hand- or foothold on the quilt. There seemed to be hundreds of them, chanting and singing their worship; but Sardana was plainly terrified, and she screamed louder when any of the adoring homunculi appeared to be closing on her. I could see Schmendrick so clearly wanting to crush the lot of them underfoot—but they were *him*: him, with his hungers and dreams and desires so exposed, so piteously naked. Knowing even as little of him as I did then, I knew that he would fight the creatures all night to keep them away from Sardana, but that it was no more in him to kill even one of them than it had been in me, that one time, so many years before . . . And as furious as I was at him, I could have wept for what he was having to learn about himself. Not for the knowledge—that comes seeking us all, sooner or later—but for the *way*. But there . . . everything costs.

Everything costs. It took the rest of the night to get rid of those minikins, because, as I've indicated, they were part of Schmendrick, part of his heart, connected to him in the deepest way: to destroy them out of hand, as I could have done, might well mean damaging him beyond any healing. There is, fortunately, another course—learned at my own cost—but I do not set it down here, anymore than I would detail the workings of that spell itself. I will say only that it involved unmaking the creatures, one by one, and each one's distress was reflected in Schmendrick's face as it vanished like a soap bubble. By the last, Sardana had long since stopped screaming, and was doing her best to comfort him. A good girl, and doubtless wasted on his brother.

After she had gone—with embraces, apologies, and forgiveness all around—Schmendrick and I sat long over a meager breakfast, neither of us being really hungry, but neither nearly ready to set to work. There was no further point in my upbraiding him, nor in his even bothering to propose running away to sea. So we sat silently for a good while, until I finally asked, "For what it may be worth to you, do you know why I was able to reverse that spell?"

Schmendrick shook his head wearily. The green eyes looked faded with exhaustion, for once, almost gray. I said, "Because I employed it once myself. With very nearly the same result."

The eyes brightened somewhat, and he opened his mouth to

speak, but then did not. I went on, "Your attempt, idiotically dangerous to both yourself and Sardana as it was, was at least more honorable than what I did. You acted out of love, however wrongly, while I . . ." I paused, never having spoken of this to anyone, as many years as it had been. "It was hatred, in my case. I was almost as young as you are, and there was someone whom I felt had slighted me and wounded me badly, and well deserved the worst I could do to him. It shames me to this day, and I give thanks, even now, that it failed. As should you now—as will you again and again and again in the future. However naturally powerful you may be, however heights you may—or, I must warn you, may *not*—rise to, there will come a time when you, too, will be as desperately grateful for a disaster as for a grand success. And in your case, Schmendrick cooper's-son, this may be just as well."

He smiled at me then—set this down, because it must mean something, all these years later. It was the first time I had ever seen him smile like a young man with a full life of triumphs and calamities ahead of him; and I think it was the first time he had ever smiled at someone who understood him even a little. As much as I failed to understand him, to comprehend what on earth he was—what on earth he was *doing* on earth—still I remember that smile. Oh, I do indeed.

"Not *may*," he said quietly. "Others will learn what they must from glory—I from failure. Shall we begin work, my master?"

And that is all I know of his youth, and of him, right there. I stood up and put the coffee things away. "Yes," I said. "By all means, let us go to work."

THE STORY OF KAO YU

World folklore traditions basically present three varieties of unicorn: the classic Western version (immortal, unspeakably beautiful, vulnerable to deceitful virgins), the Asian unicorn (one of the Four Significant Animals, along with the Phoenix, the Tortoise, and the Dragon), and the Karkadann of the Arabian desert (powerful, pitilessly aggressive, and ugly as fried sin, according to Marco Polo). I've written at least one tale about each species; and while I can't choose a favorite, I have a special feeling for this one—perhaps because of the manner in which, to my own surprise, the story stubbornly insisted on telling itself. Standing out of the way and leaving the narrative to its own business doesn't always work, but when it does, it makes the author look so good, so professional . . .

�֍

There was a judge once in south China, a long time ago—during the reign of the Emperor Yao, it was—named Kao Yu. He was stern in his rulings, but fair and patient, and all but legendary for his honesty; it would have been a foolish criminal—or, yes, even a misguided Emperor—who attempted to bribe or coerce Kao Yu. Of early middle years, he was stocky and wide-shouldered, if a little plump, and the features of his face were strong and striking, even if his hairline was retreating just a trifle. He was respected by all, and feared by those who should have feared him—what more can one ask from a judge even now? But this is a story about a case in which he came to feel—rightly or no—that *he* was the one on trial.

Kao Yu's own wisdom and long experience generally governed his considerations in court, and his eventual rulings. But he was unique among all other judges in all of China in that when a problem came down to a matter of good versus evil—in a murder case, most often, or arson, or rape (which Kao Yu particularly despised)—he would often submit that problem to the judgment of a unicorn.

Now the *chi-lin*, the Chinese unicorn, is not only an altogether different species from the white European variety and the menacing Persian karkadann; it is also a different *matter* in its essence from either one. Apart from its singular physical appearance—indeed, there are scholars who claim that the *chi-lin* is no unicorn at all, but some sort of mystical dragon-horse, given its multicolored coat and the curious configuration of its head and body—this marvelous being is considered one of the Four Superior Animals of good omen, the others being the phoenix, the turtle, and the dragon itself. It is the rarest of the unicorns, appearing as a rule only during the reign of a benign Emperor enjoying the Mandate of Heaven. As a result, China has often gone generation after weary generation without so much as a glimpse of a *chi-lin*. This has contributed greatly to making the Chinese the patient, enduring people they are. It has also toppled thrones.

But in the days of Judge Kao Yu, at least one *chi-lin* was so far from being invisible as to appear in his court from time to time, to aid him in arriving at certain decisions. Why he should have been chosen—and at the very beginning of his career— he could never understand, for he was a deeply humble person, and would have regarded himself as blessed far beyond his deservings merely to have seen a *chi-lin* at a great distance. Yet so it was; and, further, the enchanted creature always seemed to know when he was facing a distinctly troublesome problem. It is well-known that the *chi-lin*, while wondrously gentle, will suffer no least dishonesty in its presence, and will instantly gore to death anyone whom it knows to be guilty. Judge Kao Yu, it must be said, always found himself a little nervous when the sudden smell of a golden summer meadow announced unmistakably the approach of the unicorn. As righteous a man as he was, even he had a certain difficulty in looking directly into the clear dark eyes of the *chi-lin*.

More than once—and the memories often returned to him on sleepless nights—he had pleaded with the criminal slouching before him, "If you have any hope of surviving this moment, do not lie to me. If you have some smallest vision of yet changing your life—even if you have lied with every breath from your first—tell the truth *now*." But few there—tragically few—were able to break the habit of a lifetime; and Judge Kao Yu would once again see the dragonlike horned head go down, and would lower his own head and close his eyes, praying this time not to hear the soft-footed rush across the courtroom, and the terrible scream of despair that followed. But he always did.

China being as huge and remarkably varied a land as it is, the judge who could afford to spend all his time in one town and one court was in those days very nearly as rare as a unicorn himself. Like every jurist of his acquaintance, Kao Yu traveled the country round a good half of the year: his usual route, beginning every spring, taking him through every village of any size from Guangzhou to Yinchuan. He traveled always with a retinue of three: his burly lieutenant, whose name was Wang Da; his secretary, Chou Qingshan; and Hu Longwei, who was both cook and porter—and, as such, treated with even more courtesy by Kao Yu than were his two other assistants. For he believed, judge or no, that the more lowly-placed the person, the more respect he or she deserved. This made him much-beloved in rather odd places, but not nearly as wealthy as he should have been.

The *chi-lin*, naturally, did not accompany him on his judicial rounds; rather, it appeared when it chose, most often when his puzzlement over a case was at its height, and his need of wisdom greatest. Nor did it ever stay long in the courtroom, but simply delivered its silent judgment and was gone. Chou Qingshan commented—Kao Yu's other two assistants, having more than once seen that judgment executed, were too frightened of the unicorn ever to speak of it at all—that its presence did frequently shorten the time spent on a hearing, since many criminals tended to be even more frightened than they, and often blurted out the truth at first sight. On the other hand, the judge just as often went months without a visit from the *chi-lin*, and was forced to depend entirely on his own wit and his own sensibilities. Which, as he told his assistants, was a very good thing indeed.

"Because if it were my choice," he said to them, "I would leave as many decisions as I was permitted at the feet of this creature out of Heaven, this being so much wiser than I. I would then be no sort of judge, but a mindless, unreasoning acolyte, and I would not like that in the least." After a thoughtful moment, he added, "Nor would the *chi-lin* like it either, I believe."

Now it happened that in a certain town, where he had been asked on very short notice to come miles out of his way to substitute for a judge who had fallen ill, Kao Yu was asked to pass judgment on an imprisoned pickpocket. The matter was so far below his rank—it would have been more suited for a novice in training—that even such an unusually egalitarian person as Kao Yu bridled at the effrontery of the request. But the judge he was replacing, one Fang An, happened to be an esteemed former teacher of his, so there was really nothing for it but that he take the case. Kao Yu shrugged in his robes, bowed, assented, arranged to remain another night at the wagoners' inn—the only lodging the town could offer—and made the best of things.

The pickpocket, as it turned out, was a young woman of surpassing, almost shocking beauty: small and slender, with eyes and hair and skin to match that of any court lady Kao Yu had ever seen, all belying her undeniable peasant origins. She moved with a gracious air that set him marveling, "What is she doing before me, in this grubby little courtroom? She ought to be on a tapestry in some noble's palace, and I . . . I should be in that tapestry as well, kneeling before *her*, rather than this other way around." And no such thought had ever passed through the mind of Judge Kao Yu in his entirely honorable and blameless life.

To the criminal in the dock he said, with remarkable gentleness that did not go unnoticed by either his lieutenant or his secretary, "Well, what have you to say for yourself, young woman? What is your name, and how have you managed to place yourself into such a disgraceful situation?" Wang Da thought he sounded much more like the girl's father than her judge.

With a shy bow—and a smile that set even the chill blood of the secretary Chou Qingshan racing—the pickpocket replied humbly, "Oh, most honorable lord, I am most often called Snow Ermine by the evil companions who lured me into this shameful life—but my true name is Lanying." She offered no family surname, and when Kao Yu requested it, she replied, "Lord, I have vowed never to speak that name again in this life, so low have I brought it by my contemptible actions." A single delicate tear spilled from the corner of her left eye and left its track down the side of her equally delicate nose.

Kao Yu, known for leaving his own courtroom in favor of another judge, if he suspected that he was being in some way charmed or cozened by a prisoner, was deeply touched by her manner and her obvious repentance. He cleared his suddenly hoarse throat and addressed her thus: "Lanying . . . ah, young woman . . . this being your first offense, I am of a mind to be lenient with you. I therefore sentence you, first, to return every single *liang* that you have been convicted of stealing from the following citizens—" and he nodded to Chou Qingshan to read off the list of the young pickpocket's victims. "In addition, you are hereby condemned—" he saw Lanying's graceful body stiffen—"to spend a full fortnight working with the nightsoil collectors of this community, so that those pretty hands may remember always that even the lowest, filthiest civic occupation is preferable to the dishonorable use in which they have hitherto been employed. Take her away."

To himself he sounded like a prating, pompous old man, but everyone else seemed suitably impressed. This included the girl Lanying, who bowed deeply in submission and turned to be led off by two sturdy officers of the court. She seemed so small and fragile between them that Kao Yu could not help ordering Chou Qingshan, in a louder voice than was strictly necessary, "Make that a week—a week, not a whole fortnight. Do you hear me?"

Chou Qingshan nodded and obeyed, his expression unchanged, his thoughts his own. But Lanying, walking between the two men, turned her head and responded to this commutation of her sentence with a smile that flew so straight to Judge Kao Yu's heart that he could only cough and look away, and be grateful to see her gone when he raised his eyes again.

To his assistants he said, "That is the last of my master Fang

An's cases, so let us dine and go to rest early, that we may be on our way at sunrise." And both Wang Da and Chou Qingshan agreed heartily with him, for each had seen how stricken he had been by a thief's beauty and charm; and each felt that the sooner he was away from this wretched little town, the better for all of them. Indeed, neither Kao Yu's lieutenant nor his secretary slept well that night, for each had the same thought: "He is a man who has been much alone—he will dream of her tonight, and there will be nothing we can do about that." And in this they were entirely correct.

For Kao Yu did indeed dream of Lanying the pickpocket, not only that night, but for many nights thereafter, to the point where, even to his cook Hu Longwei, who was old enough to notice only what he was ordered to notice, he appeared like one whom a lamia or succubus is visiting in his sleep, being increasingly pale, gaunt, and exhausted, as well as notably short-tempered and—for the first time in his career—impatient and erratic in his legal decisions. He snapped at Wang Da, rudely corrected Chou Qingshan's records and transcriptions of his trials, rejected even his longtime favorites of Hu Longwei's dishes, and regularly warned them all that they could easily be replaced by more accomplished and respectful servants, which was a term he had never employed in reference to any of them. Then, plainly distraught with chagrin, he would apologize to each man in turn, and try once again to evict that maddening young body and captivating smile from his nights. He was never successful at this.

During all this time, the *chi-lin* made not a single appearance in his various courtrooms, which even his retinue, as much as they feared it, found highly unusual, and probably a very bad omen. Having none but each other to discuss the matter with, often clustered together in one more inn, one more drovers' hostel, quite frequently within earshot of Kao Yu tossing and mumbling in his bed, Chou Qingshan would say, "Our master has certainly lost the favor of Heaven, due to his obsession with that thieving slut. For the life of me, I cannot understand it—she was pretty enough, in a coarse way, but hardly one to cost *me* so much as an hour of sleep."

To which Wang Da would invariably respond, "Well, nothing in this world would do *that* but searching under your bed for a lost coin." They were old friends, and, like many such, not particularly fond of each other.

But Hu Longwei—in many ways the wisest of the three, when off duty—would quiet the other two by saying, "If you both spent a little more time considering our master's troubles, and a little less on your own grievances, we might be of some actual use to him in this crisis. He is not the first man to spend less than an hour in some woman's company and then be ridden sleepless by an unresolved fantasy, however absurd. Do not interrupt me, Wang. I am older than both of you, and I know a few things. The way to rid Kao Yu of these dreams of his is to return to that same town—I cannot even remember what it was called—and arrange for him to spend a single night with that little pickpocket. Believe me, there is nothing that clears away such a dream faster than its fulfillment. Think on it—and keep out of my cooking wine, Chou, or I may find another use for my cleaver."

The lieutenant and the secretary took these words more to heart than Hu Longwei might have expected, the result being that somehow, on the return leg of their regular route, Wang Da developed a relative in poor health living in a village within easy walking distance of the town where Lanying the pickpocket resided—employed now, all hoped, in some more respectable profession. Kao Yu's servants never mentioned her name when they went together to the judge to implore a single night's detour on the long way home. Nor, when he agreed to this, did Kao Yu.

It cannot be said that his mental or emotional condition improved greatly with the knowledge that he was soon to see Lanying once again. He seemed to sleep no better, nor was he any less gruff with Wang, Chou, and Hu, even when they were at last bound on the homeward journey. The one significant difference in his behavior was that he regained his calm, unhurried courtroom demeanor, as firmly decisive as always, but paying the strictest attention to the merits of the cases he dealt with, whether in a town, a mere village, or even a scattering of huts and fields that could barely be called a hamlet. It was as though he was in some way preparing himself for the next time the beautiful pickpocket was brought before him, knowing that there *would* be a next time, as surely as sunrise. But what he was actually thinking on the road to that sunrise . . . that no one could have said, except perhaps the *chi-lin*. And there is no account anywhere of any *chi-lin* ever speaking in words to a human being.

The town fathers were greatly startled to see them again, since there had been no request for their return, and no messages to announce it. But they welcomed the judge and his entourage all the same, and put them up without charge at the wagoners' inn a second time. And that evening, without notifying his master, Wang Da slipped away quietly and eventually located Lanying the pickpocket in the muddy alley where she lived with a number of the people who called her "Snow Ermine." When he informed her that he came from Judge Kao Yu, who would be pleased to honor her with an invitation to dinner, Lanying favored him with the same magically rapturous smile, and vanished into the hovel to put on her most respectable robe, perfectly suitable for dining with a man who had sentenced her to collect and dispose of her neighbors' nightsoil. Wang Da waited outside for her, giving earnest thanks for his own long marriage, his five children, and his truly imposing ugliness.

On their way to the inn, Lanying—for all that she skipped along beside him like a child on her way to a puppet show or a party—shrewdly asked Wang Da, not why Kao Yu had sent for her, but what Wang Da could tell her about the man himself. Wang Da, normally a taciturn man, except when taunting Chou Qingshan, replied cautiously, wary of her cleverness, saying as little as he could in courtesy. But he did let her know that there had never been a woman of any sort in Kao Yu's life, not as long as he had worked for him—and he did disclose the truth of the judge's *chi-lin*. It is perhaps the heart of this tale that Lanying chose to believe one of these truths, and to disdain the other.

Kao Yu had, naturally, been given the finest room at the inn, which was no great improvement over any other room, but did have facilities for the judge to entertain a guest in privacy. Lanying fell to her knees and kowtowed—knocked head—the moment she entered, Wang Da having simply left her at the door. But Kao Yu raised her to her feet and served her Dragon In The Clouds tea, and after that *huangjiu* wine, which is made from wheat. By the time these beverages had been consumed— time spent largely in silence and smiles—the dinner had been prepared and brought to them by Hu Longwei himself, who had pronounced the inn's cook "a northern barbarian who should be permitted to serve none but monkeys and foreigners." He set the trays down carefully on the low table, peered long and rudely into Lanying's face, and departed.

"Your servants do not like me," Lanying said with a small, unhappy sigh. "Why should they, after all?"

Kao Yu answered, bluntly but kindly, "They have no way of knowing whether you have changed your life. Nor did I make you promise to do so when I pronounced sentence." Without further word, he fed her a bit of their roast pork appetizer, and then asked quietly, "Have you done so? Or are you still Lanying the Pickpocket?"

Lanying sighed again and smiled wryly at him. "No, my lord, these days I am Lanying the Seamstress. I am not very good at it, in truth, but I work cheaply. Sometimes I am Lanying the Cowherd—Lanying the Pig Girl—Lanying the Sweeper at the market." She nibbled daintily at her dish, plainly trying to conceal her hunger. "But the pickpocket, no, nor the thief, nor . . ." And here she looked directly into Kao Yu's eyes, and he noticed with something of a shock that her own were not brown, as he had remembered them, but closer to a kind of dark hazel, with flecks of green coming and going. "Nor have I yet been Lanying the Girl on the Market, though it has been a close run once or twice. But I have kept the word I never gave you—" she lowered her eyes then—"perhaps out of pride, perhaps out of gratitude—perhaps . . ." She let the words trail away unfinished, and they dined without speaking for some while, until Lanying was able to regard Kao Yu again without blushing.

Then it was Kao Yu's turn to feel his cheeks grow hot, as he said, "Lanying, you must understand that I have not been much in the society of women. At home, I dine alone in my rooms, always; when I am traveling, I am more or less constantly in the company of my assistants Wang, Chou, and Hu, whom I have known for many years. But since we met, however unfortunately, I have not been able to stop thinking of you, and imagining such an evening as we are enjoying. I am certain that this is wrong, unquestionably wrong for a judge, but when I look at you, I cannot breathe, and I cannot feel my heart beating at all. I am too old for you, and you are too beautiful for me, and I think you should probably leave after we finish our meal. I do."

Lanying began to speak, but Kao Yu took her wrists in his hands, and she—who had some experience in these matters—felt his grip like manacles. He said, "Because, if you never make away with another purse in your life, Lanying the Pickpocket is still there in the back of those lovely eyes. I see her there even now, because although I am surely a great fool, I am also a judge."

He released his hold on her then, and they sat staring at one another—for how long, Kao Yu could never say or remember. Lanying finally whispered, "Your man Wang told me that a unicorn, a *chi-lin*, sometimes helps you to arrive at your decisions. What do you think it would advise you if it were here now?"

Nor was Kao Yu ever sure how many minutes or hours went by before he was finally able to say, "The *chi-lin* is not here." And outside the door, Chou Qingshan held out his open palm and Wang Da and Hu Longwei each grudgingly slapped a coin into it as the three of them tiptoed away.

Lanying was gone when Kao Yu woke in the morning, which was, as it turned out, rather a fortunate thing. He was almost finished tidying up the remains of their meal—several items had been crushed and somewhat scattered, and one plate was actually broken—when Wang Da entered to tell him that his dinner guest had stopped long enough while departing the inn in the deep night to empty the landlord's money box, leaving an impudent note of thanks before vanishing. And vanish she certainly had: the search that Kao Yu organized and led himself turned up no trace of her, neither in her usual haunts nor in areas where she claimed to have worked, or was known to have friends. Snow Ermine had disappeared as completely as though she had never been. Which, in a sense, she never had.

Kao Yu, being who he was, compensated the landlord in full—over the advice of all three of his assistants—and they continued on the road home. No one spoke for the first three days.

Finally, in a town in Hunan province, where the four of them were having their evening meal together, Kao Yu broke his silence, saying, "Every one of you is at complete liberty to call me a stupid, ridiculous old fool. You will only be understating the case. I beg pardon of you all." And he actually kowtowed— knocked head—in front of his own servants.

Naturally, Chou, Wang, and Hu were properly horrified at this, and upset their own dishes rushing to raise Kao Yu to his feet. They assured him over and over that the robbery at the inn could not in any way be blamed on him, even though he *had* invited the thief to dinner there, and she *had* spent the night in his bed, taking fullest advantage of his favor . . . the more they attempted to excuse him of the responsibility, the more guilty he felt, and the angrier at himself for, even now, dreaming every night of the embraces of that same thief. He let his three true friends comfort him, but all he could think of was that he would never again be able to return the gaze of the unicorn in his courtroom with the same pride and honesty. The *chi-lin* would know the truth, even of his dreams. The *chi-lin* always knew.

When they returned without further incident to the large southern city that was home to all four of them, Kao Yu allowed himself only two days to rest, and then flung himself back into his occupation with a savage vengeance aimed at himself and no one else. He remained as patient as ever with his assistants—and, for the most part, with the accused brought to him for judgment. Indeed, as culpable as his dreams kept telling him he was, he sympathized more with these petty, illiterate, drink-sodden, hopeless, useless offscourings of decent society than he ever had in his career—in his life. Whether the useless offscourings themselves ever recognized this is not known.

Wang Da, Chou Qingshan, and Hu Longwei all hoped that time and work would gradually free his mind of Snow Ermine—which was the only way they spoke of her from then on—and at first, because they wanted it so much to be true, they believed that it must be. And while they were at home in the city, living the life of a busy city judge and his aides, dining with other officials, advising on various legal matters, speaking publicly to certain conferences, and generally filling their days with lawyers and the law, this did indeed seem to be so. Further, to their vast relief, Kao Yu's unicorn paid him no visits during that time; in fact, it had not been seen for more than a year. In private, he himself regarded this as a judgment in its own right, but he said nothing about that, considering it his own harsh concern. So all appeared to be going along in a proper and tranquil manner, as had been the case before the mischance that called him to an all-but-nameless town to deal with the insignificant matter of that wretched—and nameless—pickpocket.

Consequently, when it came the season for them to take to the long road once more, the judge's assistants each had every reason to hope that he would show himself completely recovered from his entanglement with that same wretched pickpocket. Particularly since this time, they would have no reason to pass anywhere near that town where she plied her trade, and where Kao Yu might just conceivably be called upon again to pass sentence upon her. It was noted as they set out, not only that the weather was superb, but that their master was singing to himself: very quietly, true—almost wordlessly, almost in a whisper—but even so. The three looked at each other and dared to smile; and if smiles made any sound, that one would have been a whisper, too.

At first the journey went well, barring the condition of the spring roads, which were muddy, as always, and sucked tiresomely at the feet of their horses. But there were fewer criminal cases than usual for Kao Yu to deal with, and most of those were run-of-the-mill affairs: a donkey or a few chickens stolen *here*, a dispute over fishing rights or a right of way *there*, a wife assaulting her husband—for excellent reasons—over *there*. Such dull daily issues might be uninteresting to any but the participants, but they had the distinct advantage of taking up comparatively little time; as a rule, Kao Yu and his retinue never needed to spend more than a day and a night in any given town. On the rare occasions when they stayed longer, it was always to rest the horses, never themselves. But that suited all four of them, especially Wang Da, who, for all his familial responsibilities, remained as passionately devoted to his wife as any new bridegroom, and was beginning to allow himself sweet visions of returning home earlier than expected. The others teased him rudely that he might well surprise the greengrocer or the fishmonger in his bed, but Kao Yu reproved them sharply, saying, "True happiness is as delicate as a dragonfly's wing, and it is not to be made sport of." And he patted Wang Da's shoulder, as he had never done before, and rode on, still singing to himself, a very little.

But once they reached the province where the girl called Snow Ermine lived—even though, as has been said, their route had been planned to take them as far as possible from her home—then the singing stopped, and Kao Yu grew day by day more silent and morose. He drew apart from his companions, both in traveling and in their various lodgings; and while he continued to take his cases, even the most trifling, as seriously as ever, his entire courtroom manner had become as dry and sour as that of a much older judge. This impressed very favorably most of the local officials he dealt with, but his assistants knew what unhappiness it covered, and pitied him greatly.

Chou Qingshan predicted that Kao Yu would return to his old self once they were clear of the province that had brought him to such shame and confusion; and to some degree that was true as they rode on from town to village, village to town. But the soft singing never did come again, which in time caused the cook Hu Longwei to say, "He is like a vase or a pot that has been shattered into small bits, and then restored, glued back together, fragment by fragment. It will look as good as new, if the work is done right, but you have to be careful with it. *We* will have to be careful."

Nevertheless, their progress was so remarkable that they were almost two weeks ahead of schedule when they reached Yinchuan, where they were accustomed to rest and resupply themselves for a few days before starting home. But within a day of their arrival, Kao Yu had been approached by both the mayor of the town and the provincial governor, each asking him if he would be kind enough to preside over a particular case for them tomorrow. A Yinchuan judge had already been chosen, of course, and would doubtless do an excellent job; but, like every judge available, he had no experience handling such a matter as murder, and it was well-known that Kao Yu—

Kao Yu said, "Murder? This is truly a murder case you are asking me to deal with?"

The mayor nodded miserably. "We know that you have come a long journey, and have a long journey yet before you . . . but the victim was an important man, a merchant all the way from Harbin, and his family is applying a great deal of pressure on the entire city administration, not me alone. A judge of your stature agreeing to take over . . . it might calm them somewhat, reassure them that something is being done . . ."

"Tell me about the case," Kao Yu interrupted brusquely. Hu Longwei groaned quietly, but Chou and Wang were immediately excited, though they properly made every effort not to seem so. An illegally-established tollgate—a neighbor poaching rabbits on a neighbor's land—what was that to a real murder? With Kao Yu, they learned that the merchant—young, handsome, vigorous, and with, as even his family admitted, far more money than sense—had wandered into the wrong part of town and struck up several unwise friendships, most particularly one with a young woman—

"A pickpocket?" Kao Yu's voice had suddenly grown tight and rasping.

No, apparently not a pickpocket. Apparently her talents lay elsewhere—

"Was she called . . . Snow Ermine?"

"That name has not been mentioned. When she was taken into custody, she gave the name 'Spring Lamb.' Undoubtedly an alias, or a nickname—"

"Undoubtedly. Describe her." But then Kao Yu seemed to change his mind, saying, "No . . . no, do not describe her to me. Have all the evidence in the matter promptly delivered to our inn, and let me decide then whether or not I will agree to sit on the case. You will have my answer tonight, if the evidence reaches the inn before we do."

It did, as Kao Yu's assistants knew it would; but all three of them agreed that they had never seen their master so reluctant even to handle the evidence pertaining to a legal matter. There was plenty of it, certainly, from the sworn statements of half a dozen citizens swearing to having seen the victim in the company of the accused; to the proprietor of a particularly disreputable wine shop, who had sold the pair enough liquor, jar on jar, to float a river barge; let alone the silent witness of the young merchant's slit-open purse, and of the slim silver knife still buried to the hilt in his side when he was discovered in a trash-strewn alley with dogs sniffing at his body. There was even—when his rigor-stiffened left hand was pried open, a crushed rag of a white flower. Judge Kao Yu's lamp burned all night in his room at the inn.

But in the morning, when Wang Da came to fetch him, he was awake and clear-eyed and had already breakfasted, though only on green tea and sweetened *congee*. He was silent as they walked to the building set aside for trials of all sorts, where Hu Longwei and Chou Qingshan awaited them, except to remark that they would be starting home on the day after tomorrow, distinctly earlier than their usual practice. He said nothing further until they reached the courtroom.

There were two minor cases to be disposed of before the matter of the young merchant's murder: one a suit over a breach of contract, the other having to do with a long-unpaid family debt. Kao Yu settled these swiftly, and then—a little pale, his words a bit slower, but his voice quiet and steady—signaled for the accused murderer to be brought into court.

It was Lanying, as he had known in his heart that it would be, from the very first mention of the case. Alone in his room, he had not even bothered to hope that the evidence would prove her innocent, or, at the very least, raise some small doubt as to her guilt. He had gone through it all quickly enough, and spent the rest of the night sitting very still, with his hands clasped in his lap, looking toward the door, as though expecting her to come to him then and there, of her own will, instead of waiting until morning for her trial. From time to time, in the silence of the room, he spoke her name.

Now, as the two constables who had led her to his high bench stepped away, he looked into her calmly defiant eyes and said only, "We meet again."

"So we do," Lanying replied equably. She was dressed rakishly, having been seized before she had time to change into garments suitable for a court appearance; but, as ever, she carried herself with the pride and poise of a great lady. She said to Kao Yu, "I hoped you might be the one."

"Why is that? Because I let you off lightly the first time? Because I . . . because it was so easy for you to make a fool of me the next time?" Kao Yu was almost whispering. "Do you imagine that I will be quite as much of a mark today?"

"No. But I did wish to apologize."

"Apologize?" Kao Yu stared at her. "*Apologize?*"

Lanying bowed her head, but she looked up at him from under her long dark eyelashes. "Lord, I am a thief. I have been a thief all my life. A thief steals. I knew the prestige of your invitation to dine would give me a chance at the inn's money box, and I accepted it accordingly, because that is what a thief does. It had nothing to do with you, with my . . . liking for you. I am what I am."

Kao Yu's voice was thick in his throat. "You are what you have become, which is something more than a mere thief and pickpocket. Now you are a murderer."

The word had not been at all hard to get out when he was

discussing it with the mayor, and with his three assistants, but now it felt like a thornbush in his throat. Lanying's eyes grew wide with fear and protest. "*I?* Never! I had *nothing* to do with that poor man's death!"

"The knife is yours," Kao Yu said tonelessly. "It is the same one I noticed at your waist when you dined with me. Nor have I ever seen you without a white flower in your hair. Do not bother lying to me any further, Lanying."

"But I am not lying!" she cried out. "I took his money, yes—he was stupid with wine, and that is what I do, but killing is no part of it. The knife was stolen from me, I swear it! Think as little of me as you like—I have given you reason enough—but I am no killer, you *must* know that!" She lowered her voice, to keep the words that followed from the constables. "Our bodies tell the truth, if our mouths do not. My lord, my judge, you know as much truth of me as anyone does. Can you tell me again that I am a murderer?"

Kao Yu did not answer her. They looked at each other for a long time, the judge and the lifelong thief, and it seemed to Chou Qingshan that there had come a vast weariness on Kao Yu, and that he might never speak again to anyone. But then Kao Yu lifted his head in wonder and fear as the scent of a summer meadow drifted into the room, filling it with the warm, slow presence of wild ginger, hibiscus, lilacs, and lilies—and the *chi-lin*. The two constables fell to their knees and pressed their faces to the floor, as did his three assistants, none of them daring even to look up. The unicorn stood motionless at the back of the courtroom, and Kao Yu could no more read its eyes than he ever could. But in that moment, he knew Lanying's terrible danger for his own.

Very quietly he said to her, "Snow Ermine, Spring Lamb, thief of my foolish, foolish old heart . . . nameless queen born a criminal . . . and, yes, murderer—I am begging you now for both our lives. Speak the truth, if you never do so again, because otherwise you die here, and so do I. Do you hear me, Lanying?"

Just for an instant, looking into Lanying's beautiful eyes, he knew that she understood exactly what he was telling her, and, further, that neither he nor the *chi-lin* was in any doubt that she had slain the merchant she robbed. But she was, as she had told him, what she was; and even with full knowledge of the justice waiting, she repeated, spacing the words carefully, and giving precise value to each, "Believe what you will. I am no killer."

Then the judge Kao Yu rose from his bench and placed himself between Lanying and the unicorn, and he said in a clear, strong voice, "You are not to harm her. Everything she says is a lie, and always will be, and still you are not to harm her." In the silence that followed, his voice shook a little as he added, "Please."

The *chi-lin* took a step forward—then another—and Lanying closed her eyes. But it did not charge; rather, it paced across the courtroom to face Kao Yu, until they were standing closer than ever they had before, in all the years of their strange and wordless partnership. And what passed between them then will never be known, save to say that the *chi-lin* turned away and was swiftly gone—never having once glanced at Lanying—and that Kao Yu sat down again and began to weep, without ever making a sound.

When he could speak, he directed the trembling constables to take Lanying away, saying that he would pass sentence the next day. She went, this time without a backward glance, as proudly as ever, and Kao Yu did not look after her, but walked away alone. Wang Da and Chou Qingshan would have followed him, but Hu Longwei took them both by the arms and shook his head.

Kao Yu spent the night alone in his room, where he could be heard pacing constantly, sometimes talking to himself in ragged, incomprehensible tatters of language. Whatever it signified, it eliminated him as a suspect in Lanying's escape from custody that same evening. She was never recaptured, reported, or heard of again—at least, not under that name, nor in that region of China—and if each of Kao Yu's three friends regarded the other two skeptically for a long time thereafter, no one accused anyone of anything, even in private. Indeed, none of them ever spoke of Lanying, the pickpocket, thief, and murderer for whom their master had given up what they knew he had given up. They had no words for it, but they knew.

For the *chi-lin* never came again, and Kao Yu never spoke of that separation either. The one exception came on their silent road home, when darkness caught them between towns, obliging them to make camp in a forest, as they were not unaccustomed to doing. They gathered wood together, and Hu Longwei improvised an excellent dinner over their fire, after which they chatted and bantered as well as they could to cheer their master, so silent now for so many days. It was then that Kao Yu announced his decision to retire from the bench, which shocked and dismayed them all, and set each man entreating him to change his mind. In this they were unsuccessful, though they argued and pleaded with him most of the night. It was nearer to dawn than to midnight, and the flames were dwindling because everyone had forgotten to feed them, when Chou Qingshan remarked bitterly, "So much for justice, then. With you gone, so much for justice between Guangzhou and Yinchuan."

But Kao Yu shook his head and responded, "You misunderstand, old friend. I am only a judge, and judges can always be found. The *chi-lin* . . . the *chi-lin* is justice. There is a great difference."

He did indeed retire, as he had said, and little is known of the rest of his life, except that he traveled no more, but stayed in his house, writing learned commentaries on curious aspects of common law, and, on rare occasions, lecturing to small audiences at the local university. His three assistants, of necessity, attached themselves to other circuit-riding judges, and saw less of one another than they did of Kao Yu, whom they never failed to visit on returning from their journeys. But there was less and less to say each time, and each admitted—though only to himself—a kind of guilt-stricken relief when he died quietly at home, from what his doctors termed a sorrow of the soul. China is one of the few countries where sadness has always been medically recognized.

There is a legend that after the handful of mourners at his funeral had gone home, a *chi-lin* kept silent watch at his grave all that night. But that is all it is, of course, a legend.

MY SON HEYDARI
AND THE KARKADANN

The Mideastern image of the ferocious, implacably murderous Karkadann, lacking the grace and beauty of the classic Western unicorn and the spirituality of its Asian cousin, is clearly drawn from the rhinoceros, and this is the only story I know that deals with the creature at all. As for the hero's name, Heydari, it's in there as a tribute to my long-ago Iranian friend Abbas, with whom I used to go for long walks in the warm spring nights of Pittsburgh in the 1950s. As I remember him, Abbas could never quite decide whether he wanted to stay in the U.S., study medicine, and make a million dollars, or return to Iran and kill the Shah. I thought of him often during the Iranian Revolution of 1979, and I prayed quietly that he had become an extremely wealthy doctor in the Midwest. A gentle-natured soul, my friend Abbas was not made for ayatollahs.

�֎

No, they are vanishing now, the karkadanns; at least they are almost gone from this part of Persia. Which is a very good thing, and you'll find no one in the land to tell you otherwise. It is an especially good thing for a man master of the only working elephant herd north of Baghdad. If your business is felling trees and hauling them off to the river, to be rafted downstream to the lumber mill and turned into palaces, ships, furniture, what you will—then you are almost bound to come to me and my elephants. It has been my family's trade for four generations, and my eldest son, Farid, will make the fifth when I am gone. It is our place in the world. It is what we do.

And it is only in this generation—my generation—that we have found ourselves increasingly free of those monsters, those terrible horned demons, the karkadanns. You have never seen one, I assume? No, not likely, coming from Turkey as you do. All the same, you must surely have heard that they are huge creatures, easily the size of Greek bulls, with double hooves, tails like lions, hides like thick leather plates—and that *horn*! Six, even seven feet long they run; and with the power of that great body behind it, they can splinter a cedar or an oak into kindling. I saw it happen just so when I was a boy.

That same horn can also split an elephant like a dumpling, I have seen that happen too.

Why karkadanns hate elephants as particularly and intensely as they do, no scholar has ever been able to explain, not to my satisfaction. I still have nightmares about seeing two karkadanns charging down out of the hills they favor, bellowing that chilling challenge of theirs—like battle horns, only deeper, and with a more carrying tone—and watching helplessly as they went through my herd, slashing left and right, literally spitting elephants on their horns like kebabs, then hurling them aside and going on to the next poor picketed beast. The elephants almost never fought back, never even tried to run away. Elephants are very intelligent, you know, and perhaps their imaginations simply paralyzed them: they could see what was going to happen, see it so clearly that they could not move. I felt the same way, watching those karkadanns coming.

They trample farmers' fields too, without a thought, most especially during the mating season. The farmers plant extra crops for just that reason, hoping to salvage *something* after the beasts get through with their wheat or their corn, their arbors or their orchards. And as for guards—if you can hire any—or dogs, if you can keep them from tucking tail and fleeing at the first distant smell of a karkadann . . . well, why even discuss it? We lost men, too, in those old days, as well as elephants.

The karkadann has no natural enemies. I am told that a thousand years ago, the dragons kept them within reasonable check; but of course, in our human wisdom, we killed off the dragons in the egg and the nest, because they cost us a lamb or a goat now and again. So—of course—the karkadanns promptly ran wild, and we could only be grateful that at least they were not carnivores, like the dragons. That was our sole blessing, for all those thousand years.

No, we did have one thing else to thank the gods for in our prayers: the fact that karkadanns never drop more than one foal at a time. As many as two . . . no, it doesn't bear considering. Two to a birth, and they would own the country by this time. And other lands, too, perhaps—who knows?

They are entirely vegetarian—though their two curving fangs imply otherwise—and entirely solitary by nature, except for those few weeks when they run mad with lust, and are then very nearly as likely to attack one another as they are elephants or humans. Even the females can be badly hurt during the rut; and more than once I have been gratified to encounter a pack of jackals feasting on the carcass of a karkadann bearing the marks of a comrade's brutal assault. All in all, an unlovely, unadmirable, and altogether detestable creature. And your fascination with it is a complete mystery to me.

But it would not be so to Heydari, my third son. You will meet him at dinner, Farid being away on business. Which is a pity, because I would like you to observe the difference between them. Farid is me in large, as you might say, being that much bigger and that much more ambitious—though not yet that much cleverer, though he thinks he is. I do not always *like* him, I suppose—do you like all *your* children all the time?—but I *understand* him, which is a comfort and a reassurance, and makes for a peaceful association. But Heydari. That Heydari.

You would never take them for brothers if you met them together. Heydari is small and slight, and much darker than Farid, and much less immediately charming. I think he makes a point of it, having seen Farid making friends everywhere, instantly, all his life. He has never been any use with the elephants, and we would be out of business in a month if I put him in charge of my accounts. Yet he is more intelligent than Farid—quite likely more intelligent than all the rest of us—but I cannot see that it has thus far done him much good. All the same, I confess to a feeling for him that I can neither explain nor defend. Especially not defend, not after the time he saved the life of a bloody karkadann.

How old was he? Thirteen or fourteen, I suppose; when else would you be that stupid, in exactly that way? As he told it in his own time—long after he *should* have told it—he found the creature high in those same foothills you came through, being drawn to it by the urgent calling of a ringdove, which, for reasons no one has ever fathomed, is the karkadann's only friend. As curious as any boy, he climbed after the bird and followed it to the entrance of a cave, where the beast lay bleeding its life away, and good riddance, through several deep wounds on its throat and flanks. It was barely breathing, he said, and the yellow eyes it tried to focus on him were seeing something else.

Like any man in this realm—any man but my son—I would either have helped the miserable monster on its way, or merely sat myself down and savored its passing. But not Heydari; not my softhearted, softheaded boy. He immediately set about fetching the karkadann water from a nearby spring, going back and forth to carry it in his cap. Apart from the stupidity of it, it was a risky matter as well, for the creature was in pain, and it lunged at him more than once with the last of its strength. He treated its injuries with what herbs he could find, and bound them with strips torn from his own clothes, while the ringdove perched on that murderous horn, cooing its approval. Then he went away, promising to return on the following day, but certain that he would find the karkadann dead when he did. I have said that he has never been of any practical use with the elephants, but he has been a kind boy from his childhood. An *idiot*, but always kind.

Well, he did return, keeping his word; and, unfortunately, the wretched beast was living yet. It was still unable to raise more than its head—which it did mostly to snap at him, even with one of those wicked fangs broken off halfway—but its wounds had stopped bleeding, and its breath was coming a bit deeper and more steadily. My son was greatly encouraged. He brought it more water, and fetched an armload or two of the fruits and vines that karkadanns favor, laying it all within reach in case the creature's appetite should revive. Then he sat close beside it, because he is a fool, and recited the old, old prayers and *sutras* most of the night before he went home.

And climbed back up the next day, and the day after that, to attend to that vile animal's recovery. Mind you, he told *us*, his own family, nothing of this—which, I must say, was the first intelligent thing he had done in the whole mad business. As many losses as we had endured over the years, in terms not merely of dead elephants, but taking into account the cost of workers, of lost time and equipment, and the timber itself, we would all probably have fallen upon him and torn him to shreds. To be nursing a karkadann back to health, in order that it might continue slaughtering, destroying . . . you see, even now I am sweating and snarling with rage at my own son. Even now.

Now if this were a fairy tale out of the *Shahnameh*, the boy and the karkadann would become such fast friends that the monster would give up all its evil ways and turn to loving and aiding humanity, even against its own folk. Hardly. It did stop trying to kill Heydari, having finally connected his ministrations with its survival and recovery; but it permitted no liberties, such as petting or grooming—only the ringdove was permitted that sort of intimacy—and it would clearly have died itself before ever taking food from his hand. He tried to explain to me once why he could not help liking that quality in the beast.

"It was so *proud*, Father," he said. "No, it was not even a matter of pride—it was just what it was, and not about to yield a fraction of itself to anyone, whatever the cost. Yes, it was a dreadful creature, wicked and heartless like all the rest of its kind . . . but oh, it was magnificent, too—splendidly terrible. Father, can you understand a little of what I am saying?"

Of course I hit him. You can't go around asking your father questions like that.

But that was later, well later. Meanwhile, he was caring for that karkadann every day—I should have been able to smell it on him; they smell like hay just starting to turn moldy—while the ringdove murmured smugly to them both, and his brothers were shouting for him to put his worthless self to some use cleaning the elephants' quarters. And now and then, so he told me, he would look up from his medicating and see those yellow eyes fixed on him, and he would wonder what the creature was thinking, what it *could* possibly be thinking at that moment. Which I, or any man with the sense of a bedbug, could have told him, but let that pass. What difference? Let it pass.

Finally there came the day when Heydari made his way to the cave and found the karkadann standing erect for the first time. It was grotesquely thin for its great size, and it seemed barely able to lift its head with that monstrous horn, but it stayed on its feet, swaying dazedly from side to side, and looking every moment as though it might crumple completely. Heydari clapped his hands and shouted encouragement, and the karkadann snarled in its chest and made a weak feint at him with the horn. The boy was wise enough to come no closer, but went off to find as much of the creature's preferred vegetation as he could carry in both arms. Then, as always, he simply sat down and watched it eat, rumbling evilly to itself. And as far as I can ever suppose, he was perfectly content.

At least, he was until Niloufar discovered them.

She was a shepherd girl, Niloufar—I knew her father well, as it happens. When I think about it, it's a wonder she had a flock to tend, as many sheep as the old man slaughtered on the day she was born. He had six sons, which was more than enough for him when he thought about the battles to come over their inheritance, and the celebration of Niloufar's arrival lasted almost a week. So she was undoubtedly spoiled, treated like a princess from her birth, shepherdess or no; but she was actually quite a good girl, when all's said and done. A little bit of a thing, but pretty with it—Farid was already eyeing her, and so was Abbas, my second boy—but I am not sure that Heydari had even noticed her, or remembered her name, for that matter. She'd noticed him, though, or I'm more of a fool than he.

Her flock had winded the karkadann, of course, and were having none of it, but fled in panic to rejoin in the little valley below the cave. Niloufar left her two dogs minding them and—being just as idiotically inquisitive as my idiot son—climbed back up to the cave mouth, having heard a familiar voice there. She knew the smell of a karkadann as surely as any sheep, and she was afraid, but she kept coming anyway. The rest of her family are quite sensible.

The karkadann growled savagely as soon as it saw her, and made as though to charge. Heydari cried out, "*No!*" and the beast halted, being still so weak that it almost fell with the first steps. But Niloufar was mightily impressed with a boy who could make a karkadann obey, and she said, "Have you actually tamed it, then? I never heard of anyone doing such a thing, not even a wizard."

It was a great temptation to Heydari to say that he had indeed done this, but he was a truthful boy, even when he *should* lie, and he explained to Niloufar how he had found the karkadann near death and done what he could for it. This impressed her even more, for all that she feared and hated the creatures as much as anyone. And then . . . well, he is not a bad-looking boy, you know—favors his mother more than me, which is as well—and between one thing and another, she said, "I think you must be a remarkable person, and very brave," which is all any boy of his age cares to hear from a girl. And I am sure he found the wit somewhere to mumble that he thought she was a remarkable person too . . . and all this while that bloody karkadann rumbling and eyeing them, ready to spear them and toss them and trample them to rags, as kind as my Heydari had been to the thing. And I suppose one compliment led to another . . .

. . . and so they began meeting at the cave—always by chance, naturally—to sit solemnly together and eat their lunches and watch the karkadann gaining strength every day. As great fools as they were, the pair of them, they knew just how dangerous the beast was, and how unchanged in its nature, for all that it owed its life to Heydari. But they were young, and stupidity is exciting when you are young. I remember better than I should.

As Heydari tells it, Niloufar was always the one asking, "But what will you do if one day it should suddenly turn on us? What is your plan?" That dreaming boy of mine with a plan—*there's* a notion for you!

But he had been thinking ahead, it turned out. Girls will have that effect on you. He said, "You and I are both quick—we will run in different directions. It cannot follow us both, and I will make certain that it follows me."

"And how will you do that?" she wanted to know. Smiling, I am sure, for what girl does not want to hear that a boy will risk his life to lure a monster away from her? "How *can* you be so sure that I will not be the one it pursues?"

To which Heydari answered her, "Because I did it a good turn. For such a creature as the karkadann, that is intolerable. It will seek to wipe away the stain on its pride along with me." Then Niloufar became genuinely frightened for him, which was doubtless exciting, too, for both of them. It is exhausting even *thinking* about the young.

So Niloufar watched over her father's sheep, and Heydari watched over the recovering karkadann; and both of them shyly watched over each other as best they knew how. I am sure she must have practiced chiding and warning him, as he must have copied me telling his mother to be quiet, in the name of all the gods, and let me *think*. I hope they did not reproduce us too closely, those children. It is uncomfortable, somehow, to imagine.

And then there was the ringdove. It is important not to forget the ringdove.

It must have had no family responsibilities, for it was there all the time, or the next thing to it. Now and then it would fly away for a little while, tending to its bird business, but it always returned within the hour. And it always perched on the karkadann's immense horn, and it always cooed the softest, gentlest melody, over and over; and the karkadann would always, sooner or later, close its yellow eyes and fall into as peaceful-seeming a sleep as you can imagine those creatures ever enjoying. Sometimes it would even lie down, Heydari said, and rest its head on its front feet, which are as much like claws as they are like hooves. It would even snore now and then, in the daintiest manner imaginable, like that teakettle we only bring out for company. "You know, the way Mother snores," he explained, and I cuffed him for it, even though she does.

Heydari sometimes dozed briefly, with his head on Niloufar's shoulder, but she herself never closed an eye in the presence of the karkadann. As she told me long afterward, it was not that Heydari trusted the creature any more than she, or that she was less fascinated by it than he was; rather, she liked knowing that he trusted *her* with his safety, his protection, which no one but a sheep had ever done before. At times her eyes would meet the karkadann's yellow glare, the one as unblinking as the other, and on a few occasions she spoke to it while Heydari slept. "Why are you what you are? Why do you and your folk have no friends, no companions—not even each other—but those birds? Is there truly nothing to you but hatred and rage and solitude? Why are you in the world at all?"

Girls ask questions like that. Sometimes they ask them of men.

The karkadann never showed any sign of interest or comprehension, of course, except for one moment, when Niloufar asked, "The song of the ringdove—does it run *so*?" and she imitated it in her throat, for she had an excellent ear for melody, like all her family, even all those boys. The karkadann made a strange, perplexed sound: it woke Heydari, who blinked from one to the other of them as Niloufar repeated the run of notes, again and again. The ringdove itself fluffed out its gray and blue-gray feathers, but remained asleep on the great horn, while the karkadann stamped its front feet, and the questioning rumble grew louder. But Niloufar kept singing.

Perhaps fortunately for my unborn grandchildren, Heydari put his hand over her mouth and held it there while he shouted at her. "Are you mad, girl? Do you think you are some sort of wizard, some sort of wisewoman? In another moment, you would have been decorating that horn like a flower, and there would have been nothing, *nothing,* I could do to save you. Get back to your accursed sheep if you are going to behave so!" I myself have never seen him so angry, but this is what Niloufar told me.

Another little girl would have burst into tears and flounced away—but looking slyly over her shoulder, expecting the boy to call her back. Not that one. She drew herself up to her full height, such as it is, and stalked out of the cave and down the hill without a backward glance. And no, Heydari did *not* call, though I am certain he wished to, very much. But he is as stubborn as I am—in that one way, at least, he is like me—so all he did was stare back at the growling karkadann, having some notion of stilling it with his eyes. And presently, for that reason or another, the beast did grow quiet, though it did not sleep again, for all the cooing of the ringdove. Neither did Heydari.

He did not leave the cave until Niloufar had driven her sheep homeward; nor did he even look to notice whether she had returned to the valley the next afternoon when he climbed to see to the karkadann. She did not come at all that day, nor the next, nor the next, when at last he *was* watching for her; and when at last he gave that up, he felt older than he was. And that *is* how we grow old, you know, waiting for whatever we insist we are not waiting for. I know this.

By and by, there was no question but that the karkadann was fully restored to wicked health, its wounds entirely healed, and its terrible strength revealed in even the smallest movement it made. It even left the cave to forage for itself, now and again, and to make its way to the spring for water. Yet it lingered on with Heydari, surely not out of need or affection, but as though it, too, were waiting for . . . something, some certain moment when it would know exactly what to do about this annoying, baffling little creature. Not that there was any mystery about what *that* was going to be. Karkadanns only do one thing.

Why Heydari continued to visit the cave and care for the creature . . . ah, if you ever solve that one, explain it to him before me, because he still can't say himself. The best he was ever able to tell me was that for him, it was like dancing on the edge of a knife blade, or a great abyss, knowing that if you keep dancing there, you will very likely fall to your death—but that if you *stop* dancing, you surely will. He said he was terrified every moment, but in a wonderfully calm way, if that made any sense to me. Which it did not, no more than anything he's ever done has made sense, but there you are. There's my son for you.

And after Niloufar stopped coming . . . oh, then nothing much really seemed to matter, living or dying. And there's a boy, if you like, any boy at all. It's a wonder any of them survive to father a new crop of idiots like themselves. He meant it, too. They all mean it. He said he almost wished the karkadann would make up its mind and kill him . . . but at the same time, he could not keep from wondering, as he stared at it day after day, whether it might not have some sort of a weak spot, a vulnerable place under all that hide and power that no one had ever discovered. He imagined it being his legacy to Persia, and to me. Boys.

I wonder now and again whether the beast truly felt no gratitude at all toward my son. I have never known an animal— human beings excepted—to be totally incapable of showing some form of appreciation for a kindness. My wife has tamed a snake enough that it will come to her and take milk from her hand; Heydari himself took such care of a baby elephant when its mother was killed by a karkadann that to this day that enormous animal—Mojtaba, biggest male in my herd—follows him around, holding Heydari's hand with his trunk. And maybe there was some way in which Heydari, all the while knowing better, believed that the karkadann—*his* karkadann—would never, at the last, actually turn on him. Mind you, I say *maybe*.

Very well. There came one hot and cloudless afternoon when the air was so still you almost had to push your way through it, like a great sticky mass of old cobwebs. The karkadann had already been to the spring twice to drink, and now it half-crouched against the cave wall, eyes half-closed, growling to itself so deeply and softly that Heydari could barely hear the sound at all. The ringdove was perched, as ever, on the tip of its horn, its rippling murmur rasping at Heydari's nerves for the first time. He felt the way you feel when a storm is coming, even though it may yet be a day, or even two days, from reaching you: there is a *smell*, and there is a kind of stiff crackle, like invisible lightning, racing up and down your arms, and you have to think about each breath you take. He found that he was crouching himself, ready to spring in any direction; and at the same time—so he told me—thinking, as he studied the light and shadow playing over the brutal majesty of the beast's flanks and high shoulders, that if it had to be, now would be the time to go. Did you ever think such a thought when you were fourteen years old? I never thought anything like that.

But the boy isn't a total fool, not even then—not all the way through. When the yellow eyes seemed to have closed completely, under the influence of the ringdove's endless cooing, Heydari began edging toward the cave mouth on his haunches, inch by inch, watching the karkadann every moment. He's never said what instinct made him do it; only that it felt suddenly very close in the cave, what with that moldy-hay smell of the creature, and that birdsong going on and on, he began to feel in need of fresh air. Another foot—two feet at most—and he would simply rise and walk out and down into the little valley . . . and perhaps Niloufar would be there, even though her sheep were not. Not, you understand, that he cared a rap about *that*.

And what finally tipped the balance—what woke the karkadann and set it at last *seeing* my son as it never had before—that I don't imagine he or Niloufar or I will ever know. Heydari says it actually made that same odd puzzled sound before it charged, just as though it didn't know yet why it was being made to do this. Though I don't suppose that's true for a minute, and it wouldn't make any bloody difference if it were. It bloody *charged*.

Coming at him, absolutely silent, it looked twice as huge as it had just a moment before, for all that he had grown so used to the immensity of it in the cave. He shrieked, fell over backward, and rolled some way down the slope, stopping himself by grabbing at clumps of grass and stones. When he stumbled to his feet, the karkadann filled his entire horizon, poised at the cave mouth, staring down at him. It did not move for what he tells me is still the longest moment of his life. Once he said that it would almost have been worth dying on that horn like an elephant to know what was going through the beast's mind. I tried to hit him, but he ducked out of range.

He could see the great leg muscles gathering and swelling like thunderheads as the karkadann set itself, and he thought—or he *says* he thought—of his family, and how sad his mother would be, and how furious I would be, and he wished he were safely home with us all. That's as may be; but I've always suspected he'd have been thinking of little Niloufar, and wishing he had had time and sense enough to make it up with her. I hope he was.

In a vague kind of way, he wondered where the ringdove had gotten to. It had flown up the moment the karkadann charged him, and he could not see it anywhere. A pity, for if there was anything in the world that soothed that devil-gotten creature at all, it was the song of the dove. The strange thing was that he could have sworn he still heard it somewhere. Perched in some tree, like enough, waiting patiently for the slaughter to be over, the same as always. Ringdoves aren't smart birds, but they aren't fools either.

Then the karkadann came for him.

He says he never heard the bellow. He says what he'll remember to his last day is—of all things—the sound of the stones of the hillside surging backward under the karkadann's clawed hoofs. That, and the ringdove, suddenly sounding almost in his right ear . . . and another sound that he knew he knew, but it shouldn't be there, it mustn't be there . . .

It was Niloufar. It was Niloufar, singing her perfect imitation of the ringdove's song—and it was Niloufar riding my big Mojtaba straight at the karkadann! Now, as I think I've made abundantly clear to you, there is no elephant in the *world* who will challenge a karkadann . . . except, perhaps, one who has lost his mother to such beasts, and who sees his adoptive mother in the same danger. Mojtaba trumpeted—Niloufar swears it sounded more like a roar than anything else—laid his big ears back flat, curled his trunk out of harm's way, and charged.

As nearly as I could ever make out from their two accounts, that double impossibility—a ringdove singing sweetly where there wasn't a ringdove and an elephant half its size attacking head-on, with death in his red eyes—the karkadann must have been thrown off-guard: unable either to halt or commit to a full rush, and too bewildered to do more than brace itself for Mojtaba's onslaught. Mad with vengeance or not, the elephant knew enough to strike at an angle that made the broken fang useless as a weapon, and he crashed into the karkadann with his full weight and power, knocking the beast off its feet for—doubtless—the first time in its life. Mojtaba's tusks—five feet long, both of them, if they're an inch—drove into its side, wrenched free, drove again . . .

But poor Niloufar, flattening herself in vain against the elephant's back, was knocked from her hold and hurled through the air. And the gods only know how badly she might have been hurt, if Heydari, my son, running as fast as though the karkadann were still behind him, had not managed to break her fall with his own body. She hit him broadside, just as Mojtaba had crashed into the karkadann, and they both went down together—both, I think, unconscious for at least a minute or two. Then they sat up in the high grass and looked at each other, and, of course, that was the real beginning. I know that, and I wasn't even there.

Heydari said, "I thought I would never see you again. I kept hoping I would see your sheep grazing in the valley, but I never did."

And Niloufar answered simply, "I have been here every day. I am a very good hider."

"Do not hide from me again, please," Heydari said, and Niloufar promised.

The karkadann was dead, but it took the children some time to call Mojtaba away from trampling the body. The elephant was trembling and whimpering—they are *very* emotional, comes with the sensitivity—and did not calm down until Heydari led him to the little hill stream and carefully washed the blood from his tusks. Then he went back and buried the karkadann near the cave. Niloufar helped, but it took a very long time, and Heydari insisted on marking the grave. As well as that girl understands him, I don't think she knows to this day why he wanted to do that.

But I do. It was what he was trying to tell me, and what I hit him for, and likely still would, my duty as a father having nothing to do with understanding. The karkadann was magnificent, as he said, and utterly monstrous too, and he probably came as near to taming it as anyone ever has or ever will. And perhaps that was why it hated him so, in the end, because he had tempted it to violate its entire nature, and almost won. Or maybe not . . . talk to my idiot son, and you start thinking about things like that. You'll see—I'll seat you next to him at dinner.

No, we've never called them anything but karkadanns. Odd, a Roman fellow, a trader, he asked the same question a while back. Only other time I ever heard that word, *unicorn*.

THE QUEEN WHO
COULD NOT WALK

I'm very fond of this story, but I've never been quite sure of its origin, except for Kipling's classic story "The Miracle of Purun Bhagat," which deals with a Hindu statesman in midlife who abruptly gives up his power and position, takes up a staff and a begging-bowl, and simply disappears into the Himalayas, where he eventually becomes the revered hermit meditating above a poor hill village. My queen has no such choice in the matter; but, unlike Purun Bhagat, she does have a companion, without whom she would never have survived her own journey—and to whom she owes a terrible debt that I didn't imagine myself when I began to write the story. For good or ill, that seems to be the way I've worked for almost sixty years.

�֍

Far Away And Long Ago is a real country, older and more enduring than any bound by degrees and hours and minutes on a map. For a time there lived a king and queen there no worse than most kings and queens, and probably a little better. These two ruled their subjects kindly enough, considering that they rarely saw any of them, except for the servants who assured the king and queen that they were better rulers than the ruled deserved. When they rode abroad on their semiannual passages, the streets were lined with ranks of cheering people who waved their caps, if they owned any, and threw flowers, if they could afford them, and kisses if they could not. And the affection and loyalty displayed were reasonably genuine, for the people knew well how much worse things could be, and often had been, and were thus grateful.

Part of their tenderness for the queen undoubtedly stemmed from the well-known fact that she was crippled, her legs stricken useless from the very day of her wedding. Her affliction caused her no pain—indeed, her health otherwise was remarkably vigorous—but no doctor was ever able to provide cause or cure, nor could any wisewoman mumble and chant her way through the mystery, however many chickens she slaughtered. So the queen sat all day on her padded throne, or reclined gracefully on a specially-built divan; she was carried everywhere within the palace and its great crystal-roofed gardens by the king himself; and, of course, she traveled in a closed sedan chair whenever she went outside. Everything was done for her comfort that might be done, and if sometimes that constant awareness was an ache in itself, she kept it close and never let it show. For she had been raised properly, and she knew how queens properly dealt with aches.

It says a good deal for the king that it never occurred to him to reject his wife, to return her to her family as damaged goods, as many advised him. On the contrary, he had both sense and wit enough to treat her altogether as his partner and companion in all matters: ruling in sorrow at times, and in discomfort always, but ruling. And, as has been said, they were at least better than the average run of those who had come before them.

Now it is to this day a curious aspect of the governance of that realm that kings and queens are not born to royalty, but selected in earliest childhood, and at a certain mirror point in life—a time never known until it arrives, until certain priests have cast their bones and consulted uncharted stars—they must step down, exchanging jeweled crown and stately robes for loincloth and begging-bowl, and go out into the world far beyond the sheltered world they have known since first being raised up. None was encouraged to linger in his or her old surroundings, and few ever did, but drifted away silently along every curve of the round earth. Once in a great while, word would come of a lost king being worshipped as a holy man in some spiny mountain village, or rumor might whisper of a former queen achieving rural renown as a cook in a village inn. But in the main they simply wandered off into absence without protest or complaint. Some were quickly forgotten; others—for good or ill—never were.

When the end came for this particular king, announced for his ears alone by a wizened, sour-faced old priest with a lisp, he grieved deeply to leave his wife to the mercy of time and her ruined legs. But he had prepared as well as he could, hiring, at great expense, the finest deviser he could seek out to design a chair with wheels for her, a sort of mobile throne: the first ever seen, as it happens, in the land of Far Away And Long Ago, where all moves slowly. The king disliked the result, as he had known he would, having always taken great delight in carrying the queen in his arms himself wherever in the palace she desired to go. But the queen, in fact, was quite pleased, and played with her new wheelchair like a child, rolling and spinning and turning in circles. And when she did notice the sadness in her husband's eyes as he looked on, she said to him quickly, "But you will always have to push me, you know. I cannot make this thing go very far by myself." And the king smiled and nodded, and kissed her, and said nothing.

He also spoke privately to a servingman he trusted, and whom he knew to be fond of the queen, asking him to look after her in his place when he should be gone forever. The man promised to do all that one that of his lowly status could do to aid and comfort a royal personage, and allowed himself the liberty of rejecting the handsome payment that the king offered him. "My services are for sale, Majesty," he rebuked the king gently. "The strength of my arms and my back is for sale. My friendship is not." And the king was much shamed by this, and asked his pardon.

When the king left, quietly, in the night, so as not to awaken the queen to grief quite so soon, she was inconsolable as she had not been since she lost the use of her legs. The servingman was too wise to attempt to comfort her—which would not have been his place, in any event—but he did what he knew how to do, keeping palace officials and family members alike graciously and dexterously away from her until she felt herself at least a little recovered and able to deal with such matters. For she must now be queen in full measure, reigning alone, with no guide and no true knowledge of those she governed. She could only do her best, he counseled her, as he and her many other servants did.

And so she lived, ruling as she imagined her husband would have done—*Where could he be now? Sleeping cold in what hayfield? Begging his evening meal along what road?*—until her own time of stars and runes and farseeing priests came. She was aged then, though not as old as many had been who obediently cast aside power and took up holy homelessness. Her servant—old himself now, but long ascended to the highest rank in her household— fiercely pleaded her case for unique consideration, on the grounds of her disability; but the gods were the gods, implacable as ever. The only mercy allotted her was permission to take her special chair along with her into the wild. It was the last service her old friend could perform; she never saw him again.

There she sat, day after day: one old woman among the throng of beggars, hawkers, and petitioners who crowded the courtyard of the palace that had for so long, and so recently, been her home and her life. It was the hot season, and she suffered greatly; but to wheel herself back into the blessed shade of a god's statue meant making herself less visible to those passersby who wished to gain merit by placing coins in pleading hands. Most would have offered alms gladly to one who had lately been their ruler; but few of those had ever seen her face, and fewer still recognized her in her dusty rags. She went thirsty most days, and hungry many a night; and still she sat on alone on her wheeled throne.

Then the rains came. Within a day, they had driven half the courtyard swarm to cover; within two, they had beaten down all flowering growth and battered every leaf off the ornamental trees that ringed the palace. In three days, the cracked and withered earth, soaked beyond absorbing, had become a hungry, gummy marsh, sucking boots and sandals off their wearers' feet, and making it impossible for the wheels of the old queen's chair to turn at all. Prisoned on her throne, her begging-bowl full only of water, her condition more hopeless than that of the lowest beggar in her former realm, she bowed lower and lower beneath the pitiless lash of the rain, and waited to die.

She never really remembered the beggar woman coming to her, though sometimes she thought she recalled a voice out of the wind and rain, and rough, strong hands over hers on the arms of the wheelchair. But when she opened her eyes fully, it was to the steamy, pungent warmth of a cowshed, and the hands were drying her face and hair and body as they stripped her few scraps of clothing from her starving body and lifted her out of her chair to set her down, curled like a child, against a warm, breathing flank and covered her with straw, piles and piles of straw. She fell asleep with the soft, comforting murmur that cows make to their newborns in her ears, and she did not wake until the storm had passed and sunlight was shining in her eyes through the chinks in the shed walls.

The beggar woman was sitting on a hay bale, knees drawn up to her chest, greedily munching a fruit in its skin. Her voice, when she saw the queen reaching feebly for her chair, was as rough as her hands. "Lie still—you haven't the strength of a blind kitten. Show some sense now, and lie still!"

The queen could not tell the woman's age. Her brown face and bare arms were streaked with dried mud, and her hair was so dirty and tangled that it was impossible to be sure of what color it was. As for her dress, it was little better than the queen's rags, and she wore no shoes at all. She finished the fruit, tossed away the core with a grunt of disgust, hopped down from the hay bale, and rummaged to find a bucket lying loose in one of the stalls. With this in hand, she addressed herself to the cow who had kept the queen warm and alive all night, and quickly returned with new milk all but spilling over the bucket's rim. "You'll have to sit up and lap it as it stands. This inn's well enough for bed, but it's not much for breakfast."

The beggar woman strolled close to look at the wheelchair, propped against the stall door. "A pretty thing," she remarked, "but not much good without a dog or a goat to pull it, I'd think. Or maybe—" and here she turned and smiled sardonically at the exhausted and bewildered queen—"some poor fool to push it? Drink your milk while it's warm, best thing for you." She scraped with a dirty forefinger at the mud caking the chair's wheels. It fell away in long flakes and wrinkled clods. "Pretty, though, I'll say that . . ."

The queen drank as much as she could manage of the sweet milk, and only then found the strength to ask, "Who are you?"

The beggar woman shrugged. "No one you'd know." But the queen had fallen back to sleep, and the beggar woman put more straw over her; then picked up the begging-bowl, fallen to the dirt floor, and studied it thoughtfully for some time. "Pretty," she said again, and left the shed with the bowl under her arm.

The queen drowsed away the rest of the day under the straw, waking only to sip more of the milk and sleep again. Waking at last, warm and hungry, she saw the beggar woman crouched nearby, sorting through loaves of bread, entire rounds of cheese, sacks of dried lentils and peas, two bottles of wine, and even a packet of salt fish. When she saw that the queen was awake and watching her, she smiled proudly—the queen noticed that several of her lower teeth were gone—gesturing grandly over her treasure. "There's money, too," she announced, jingling coins in her hand. "All enough to see us on our way, I should think."

"On our way to where?" the queen asked dazedly. "And where is my bowl? You have saved my life, and I must beg for both of us now—it is the least I can do to repay you. If you will help me into my chair . . ."

The beggar woman laughed as harshly as she seemed to do everything else. "We'll neither of us need be seeking alms for a while now, my fine lady; how on earth did you come by a begging-bowl lined with silver?" Not waiting for an answer, she went on, "Well, we're not bound off anywhere tonight—nor tomorrow, either, until you get some strength into you. But winter's coming on, and there's too many sparrows pecking for crumbs around a palace, if you take my meaning. We'll do better in the hill country, where folk see fewer of our kind." She peered sharply at the queen then, out of shrewd, quick dark eyes. "Not but what it'll take wiser than I to ponder what your kind *is*. But you're some somebody, anyway, with your silver-lined bowl and that bloody chair that I'll be forever pushing and pulling out of every rut, I've no doubt. And maybe that . . . that *air* of yours will pay for itself along the way. Here—" she handed the queen a torn-off heel of bread and a chunk of cheese to go with it. "Eat and sleep for a few days, until the roads are dry. Eat and sleep."

The queen took her at her word, doing nothing for three days but dozing and waking, nibbling this or that of the beggar woman's bounty, and turning back to the deep comfort of the cow's warmly receptive side. In the night, vaguely roused by her companion's snoring a few feet from her, she tried hard to think about her lost life and her lost husband . . . but even he seemed as distant as though he had never been anything but a story that she had told herself in her childhood. She dreamed often during those days and nights, and while some of the dreams were sad, and some were frightening, in all of them she walked, as she had walked before her wedding day. But in those dreams she was always alone.

The beggar woman herself came and went as she chose: always cheerful, in her odd, half-mocking way, most often unwashed, sometimes with food or a few coins and sometimes not, but frequently, as the queen's vision cleared, bearing bruises on her legs and arms, or even on her face. When the queen pressed her for an explanation, she would either turn the question aside with a snort and a gesture, or say simply, "Minor disagreement." From somewhere she procured a sailor's needle and thread in order to mend the queen's torn and fouled clothes as best she could. Being no seamstress, she pricked her fingers often and swore interestingly each time; but she kept at the work with a gruff patience that belied the perennial half-derisive air with which she otherwise tended the queen. She spent a good deal of time squatting by the chair, cleaning the mud off the wheels and adding soft rags and feathers to the cushion that padded the seat. Now and then she would look up to growl wonderingly, "Tell me again who made this bloody ridiculous thing for you?

He must have taken you for a monkey—you need two sets of hands and a tail just to steer."

"It was my husband who had it made," the queen answered her. "He wanted me to have at least that much control over my life when he should be . . . when he must take up his new way." She had long been too old to weep, but her eyes still ached where the tears would have been.

"And you lost your legs on your wedding day?" The beggar woman cackled, rudely and raucously. "That must have been a bridal night indeed."

"Indeed," the queen said quietly, and the beggar woman laughed again.

One morning the queen woke to sunlight, and saw that the cowshed doors stood open and small birds were flying in and out. The beggar woman was busily arranging their food supplies for travel, doing it with astonishing inventiveness. Sacks of varying sizes were slung around a rod at the back of the wheelchair; other pouches and packages were bundled in wherever there was any secure space for them; and somehow there was still room for the queen, when the beggar woman lifted her in strong, skinny arms and deposited her on the cushioned seat with an exasperated grunt of "Sitting on it half your life didn't make it any smaller, I'll tell you that." But she took firm hold of the chair's handles and guided them out of the cowshed, where they both paused to take a long last look toward the storm-washed palace glinting in the sun. The beggars were returning, their wheedling voices audible from the cowshed as they crowded close, quarreling savagely over the handful of alms distributed every morning. The beggar woman's voice was oddly gentle for a moment as she said, "I was born there. Just behind that horse trough, in a mud puddle." Her usual hoarse chuckle displaced any wistfulness. "At least my mam told me it was mud."

The queen said, "I was born on the steps of the palace. The pains overtook my mother there."

She did not mention that her mother, a wealthy merchant's wife, had come out with her attendants and nurses to enjoy a last breath of free air before her confinement. The beggar woman looked at her with something like a new respect. "Aye, well, you know then. That would be where you get that hoity-toity style, no doubt of it. Didn't make you much good at it, though, did it? I watched you out there, you know—watched you for some little while—and you'd have thought you'd never begged in your life." She laughed again, rooting in one ear with a broken-nailed forefinger. "Well, time we started. It's a long way to the hills, and it'll be longer pushing my lady's bloody carriage and pair." She gripped the chair handles and thrust her weight forward. "Sit *still*, now!"

As the wheelchair jolted over ruts and naked tree roots, the queen asked the beggar woman, "Why did you save me, there, in the rain? I am nothing to you—why now are you making yourself responsible for my life?"

The beggar woman seemed to ponder the question quite seriously, scratching her frowsy head and wrinkling her invariably smudged nose. She said finally, "Just never saw anyone drown sitting up before. So stupid, I took it for a sign." And the queen laughed for the first time in a very long while.

They covered very little distance that first day, despite the fact that the roads were fairly level, with few deep holes, and no obstacles that the wheelchair could not be guided around. The hills, glistening cool invitation on the horizon, yet drew no closer, and the beggar woman was only able to cozen a few morsels of bread and honey out of a wary farmer eating his lunch beside the road. But the night was warm, and the queen slept well in a bed of soft grasses arranged for her by the beggar woman, who grumbled constantly as she did so. "You needn't think we'll be going on like this, my lady, just because you're too lazy to walk. Come a time, there will, when I'll be the one lounging in this idiot contraption, while you wheeze your guts out pushing me uphill. Tomorrow, next day, I'll be sitting there before you're even awake, just waiting my turn. Fair's fair, and it's a long way yet to the hills."

She said that often—*it's a long way yet to the hills*—even when they were deep among them, with the winding roads becoming steeper and rougher every day, and every other breath she panted was a curse as she toiled to keep the wheelchair from slipping back down a stony trail at her, or from running away with the helpless queen when the path suddenly dropped off. But for all her oaths and weary threats, she pushed the cumbersome chair and its usually terrified passenger farther on and farther up into country where cows grazed precariously on slanting rooftops, and gardens grew on carved terraces designed to take advantage of every single foot of ground. The hill people, as the beggar woman had foretold, indeed showed more generosity to strange travelers than city folk had done; but all the same, they proved just as anxious to see them on their way, rarely allowing them to rest so much as a night in their barns or cellars. Only during a storm—and not always then—were they likely to be granted shelter; and the queen, who already knew how to be grateful for the dumb kindness of a cow, came to appreciate dry firewood and a daughter's outworn clothes. Once a blacksmith repaired a broken wheel of the chair, and asked nothing for his labor; once a fisherman went out of his way to point out a safer road than the bandit-plagued one they were traveling. The queen learned to accept whatever strange gifts came their way with the courtesy she would have shown an ambassador from a greater kingdom, and to give back what she could—a smile— with her whole full heart.

It became more difficult every day for her to remember palace beds and palace meals, servants—except for the one, out of so many—and grand festivals in honor of neighboring rulers; even such tiny joys as reading poetry aloud to her husband the king, or being carried by him through the palace grounds on a cool blue evening. Whenever she realized that she had forever lost one or another such cherished moment, then she would mourn bitterly, while the beggar woman mocked her. "And what are you grizzling for this time? A man, was it?—some sturdy rogue, liked the notion of a woman who could never run away from him? Sit up and stop mewling—it's a long way yet to the hills."

She herself appeared stringy-muscled and tireless, which the queen knew was not so. Almost every night, she could hear the deep whine in her companion's splintering breath as they lay by each other on cold ground or a stable's gritty floor, after another day of stubbornly wrestling the battered wheelchair still farther on toward . . . toward what hills, what goal?

For that the beggar woman had some definite objective beyond seeking more generous almsgivers, the queen had long ceased doubting. They were bound *somewhere*, if it cost the beggar woman the last strength in her body, which the queen could see happening in the frighteningly wide eyes that seemed to sink deeper into the thinning face day by day, feel in the raw hands that forced the chair onward. If guilt and sympathy could have brought her up out of her chair, the beggar woman would indeed have been riding in her place; as it was, the best she could do was to urge her to lie up for a day, two days, in some cave or—better—an abandoned barn, which she angrily refused to do. "Maybe you've some martyr's notion of dying in the filthy rain, as you began, but I surely don't. Winter's coming round again, and we'll go to earth when we reach our earth. Hold your peace, therefore—and stop squirming so when I pick you up." And the skinny, trembling arms raised her, and the chapped and bleeding hands eased her once more into the chair with the old surprising dexterity, determined gentleness, and the equally familiar snarling, "O bloody woman, didn't anyone at least teach you to hold your head up? Sit straight, blast you!" The blanket tucked so precisely around her was, at the last, the only one they had.

There came a morning, as the queen had known it must come, when it was nearly noon before the beggar woman—she who usually demanded that they be on the road by sunrise—was able to struggle to her feet, snatch up whatever scraps were left over from last night's dinner of scraps, and then at last grip the wheelchair handles. There had been soft rain in the night; the midday air was no warmer than dawn had been, and the queen clenched her teeth to keep them from chattering. But the beggar woman stepped out bravely for all of that, grumbling inaudibly as she lunged the chair along muddy paths and through heaps of dankly clinging leaves. It was not until she was endeavoring to guide it over the mild rise of a tree root that she went down slowly, fluttering and half-turning like a leaf herself. She attempted to rise, and could not, and did not try again.

The queen had never been able to afford to take any action without considering the consequences; so she never knew where she discovered the courage to twist and hurl herself out of her chair in complete thoughtlessness, falling hard enough beside the beggar woman that for a moment she could not breathe. For long minutes the two of them lay very still together, then the queen scrabbled herself into a sitting position, and pulled the poor bruised head onto her thigh.

Only when the beggar woman opened her eyes did the queen fully realize how old she was. It was not a matter of lines never observed before, or of another missing tooth or two, or hair that seemed suddenly to have become grayer and thinner than when they had stopped the night before, but layers of ancient grief and rage and weariness, all laid down one atop another, like geological strata. The beggar woman's words sounded like stones in her throat, but they came clearly to the queen's ears. She said, "A long way to the hills. At last, it is all to end in the hills."

"Nonsense," the queen said with a firmness she wished with all her heart to feel. "There is a village within a mile—you told me so yourself yesterday. We can reach it easily, and we will rest there until you are better. Rest now, and I will wait as long as you need, until we are ready to go on." She took the beggar woman's hands in her own and held them to her breast. "Only rest now, dear friend."

But the beggar woman shook her head, smiling, and for the first time her smile was neither mocking nor mean, but oddly rueful. "I go no farther. It was too long a way . . . longer than you think." She coughed and spat, and the queen wiped her mouth with her own ragged sleeve. The beggar woman said, "You are the queen." She had never spoken the word before.

The queen tried to laugh. "You must have known that the day we met, because I was such a bad beggar." Her own throat was hurting more and more.

"Long before." The beggar woman managed to raise herself slightly in the queen's lap, her eyes like coals in her ashen face. She said, "Your husband was the king."

"Yes," the queen whispered in answer. "Until he was not. Until he had to go away. Into the wilderness, like me." She could not hear the last words herself.

"He was a hunter. A great hunter." The beggar woman's voice had grown stronger and harsher. "He killed a deer, do you remember?"

The queen frowned. "He loved to hunt." She made another attempt at laughter. "I used to tell him that he loved the hunt more than he loved me. And he would kiss me and say, *'Not quite, heart of mine . . . never quite.'* But he killed so many deer—I am sorry . . ."

The beggar woman said, "You would remember this deer. It was a great red buck, and its antlers rose up like a forest, like a garden. It was killed on the day before your wedding."

"*The offering . . .*" The queen dropped the hands she had been gripping so warmly and put her own fingers to her lips. "My husband fed a whole village with that magnificent animal. He told me it was an offering to the gods, so that we would be happy together, always. And so we were—so we were, even when . . ."

"That deer was my husband." The words came very quietly, almost without expression. The beggar woman said, "He was a shapeshifter—a master—but he never used his gift to harm anyone. He just liked being an animal from time to time—a fox, an otter, an owl, a salmon. But the deer . . ." Now it was she who gripped the queen's wrists, so strongly that the queen opened her mouth in pain. "The deer was his favorite, his best making. He always wanted me to change myself into a doe, so that we could run away into the deepest woods together, and perhaps . . . perhaps not come back. But I never could, though I tried. I was never witch enough, not for that."

The queen recoiled from her words, but then realized that to pull away as her whole body desired would spill the beggar woman's head and shoulders back onto the damp ground, so she forced herself to remain still. She said, "I am sorry. My husband would never, never . . . if he had known. If he had only *known* . . ."

"Yes," the beggar woman said, but she hardly seemed to be listening. She said, "My heart left me on that day. It crawled away and died, and there was nothing left but revenge to fill the empty place. Your husband had taken my man—I would have taken yours on that same day, if I could . . . not witch enough for that, either . . ." Her voice fell away to a forlornly bitter mumble. "Took you from him, anyway . . . next best . . ."

A strange quietness had settled over the queen: a calm as far beyond anger or fear as it was beyond the loss that had lived with her for half her life. She said softly, "My legs. You cursed me, you poor thing." She brushed the beggar woman's dirty, tangled hair back from her face.

"Always a price," the beggar woman whispered. "For all we take, we pay . . ." Her eyes and voice were far away, but the words were clear. "When I spoke my curse on you, I lost my power . . . all of it, all my nice little gift . . . gone forever." Her sudden raking laughter had the sound of blood in it. "Curses come high. Beggar ever since, just like you . . . and no vengeance to show for it, not a day, not a day . . ."

She began to weep then, raggedly and tearlessly, as though she had forgotten how. This the queen could not bear; and almost against her will she found herself holding the beggar woman in her arms, crooning, "Hush—oh, *hush*, do, please hush! You never harmed me—you could not . . . I lost nothing, nothing that mattered—you lost everything, and I am so sorry! Please— *please* forgive my husband! He did not *know* . . ."

But still the terrible dry weeping continued, shaking the queen's body as much as it convulsed the exhausted body that she rocked like the child she had never had. At last in desperation, she cried out, "I forgive you! If you will only forgive my husband, then fully and freely do I forgive you!"

And with these words she screamed, because feeling had begun to return to her legs, and with it pain such as she had never known in all her life. The agony crept steadily upward from her feet, long since bare, and she screamed, *"Make it stop! O, gods, make it stop!"* while the beggar woman wept and coughed and cried out, calling a name the queen did not know; and so they rocked and moaned together, scattering the dank leaves.

But finally the queen's new legs hurt her less and less, and the pain seemed to flow into the wobbly strength of a fawn. She stood up for the first time since her wedding day—promptly fell down—then stood again, swaying, feeling herself thin as rain. She said, "It is your turn to ride," and stooped to lift the beggar woman into the wheelchair. But the other shook her head weakly, and the queen stepped back, still cautious on her feet. Staring down, she saw the beggar woman's face seemingly growing younger, as happens sometimes when death is close, the rumples of a life smoothed away like a bedsheet. The queen said again, "Please. You must ride now."

"I have done all things that I must do," replied the beggar woman. "All but one."

Then the queen dropped on her knees beside her, as she could not have done only minutes before, and she pleaded, "I would have died but for you. Not merely in the rain, that first day, but in every way, from the inside out. Wherever we have journeyed, you have sheltered me, you have gone without that I might have, gone cold that I might sleep warm. What you did to me you have atoned for again and again, and I have gladly forgiven you . . . no, we have forgiven each other, we two old women." She stroked the beggar woman's dirty cheek and kissed her forehead, saying, "Come—the village is close enough that I can carry you. Never mind the poor old chair, we'll not need it any more. I would be proud to carry you."

"No," whispered the beggar woman as the queen began to lift her where she lay. "No—too long a way . . . I thought if I brought you . . . if you forgave, my power . . . but curses come high, and it is too long, too long to the hills . . ." But there was no resistance in her, nor breath, either; when the queen stood up with the body in her arms that was almost weightless, even when she freed one hand to close the beggar woman's eyes. She said no farewell, neither made any prayer, but she stood so for a long time.

If there had not been rain, the queen would never have been able to claw out a grave with her bare hands. Even so, it took her most of the day before she felt it deep enough to protect the beggar woman's body from weather and animals. She marked the grave with the wheelchair, promising silently to return with a stone once the ground had settled. Then she wiped her hands on the cleanest of her rags, and started on alone, still on trembling fawn's legs.

On the outskirts of the village, she met an old man gathering firewood. She knew him, but he did not know her; and she realized from his wondrously sweet faraway smile that he never would. But he clucked pityingly at her bleeding hands, and she helped him arrange the broken branches more comfortably in the three slings he bore on his back, and she carried all she could herself, and so they walked on together. He took her hand trustingly, and smiled again when she called him by a name that he did not recognize. And the queen rested her head gently against his white head, and they went on.

TRINITY COUNTY, CA:
YOU'LL WANT TO COME AGAIN
AND WE'LL BE GLAD TO SEE YOU!

My late friend Pat Derby (with whom I wrote my one as-told-to book, The Lady and Her Tiger) was forever rescuing half-starved wolves, bears, and mountain lions, kept as guardians of their compounds by drug dealers all over hidden wilderness camps in northern California, mostly to ward off, not so much the police and the FBI, as their fellow dealers. I lived in the Santa Cruz area for twenty-two years, during which time it became one of the major sources of marijuana and—far worse—crystal methedrine, which, by the time you read this, may have been officially recognized as the leading cash crop of the state. I knew Trinity County in those days less well than I knew Santa Cruz, Alpine, El Dorado, and Monterey, but the underground economy was the same, and everyone from Sacramento officialdom to boardwalk hippies knew it. This story merely takes the hidden world that Pat Derby showed me a notch further: what if drug dealers employed dragons, instead of lions. . . ?

�֍

"This stuff *stinks*," Connie Laminack complained. She and Gruber were dressing for work in the yard's cramped and makeshift locker room, which, thanks to budget cuts, was also the building's only functional toilet. To get to the dingy aluminum sink, she had to step around the urinal, then dodge under Gruber's left arm as he forced it up into the sleeve of his bright yellow outer coverall.

"You get used to it."

"No, I won't. They let me use my Lancôme in school. *That* smells human."

"And has an FPF rating that's totally bogus," Gruber said. "Anything you can buy retail is for posers and pet-shop owners. Won't cut it out here."

Laminack unscrewed the top from the plain white plastic jar on the shelf below the mirror, and squinted in disgust at the gray gloop inside. "I'm just saying. Gack."

Gruber smiled. Stuck with a newbie, you could still get some fun out of it. Sometimes. "Make sure you get it every damn place you can reach. Really rub it in. State only pays quarter disability if you come home Extra Crispy."

"Nice try, but some of us actually do read the HR paperwork we sign."

"Oh, right," Gruber said. "College grad." She gave him a hard look in the mirror, but dutifully started rubbing the D-schmear on her hands and arms anyway, then rolled up her pants legs to get at her calves.

"Face, too. Especially your face, and an inch or two into the hairline. Helps with the helmet seal."

"Just saving the worst for last."

Gruber laughed wryly. "It's all the worst."

"You'd be the one to know, wouldn't you?"

"Got *that* right, trainee."

By the time they headed out to the Heap, he was throwing questions at her, as per the standard training drill, but not enjoying it the way he usually did. For one thing, she'd actually done a good job with the D-schmear, even getting it up into her nostrils, which first-timers almost never did. For another, she seemed to truly know her shit. Book shit, to be sure, not the real-world shit she was here to start learning . . . but Gruber was used to catching new kids in some tiny mistake, then pile-driving in to widen the gap, until they were panicked and stammering. Only Laminack wasn't tripping up.

It had begun to bug him. That, and the fact that she bounced. Like he needed *perky* to deal with, on top of everything else.

He waved back to Manny Portola, the shift dispatcher, who always stood in the doorway to see the different county crews off. It was one of Manny's pet superstitions, and in time it had become Gruber's as well, though he told himself he was just keeping the old guy happy.

Laminack waved to the dispatcher as well, which irritated Gruber, even though he knew it shouldn't. He slapped the day-log clipboard against his leg.

"Next! Name the three worst invasives in Trinity."

"Trick question."

"Maybe, maybe not."

"No," she insisted. "Definitely. You didn't define your terms." Her bland smile didn't change, but Gruber thought he heard a tiny flicker of anger. Maybe he was finally getting to her. "Are we talking plants or animals here? 'Cause Yellow Star Thistle and Dalmatian Toadflax and Kamathweed are hella invasive, even if the tourists do like the pretty yellow flowers. And if we *are* talking animals, not plants, do you want me to stick to the Ds, or do you want me to rattle off the three worst things that have ever crawled or flown or swum in here from somewhere they shouldn't? Which I could. And what do you mean by 'worst,' anyway? Because for my money, jet slugs are about as yucky as it gets, and there are a lot more of them up here now than there are China longs. So yeah, I call trick question."

Gruber definitely wasn't ready for two weeks of this. "Nobody likes a show-off, Laminack."

"No, sir."

"We're not County Animal Control, and we're damn well not the State Department of Food and Agriculture or the California Invasive Plant Council. So what do you think I wanted to hear when I asked that question?"

Reaching the Heap, Laminack opened the driver's-side door for him and stepped back. She didn't exactly stand at attention, but near enough.

"I think you wanted me to tell you that last year's baseline survey put quetzals, China longs, and Welsh reds at the top of the list in Trinity, but winter was rough, so it's too early to know yet what we'll be dealing with this season. Especially with the pot growers and meth labs upping their black-market firepower."

"Hunh." Without meaning to, he found himself nodding. "Not bad, Laminack."

"Call me Connie, okay? My last name sounds like a duck call."

Great, Gruber thought. *She even bounces standing still.*

First scheduled stop of the day was more than thirty miles out of Weaverville, up 299 into the deep woods of Trinity National Forest, almost all the way to Burnt Ranch. Despite everything eating at him, Gruber always found the views in this corner of the county restful, an ease to the soul, and he enjoyed watching Connie begin to get clear on just how big the place was, even in this first tiny taste: 3,200 square miles by outline, same size as Vermont on the map—or all of Texas, if ever God came along and stomped the Trinity Alps out flat—and only 13,000 people to get in the way, the majority of whom lived in Weaverville and Lewiston and Hayfork. The rest were so spread out that words like "sparse" and "isolated" didn't do the situation justice. Gruber had been on the job for sixteen years, and he knew there were people living in corners of these woods so deep he still hadn't been there yet.

They turned off onto a tributary road that wasn't shown on the state-supplied map, and wound uphill for five snaky miles before Gruber stopped the Heap and killed the engine.

"Welcome to your first block party. Another mile or so up, we're going to do a little Easter egg hunt. You want to guess what kind?"

For the first time this morning, Connie hesitated. Then she caught herself and said, firmly, "Belgian wyverns. I thought maybe doublebacks, for a minute, but that would have been a couple of weeks ago at this latitude. Right?"

Gruber nodded. "Almost all the other Ds are late-summer, early-autumn layers, but wyverns and doublebacks—and Nicaraguan charlies, only we don't have those up here, not yet, thank God—they lay their eggs in the spring, so they'll hatch and be ready in time to eat the other Ds' eggs. Just this side of parasites, you ask me. But some elements of the Asian community think ground-up prepubescent wyvern bones are an aphrodisiac, so there's always some idiot in the woods willing to try and raise the little bastards. We got an anonymous tip on this place a week ago."

"So let's go. I'm ready."

Gruber shook his head. "Ground rules, first. And fair warning: say anything but yes—and I do mean *anything*—and we're home in Weaverville before lunch, with your ass planted firmly on the next bus back to UC Davis. This is not a joke up here. This isn't the classroom. Mostly we don't run into trouble, but that's *mostly*, and you can't let that get in the way of being ready for everything else."

Connie didn't say a word. She looked at Gruber for a moment, and then nodded.

"First rule," Gruber continued. "What I tell you to do, you do. If I say 'run,' you damn well *sprint*, and you don't look back. If I shout, 'Get back in the Heap!' you jump in here and hit the autolock, even if I'm still outside."

"Yes," Connie said.

"Second rule. If you're in here and I'm in trouble, you hit the screechers."

"Yes."

"Third rule. If that doesn't help, then you drive the hell out of sight as fast as you can, and you keep calling in to the sheriff's office for backup until you finally reach a live zone and get through. Then you *sit and wait for somebody to show up*. This is not—I repeat *not*—some reality TV show. There are reasons Manny's got that NO HEROES sign on his desk."

"Got it." She blinked and corrected herself. "Yes."

"Fourth rule, you see even a hint of a gun, you don't wait for me to yell. You get your butt back in the Heap and duck down. The plate on this thing can handle pretty much anything one of the locals is likely to be carrying." He didn't wait for her to respond before he went on. "And finally, fifth rule, today you don't say anything to anybody without checking with me first. Walk straight, stand tall, and make like you're Clint Eastwood with laryngitis. Got that?"

She nodded once.

Not so bouncy now. Good.

"Helmet and gloves on, then. Let's go."

The road wound on a while longer, then turned left over a ridge and started down. As it did, the landscape changed, the usual Trinity mix of tall oak, pine, and fir trees giving way to high pasture and orchards, green and peaceful as a children's book.

The farmhouse wasn't out of a picture book, but a new coat of paint masked its aged and fraying condition. An old woman in a sun hat was down on both knees, pruning roses and humming to herself, not even looking at the Heap as it pulled in. There was a one-gallon lawn and garden sprayer sitting next to her.

"Deaf or on guard," Gruber said. "And you know how I vote. Keep your tapper handy, but stay behind me."

The old woman only looked up when Gruber opened the Heap's door and stepped out, his coverall a bright yellow blotch in the middle of a bright blue day. He checked her out. Pure Grandma. Straw hat, pink cheeks, worn old flannel shirt, muddy-kneed jeans . . . no jury would convict her of stealing cookies, let alone raising Ds.

"Can I help you?" she asked.

Gruber turned on the big bland smile that came packaged with the uniform and started forward, nice and easy. He heard Connie fall into line.

"Ma'am, good morning. My name is Mike Gruber, and this is my partner, Connie Laminack. We're D Patrol for the county." He pointed at the big agency patch on the front of his coverall, the one just below the California state seal, then made a show of checking his clipboard. "Are you Mrs. Johanna Watkins?"

The woman leaned back on her haunches, shading her eyes with one hand, even though the sun was behind her.

"That's me. Beautiful day, isn't it?"

"Yes, ma'am. Surely is."

"Nice to be outside. Have to spray these roses every day, you know, or else the deer eat them. What can I do for you?"

"Well . . ." Gruber paused. "The thing of it is, Mrs. Watkins,

Johanna, we have reliable information that you and Mr. Watkins have been breeding wyverns—Belgian wyverns, to be precise—and selling the younglings to a crew down in Douglas City. Now, as I'm sure you know, there are both state and federal statutes against wyvern trafficking of any kind: live or dead, eggs, skins, organs, you name it. It's illegal."

The Watkins woman was good: Gruber had to give her that. She flashed a crinkly smile straight out of a biscuit-mix commercial and said, "Oh, but everyone does it, surely—that's just one of those laws, you know, like they say, more honored in the breach than the observance—"

Gruber interrupted her. "Well, actually no, ma'am, everybody *doesn't* do it, whatever you've been told. And the laws *are* enforced, as I'm afraid you're about to find out. Now I'm going to need to speak to your husband—and then, if you two could give us a brief walking tour of your operation—"

Johanna Watkins was on her feet, periwinkle-blue eyes wide, moving smoothly into Plan B: shocked and trembling innocence. "Officer, we really didn't . . . I mean, Eddie, my husband, Eddie and I, we're just two old people living on a fixed income, and it seemed . . . I mean, nobody really told us, and we were just trying . . . we didn't want to be a burden on our son—"

Gruber stopped her as courteously as he could, keeping one eye on the garden shears dangling in her left hand. He had once been attacked by an old man swinging a fan belt studded with bits of broken glass, and the event had left him with a certain wariness regarding senior citizens. "Well, ma'am, all I'm required to do is write you up a citation, like a traffic ticket—the rest'll be up to Sheriff Trager's discretion. So if Mr. Watkins is home . . ." He had always found it better—and often safer—to leave commands implied.

"Yes," Mrs. Watkins stammered, letting her voice tremble affectingly. "Yes, yes, of course. If you'll just wait here, I'll be, I'll get . . ." She too left the sentence unfinished, dropping the shears and wandering toward the house in a seeming daze.

Behind him, Connie murmured, "Permission to speak, sir?"

"Only 'til Sweetie Bat gets back." He took a few steps and craned his neck to observe the surprisingly large stretch of tightly-fenced paddock that was located south and downslope from the house. Several rough-hewn wooden poles sporting a makeshift power line ran between the two. Beyond the paddock, the woods began.

Connie said, "I know it's silly—I guess—but she does look like my grandmother. She really does."

Gruber shrugged. "She's *somebody's* grandmother. Retirement, kids gone, a little problem with cash flow . . . we see a lot of that. Sometimes they're just bored, you'd be surprised."

"She looked so scared," Connie sighed. "I just wanted to tell her, *'It's okay, it'll be all right'*—"

She was interrupted by the sound of a slamming door at the back of the house, followed immediately by a stumbling clatter and scraps of a shrill and breathless quarrel—then the unmistakable growl of a two-stroke engine. Gruber said mildly, "Well, *shit*." Loping around the corner of the old farmhouse, he saw Johanna Watkins and a lanky old man wearing checked pants and a yellow sweater racing toward the tree line on a metallic green minibike. Gruber halted, scratching his head, and began to laugh.

Connie came up beside him, staring after the sputtering little bike as it vanished into the trees. "Shouldn't we go after them, or something?"

"Not our job, I'm happy to inform you. We're contraband, not perps. Trager's boys can track them later, or maybe nab them when they sneak back to the house, likely tonight. They weren't carrying anything, and it gets *cold* up here after sunset."

He flipped his tapper to trank and started toward the paddock, saying over his shoulder, "Stay back 'til I call you." The gate was clearly meant to be opened by a remote switch—*probably in the kitchen, right next to the cookie jar*—but the lock was cheap, and Gruber forced it easily. The two wyverns came out of hiding as soon as he opened the gate, bounding toward him like little kangaroos on their powerful hind legs. Red, with dark-gold chests and bellies, they stood just under three feet high; three-foot-six was a King Kong among wyverns. "Geese with teeth," Manny called them, but for all that they could do damage. The wings—a much deeper red, almost black—were useless for flying, but tipped with sharp, curving claws. Gruber had always considered them more dangerous than the fangs, which were just as sharp, and more numerous, but easier to keep track of.

He let the wyverns get close, having no illusions regarding his own ability with hand-held weapons, but then he dropped them with one dart apiece. They were out before they hit the ground, and would stay that way for ten, maybe twelve hours: the current generation of tranquilizers was a lot more reliable than what he'd started the job with, and good for a wider range of Ds, no matter how many hearts they had, or whether their blood was acid or base. Gruber had no nostalgia for the old days, except as they involved long-gone movies and breweries.

"Easter Bunny time," he called over his shoulder. Connie approached the paddock slowly, casting a wary eye toward the sedated wyverns. Watching her, Gruber said, "No, I take it back, it's May. Time to go gathering nuts."

"They actually do look like nuts, don't they?" Connie frowned, remembering. "We had a whole extra series on protective color-ation just in eggs."

"Yeah, they look like coconuts," Gruber said. "Except for the ones that don't. Belgian wyverns can be weird. So you watch where you're putting your feet." Remembering altogether too well how long it had taken him to get the knack, he kept a close eye on Connie as they worked through the paddock together, never letting her get too far from him. What worried him more, as they loaded the eggs into the standard McNaughton keeper—clumsier to carry than the old Dorchester, but it could hold twice as many eggs as their thirty-seven in perfect thermal stasis as long as its battery pack held out—was feeling their rising warmth in his palms, and realizing just how close they had been to hatching.

When a third pass didn't turn up anything new, he had Connie drive the Heap down to the paddock while he tagged and chipped the wyverns, then bound their wings and legs with Thermo-Kevlar banding. It took a shared effort to get the sleeping creatures locked away in the back, him lifting and her pushing. The male was particularly troublesome: its head and neck kept flopping in the wrong direction as they tried to angle it into the Heap's fireproofed main containment module. After they finally managed the trick, Gruber took Connie with him to the farmhouse. He showed her how to fill out the official citation form, and had her tape it to the front door with four strips of bright orange waterproof tape, one strip per side.

Back in the Heap, he took the wheel while Connie stored the McNaughton under her seat. Gruber would have sworn that he saw her pat it once, quickly and shyly.

As they headed out, Connie asked, "Where do you suppose the proud parents went?"

"Hiding out with family, maybe. Calling lawyers. Not a lot of options when it gets to this point. When we hit a place where my cell works, I'll call Manny. Trager's people will make things plain to them, one way or another." The Watkins farm disappeared from the rearview mirror as he spoke. "How you liking it so far?"

"Is that another trick question?" Her voice was quiet and subdued, all the early-morning attitude gone. She said, "They were little, but they were scary. The way they went straight for you . . ."

"They can hurt you," Gruber said. He glanced sideways at her. "Not like class, huh? Not like field trips, even."

Connie was silent for some time. In this stretch, the narrow old road was rough, all pebbles and potholes. They passed a couple of abandoned trailers, and a lean, ugly dog chased along after the Heap for a while, until it got bored. She said finally, "What are they like . . . the big ones? What does it *feel* like?"

Gruber shrugged. "Not that different, you been doing it long enough. Sure, you wet your pants, first time it's a quetzal coming at you, first time you look right into the eyes of a China long. But there aren't as many in the county as people think—I went two years one time, never saw anything bigger than a doubleback— and as long as you stay cool, long as you treat each and every damn D as though it was twelve feet tall, you're pretty much okay. Usually."

"Usually," Connie said. "Right."

"I'm forty-seven years old," Gruber said, smiling at her before he could stop himself. "Forty-eight in three weeks. Believe me, *usually* is as good as it gets. Ds, anything else. I'll settle for *usually* any time."

He turned his head away quickly to watch the road; you could break an axle as easily as an ankle in this country. Connie had her back to him, looking out, one elbow braced on the window frame. She said, half to herself, "Looks just like eastern Mendocino."

"Spent some time there?"

"Visited my cousins, growing up. They're over in Ukiah."

"Mendocino's got the same troubles we have. The farms mostly don't pay worth a damn anymore, so a lot of folks either sell out to the pot growers and meth makers or go into the business themselves."

"Will—my older cousin—he told me stories." She shook her head. "But I never saw anything. No Ds, for sure, though I heard they were there. Sheltered life, I guess."

"Pot farms aren't on your typical family-outing list."

She laughed, a bit shakily, and replied, "I liked the trees and the space okay, but I was a city kid. I just wanted a Barbie. A Barbie and a utility belt, like Batman's." Gruber looked at her. "I had to know how he got all that *stuff* into all those little compartments. And what about the gadgets and things we never saw? I had to *know*, that's all."

"Permission to speak revoked," Gruber said. "Forever."

The rest of the morning went smoothly, standard drill-and-drop-in for every live report like the Watkins' place: drive the neighboring roads, watch for burn marks or D scat, stop every few miles to let the pheromone detectors take a sniff, and knock on whatever doors they could find. In that fashion, they checked out half a dozen farms and isolated cabins, the Heap toiling up one barely-visible dirt track to break into briefly-dazzling alpine blue, and then plunging straight down another into a hemlock valley dense with a heavy, motionless dark green. Only one place was harboring a D, a pitiful little half-starved sniggerbit that might actually have been a family pet, like the kids clinging to their silent father's legs claimed. The man himself said nothing. He just looked at Gruber and Connie and the filled-out citation as though they were all different kinds of snakes, then led his kids inside so they wouldn't have to see the sniggerbit tranked and taken away.

In the ordinary manner, Gruber reported back to Manny in Weaverville as soon as he got up high enough on some hill to see a bar or two on his cell. Life would have been easier with a sat phone, but the county wouldn't spring for the service plan.

Manny's voice sounded like he was on the other side of the moon, or maybe trapped in a room full of rabid washing machines.

"... *ob's guys say they need ... back at the Watkins' ...*"

"Say again, please, Manny. This connection sucks."

"Who's 'ob'?" asked Connie.

"Sheriff Trager," he told her. Then back into the cell: "Say again, please. I'm not getting this."

"... *burned down. Whole house gone. Big ... tracks, fire score, maybe some tail marks. Bob wants you there for a walkaround. Meet ... 299 south of—*"

That was it. Gruber looked at the cell phone in his hand. No bars, just a lot of crackling noise. No point in even trying to call back. Briefly he considered going higher, trying to get back in touch, but to do that he'd have to get out and climb for who knows how long, or else head downhill in the Heap and hope he could find the forest service road that tracked the facing ridge.

"Was that about the Watkins' place? It's *burned down?*"

"You heard what I heard," he said. Then: "County map. Glove compartment." She fumbled for it even as he kept speaking. "Sheriff Trager is not exactly a patient man, so let's see if we can find a shortcut."

❉ ❉ ❉

They were still several miles away, by the map, headed down-hill on a road that didn't deserve the name, when a yellow light started blinking on the dashboard. Gruber slammed on the brakes. The Heap skidded to a halt, and he and Connie were jolted against their shoulder belts so hard Gruber knew they'd be feeling it the next day.

Connie shot him a look. "What's wrong?"

"Stay here. I'll be right back." He threw the Heap into park but left it running. With one hand, he unstrapped himself as fast as he could; with the other, he pushed the door open wide.

"Gruber?"

"Just *stay here*."

He shut the door behind him as gently as he could, but the *clatch* sound still seemed like a gunshot in the quiet under the trees. Gruber held his breath and listened. He heard the Heap's low idling and some distant bird sounds, but nothing else. He looked down the rough road in the direction they were going, then back the way they'd come, and off to either side. All the time, he kept his eyes vague and unfocused, paying attention mainly to his peripheral vision, trying to tease some hint of motion out of the tangle of trees and leaves and brush. Nothing that way, either. He did get detailed then, leaving the side of the Heap to explore a little way into the woods, peering low on the tree trunks and high into the branches, looking for firesign or fresh breaks.

After five minutes, he came back to the Heap, opened the driver's-side door, and stood there without getting in, frowning at the still-blinking yellow light.

"You are seriously freaking me out," Connie said, not even

trying to hide the worry in her voice. "What's going on? Why'd you stop?"

"That," Gruber said, pointing at the light.

"What, do we have engine trouble?"

"No," he said, getting back in the Heap. He pulled the door shut normally and started to belt himself back in. "That's the emergency telltale for the passive pheromone traps. Manny calls it the 'oh shit' light."

"You mean—"

"Oh yeah," he nodded. "I can't find any sign of it out there, but we just crossed serious D trail. That or the damn sensor is showing a false positive, which could be, given the jouncing it's gotten today."

"What do we do?"

"We check it out. Burnt house in the neighborhood, that might have been Grandma and Grandpa coming back to get rid of evidence. But Manny said Trager spotted fire score . . . so we check it out. Cautiously."

She shook her head. "My folks are going to call me at the motel tonight and ask me how my first day went, and I'm so going to have to lie to them. They never wanted me doing this."

"That's not your big problem," Gruber said.

"It isn't?"

"Nope." His lips pulled back in a flat grin as he put the Heap back into drive, then eased down on the gas. "Didn't I tell you? Newbies have to write the first drafts of the incident reports. You're going to be up to your eyebrows in paperwork 'til midnight."

"Thanks."

When he saw her expression, he wanted to laugh, but the light that was still blinking on the dash wouldn't let him.

❊ ❊ ❊

Connie spotted them before he did—a scattering of trees, all firs, all fairly close together, bearing the unmistakable fingerprint of fire: scorch marks like whip weals, ten or twelve feet off the ground. On the ground next to the trees was what would have looked like an abandoned turnoff, except for the fresh tire tracks vanishing into it. Gruber shifted to four-wheel drive and turned the Heap to follow, doggedly pushing it through clinging, scraping underbrush that grabbed at the tires and fenders and menacingly low boughs that actually blocked the way. He coaxed and cajoled the truck over logs that had obviously been hauled into position. Finally, around a hundred yards in, things eased off, and he found himself driving on a well-tended trail, flat and easy and wide enough for a commercial trailer.

Without turning his head, Gruber said, "Name the seven major Ds that actually breathe fire."

Connie welcomed the distraction. "Uh . . . Welsh reds, quetzals, China longs—the North China subgenus, *not* the southern longs."

"Keep going."

"Himalayans, the San Ysidro group, the Yilbegan . . . and the Chuvash. Right?"

"Right. So what do we have here? Consider the evidence."

Gruber swung the Heap past a couple of trees burnt charcoal-black, as though they had been through a forest fire. Connie said quickly, "Anything could have done those: they burned from the ground up. But the fire marks back there, those were pretty high. A *humungous* Welsh red could do it, maybe, but more likely a quetzal or a China long. I'm betting on a long."

Gruber nodded. "Agreed. But why *not* a quetzal? Why not any of the others?"

"Well . . ." She swallowed hard. Her voice sounded dry and rough to him, like it hurt to speak. "They've never been reported up here, not even once. And longs outnumber quetzals and reds six to one in the reclamation stats. The longs have been invasive up here since '82, they're a lot easier to get hold of . . . no, it's got to be a long."

A rambling, ranch-style house was coming into view through the trees, and Gruber braked the Heap to an easy stop at the first sight of it. "Guess we're going to find out."

He put on his helmet and gloves and opened the driver's-side door. Keeping his voice low, he said, "Rules still apply. You lock up after me, stay right where you are, and if I get into trouble, you are solid *gone*, yelling for help all the way."

She said, "I thought we were contraband, not perps."

"All I'm going to do is look around a little bit, size up the operation—then we're out of here. Just keep your eyes open and the engine running."

"All right." Her voice was almost inaudible, a child's mumble. She said, "I wish you didn't have to do this."

Gruber said, "It's not the D I'm worried about, not so much—it's the people. People are always scarier than Ds, that's the first rule of the job. I'll be fine. You sit *tight*, you got that? You got it, Connie?" It was the first time he had actually called her by her name.

"I said all right, didn't I?" She frowned at him.

"Back in a flash." He popped a rack of Winged Monkeys out of the holder in the door and stuffed all six into different pockets of his coverall. The little handball-sized spheres were a cross between an insect fogger and a grenade, only with a payload of burst-release broad-spectrum tranquilizers. Gruber hated them, fully trusting neither their accuracy nor their cargo, but at least this way he could go in without looking aggressively armed, while still carrying something useful at longer range than the standard tapper.

Walking alone toward the house, he knew from just tasting the air that one of the big Ds was nearby, though he couldn't yet make out which breed. *They always smell like garbage-dump fires, just different kinds.* Part of him wanted to bolt back inside the Heap and head straight for Weaverville, but he knew the grief he'd catch from Trager's boys if something like *that* ever got around. So he turned, with the Heap already barely visible among the dark trees, and gave Connie a jaunty little wave.

That's when he saw the green minibike parked off to one side, near the bushes. He'd walked right by it, but hadn't noticed because the angle had been wrong.

Well, he thought. *That answers that.*

He turned without letting his face show anything, then walked the rest of the way to the ranch house. When he got there, he climbed the three steps to the low veranda, knocked on the front door, and stood quickly to one side, just in case.

He was not especially surprised when the door was answered fairly promptly, but the wispy, pallid creature who opened it did catch him off-guard. Not quite an albino, having watery blue eyes and watery red hair, the man was still pale as the liquid that pours off yogurt or tofu when the container is first opened. Clearly in his early twenties, he already had the ruined mouth and teeth of a scrofulous old man. But his voice was guilelessly friendly as he inquired, "Yes? What can I do for you?" He stepped over the threshold toward Gruber, pulling the door almost shut behind him.

"D Control, sir," Gruber said. "Not here for you, just trying to trace a couple of elderly persons, last seen heading in this direction on a motorbike." He gestured vaguely behind him. "Kind of like that one out there, actually. We have some reason to believe that they were running a breeding operation out of their farm. Belgian wyverns, to be precise. Would they be here with you presently, by any chance?"

"Elderly persons." The young man wrinkled his genuine alabaster brow and uttered a light, soft chuckle. "Well, I suppose that could be Mr. and Mrs. Edward J. Watkins, my grandparents—I'm Larry Watkins—but breeding Ds? *Please*— those two couldn't cross the street on a red light. Can't help you, I'm afraid. That's my minibike, and I haven't seen the grandsters for at least a month, not a close family, sorry." He turned back toward the house, saying apologetically, "I'd invite you in, but I've got company just now. Old friends getting together, you know how it is. Please do say hello to my supposedly felonious grandparents for me, should you ever find 'em." He vanished through the door, still chuckling.

Gruber knew he'd already pushed his luck as far as it was going to stretch. The sane thing to do was leave, consult with Trager, and not return until he had proper support. But the snotty little shit had put his back up, so instead of hightailing it straight for the Heap, he found himself moving around the side of the house as carefully and quietly as he could.

Just a quick little look-see . . .

There were two buildings up the overgrown rise to the rear: Quonset-type huts, like man-sized culverts closed at both ends. One sniff told him what they were making there, and how they were making it. Nobody was ever going to confuse the rotting-fish smell of phosphine gas with anything else.

He had just enough time to feel really stupid before the first shot rang out. It didn't come anywhere close to him—tweakers didn't tend to be Olympic marksmen—but it was definitely large-caliber, and the next one whanged off a rock and ricocheted by his left ear. He bellowed, "D Control! Not after you!" but he might as well have yelled, "Hey, who ordered the Extra-Large with sausage and mushrooms?" for all the good it did him. People were spilling out of the nearest Quonset now: a couple of large guys with muscle shirts and walrus mustaches, followed by a slighter Latino. Gruber counted two automatic rifles and a shotgun between them, before he spun and ran, praying not to turn an ankle on the tangly, pebbly slope.

He skidded around the house and came face to face with a nightmare.

As many years as Gruber had been with D Control, he had never seen anything like it, not in real life—just in YouTube videos, which definitely didn't do the beast justice. It was deep, deep ebony all the way, even the wings, at least nine feet tall at its breastbone, easily thirty feet long from head to tail-tip, and spiked *everywhere*, with a flattened viperine head that looked too big for its body, and yellow-orange eyes that blazed in the twilight like amber stars. The fire dancing in its open mouth seemed redder than any other flame in the world, and different as well, as though *it* was the D's real tongue, ready to lick and caress and savor.

Gruber froze. *How in hell had they gotten a full-grown San Ysidro Black up here without anyone knowing? And how in hell had they trained it?* He'd only ever heard of three San Ysidros getting past Homeland Security, all *eggs*, for Christ's sake, all in Florida, and every one of the animals was recovered when the hatchlings ripped up the fools who'd bought them.

It wasn't possible. But here it was, planted firmly between him and the Heap—dammit, couldn't Connie see the thing?

Why wasn't she gone already?—while assorted bad people with large guns converged on his aging tail. Gruber was suddenly less concerned about them, at the moment. They'd most likely just watch while the San Ysidro did its job and gave Connie her very first experience of watching a partner vanish in fire.

But he couldn't worry about Connie just now. *Or* the meth-lab commandos. Not if he wanted to live more than a few seconds.

"Hey, Big D," Gruber said casually, stepping backward, slipping both hands into his pockets. The San Ysidro ran out its blazing red tongue and seemed to grin at him.

He threw the first Flying Monkey at it left-handed, then turned without waiting to see what happened and fired the second one straight at the front window of the house. It shattered the glass, and as it did, he beat feet for the door. Fore and aft, he heard two loud *whumps*—the internal CO_2 cartridges going off— and the hissing spray of the tranquilizer release. He saw thick white tendrils of it coming through the broken window, and for a moment he thought his crazy improvisation might actually work. He didn't expect one half-assed throw to take down the San Ysidro, and the drug mist wouldn't knock out people, just make them cough a lot and tear up badly. But they had to have guns in the house, and obviously the beast was trained to leave the occupants alone. If he could just get inside while the Watkins clan was distracted, grab himself a real weapon—

As a rule, firebreathers weren't big on accuracy; they didn't have to be, not when they could burn down a whole forest to get at the one thing they were after. The San Ysidro's first blast missed Gruber, but took out a sizable chunk of the veranda, and he had to duck away to keep splashes of the clinging, fiery fluid from lighting him up, too. His straight path to the door vanished behind a wall of heat and smoke.

"Crap!" he shouted, then ran uphill in the only clear direction left to him. He could feel the D turn slowly to follow. The guys with guns didn't. In the quick glimpse he allowed himself, he saw them shouting at Larry Watkins, who was out on the veranda with a halon fire extinguisher, spinning like a dervish as he tried to quench the flames.

Gruber jumped over a couple of fallen trees and kept moving. The San Ysidro glided slowly in pursuit, quick and graceful for its size, coming at an angle. Gruber realized that the thing was *trying* to drive him into the undergrowth, where he'd be surrounded on all sides by easily flammable material. "What, you had to be smart as well as big?" he muttered to himself. Meanwhile it came on without making a sound, though he could hear the fire building in its throat and chest, rustling like terrible wings.

Gruber knew his tapper was useless against something this large, even if it let him get close enough to try it. The four Winged Monkeys were all he had. He got another one ready, turning it over and over again in his right hand as he watched the D come on, banging its way through the trees as if it barely knew they were there.

When the San Ysidro had a clear path, it sped up, closing fast as it prepared to let loose another blast. Gruber got a proper two-seam cut fastball grip on the Winged Monkey and reared back, hurling it dead-center straight into the flames and fangs of the thing's open mouth. He didn't wait to see it go down the San Ysidro's gullet, being far too busy hurling himself to one side. Flames shot over him as he tumbled backward down the hillside, trying to spot some cover somewhere as he rolled. He fetched up hard against a tree and sat up slowly, struggling to catch his breath. He'd lost his helmet, and one of his overall sleeves was on fire. He rubbed the yellow fabric in the dirt until it was out, barely noticing what he was doing. Other things had his attention.

The *whump*, when he heard it, was barely audible. He saw the San Ysidro stop still, not dead or disabled, by any means, but definitely looking puzzled. It hacked once, like a cat with a hairball, then bellowed in decided discontent. The trickle of fire that splashed out this time had a flickering green streak to it.

Gruber pushed himself to his feet and let the tree trunk keep him there. His shoulder hurt like hell. He whispered, "Hold *still*, you bastard," and threw two more Monkeys, one after the other, as fast and hard as the pain would let him. The first bounced off when the San Ysidro raised its head, and blew uselessly when it hit the ground; but the other one played crazy pinball in a nest of cranial spikes and burst right above the thing's left eye, surrounding its whole head and torso in a thick gray-white fog. The San Ysidro started to take a step, but didn't finish; instead, both hind legs jerked stiff and stopped moving, causing it to fall over on one side. The spikes on its right hip and shoulder plowed deep furrows in the soil, and it shook its head up and down, rumbling to itself. Gruber had seen horses in pain do the same thing.

For whatever reason, the Heap was still parked where he'd left it, so he began to circle back through the trees, hoping to get there without being spotted by any of the meth-heads standing around the wrecked and smoking veranda. No such luck; fifty yards short of his goal, he heard the jagged tear of a semiautomatic rifle firing, and sprays of dirt and splintering tree bark stitched a line between him and his goal. Gruber found himself pinned down behind a fallen sapling that wasn't nearly big enough to be good cover. Every time he moved, every time he showed so much as his bald spot, the chips flew; and that log couldn't afford to lose too many chips. He had one Winged Monkey left, but bitterly concluded that it was no help. He couldn't have reached the gunmen from here anyway, even if his shoulder wasn't screaming; and standing up to try would be suicide.

"Quit firing, already!" he shouted. "The sheriff knows I'm here! You want to get the needle for a murder charge, instead of six years on some punkass meth conviction?"

"Go to hell, asshole!" It was the Watkins kid shouting. "You wouldn't even be my first today!"

Gruber thought about meth paranoia and burned-down houses, abruptly certain that Johanna and Eddie Watkins were never going to see the inside of the Trinity County Courthouse. He shivered.

Then he heard the Heap's engine suddenly rev to a roar, and had his mouth open to yell to Connie not to try and pick him up, that they'd both be exposed the moment she opened the door for him. But in a moment, he realized that wasn't her plan.

The nerve-rending wail of screechers came on as she gunned the Heap straight for the house, picking up speed fast. The tweakers fired at it, of course, but the Heap had been built to withstand flames, claws, fangs, and pretty much anything short of an RPG. When the guys with the walrus mustaches realized the howling metal monster wasn't slowing down, not even a little bit, they threw away their guns and bailed, running for the trees. The Latino followed a moment later. Only Larry Watkins kept firing, his eyes wide and insane.

With nobody paying attention to him anymore, it was safe for Gruber to stick his head out: even at this distance, the screechers were so loud he had to put his hands over his ears. He watched the whole scene in disbelief, tensing at the inevitable collision. Then—not twenty feet from the house—Connie must have braked hard and spun the steering wheel all the way to the left, or nearly so, because the Heap suddenly went into a great skidding turn that almost tipped it over, trading back for front as the rear end came round and three tons of reinforced metal hammered what was left of the veranda into kindling. Watkins vanished somewhere in the debris.

The Heap came to a stop. So did the screechers.

Gruber jumped to his feet and ran full-tilt toward the house. He couldn't see Connie through the fissured, pockmarked glass of the Heap's front window, and for a moment he was certain that one of the bullets had gotten through, that she was lying dead on the floor of the cab and it was all his goddamn fault. But before he got there, the Heap lurched once, then again, and finally detached itself from whatever piece of the house it had gotten caught on, moving forward smoothly. In a dim, distant way, he realized he was shouting.

Connie slowed the Heap to a crawl when she spotted him. As Gruber pulled open the driver's-side door and jumped in, she moved over, making room for him to take the wheel. He stomped on the gas without bothering to belt himself in.

"You better be okay to drive, and not in shock or anything," she said. "I've got something to take care of here."

He turned to look at her and ask what, but a shadow at the corner of his eye made him pull his head back just in time to see the San Ysidro standing smack in the middle of the flattened dirt road they'd driven up, a century or so earlier. It looked profoundly pissed-off, and if it didn't know that Gruber was the human being responsible for its pain and confusion, then he was in the wrong line of work.

Two seconds, three choices. He could jam on the brakes and pulp both of them against the windshield—Connie wasn't belted in, either—or he could ram the D and make it even angrier, or he could veer round it one way or the other and pray not to front-end a tree before he managed to pull the Heap back onto the road. Connie had the McNaughton on her lap, messing with it, doing something he couldn't figure, but Gruber knew she hadn't seen the San Ysidro yet, and there was no time to shout an explanation. He picked Door Number Three, threw all his weight on cranking the wheel to the right, crashed into a blackberry bramble, and came out the other side just as a blast from the San Ysidro sent it up in flames. Gruber had the wheel to hold on to. Connie didn't. She screamed as inertia threw her against his aching right shoulder, and *he* yelled as she hit him, the pain causing him to white out for a moment. His foot slipped off the accelerator and the Heap slowed down, half on the road and half off.

When he could focus again, the Heap had stopped, and the San Ysidro had climbed on top of it. The D was hammering on the cab with everything it had—wings, spikes, tails, and claws—trying to get in. It brought its head down even with the side window, and Gruber found himself staring straight into one of its glaring yellow eyes from ten inches away.

It knew, all right. It knew who he was, why he was there, what he had done to it, how he had felt about doing it; and it knew he wasn't going to get away. Not this time.

It reared its head back, opened its jaws, and let loose hell.

The Heap was completely fireproof, of course, like every D-retrieval vehicle—flames couldn't even get under the door, normally—but the designers hadn't done any tests after shooting one all the hell up, slamming it into a house, and driving it through a bunch of scrub and fallen tree limbs. Gruber saw tiny fingers of flame squeezing through cracks in the windshield, and smelled insulation and wiring burning inside the dash. The air in the cab was so hot it hurt to breathe: Gruber couldn't guess what was going to kill them first, roasting to death or smoke inhalation. He turned the key in the ignition, but couldn't even hear the starter motor turning over. If the San Ysidro's fire had gotten through the engine compartment seals, it was all over.

For a single moment, he rested his head on the wheel and—only for a moment—closed his eyes.

A sudden raw blast of heat on his face made him aware that Connie had opened the window on her side. He looked and saw her leaning out through it, hurling wyvern eggs at the San Ysidro as fast as she could pull them out of the keeper. No, not eggs—blazing orange hatchlings, literally biting at her fingers as she scooped them up and threw them. Gruber screamed at her to get down, but she paid him no heed, not until the McNaughton was completely empty. Then she slumped back onto her seat and tried to roll the window up, but couldn't get a grip on the handle. Despite the D-schmear, her crabbed-up fingers were a mass of red and blistered burns, and both hands bled from a dozen bad nips and slices. He reached past and rolled the window up for her, certain that any second they were both going to be incinerated by the San Ysidro's fire.

Only that wasn't happening. Something else was.

The San Ysidro was howling. The cab shook hard as it lurched away, letting go. Gruber saw it rolling and thrashing on the ground, speckled with bright moving sparks, as if its own fire was leaking out from the inside.

Connie was laughing hysterically, her wounded hands curled in her lap. "How do *you* like being on the receiving end for once, hey? You like that?"

Gruber finally understood what she had done. Ds—*all* the Ds—were as fiercely territorial as different species of ants . . . and newborn wyverns had teeth that could puncture Kevlar, a mean body temperature hotter than boiling water, and a drive to eat that wouldn't stop until they'd consumed five or six times their own body weight. One of them, the San Ysidro could have handled. Seven or eight, even, with some permanent damage. But more than thirty, and every single tiny mouth eating its way straight in from wherever it started?

Gruber and Connie sat in the Heap's cab, saying nothing, and watched the San Ysidro die by inches. It took nearly an hour before it stopped moving. Somewhere in there Gruber got out the first-aid kit and did what he could for Connie's hands.

It was full night out by the time it was over. Connie was slumped beside him, almost bent double, her arms crossed palm-up in front of her chest. They both felt hollow, still half in shock and no longer amped on adrenaline.

She mumbled, "Nobody should be allowed to have them."

"Nobody is," Gruber said. "But they have them anyway." Connie did not seem to have heard him.

"You're a walking mess," he said with weary affection. Her dark-brown hair was scorched short on the right side, just as her right cheek and ear were singed, and all of her right arm had a first-degree burn inside her coverall sleeve. He didn't want to think about what was under the bandages on both her hands, but for now the kit's painkiller was keeping the nerves properly numb. That was good. "Thanks for saving my dumbass life. Twice, even."

Connie gave him a wary sideways glance. Most of her right eyebrow was gone too. "Trick compliment?"

"No trick. That was smart, cranking up the McNaughton so

the wyverns would hatch out faster. I wouldn't have thought of that one." He rubbed his right shoulder, which was out-and-out killing him, now that it had regained his attention.

"I had to do *something* when the San Ysidro showed up. It was the only thing that occurred to me."

"You could have peeled out of there, like I told you to."

She shook her head. "I'm not actually so good about following orders. I was going to tell you that tomorrow."

He thought for a silent while. "Consider the message conveyed."

A minute later, he pushed the door open and stepped out. "Come on. The Heap's not going anywhere, and we've got a job to finish."

"What, we're going back?" She stiffened in the seat, leaning away from his extended hand.

"Not a chance. I think you must have creamed Junior pretty good, or else we'd have had company by now. But it's anybody's guess whether those other idiots came back or not." He made a brusque *hurry-up* gesture, and turned away once he saw she was finally starting to move. "So no, we're not going back. What we're going to do is hike down to 299. Somewhere around the turnoff, we're going to find Trager or one of his guys. They were expecting us hours ago, they'll be looking. After we tell them what went down, we can get you to Mountain Community Medical."

"You too," Connie said.

"Yeah, me too."

He stood where the San Ysidro had finally ceased thrashing, and looked down at the bloody, riddled corpse. Somehow it looked even bigger, splayed out dead in the darkness. Connie stopped a few feet behind him.

"Hey, trainee. How long before the baby wyverns wake up and start eating their way back out?"

"I have no idea," she said, looking a little worried.

"Good to learn there's *something* about Ds you don't know." Despite the pounding snarl in his shoulder, he realized he felt happier than he had in months. Maybe years. "The answer, for your information, is twelve to fifteen hours. Plenty of time for somebody else to come here and handle this mess, and good luck to them."

He started off the way they'd first come, hunching forward slightly as he walked to keep his torso from swinging too much. Connie caught up with him, matching his pace. The stars were out, and it wasn't hard to find their way.

Neither of them said anything for more than twenty minutes. Then Connie spoke up. "They had a *San Ysidro black*. Can you *believe* it?"

"There's a lot of people who'll be asking that one," Gruber nodded. "From the Feds on down. Get ready to star in one hell of an investigation."

Connie stopped walking. "Oh my god," she whispered. "Oh no. What are my parents going to say? I can't tell them about this! I mean—"

"Nice try," Gruber grinned at her. "Parents or no, hands or no, you're still writing up the report. If you can't type, you can dictate."

She tried to kick him in the shin, but he managed to get out of range. The first time, anyway.

THE WAY IT WORKS OUT
AND ALL

Okay, it's my fault. I'm largely the one who spread the rumor, so I'm responsible to put it to rest. Avram Davidson did not know everything in the world. Almost . . . but not quite. I have a distinct memory of doing a reading at U.C. Irvine, where Avram was teaching at the time, to find him sitting in a front row, holding a frisky helium balloon in one hand, and a pretty young student's hand in the other. After I finished my gig (somewhat distracted by performing in front of one of my major heroes, old friend or no), Avram came up to give me a hug and to inquire, quite seriously, "What do you know about feral camels?" As it happened, I did know something about a tentative attempt by the American Army, in the days after the Civil War, to introduce a small force of camels into the deserts of the Southwest. The attempt was soon abandoned; but for many years afterward, soldiers and nineteenth-century tourists alike would report having seen impossible ghostlike creatures materializing out of a sandstorm, and vanishing again just as swiftly. I still find it unlikely that Avram really didn't know something that I, with my ragbag, hit-or-miss education, actually knew. More than likely, he was just being kind to my ego.

However, it would certainly have been Avram who discovered the Overneath. He would.

❧

In the ancient, battered, altogether sinister filing cabinet where I stash stuff I know I'll lose if I keep it anywhere less carnivorous, there is a manila folder crammed with certain special postcards—postcards where every last scintilla of space not taken by an image or an address block has been filled with tiny, idiosyncratic, yet perfectly legible handwriting, the work of a man whose only real faith lay in the written word (emphasis on the *written*). These cards are organized by their postmarked dates, and there are long gaps between most of them, but not all: thirteen from March of 1992 were mailed on consecutive days.

A printed credit in the margin on the first card in this set identifies it as coming from the W. G. Reisterman Co. of Duluth, Minnesota. The picture on the front shows three adorable snuggling kittens. Avram Davidson's message, written in his astonishing hand, fills the still-legible portion of the reverse:

March 4, 1992

Estimado Dom Pedro del Bronx y Las Lineas subterraneos D, A, y F, Grand High Collector of Revenues both Internal and External for the State of North Dakota and Points Beyond:

He always addressed me as "Dom Pedro."

Maestro!

I write you from the historic precincts of Darkest Albany, where the Erie Canal turns wearily around and trudges back to even Darker Buffalo. I am at present engaged in combing out the utterly disheveled files of the New York State Bureau of Plumbing Designs, Devices, Patterns, and Sinks, all with the devious aim of rummaging through New York City's dirty socks and underwear, in hope of discovering the source of the

There is more—much more—but somewhere between his hand and my mailbox it had been rendered illegible by large splashes of something unknown, perhaps rain, perhaps melting snow, perhaps spilled Stolichnaya, which had caused the ink of the postcard to run and smear. Within the blotched and streaky blurs I could only detect part of a word which might equally have read *phlox* or *physic*, or neither. In any case, on the day the card arrived even that characteristic little was good for a chuckle, and a resolve to write Avram more frequently, if his address would just stay still.

But then there came the second card, one day later.

March 5, 1992

Intended solely for the Hands of the Highly Esteemed and Estimated Dom Pedro of the Just As Highly Esteemed North Bronx, and for such further Hands as he may Deem Worthy, though his taste in Comrades and Associates was Always Rotten, as witness:

Your Absolute Altitude, with or without mice . . .

I am presently occupying the top of a large, hairy quadruped, guaranteed by a rather shifty-eyed person to be of the horse persuasion, but there is no persuading it to do anything but attempt to scrape me off against trees, bushes, motor vehicles, and other horses. We are proceeding irregularly across the trackless wastes of the appropriately-named <u>Jornada del Muerto</u>, *in the southwestern quadrant of New Mexico, where I have been advised that a limestone cave entrance makes it possibly possible to address*

Here again, the remainder is obliterated, this time by what appears to be either horse or cow manure, though feral camel is also a slight, though unlikely, option. At all events, this postcard too is partially, crucially—and maddeningly—illegible. But that's really not the point.

The next postcard showed up the following day.

March 6, 1992

To Dom Pedro, Lord of the Riverbanks and Midnight Hayfields,

Dottore of Mystical Calligraphy, Lieutenant-Harrier of the Queen's Coven—greetings!

This epistle comes to you from the Bellybutton of the World— to be a bit more precise, the North Pole—where, if you will credit me, the New York State Civic Drain comes to a complete halt, apparently having given up on ever finding the Northwest Passage. I am currently endeavoring, with the aid of certain Instruments of my own Devising, to ascertain the truth—if any such exists—of the hollow-Earth legend. Tarzan says he's been there, and if you can't take the word of an ape-man, I should like to know whose word you can take, huh? In any case, the entrance to Pellucidar is not my primary goal (though it would certainly be nice finally to have a place to litter, pollute, and despoil in good conscience). What I seek, you—faithful Companion of the Bath and Poet Laureate of the High Silly—shall be the first to know when/if I discover it. Betimes, bethink your good self of your bedraggled, besmirched, beshrewed, belabored, and generally verklempt old friend, at this writing attempting to roust a polar bear out of his sleeping bag, while inviting a comely Eskimo (or, alternatively, Esquimaux, I'm easy) in. Yours in Mithras, Avram, the A. K.

Three postcards in three days, dated one after the other. Each with a different (and genuine—I checked) postmark from three locations spaced so far apart, both geographically and circumstantially, that even the Flash would have had trouble hitting them all within three days, let alone a short, stout, arthritic, asthmatic gentleman of nearly seventy years' duration. I'm as absent-minded and unobservant as they come, but even I had noticed that improbability before the fourth postcard arrived.

March 7, 1992

Sent by fast manatee up the Japanese Current and down the Humboldt, there at last to encounter the Gulf Stream in its mighty course, and so to the hands of a certain Dom Pedro, Pearl of the Orient, Sweetheart of Sigma Chi, and Master of Hounds and Carburetors to She Who Must Not Be Aggravated.

So how's by you?

By me, here in East Wimoweh-on-the-Orinoco, alles ist maddeningly almost. I feel myself on the cusp (precisely the region where we were severely discouraged from feeling ourselves, back in Boys' Town) of at last discovering—wait for it—the secret plumbing of the world! No, this has nothing to do with Freemasons, Illuminati, the darkest files and codexes of Mother Church, nor—ptui, ptui—the Protocols of the Learned Elders of Zion. Of conspiracies and secret societies, there is no end or accounting; but the only one of any account has ever been the Universal International Brotherhood of Sewer Men (in recent years corrected to Sewer Personnel) and Plumbing Contractors. This organization numbers, not merely the people who come to unstop your sink and hack the tree roots out of your septic tank, but the nameless giants who laid the true underpinnings of what we think of as civilization, society, culture. Pipes far down under pipes, tunnels beyond tunnels, vast valves and connections, profound couplings and joints and elbows—all members of the UIBSPPC are sworn to secrecy by the most dreadful oaths and the threat of the most awful penalties for revealing . . . well, the usual, you get the idea. Real treehouse boys' club stuff. Yoursley yours, Avram

I couldn't read the postmark clearly for all the other stamps and postmarks laid over it—though my guess would be Brazil—but you see my point. There was simply no way in the world for him to have sent me those cards from those four places in that

length of time. Either he had widely scattered friends, participants in the hoax, mailing them out for him, or . . . but there
wasn't any *or*, there couldn't be, for that idea made no sense.
Avram told jokes—some of them unquestionably translated
from the Middle Sumerian, and losing something along the
way—but he didn't *play* jokes, and he wasn't a natural jokester.

Nine more serially dated postcards followed, not arriving
every day, but near enough. By postmark and internal
description they had been launched to me from, in order:

Equatorial Guinea

Turkmenistan

Dayton, Ohio

Lvov City in the Ukraine

The Isle of Eigg

Pinar del Río (in Cuba, where Americans weren't permitted
to travel!)

Hobart, capital of the Australian territory of Tasmania

Shigatse, Tibet

And finally, tantalizingly, from Davis, California. Where
I actually lived at the time, though nothing in the card's text
indicated any attempt to visit.

After that the flurry of messages stopped, though not my
thoughts about them. Trying to unpuzzle the mystery had me
at my wits' rope (a favorite phrase of Avram's), until the lazy
summer day I came around a corner in the Chelsea district of
New York City . . .

. . . and literally ran into a short, stout, bearded, flatfooted
person who seemed almost to have been running, though that
was as unlikely a prospect as his determining on a career in
professional basketball. It was Avram. He was formally dressed,
the only man I knew who habitually wore a tie, vest, and jacket

that all matched; and if he looked a trifle disheveled, that was equally normal for him. He blinked at me briefly, looked around him in all directions, then said thoughtfully, "A bit close, that was." To me he said, as though we had dined the night before, or even that morning, "I did warn you the crab salad smelled a bit off, didn't I?"

It took me a moment of gaping to remember that the last time we had been together was at a somewhat questionable dive in San Francisco's Mission District, and I'd been showing signs of ptomaine poisoning by the time I dropped him off at home. I said meekly, "So you did, but did I listen? What on earth are you doing here?" He had been born in Yonkers, but felt more at home almost anyplace else, and I couldn't recall ever being east of the Mississippi with him, if you don't count a lost weekend in Minneapolis.

"Research," he said briskly: an atypical adverb to apply to his usual rambling, digressive style of speaking. "Can't talk. Tomorrow, two-twenty-two, Victor's." And he was gone, practically scurrying away down the street—an unlikely verb, this time: Avram surely had never scurried in his life. I followed, at an abnormally rapid pace myself, calling to him; but when I rounded the corner, he was nowhere in sight. I stood still, scratching my head, while people bumped into me and said irritated things.

The "two-twenty-two" part I understood perfectly well: it was a running joke between us, out of an ancient burlesque routine. That was when we always scheduled our lunch meetings, neither of us ever managing to show up on time. It was an approximation, a deliberate mockery of precision and exactitude. As for Victor's Café, that was a Cuban restaurant on West 52nd Street, where they did—and still do—remarkable things with unremarkable ingredients. I had no idea that Avram knew of it.

I slept poorly that night, on the cousin's couch where I always crash in New York. It wasn't that Avram had looked frightened—I had never seen him afraid, not even of a bad review—but *perturbed*, yes . . . you could have said that he had looked perturbed, even perhaps just a touch *flustered*. It was distinctly out of character, and Avram out of character worried me. Like a cat, I prefer that people remain where I leave them—not only physically, but psychically as well. But Avram was clearly not where he had been.

I wound up rising early on a blue and already hot morning, made breakfast for my cousin and myself, then killed time as best I could until I gave up and got to Victor's at a little after 1 P.M. There I sat at the bar, nursing a couple of Cuban beers, until Avram arrived. The time was exactly two-twenty-two, both on my wrist, and on the clock over the big mirror, and when I saw that, I knew for certain that Avram was in trouble.

Not that he showed it in any obvious way. He seemed notably more relaxed than he had been at our street encounter, chatting easily, while we waited for a table, about our last California vodka-deepened conversation, in which he had explained to me the real reason why garlic is traditionally regarded as a specific against vampires, and the rather shocking historical misunderstandings that this myth had occasionally led to. Which led to his own translation of Vlad Tepes's private diaries (I never did learn just how many languages Avram actually knew) and thence to Dracula's personal comments regarding the original Mina Harker . . . but then the waiter arrived to show us to our table; and by the time we sat down, we were into the whole issue of why certain Nilotic tribes habitually rest standing on one foot. All that was before the *Bartolito* was even ordered.

It wasn't until the entrée had arrived that Avram squinted

across the table and pronounced, through a mouthful of sweet plantain and black bean sauce, "Perhaps you are wondering why I have called you all here today." He was doing his mad-scientist voice, which always sounded like Peter Lorre on nitrous oxide.

"Us all were indeed wondering, Big Bwana, sir," I answered him, making a show of looking left and right at the crowded restaurant. "Not a single dissenting voice."

"Good. Can't abide dissension in the ranks." Avram sipped his wine and focused on me with an absolute intensity that was undiluted by his wild beard and his slightly bemused manner. "You are aware, of course, that I could not possibly have been writing to you from all the destinations that my recent missives indicated."

I nodded.

Avram said, "And yet I was. I did."

"Um." I had to say something, so I mumbled, "Anything's possible. You know, the French rabbi Rashi—tenth, eleventh century—he was supposed—"

"To be able to walk between the raindrops," Avram interrupted impatiently. "Yes, well, maybe he did the same thing I've done. Maybe he found his way into the Overneath, like me."

We looked at each other: him waiting calmly for my reaction, me too bewildered to react at all. Finally I said, "The Overneath. Where's that?" Don't tell *me* I can't come up with a swift zinger when I need to.

"It's all around us." Avram made a sweeping semi-circle with his right arm, almost knocking over the next table's excellent Pinot Grigio—Victor's does tend to pack them in—and inflicting a minor flesh wound on the nearer diner, since Avram was still holding his fork. Apologies were offered and accepted, along with a somewhat lower-end bottle of wine, which I had sent over. Only then did Avram continue. "In this particular location, it's about forty-five degrees to your left, and a bit up—I could take you there this minute."

I said *um* again. I said, "You *are* aware that this does sound, as directions go, just a bit like 'Second star to the right, and straight on till morning.' No dissent intended."

"No stars involved." Avram was waving his fork again. "More like turning left at this or that manhole cover—climbing this stair in this old building—peeing in one particular urinal in Grand Central Station." He chuckled suddenly, one corner of his mouth twitching sharply upward. "Funny . . . if I hadn't taken a piss in Grand Central . . . hah! Try some of the *vaca frita*, it's really good."

"Stick to pissing, and watch it with that fork. What happened in Grand Central?"

"Well. I shouldn't have been there, to begin with." Avram, it could have been said of him, lived to digress, both as artist and companion. "But I had to go—you know how it is—and the toilet in the diner upstairs was broken. So I went on down, into the *kishkas* of the beast, you could say . . ." His eyes had turned thoughtful and distant, looking past me. "That's really an astonishing place, Grand Central, you know? You ought to think about setting a novel there—you set one in a graveyard, after all—"

"So you were in the Grand Central men's room—*and?*" I may have raised my voice a little; people were glancing over at us, but with tolerant amusement, which has not always been the case. "*And, maître?*"

"Yes. And." The eyes were suddenly intent again, completely present and focused, his own voice lower, even, deliberate. "And I walked out of that men's room through that same door where in I went—" he could quote the *Rubáiyát* in the damnedest contexts—"and walked into another place. I wasn't in Grand Central Station at all."

I'd seen a little too much, and known him far too long, not to know when he was serious. I said simply, "Where were you?"

"Another country," Avram repeated. "I call it *the Overneath,* because it's above us and around us and below us, all at the same time. I wrote you about it."

I stared at him.

"I *did*. Remember the Universal International Brotherhood of Sewer Persons and Plumbing Contractors? The sub-basement of reality—all those pipes and valves and tunnels and couplings, sewers and tubes . . . the everything other than everything? That's the Overneath, only I wasn't calling it that then—I was just finding my way around, I didn't know *what* to call it. Got to make a map . . ." He paused, my bafflement and increasing anxiety obviously having become obvious. "No, no, stop that. I'm testy and peremptory, and sometimes I can be downright fussy—I'll go that far—but I'm no crazier than I ever was. The Overneath is real, and by gadfrey, I *will* take you there when we're done here. You having dessert?"

I didn't have dessert. We settled up, complimented the chef, tipped the waiter, and strolled outside into an afternoon turned strangely . . . not foggy, exactly, but *indefinite,* as though all outlines had become just a trifle uncertain, willing to debate their own existence. I stopped where I was, shaking my head, taking off my glasses to blow on them and put them back on. Beside me, Avram gripped my arm hard. He said, quietly but intensely, "Now. Take two steps to the right, and turn around."

I looked at him. His fingers bit into my arm hard enough to hurt. "Do it!"

I did as he asked, and when I turned around, the restaurant was gone.

I never learned where we were then. Avram would never tell me. My vision had cleared, but my eyes stung from the cold, dust-laden twilight wind blowing down an empty dirt road. All of New York—sounds, smells, voices, texture—had vanished with Victor's Café. I didn't know where we were, nor how we'd gotten there; but I suppose it's a good thing to have that depth of terror over with, because I have never been that frightened, not before and not since. There wasn't a living thing in sight, nor any suggestion that there ever had been. I can't even tell you to this day how I managed to speak, to make sounds, to whisper a dry-throated *"Where are we?"* to Avram. Just writing about it brings it all back—I'm honestly trembling as I set these words down.

Avram said mildly, "Shit. Must have been *three* steps right. Namporte," which was always his all-purpose reassurance in uneasy moments. "Just walk *exactly* in my footsteps and do me after me." He started on along the road—which, as far as I could see, led nowhere but to more road and more wind—and I, terrified of doing something wrong and being left behind in this dreadful place, mimicked every step, every abrupt turn of the head or arthritic leap to the side, like a child playing hopscotch. At one point, Avram even tucked up his right leg behind him and made the hop on one foot; so did I.

I don't recall how long we kept this up. What I *do* recall, and wish I didn't, was the moment when Avram suddenly stood very still—as, of course, did I—and we both heard, very faintly, a kind of soft, scratchy padding behind us. Every now and then, the padding was broken by a clicking sound, as though claws had crossed a patch of stone.

Avram said, "Shit" again. He didn't move any faster—indeed, he put a hand out to check me when I came almost even with him—but he kept looking more and more urgently to the left, and I could see the anxiety in his eyes. I remember distracting myself by trying to discern, from the rhythm of the sound, whether our pursuer was following on two legs or four. I've no idea today why it seemed to matter so much, but it did then.

"Keep moving," Avram said. He was already stepping out ahead of me, walking more slowly now, so that I, constantly looking back—as he never did—kept stepping on the backs of his shoes. He held his elbows tightly against his body and reached out ahead of him with hands and forearms alone, like a recently blinded man. I did what he did.

Even now . . . even now, when I dream about that terrible dirt road, it's never the part about stumbling over things that I somehow knew not to look at too closely, nor the unvarying soft *clicking* just out of sight behind us . . . no, it's always Avram marching ahead of me, making funny movements with his head and shoulders, his arms prodding and twisting the air ahead of him like bread dough. And it's always me tailing along, doing my best to keep up, while monitoring every slightest gesture, or what even *looks* like a gesture, intentional or not. In the dream, we go on and on, apparently without any goal, without any future.

Suddenly Avram cried out, strangely shrilly, in a language I didn't know—which I imitated as best I could—then did a complete hopscotch spin-around, and actually flung himself down on the hard ground to the left. I did the same, jarring the breath out of myself and closing my eyes for an instant. When I opened them again, he was already up, standing on tiptoe—I remember thinking, *Oh, that's got to hurt, with his gout*—and reaching up as high as he could with his left hand. I did the same . . . felt something hard and rough under my fingers . . . pulled myself up, as he did . . .

. . . and found myself in a different place, my left hand still gripping what turned out to be a projecting brick in a tall pillar. We were standing in what felt like a huge railway station, its ceiling arched beyond my sight, its walls dark and blank, with no advertisements, nor even the name of the station. Not that the name would have meant much, because there were no railroad tracks to be seen. All I knew was that we were off the dirt road; dazed with relief, I giggled absurdly—even a little crazily, most likely. I said, "Well, I don't remember *that* being part of the Universal Studios tour."

Avram drew a deep breath, and seemed to let out more air than he took in. He said, "All right. That's more like it."

"More like *what?*" I have spent a goodly part of my life being bewildered, but this remains the gold standard. "Are we still in the Overneath?"

"We are in the *hub* of the Overneath," Avram said proudly. "The heart, if you will. That place where we just were, it's like a local stop in a bad part of town. This . . . from here you can get anywhere at all. Anywhere. All you have to do is—" he hesitated, finding an image—"*point* yourself properly, and the Overneath will take you there. It helps if you happen to know the exact geographical coordinates of where you want to go—" I never doubted for a moment that he himself did—"but what matters most is to focus, to feel the complete and unique reality of that particular place, and then just . . . *be* there." He shrugged and smiled, looking a trifle embarrassed. "Sorry to sound so cosmic and one-with-everything. I was a long while myself getting the knack of it all. I'd aim for Machu Picchu and come out in

Capetown, or try for the Galapagos and hit Reykjavik, time after time. Okay, *tovarich*, where in the world would you like to—"

"Home," I said before he'd even finished the question. "New York City, West Seventy-ninth Street. Drop me off at Central Park, I'll walk from there." I hesitated, framing my question. "But will we just pop out of the ground there, or shimmer into existence, or what? And will it be the real Seventy-ninth Street, or . . . or not? *Mon capitaine*, there does seem to be a bit of dissension in the ranks. Talk to me, Big Bwana, sir."

"When you met me in Chelsea," Avram began; but I had turned away from him, looking down to the far end of the station—as I still think of it—where, as I hadn't before, I saw human figures moving. Wildly excited, I waved to them, and was about to call out when Avram clapped his hand over my mouth, pulling me down, shaking his head fiercely, but speaking just above a whisper. "You don't want to do that. You don't ever want to do that."

"Why not?" I demanded angrily. "They're the first damn *people* we've seen—"

"They aren't exactly people." Avram's voice remained low, but he was clearly ready to silence me again, if need be. "You can't ever be sure in the Overneath."

The figures didn't seem to be moving any closer, but I couldn't see them any better, either. "Do they live here? Or are they just making connections, like us? Catching the red-eye to Portland?"

Avram said slowly, "A lot of people use the Overneath, Dom Pedro. Most are transients, passing through, getting from one place to another without buying gas. But . . . yes, there *are* things that live here, and they don't like us. Maybe for them it's 'there goes the neighborhood,' I don't know—there's so much I'm still learning. But I'm quite clear on the part about the distaste . . . and I think I could wish that you hadn't waved quite so."

There *was* movement toward us now—measured, but definitely concerted. Avram was already moving himself, more quickly than I could recall having seen him. "This way!" he snapped over his shoulder, leading me, not back to the pillar which had received us into this nexus of the Overneath, but away, back into blind dark that closed in all around, until I felt as if we were running down and down a subway tunnel with a train roaring close behind us, except that in this case the train was a string of creatures whose faces I'd made the mistake of glimpsing just before Avram and I fled. He was right about them not being people.

We can't have run very far, I think now. Apart from the fact that we were already exhausted, Avram had flat feet and gout, and I had no wind worth mentioning. But our pursuers seemed to fall away fairly early, for reasons I can't begin to guess— fatigue? boredom? the satisfaction of having routed intruders in their world?—and we had ample excuse for slowing down, which our bodies had already done on their own. I wheezed to Avram, "Is there another place like that one?"

Even shaking his head in answer seemed an effort. "Not that I've yet discovered. Namporte—we'll just get home on the local. *All will be well, and all manner of things shall be well.*" Avram hated T. S. Eliot, and had permanently assigned the quotation to Shakespeare, though he knew better.

I didn't know what he meant by "the local," until he suddenly veered left, walked a kind of rhomboid pattern—with me on his heels—and we were again on a genuine sidewalk on a warm late-spring afternoon. There were little round tables and beach umbrellas on the street, bright pennants twitching languidly in a soft breeze that smelled faintly of nutmeg and ripening citrus, and of the distant sea. And there were *people*: perfectly ordinary men and women, wearing slacks and sport coats and sundresses, sitting at the little tables, drinking coffee and wine, talking, smiling at each other, never seeming to take any notice of us. Dazed and drained, swimming in the scent and the wonder of sunlight, I said feebly, "Paris? Malaga?"

"Croatia," Avram replied. "Hvar Island—big tourist spot, since the Romans. Nice place." Hands in his pockets, rocking on his heels, he glanced somewhat wistfully at the holidaymakers. "Don't suppose you'd be interested in staying on awhile?" But he was starting away before I'd even shaken my head, and he wasn't the one who looked back.

Traveling in darkness, we zigzagged and hedge-hopped between one location and the next, our route totally erratic, bouncing us from Croatia to bob up in a music store in Lapland . . . a wedding in Sri Lanka . . . the middle of a street riot in Lagos . . . an elementary-school classroom in Bahia. Avram was flying blind; we both knew it, and he never denied it. "Could have gotten us home in one jump from the hub—I'm a little shaky on the local stops; really *need* to work up a proper map. Namporte, not to worry."

And, strangely, I didn't. I was beginning—just beginning—to gain his sense of landmarks: of the Overneath junctures, the crossroads, detours, and spur lines where one would naturally turn left or right to head *here*, spin around to veer off *there*, or trust one's feet to an invisible stairway, up or down, finally emerging in *that* completely unexpected landscape. Caroming across the world as we were, it was difficult not to feel like a marble in a pinball machine, but in general we did appear to be working our way more or less toward the east coast of North America. We celebrated with a break in a Liverpool dockside pub, where the barmaid didn't look twice at Avram's purchase of two pints of porter, and didn't look at me at all. I was beginning to get used to that, but it still puzzled me, and I said so.

"The Overneath's grown used to me," Avram explained. "That's one thing I've learned about the Overneath—it grows, it adapts, same as the body can adapt to a foreign presence. If you keep using it, it'll adapt to you the same way."

"So right now the people here see you, but can't see me."

Avram nodded. I said, "Are they real? Are all these places we've hit—these local stops of yours—are *they* real? Do they go on existing when nobody from—what? *outside*, I guess—is passing through? Is this an alternate universe, with everybody having his counterpart here, or just a little something the Overneath runs up for tourists?" The porter was quite real, anyway, if warm, and my deep swig almost emptied my glass. "I need to know, *mon maître*."

Avram sipped his own beer and coughed slightly; and I realized with a pang how much older than I he was, and that he had absolutely no business being a pinball—nor the only true adventurer I'd ever known. No business at all. He said, "The alternate-universe thing, that's bullshit. Or if it isn't, doesn't matter—you can't get there from here." He leaned forward. "You know about Plato's Cave, Dom Pedro?"

"The people chained to the wall in the cave, just watching shadows all their lives? What about it?"

"Well, the shadows are cast by things and people coming and going outside the cave, which those poor prisoners never get to see. The shadows are their only notion of reality—they live and die never seeing anything but those shadows, trying to understand the world through shadows. The philosopher's the one who stands outside the cave and reports back. You want another beer?"

"No." Suddenly I didn't even want to finish the glass in my hand. "So our world, what we call our world . . . it might be nothing but the shadow of the Overneath?"

"Or the other way around. I'm still working on it. If you're finished, let's go."

We went outside, and Avram stood thoughtfully staring at seven and a half miles of docks and warehouses, seeming to sniff the gray air. I said, "My mother's family set off for America from here. I think it took them three weeks."

"We'll do better." He was standing with his arms folded, mumbling to himself: "*No way to get close to the harbor, damn it . . . too bad we didn't fetch up on the other side of the Mersey . . . best thing would be . . . best thing . . . no . . . I wonder . . .*"

Abruptly he turned and marched us straight back into the pub, where he asked politely for the loo. Directed, he headed down a narrow flight of stairs; but, to my surprise, passed by the lavatory door and kept following the stairway, telling me over his shoulder, "Most of these old pubs were built over water, for obvious reasons. And don't ask me why, not yet, but the Overneath likes water . . ." I was smelling damp earth now, earth that had never been quite dry, perhaps for hundreds of years. I heard a throb nearby that might have been a sump pump of some sort, and caught a whiff of sewage that was definitely *not* centuries old. I got a glimpse of hollow darkness ahead and thought wildly, *Christ, it's a drain! That's it, we're finally going right down the drain . . .*

Avram hesitated at the bottom of the stair, cocking his head back like a gun hammer. Then it snapped forward, and he grunted in triumph and led me, not into my supposed drain, but to the side of it, into an apparent wall through which we passed with no impediment, except a slither of stones under our feet. The muck sucked at my shoes—long since too far gone for my concern—as I plodded forward in Avram's wake. Having to stop and cram them back on scared me, because he just kept slogging on, never looking back. Twice I tripped and almost fell over things that I thought were rocks or branches; both times they turned out to be large, recognizable, disturbingly splintered bones. I somehow kept myself from calling Avram's attention to them, because I knew he'd want to stop and study them, and pronounce on their origin and function, and I didn't need that. I already knew what they were.

In time the surface became more solid under my feet, and the going got easier. I asked, half-afraid to know, "Are we under the harbor?"

"If we are, we're in trouble," Avram growled. "It'd mean I missed the . . . no, *no*, we're all right, we're fine, it's just—" His voice broke off abruptly, and I could feel rather than see him turning, as he peered back down the way we had come. He said, very quietly, "Well, *damn . . .*"

"What? *What?*" Then I didn't need to ask anymore, because I heard the sound of a foot being pulled out of the same mud I'd squelched through. Avram said, "All this way. They *never* follow that far . . . could have sworn we'd lost it in Lagos . . ." Then we heard the sound again, and Avram grabbed my arm, and we ran.

The darkness ran uphill, which didn't help at all. I remember my breath like stones in my lungs and chest, and I remember a desperate desire to stop and bend over and throw up. I remember Avram never letting go of my arm, literally dragging me with him . . . and the panting that I thought was mine, but that wasn't coming from either of us . . .

"Here!" Avram gasped. "*Here!*" and he let go and vanished between two boulders—or whatever they really were—so close together that I couldn't see how there could be room for his stout figure. I actually had to give him a push from behind, like Rabbit trying to get Pooh Bear out of his burrow; then I got stuck myself, and he grabbed me and pulled . . . and then we were both stuck there, and I couldn't breathe, and something had hold of my left shoe. Then Avram was saying, with a calmness that was more frightening than any other sound, even the sound behind me, "Point yourself. You know where we're going—point and *jump* . . ."

And I did. All I can remember is thinking about the doorman under the awning at my cousin's place . . . the elevator . . . the color of the couch where I would sleep when I visited . . . a kind of hissing howl somewhere behind . . . a *shiver*, as though I were dissolving . . . or perhaps it was the crevice we were jammed into dissolving . . .

. . . and then my head was practically in the lap of Alice on her mushroom: my cheek on smooth granite, my feet somewhere far away, as though they were still back in the Overneath. I opened my eyes in darkness—but a warm, different darkness, smelling of night grass and engine exhaust—and saw Avram sprawled intimately across the Mad Hatter. I slid groggily to the ground, helped to disentangle him from Wonderland, and we stood silently together for a few moments, watching the headlights on Madison Avenue. Some bird was whooping softly but steadily in a nearby tree, and a plane was slanting down into JFK.

"Seventy-fifth," Avram said presently. "Only off by four blocks. Not bad."

"Four blocks and a whole park." My left shoe was still on—muck and all—but the heel was missing, and there were deep gouges in the sole. I said, "You know, I used to be scared to go into Central Park at night."

We didn't see anyone as we trudged across the park to the West Side, and we didn't say much. Avram wondered aloud whether it was tonight or tomorrow night. "Time's a trifle hiccupy in the Overneath, I never know how long . . ." I said we'd get a paper and find out, but I don't recall that we did.

We parted on Seventy-ninth Street: me continuing west to my cousin's building, and Avram evasive about his own plans, his own New York destination. I said, "You're not going back there." It was not a question, and I may have been a little loud. "You're *not.*"

He reassured me instantly—"No, no, I just want to walk for a while, just walk and think. Look, I'll call you tomorrow, at your cousin's, give me the number. I promise, I'll call."

He did, too, from a pay phone, telling me that he was staying with old family friends in Yonkers, and that we'd be getting together in the Bay Area when we both got back. But we never did; we spoke on the phone a few times, but I never saw him again. I was on the road, in Houston, when I heard about his death.

I couldn't get home for the funeral, but I did attend the memorial. There were a lot of obituaries—some in the most remarkable places—and a long period of old friends meeting, formally and informally, to tell stories about Avram and drink to his memory. That still goes on today; it never did take more than two of us to get started, and sometimes I hold one all by myself.

And no, I've never made any attempt to return to the Overneath. I try not to think about it very much. It's easier than you might imagine: I tell myself that our adventure never really happened, and by the time I'm decently senile, I'll believe it. When I'm in New York and pass Grand Central Station, I never go in, on principle. Whatever the need, it can wait.

But *he* went back into the Overneath, I'm sure—to work on his map, I suppose, and other things I can't begin to guess at. As to how I know ...

Avram died on May 8th, 1993, just fifteen days after his seventieth birthday, in his tiny dank apartment in Bremerton, Washington. He closed his eyes and never opened them again. There was a body, and a coroner's report, and official papers and everything: books closed, doors locked, last period dotted in the file.

Except that a month later, when the hangover I valiantly earned during and after the memorial was beginning to seem merely colorful in memory rather than willfully obtuse, I got a battered postcard in the mail. It's in the file with the others. A printed credit in the margin identifies it as coming from the Westermark Press of Stone Heights, Pennsylvania. The picture on the front shows an unfrosted angel food cake decorated with a single red candle. The postmark includes the flag of Cameroon. And on the back, written in that astonishing, unmistakable hand, is an impossible message.

May 9, 1993

To the Illustrissimo Dom Pedro, Companero de Todos mis Tonterias and Skittles Champion of Pacific Grove (Senior Division), Greetings!

It's a funny thing about that Cave parable of Plato's. The way it works out and all. Someday I'll come show you.

Years have passed with nothing further . . . but I still take corners slowly, just in case.

All corners.

Anywhere.

KASKIA

I don't see "Kaskia," in honesty, as one of my best stories, but I have a tenderness for its protagonist, Martin, the produce manager at some place like Safeway or Lucky. As with most writers, there's almost always something of myself in most of my characters: young or old, male or female, fable-born or as straight outta Gunhill Road as I could draw them. Martin's need to keep contact with an alien being on the other side of this galaxy or another—perhaps even on the other side of time—and the forlorn candor of his attempt to comfort Kaskia came straight out of myself, as I realized when I reread the story some while later. And his own surprising comforting . . . well, that's perhaps what artists find in their work, when it's going well. Perhaps.

❁

Even afterward, Martin never could bring himself to blame the laptop. Rather, he blamed his foolishness in buying a computer at once so far beyond his means, his needs, and his abilities. "Goddamn bells and whistles," Lorraine told him scornfully at the time. "LEDs, apps, plug-ins, backup gadgets—you've always been a fool for unnecessary extras. You think people will look at that thing and think you're a real computer geek, an *expert*." She gave that little sneeze-laugh he'd once found endearing and went off to call her buddy Roz and relate his latest idiocy in detail. Sucking a forefinger, cut while he was struggling to open the box, he heard Lorraine saying on the phone, "And on top of that, he bought the thing from his cousin Barry! *That* asshole.

You remember—right, right, anything that falls off a truck is legally Barry's. I am *telling* you, Roz . . ."

The trouble was, of course, that she'd been right. Martin was fond of Barry—if he thought about it, he'd have to say that Barry had been his closest friend since childhood, given a very limited experience with close friends. But he had few illusions about his cousin's probity or loyalty: even in the first flush of his infatuation with the new computer, he'd known that nothing Barry told him about it was likely to be true. The brand was completely unfamiliar, the keyboard had too many function keys beyond the usual twelve, and there were other keys and markings with strange symbols that Barry never even tried to explain to him. "It's one of a kind, absolutely unique, same as you. I feel like I'm in Shakespeare, bringing two great lovers together."

Directions had not been included, but Jaroslav, the amiable graduate student two doors down the hall, who actually *did* know quite a lot about computers, came over to set up Martin's laptop for him. It took considerably longer than expected, due in part to Jaroslav's unfamiliarity with the operating system, and in equal measure to his fascination with the computer's programs and connections. "No, that cannot be it, that makes no *sense*. Well, I suppose that would work, it *seems* to work, but I cannot understand . . . yes, *that* works, but *why*. . . ?" He made no more sense out of the keyboard than Barry had, and was clearly only half-joking when he muttered, "With this thing, I am lucky to know to set the clock, where to plug in the mouse." By the time he was done, his Iron Man T-shirt was sweated through, and he was talking to himself in Serb. Afterward, Martin noticed—on the occasional times they passed in the lobby or hall, or outside the building's laundry room—that Jaroslav avoided meeting his eyes.

Despite Martin's vast ignorance of the workings of his new computer, however, it functioned better than any machine he had ever owned since a beloved bathtub motorboat that ran up a flag and fired pellets at his rubber ducks. Lorraine had once commented that electronic devices seemed to commit suicide in Martin's presence, and it was a hard point to argue. Yet the strange laptop never misbehaved: never froze, never crashed, never devoured work he had forgotten to back up—never, in short, treated him with the kind of spitefulness that had always been his lot from anything involving electrons and wires. He realized that he was actually grateful, and from time to time found himself thinking of it not as a machine, but as a quiet and singular friend.

Often now, when he came home in the evening from the large chain grocery where he was the produce manager, he would sit at his worktable (dinner having long since evolved into a solitary pursuit for both Lorraine and himself) and let the computer talk to him, either onscreen or through the excellent earphones that Barry had grandly thrown into the deal. The computer had a sound system, with built-in speakers, but Lorraine complained about the noise, and Martin liked the earphones better anyway. They gave him a curious private peacefulness that made him feel as though he were at the bottom of the ocean in an old-fashioned diving suit, talking with a companion he could not see. Not that he had ever worn any sort of diving suit, or actually been in water deeper than his high school swimming pool. Martin had not been to very many places in his life.

He did no store work on the new computer; there was an intimidating, unforgiving desktop model in his backroom cubicle for that. The laptop was for telling him stories at the swirl of a mouse: it was for bringing him news, delivering such email as he ever received—while most considerately eliminating all junk and spam—and for showing him not only the old *films noir* and television episodes of his youth, but a wider, richer world, a world he had resigned himself early in life to seeing in snippets at best, but never to know in all its sprawling, vulgar magnificence. The laptop seemed genuinely to care for him: *him*, Martin Gelber, forty-one years old, balding and lonely, spending his days with fruits and vegetables, and his nights with a wife long since a stranger. Absurdly—and he knew bitterly well just how absurd it was—Martin began to feel cherished.

He was also aware that he had no more than scratched the surface of the laptop's talents and capacities. There were keys he carefully avoided touching, software settings he never once changed from how Jaroslav had left them, areas of the screen where he never let the mouse wander. Now and then he was tempted to click on some mysterious button—just to *see*—but Martin had the sad virtue of understanding his own capacity for disaster, and the allure of adventure always faded quickly. He was more than happy with the computer the way it was, and the way they were together.

Except for the One Key.

Martin called it that, having seen *The Lord of the Rings* and read Tolkien's books as well. The One Key lived alone on the upper right corner of the keyboard, well past *Print Screen* and *Scroll Lock* and *Pause/Break* . . . past the tiny blue lights indicating that *Num Lock* or *Caps Lock* or *Scroll Lock* was engaged . . . an ordinary key, no different from any other, except for being without a letter, a number, or—as far as Martin could discern—any obvious purpose. It was simply the One Key: it was just *there*, like a wisdom tooth, and it drew him from the first as the little closet had drawn Bluebeard's seventh wife, or the chest full of plagues had enticed Pandora. Martin, being Martin, and aware that he was Martin, left it strictly alone.

And left it alone.

And went on leaving it alone, until the afternoon of his day off, when there was nothing on TV—not that he ever watched television much anymore—and Lorraine was away with this or that shopping friend . . . and the One Key was now somehow looking as big as the lordly *Backspace* or *Enter*. Martin stared at it for quite a while, and then said, suddenly, loudly, and defiantly, "What the *hell!*" and pushed it.

Nothing happened.

Martin had, of course, no idea what he had expected to happen. He had a reasonable assumption that there wouldn't be an explosion—that the computer wouldn't either levitate or fall completely to pieces—and that a cuckoo wouldn't pop out of the screen with a message from something eternal in its beak. But he had rather anticipated that a deep-toned bell would ring somewhere, surely, and that it would be answered. Every key has a function, he told himself, a programmed reason for existing: there *would* be a response. Martin waited.

A green spark appeared in the center of the computer screen, slowly swelling and swirling, taking on the aspect of a sparkling pinwheel galaxy as it filled the screen. Martin clapped the earphones on his head, hearing a staticky crackle that was not at all like static, but fell into rhythmic, distinctly repetitive patterns that seemed to be trying to form words. The green galaxy revolved dizzyingly before his eyes.

"I don't understand," Martin said aloud, startled to hear himself speak. Suddenly frightened, he considered turning off the laptop. But he didn't, and the vision continued to dazzle his eyes and sizzle in his ears. On an impulse, he moved to the keyboard and typed the same words: *I don't understand.*

This time the response was immediate. The sparkling scene vanished, to be replaced by the image of a face. It was not a human face. Martin knew that immediately, for while it provided the usual allotment of features, they were arranged in a configuration that could only be described as shockingly, impossibly beautiful—Martin actually lurched back, as though hit in the stomach, and made a softer version of the sound that one makes on such occasions.

Words formed under the face. Martin recognized them as words: they were the equivalent in pixels of the sputtering that had been shaping itself into language in his earphones. To him, dazed as he certainly was, it seemed the speech of space, the common dialect of planets and comets alike. All he could think to do was to type his own words over once again, staring at the lovely, terrifying, utterly perfect alien face as he did so. *I don't understand.*

Nothing changed on the screen for some time. Martin occupied himself primarily in praying that Lorraine would not return just then, but also in marveling that a face so beautiful could simultaneously reveal itself as obviously unhuman, yet lose none of its appeal. Nor could he pinpoint the exact reason he knew what he knew—but he knew, and he went on waiting for an answer.

The laptop screen changed again. The face vanished—Martin found himself reaching helplessly toward where it had been— and the screen filled once more with the characters of that otherworldly language. Martin groaned . . . but in almost the same moment, the words dissolved and reformed themselves into something approximating English. He leaned close to the computer, squinting to read them.

Me what
You
Hel who lolo
Me me

First Contact! Martin had seen enough science-fiction movies to know about first contact. The ludicrousness of a computer—a laptop, at that—connecting a suburban produce manager with another world and another life-form was not lost on him, as stunned and overwhelmed as he was. "Why me?" he demanded aloud. "Why not a scientist, an astronomer, whatever? Come *on*, for goodness' sake!" But all the same, he typed onto the screen *Where are you? What is your name?*

There was no response for what seemed a very long while, as excited and impatient as he was. He tried to calm himself, thinking that he and the alien—*his* alien, if he was the first to discover her, like an island or a mountain—might likely be communicating over light-years, not mere miles. This was hardly instant messaging, after all. Even so, he was fidgeting like a child, unable to sit still, by the time the reply came back.

You what
Talk
Who no gone gone
Me

The next word, which Martin thought must have been an attempt at a name, dissolved back into a flurry of words—or sounds? or mathematical symbols? or plain lunatic gibberish?—in the original possibly cosmic tongue. In turn, he went back to his own first-contact cry: *I don't understand.*

"Story of your life, Gelber," he said aloud to the computer. "Find a girl to go to the prom with, she lives too far away for a cab ride, and she doesn't speak English. Your life in one line, I swear."

The computer said back to him in what was still a braver try at his language than any attempt he had yet made at hers:

Me belong Kaskia

Belong who you

Kaskia. Her name was Kaskia, or else she—belonged? a slave?—to someone of that name. Martin refused to believe that anyone who looked like that could be anyone's servant, let alone a slave. He took a long breath and typed back *Martin. My name is Martin.*

He heard nothing back for the rest of the day, even though he forlornly pressed the One Key again and again. Lorraine came home in a good mood, the one benign side effect of her shopping expeditions, and they enjoyed a relatively placid evening, practically together. Martin yearned to get back to the laptop, and Lorraine clearly had phone calls to make—Martin knew the look—but instead they watched a public-television documentary on the history of the Empire State Building, even sitting still through the semiannual fundraising supplications. *Maybe having a special secret makes you nicer,* Martin thought. *Easier to get along with.* He wondered what Lorraine's secret might be.

When Lorraine went to bed, he booted up the laptop and tried, cautiously and apprehensively, to contact the being who called herself—itself?—Kaskia, but to no avail. Applying the One Key repeatedly summoned no starry crackle to his screen, nor did appealing directly to the computer's elaborate message-tracing systems produce any unearthly footprints at all. The entire contact—the entire vision—might never have occurred.

Martin mourned it all through the next day's work at the supermarket. Unlike the protagonists of any number of films and stories, he never for a moment took his encounter with the unearthly for a hallucination or a dream. There had been a connection, however fragmented, with a creature from another place or reality; and the idea of such a wonder never occurring again for the rest of his life made that life seem to him even duller and more pointless than he already knew it to be. "I won't stand for it," he said aloud to himself, while showing Jamil the proper way to stack the red cabbages. "I won't." Jamil took it as a slight to his cabbage-stacking technique, and was deeply wounded.

Three further days passed, during which Martin spoke less and less, both at home and at work, and spent more and more time trying to coax the strange laptop to find Kaskia's world for him again. The computer remained not so much mutinous as regretfully firm, almost parental, as though it had decided that passing the borders of his own understanding was simply bad for him. The One Key remained so unresponsive that he came to fear that he might have damaged it by punching it in frustration when he lost contact with Kaskia. During that time, he could hardly endure to look at the laptop, which Lorraine noticed, teasing him about it. "What happened? Novelty wear off? Barry'll sell you a new toy anytime, if you can find him." Martin hardly heard her.

On the fourth night, sleepless, he finally wandered to his worktable, sat down at the laptop, and played several games of solitaire, as he could have done at any of the store computers. Then he reread his email, browsed a favored newsletter, played a round of *Battleship* against himself, and tapped the One Key, almost diffidently, with his head turned away from the screen. He had not even put his earphones on.

When he heard the static of the spheres, he did not turn immediately, but moved very slowly, as though that other place were a wild bird he was trying not to startle away. The screen was, as before, aswarm with wheeling green sparks, and though

Martin waited patiently, neither words nor the image of the wondrously alien beauty appeared. Finally, he was unable to resist typing once again *My name is Martin*, and then, after some thought, adding boldly *Your name is Kaskia*.

The reply was long in coming, leaving him to fear that he really had frightened her off, and then to speculate on whether an astronomer or mathematician could work out, just from the time it took his electronic missive to receive an answer, how distant Kaskia's world actually might be. He vaguely recalled Barry as having been good with algebra and trigonometry in high school, and thought about setting him the problem.

Words shivered into place on the screen.

Kaskia. You Martin. Where you.

Martin slapped his palms exultantly on the table, and then quickly deadened the vibrations, for fear of waking Lorraine. "It's real!" he whispered, raising his head to look toward the ceiling, and far past it. "Oh, sonofabitch, it's real!" And either her English or the transmission was clearly improving, along with her comprehension. She must have one of those universal translators, like on *Star Trek* and those other shows. Or maybe she was just a fast learner.

He was up most of that night, happily reenacting all the first-contact scenes and dialogue he remembered from movies and television. He placed himself and his planet in the universe for her, as best he could (though she seemed, to his chagrin, to have little knowledge of her own world's relation to any other); and he even told her, out of his own small store, something of the Earth's history and geography. Kaskia was rather less informative, which he put down to her continuing difficulties with the language and her consequently understandable reticence. He did learn that she lived in some sort of grandly sprawling

extended-family setting, that she was a singer and musician—
apparently quite well-known, as far as he could make out—and
that she felt happy and fortunate (if that was what the word she
used meant) to find him a second time. The galaxy was very big.

The contact began to break up toward morning, presumably
due to the rotation of both worlds and the slow, endless drift of
the entire cosmos. But he understood by now when it would be
possible for them to speak again; and when he asked her shyly
if he might see her image once more—it took her some little
time to grasp the meaning of the request—the face that had
so literally made him forget how to breathe reappeared for a
moment, sparkling against the stars. Then it was gone, and the
screen of the laptop went blank.

Sleep was neither an issue nor an option. He lay down on
the living-room couch—not for the first time—and stared
at the ceiling, consumed by a need to tell *someone* about his
discovery, whether or not he was believed. Lorraine was out
of the question, for a good many reasons, while Jaroslav was
still avoiding him in the hall, and shopping elsewhere. As for
his fellow workers, matters of authority forbade his taking
any of them into his confidence . . . except perhaps for Ivan,
the black security guard. Ivan read on the job, whenever he
could get away with it—he had often been seen reading as he
walked through the parking lot—and Martin, as management,
should not have sympathized with him, or protected him, for a
moment. But he did. Most of the books Ivan read were science
fiction; and Martin had a growing feeling that, out of all the
people he knew, Ivan might very well be the only one who might
sympathize with *him*, for a change.

Ivan did. Ivan said, "Wow, man, that is a *good* story." He slapped
Martin's shoulder enthusiastically. "That's like Niven writing

Bradbury. I didn't know you were into that stuff. You got any others?"

Martin did not waste time protesting the complete truthfulness of his account. He said, "Well, I'm not a writer, you know that—I'm just fooling around. You think I ought to change anything? I mean, if *you* were writing it?"

Ivan considered. "One thing, I'd find a way for them to meet up. Not rocket ships, no Buck Rogers shit like that, I'm thinking transporters or some such. I mean, that's exciting, man—that's *risky*. Yeah, he's seen her picture, he's seen *somebody's* picture, but what if she turns out to have a tail and horns and six-inch teeth? Mail-order brides, you know?"

"Well, I don't think the guy's thinking about getting together with her. I mean, she's sort of famous on her world, and he's married, and he could be a lot older—"

"Or *she* could. He don't know how long it takes her planet to get around the sun, or anything about the biology. She could be seven hundred or something, you never know." Ivan patted Martin's shoulder again. "Tell you one thing, *I'd* sure like to have a laptop like the one you thought up. Dell ever makes that puppy, I'm first in line."

Martin spent a good deal of time looking at the computer himself, even when the link to Kaskia was not open. His growing sense of the laptop's true potential had, paradoxically, begun to distance him from the machine that he still believed loved and cared for him. "You scare me," he said aloud to it more than once. "You're with the wrong guy, we both know that." To his mind, the One Key, employed skillfully by someone who knew what he was doing, could probably open channels quite likely beyond the reach of the Hubble telescope. "But that's just not me," Martin said sadly. "I wish it were. I really do."

He did finally get in touch with Barry, who, as expected, claimed absolute ignorance of the laptop's provenance, and could offer no clues toward tracing its history. "I told you everything I know the day I put it in your hands, kid." He gave Martin the warm, confiding smile that not only attracted new victims every day, but continued to re-seduce the old ones, who knew better. "I told you, you belonged together. Was I wrong? Tell me I was wrong."

Martin sighed. "It's like the time you sold me the motorcycle."

Barry's grin widened. "The Triumph. The Bonneville T100. You looked great on it."

"I almost killed myself on it. It was way too much power for me. I sold it two weeks later and only got half what I paid you for it." Martin rubbed his left shoulder reflectively. "This computer's the same way."

"I can't take it back," Barry said quickly. He looked alarmed, which was exceedingly rare for him, and it was Martin's turn to smile reassuringly.

"I don't want to sell it. I just wish I could live up to it." He sighed again. "I wish we really did belong together."

Lorraine came home from work then, and Barry promptly disappeared without a further word. Martin thought, *Those two understand each other better than I understand either one of them.* He wondered whether Lorraine had heard the last thing he said to his cousin. He wondered whether he cared.

The link, or channel, or the hailing frequency, or whatever it actually was, seemed to be open to wherever Kaskia was every five days, sometimes in the afternoon, like that first time, but most often at one or two in the morning. He often asked Kaskia what time it was there, but she seemed to have no concept of measuring time that Martin could translate into his mind. They usually spoke, through the good offices of the laptop screen, until nearly dawn, when Martin would slip quietly into bed beside Lorraine and try to catch at least two or three hours of sleep before heading off to work. It was a wearying regime, but generally manageable.

Kaskia's English had improved further each time they communicated. When Martin questioned how she could be learning the language so fast, since she had not known of its existence until a few weeks before, she replied lightly, *Must be good teacher you.* Asked whether Martin could possibly learn her language in the same way, her answer was a somewhat puzzled *How could you.* She had not yet mastered question marks, or else there was a translation issue involved that he did not understand.

Which did not mean that she did not ask questions. She asked constantly and charmingly—if sometimes startlingly— about the smallest details of Martin's life, from when and where and how he slept, to the names of every fruit and vegetable he handled in his work, and whether there were *nildrys* on his planet. Martin never found out what *nildrys* were, but retained the distinct impression that a planet—or did she mean a house?— without *nildrys* was beneath contempt.

She herself liked best to talk about her pet, whose name on the computer screen was *Furtigosseachfurt*, and who sounded, in Kaskia's description, like a cross between a largish ferret and a squirrel. He was quick and affectionate, liked to have his back scratched and his belly tickled, and on occasion he hid from her behind a rock or high in a tree, and then she had to find him. Her messages regarding the creature took up so much time that Martin would rather have spent on many other matters, and he even found himself skimming a bit over writing from the stars. But they were also so tender and guilelessly touching that they brought Martin just as often close to tears. Once she wrote *Sometimes he is all I have. Sometimes not. You.* Because of the lack of question marks, you could imagine, if you wanted to, that she might be saying that Martin was at times all she had. Martin wanted to think so.

One day the green sparks on the screen formed one word and nothing more. *Dead.*

Martin never thought for a moment that she was speaking of anything but the ferret-squirrel. She never mentioned family at all, and only rarely spoke of friends or acquaintances. He wrote as earnest a condolence as he knew how, sent it off into space expecting no reply, and got none. He wrote another.

Not being an obsessive person by nature, it never occurred to him that his concern for the sorrow of a person infinitely far away across the galaxy might in any way affect his work, or concern anyone else. But, in fact, his increasing distraction had indeed been noticed by his superiors at the market, and by Lorraine as well. This was less of a worry for her than it might have been—Lorraine had survived far worse disasters, and had already chosen her parachute and a cozy landing strip. But she retained a certain rough fondness for Martin, and actually wished him well; so when she confronted him for the last time, it was without much malice that she said, "I have a bet with myself. Twelve to seven that when I walk out of here, you won't notice for three days. Want to cover it?"

Martin's response was as distant as Kaskia's planet, though, of course, Lorraine couldn't know that. He said quietly, "You left a long time ago. I did notice."

Somewhat off balance, Lorraine snapped, "Well, so did you. I'm not even sure you were ever here. Stop playing with that damn computer and look at me—you owe me that much. I'm at least more interesting than a blank screen!" For Martin had the laptop open and was indeed staring at the empty screen, only now and then cutting a quick peripheral glance at her. Lorraine demanded, "What the hell are you looking at? There's nothing there!"

"No," Martin agreed. "Nothing there at all. Good-bye, Lorraine. My fault, I know it, I'm really sorry." But the last words were entirely by rote, and he was looking at the computer screen again while he was speaking them. Lorraine, who had not planned to leave quite this soon, gave a short sneeze-laugh and went to make a phone call.

She would have collected on her bet, for Martin was too occupied with the One Key to be paying attention when she did leave the next day. They were into the second five-day cycle since his last communication from Kaskia, and he was growing anxious, as well as frustrated. He had reached the point lately of stepping outside when the night was at its darkest, and staring until his eyes blurred and burned up at the black, empty sky, currently just as much help to him as the empty computer screen. He would never have said—and never once did—that nothing else mattered but hearing once again from a non-human woman unimaginably far away on the other side of the other side, and he could not make anything else be real. All he could do, at this point, was simply to keep saying her name as though that would make her appear.

And when he returned to the laptop, she was there. Rather, the green sparks were crowding his screen, leaping this way and that, like salmon fighting their way home. And there was that unchanging alien face that chilled and haunted him so . . . and there was a message, as the sparks flew upward into words:

I miss
so much so much

I miss

help me

It was as though her grief had driven her language back to the basics with which their conversation across the night had begun—how long ago it seemed now to Martin. Nevertheless, the cry for comfort was clear; and he, whom so few had ever truly needed or called on for aid, would respond. He began to type, letting the words come without reading over them:

Dear lovely Kaskia,

I too know something about loss.

I never had such a pet as yours—

I cannot have pets, because I have

always been allergic to animals.

Do you know what that means,

allergic?

It means that the skin and the fur

and the hair of most animals

makes you ill,

sometimes very ill indeed.

I think sometimes that I have been

allergic to people,

even to my customers in the produce department,

and to my fellow workers.

I think I would do better with animals than people,

if I were not so allergic.

You have lost a great friend,

but at least you let yourself have him,

you took the risk of having a friend,

and he had you,

so you cannot ever really lose each other.

The words rolled steadily up the screen and disappeared into the night, and the stars beyond. Martin wrote on, haltingly, but never looking back.

> *I have not been as brave as you,*
> *so I have no friend like that,*
> *except you.*
> *We cannot really know each other,*
> *and I suppose we never will,*
> *but I have come to think of you as a dear friend,*
> *and I cannot bear to think of you so unhappy.*

He took a deep breath here, paused just for a moment, and went on.

> *I am very lonely.*
> *I have always been lonely.*
> *It is my fault.*
> *Do not let your grief shut you off.*
> *It is too easy,*
> *and it lasts too long.*
> *Oh, Kaskia, so far away*

The screen, with his last words still on it, went abruptly blank. Martin stared. The laptop was vibrating under his hands, making a sound like an old-fashioned sewing-machine, or a car about to throw a rod. It stopped presently, and new words began to appear on the screen. They were like the sparkling pixel words that Kaskia had first tried before she began to absorb English, but the hand—and, somehow, the tone—was definitely not hers. Martin typed, as before, *My name is Martin Gelber,* and added, with a touch of defiance, *I am Kaskia's friend.*

That got somebody's attention immediately. He was answered by what came across the screen as a bellow of fury.

> *YOU.*

Martin repeated, *My name is Martin Gelber. I am a friend of Kaskia's—*

I KNOW YOU.

The laptop seemed to shiver in the face of such outrage, however faraway.

THE ONE TRIES COMMAND MY CHILD.

Martin stared at the screen in bewilderment and horror. He typed back *Child? I'm talking about Kaskia!*

The new voice was slower to reply this time, and not quite as accusatory.

MY CHILD. MY DAUGHTER.

Martin thought of Ivan at the supermarket. Then he typed *I didn't know.*

The voice on the laptop screen still resolved in capitals, but the tone no longer came across as menacing.

WOULD NOT. KASKIA LIKES TALK. STORIES. LIKES STORIES.

"Yes," Martin said softly, remembering; and then typed *Yes. So then she is not a famous singer and musician?*

LIKES SINGING.

Of course, he replied. *The sad story about her pet dying?*

DEAD. YES. OLDER SISTER'S.

Martin said, "Oh dear."

GOOD GIRL. GOOD GIRL.

Yes, Martin typed again. *Smart girl. Don't punish, please.*

The voice did not answer. Martin wrote, slowly now, *Your daughter changed me. I don't know how, or in what way. But I am different because of her. Better, perhaps—different, anyway. Tell her so.*

Still no answer. Martin was no longer sure of the voice's presence, but he asked, *One other question. Every time we spoke,*

Kaskia and I, there was an image of the most beautiful woman I have ever seen. I thought it was a picture of her. Not?

GOODBYE KASKIA FRIEND.

"Good-bye," Martin said softly. "Good-bye, Kaskia."

The laptop went dark and still. Martin touched the One Key, but nothing happened. He had an odd feeling that nothing would again; the computer had served its purpose, at least for him. He shut it off, unplugged it, wrapped the power cord around it, and put it in a drawer.

After two cups of strong percolated coffee, he called Barry. When his cousin—hungover and grumpy, by the sound of him—answered the phone, Martin said, "Barry? Do you remember the old Prince Albert sting?"

"Prince *Albert?*" Barry was definitely hungover. "Say *what?*"

"You remember. Big fun for bored kids on rainy afternoons. Call up a smoke shop, a candy store, ask them if they've got Prince Albert in a can. Remember now?"

A hoarse chuckle. "Right, sure, yeah. They say yes, and we say, 'Well, let him out right now, he can't breathe in there!' Then we giggle like mad, and they call us little motherfuckers and hang up. What the hell put *that* in your head?"

"Just Memory Lane, I guess."

"Hey, I heard about Lorraine. That really sucks. You okay?"

"I guess. Not really sure what okay is right now. I guess so."

"Okay means there's better out there, lots better. Seize the weekend, like they say in Rome—old Cousin Barry's going to hook you up with one of his Midnight Specials. Meanwhile you're crazy free, right?"

"Crazy, anyway." To his own surprise, Martin realized he was smiling. "We'll see about the free part."

There were bathroom-sink noises at the other end. "'Scuse

me—trying to make an Alka-Seltzer one-handed. Hey, you still happy with that computer I sold you? I got a buyer, if you're not."

Martin hesitated only briefly. "No, I'm fine with it. Great little machine."

Barry cackled triumphantly. "*Told* you it'd change your life, didn't I?"

"No, you didn't. But thanks anyway."

Martin's smile widened slowly. Standing alone in the kitchen, he closed his eyes and listened to the stars.

SCHMENDRICK ALONE

In The Last Unicorn, *there is a scene in which Schmendrick, attempting to free the unicorn from her cage in Mommy Fortuna's Midnight Carnival, summons a demon beyond his own power and barely avoids a terrible disaster. He mentions at the time that he had called the same demon once before, "and I couldn't control him then, either." This is that same demon; and this is Schmendrick at the age of twenty or so, set on the road and on his way by the wizard Nikos, who has taught him everything he can, and everything a wizard needs to know. The rest is up to the green-eyed boy himself . . . and to a unicorn . . . and to a fierce, stubborn woman named Molly Grue . . .*

❦

When the door closed behind him with, as always, never a click of the lock nor any crack or separation where it merged into the hillside, Schmendrick stood facing it for some while. "Well," he said, and, by and by, "Well" again. He shook his head slowly, as though to quiet the ringing of Nikos's somber final words to him. "I tremble at your doom . . ." He had always known the old wizard as a plainspoken man, far less given to darkly mystic utterances than the general run of his colleagues . . . *but why did he say that?*

The noon sun was high, and the day fair, but the tall, thin young man shivered in a cold he had never known, even as the born foreigner in a family he had never truly belonged to for a single day in his nineteen years. Only a certain gawky dignity kept him from banging frantically on the door he could no longer see, begging to be let through, to be allowed home. *Don't be more of a fool than he already thinks you are.* There were no tears in his eyes, but they hurt all the same.

Reaching back to settle his knapsack more firmly on his shoulders, his hand encountered a strange other hand, already immersed to the wrist among his belongings. Dazed and lonely as he was, he still gripped the intruder hard enough to fetch a yelp from its owner as he turned to confront him. Deepening his voice—which had been late in breaking, adding one more target for his three brothers' mimicry—he demanded, "What do you think you are doing, fellow?"

A weedy man of indeterminate years, with a pumpkin-orange face under thinning grayish hair—gaped back at him in genuine, if momentary, disbelief. "What do you *think* I'm doing? I'm picking your pack, stealing your every cherished possession. Or I would have been, if age had not robbed me of my skill, as I would have robbed you of whatever you've got in there that smells like goat cheese. Which you had better eat quickly, by the way, for it will be a public menace in two days' time." As though recalling an interrupted task, he dropped to his knees, clasping his hands in piteous supplication. "Pity, oh, pity, gentle lord, for a harmless, helpless, obsolete old thief, with no family, no morals—and now without the one talent that has served these many years to keep his skin and bones from abandoning him altogether in this heartless world. *Pity,* I pray you!"

Schmendrick drew himself up, puffing his chest out just a bit and smoothing his blue cloak—Nikos's parting gift, along with a strange, many-pointed hat—about himself. "Wretch, do you not realize that I am a mighty and powerful wizard? I sensed your sneaking approach while you were yet making up your mind whether to rob me or no. And now *I* am the one debating whether to turn you into toad, worm, or fire-dwelling salamander." He narrowed his eyes, as he had seen Nikos do on certain occasions, none of which he wanted to remember. "Peradventure, out of kindness, I should leave the choice to you, hey? How like you *that*, Master Thief?"

The pack-picker howled even louder. "Mercy, great lord! I had no idea . . . I didn't know . . . I would *never* . . ." He went on in that vein long enough that Schmendrick began to glance back toward Nikos's house, in some anxiety that the old wizard might be stirred to open his door a second time and instantly know what Schmendrick and the thief both knew themselves: that it had been pure chance and blind luck that had alerted the innocent prey to the predator's intent. *My first hour in the great world, and at this rate I may not make sundown.*

He gripped the kneeling man's shoulders, shaking him, shouting, "Stop that racket, miserable knave! Leave off this instant, I order you, or the next sound out of your mouth will be the cooing of a raven, the dulcet wail of a cat in season. Do you hear me!" When the thief would not cease his crying, Schmendrick hauled him to his feet by main force, despite the fact that his body had gone completely limp, so that it was all but impossible to hold him upright without falling with him. In desperation, Schmendrick cried out himself, "Enough, I forgive you! We are quits, go your way in peace—I forgive you fully and freely!"

On the instant, the thief's body revived, straightening against him, fervently throwing his arms about Schmendrick and kissing his cheeks over and over, much to the new-fledged wizard's embarrassment and revulsion, for the thief had plainly given up bathing sometime since, for some penance or other. "Master, you will never regret this mercy, I promise you! You have changed my life, as only a god can do. From this moment, I swear myself to a career of honest poverty, pure-hearted decency—aye, even charity and chastity, where possible—eternally trudging humbly in the footsteps of my lord!" He fell to embracing and kissing Schmendrick again, until forcibly detached; following which he stepped back and inquired politely, "But I never caught your name, Master. In my former life, one didn't . . . you understand? If I may be granted such a privilege. . . ?"

"Indeed you may. I am known as Schmendrick the Magician." Schmendrick bowed grandly with a sweep of his cloak—*must practice that*—and the transformed thief returned the obeisance so profoundly that he almost fell to his knees again and was noisily grateful for a kindly hand up. They continued bowing until each was out of the other's sight; and Schmendrick set off briskly on the road to his destiny, that had appeared so lonely and forbidding only moments before. *Nikos must have known that I was ready—that it was my time. This may not be so bad, after all.*

The mood of exhilaration lasted some hours; until, taking his dinner at a wayside public house, he discovered that, while the contents of his knapsack remained untouched, the purse at his waist was completely empty, as were both pockets of his trews. The pack-picker's hands seemed, as it proved, to have lost no whit of their old skill.

Throat thick with rage, face aflame with humiliation, Schmendrick sprang to his feet, determined to retrace as many miles of his journey as required, even to Nikos's door, until he closed his hands around the neck of the scoundrel who had taken such advantage of his youth and ingenuousness. *And your vanity,* he could hear his old master mocking him. *Let us never forget to honor your vanity.*

He was nearly at the door when a notably firm grip closed

on his right arm, and the innkeeper growled at his ear, "Stay but a little, my friend. There's a trifling matter between us, to be discussed like gentlemen." The innkeeper was a burly man with discouraging eyes, and the fellow looming up silently on Schmendrick's left might have been his twin, but for the temple-to-jaw scar on his cheek. The innkeeper inquired, surprisingly courteous, "Would it interest you to learn what became of the only man who ever quit my house without paying his score?"

In a small voice, Schmendrick managed to reply, "Would it concern you at all to know that I have been robbed?"

The innkeeper shrugged. "My only concern is to maintain a certain reputation for being extremely hazardous for swindlers." He nodded to the scar-faced man, who placed his huge hands, almost caressingly, about Schmendrick's throat.

"Wait!" Schmendrick gurgled. "*Wait!*" At a glance from his master, the scar-faced man loosened his grip, at the same time placing himself between Schmendrick and the door. The innkeeper wondered thoughtfully, "Is there a reason why my friend should not twist your head off and kick it down the highroad? You are young, and I would be glad of an excuse to be kind. They are, alas, tragically rare."

"Because . . . because I am a wizard!" The declaration did not come out quite as forcefully as it had done with the thief, and the word *mighty* was nowhere involved; but all the same it did catch the innkeeper's attention, causing him to fold his arms and purse his lips. The scar-faced man scratched his head, with a sound like a plough working a stony field.

"A wizard," the innkeeper muttered. "Well, now, one would think that a wizard could easily magic up the amount of his score, surely? And a wizard's money is as good as another's . . . or am I wrong?"

"You are indeed, my good man." Schmendrick's confidence was returning with his breath. "I tell you in all honesty that any coin I placed in your hand, whether of copper or silver, would have melted into air, into thin air, before I was a mile along that same highroad. My master Nikos, greatest of enchanters, from whose tutelage I have been released but this morning, instructed me from my first day of study that magic and money are incompatible by their very natures, and forbade me any dealing with that false art, on pain of immediate dismissal . . . or worse." He felt bold enough to put his own hand on the innkeeper's hairy-muscled one. "But no one was ever the worse for a wizard's aid, even such a young wizard as myself, and I can pay the cost of my luncheon in ways you may not have considered, or yet encountered. How may I serve you, therefore? Only try me!"

The innkeeper shrugged his hand away with a seeming twitch of his skin, as a horse will do an annoying midge. But the scar-faced man spoke for the first time, in a changed voice, a slower voice like the scraping rumble of millstones, "If words alone could butter parsnips, the wizardlet might well be the perfect cat's-paw to recover your wife's ring and prove her innocence." Schmendrick was not at all certain that he enjoyed being referred to as a wizardlet, but he remained as impassive as he felt Nikos would have been. The scar-faced man went on, "You cannot be certain that she has deceived you, merely because she cannot find her wedding ring. Whether she lost it in the garden, as she says, or in the wash, or in a lover's bed . . . let the boy search it out, for the sake of your peace. After all—" and he winked horribly at Schmendrick—"there's plenty of time to feed him to the pigs if he fail. True?"

"True," the innkeeper responded slowly. When he peered at Schmendrick again, there was something in his hard eyes that had not been there before. "What says the wizard to that? Prove my wife's purity beyond doubt, and there'll be more than a meal in it for you—aye, you'll leave here fat enough to cast two shadows, and with enough in your purse to see you as far as the moon, if that's your destination. From the look of you—" and he smiled slightly for the first time—"it very well might be."

Schmendrick's head hurt. He looked from one to the other of them, noting sourly that the scar-faced man had not moved an inch from his door-blocking position, and that none of the other diners and drinkers had shown the slightest interest in his predicament. He ran through Nikos's favored finding spell in his mind, pleased at recalling it so precisely, while stroking his chin in as gravely measured a manner as he could summon, and finally announced, "Very well. It is not the sort of task I generally concern myself with, but under these present circumstances, how can a wizard refuse in good conscience?"

"Ah, how indeed?" murmured the scar-faced man. The innkeeper gestured to him to stand back and give the wizard conjuring room; but the door grew no nearer, nor the way to it any less occupied. Schmendrick sighed and closed his eyes. Nikos always did that when casting a spell.

The words he spoke were short and unimpressive, sounding neither especially resonant nor musical; he stumbled over two of them and had to start over. Such gestures as he made were hardly sweeping, rather resembling the finger-wrestling games that bored children play with their hands. To compensate for this lack of grand style, he sank to one knee with a flourish of his cloak, all the while knowing perfectly well that Nikos would have scorned such a display. He peeped up slyly under his eyelids, after a moment, to assess his employers' reactions.

Nothing had happened. Beyond the fact of two large men,

one somewhat uglier than the other, confronting with increasing annoyance a third—taller, but far less massively constructed—now rising unsteadily to his feet . . . nothing at all had changed. Except, perhaps, that the scar-faced man was flexing his fingers with a certain ominous crackling, while the innkeeper was untying his apron. His arms looked even bigger than Schmendrick remembered them.

"A pity," the innkeeper said softly. He sounded genuinely wistful.

"A great pity," the scar-faced man agreed with him. "Except for the pigs, of course."

"I can try again," Schmendrick told them, hoping earnestly that his voice sounded at least somewhat less desperate than he felt. "I don't always get things right the first time."

The scar-faced man smiled. His teeth were like blocks of granite, worn into curious shapes by centuries of wind and rain. "Discuss it with the pigs, wizardlet." He picked Schmendrick up by the collar of his cloak.

"Do not harm him." The innkeeper's own voice had turned heavy and sad.

"Kick him a few yards down the road, if you like, but nothing more. What's the theft of one meal, after all, when. . . ?" He seemed about to say more, but then shrugged wearily and turned away toward the taproom. Without turning his head, he muttered, "Go in peace, boy. Don't come back."

"A few yards it is," the scar-faced man called after him. Eagerly dragging the frantically protesting Schmendrick to the door, he announced loudly, "I doubt there's much distance in that bony bum, but we'll do what we can, won't we?" A few patrons looked up and laughed as the two of them went by, but no one followed to enjoy the spectacle. This was a good thing; because

Schmendrick was not kicked any distance at all, but set almost tenderly on his feet a short distance from the public house, and even brushed off and somewhat tidied by the scar-faced man, who growled, "My apologies, friend. It's a poor way to treat a man who's done me as good a turn as you have."

Schmendrick could do nothing but catch his breath and stare. The scar-faced man said, "If I'd thought for a single minute that you were actually wizard enough to find that ring of his wife's . . . well, I'd not have stopped running for a day and a half. Conservative estimate, let me tell you." He reached into an inner pocket and brought out a small gold circlet, which glittered in his palm for only a moment before he put it away again. "But one look at you, and I knew my secret was in good hands." He slapped Schmendrick on the shoulder, almost affectionately. "You couldn't turn cream into butter, could you, boy? Tell the truth now."

Schmendrick found his voice. "I am a disciple of the great Nikos! I studied with him for seven years!"

The scar-faced man clucked sympathetically. "Well, I can't say I know the chap, but you really ought to ask for your money back. Oh . . . speaking of which—" and he reached into a different pocket to hand Schmendrick a fistful of copper coins. "There— don't thank me, worth every penny. He'll never put faith in a wizard again, even should a real one happen along. Be on your way, my friend, and luck go with you, for you'll certainly need it." He chuckled like a landslide, thumping Schmendrick's shoulder a second time. "You had me really anxious there for a moment or two, wizardlet."

Schmendrick stared after him for a long while. Finally, with a deep, rasping sigh, he sank down into the grass at the side of the road and began to take wincing stock of his position. His purse was lost, along with every coin of Master Nikos's parting gift; his pack, left behind in the public house, had held little of value, bar clean tunic and trews and a cake of Nikos's favorite lily-of-the-valley soap. But what it had contained was without price to a "wizardlet," as he mocked himself aloud in bitterness: seven years' fragmented memories of the first true companionship, and—yes, why not?—grimly devoted fatherhood as well.

"Who else was ever so patient with my bumbling? Who else was so brusquely kind when I wept in lonely self-disgust—when even his familiar demons made game of me? Who else ever believed in me, with so little to believe? And what would he think now, to see me naked and penniless under a darkening sky?" He had more than once, journeying with his master, seen Nikos bring a small, practical shelter for the two of them into a night's existence, but such enchantment was yet as far beyond his abilities as summoning a properly cooked meal lay beyond even Nikos's competence. And, as an apprentice, he was as strictly forbidden to attempt to magic up gold, silver, or lowly copper as to create life, though he had never grasped the parallel. "When you are as old as I, you will understand—perhaps—how to do certain things, and understand as well why you must never do them. Perhaps." Even Nikos's faith had its misgivings.

Schmendrick slept cold and hungry in a dry ditch that night, under his new cloak, with his new strange hat over his face, and arose determined not to do so again.

Limping along a road rougher and more stony with every mile, he eventually begged a ride from a farmer on his way to market, who was won over, not by the company of a wizard—"I scour up a living out of soil like yesterday's dry toast, *and* I can live with my wife without strangling her; *there's* magic for you"—but by the fact that Schmendrick could read and write, and cipher as well. There was a week's board and room in that chance acquaintanceship; and by the time Schmendrick departed, he had become familiar with a number of similar folk with similar problems. Not one of them needed supernatural assistance, but help with a family's accounting was very nearly as welcome as another hand in the field, or another spade clearing a silt-clogged ditch. And a farmer's solemn-eyed children always marveled with their gruff parents at singing frogs flying up to the treetops or at flowers daintily arranging themselves on the dinner table. Setting out once more on his aimless way, Schmendrick had only to turn his head to see any number of work-roughened hands of all sizes waving him farewell. At certain times—especially when there were children—it felt very nearly like walking away again from Nikos's door.

Later one evening than he liked to be seeking shelter, he came to a cottage that was clearly no farmhouse, for he heard the rhythmic clatter of a shuttle from within. When he knocked for admission, he was greeted by an elderly couple, clearly the grandparents of the young woman who looked up from her loom by the fire as he entered. She made an effort to smile, but it was plain to Schmendrick that she had been weeping not long before; the red eyes of both of the old people told him the same thing. Begging their pardon for intruding into a house of grief, he turned again toward the door; but their courtesy was a match for his, and would not permit them to let him leave. They sat him firmly at their table, insisted on offering him the best of what little they had, and kept assuring him brokenly that their trouble was no concern of a stranger's. Schmendrick had been more at his ease in the public house—before the adulterous wedding rings started flying—being threatened with being fed to pigs.

Grandmother and Grandfather alike had warm, gentle faces, but their young granddaughter was the most beautiful woman Schmendrick had ever seen, even including Sardana, his secretly-cherished sister-in-law. Her tear-swollen eyes were the blue-green of the sea in sunlight; her flowing hair was the color of river water, and the dark-gold skin seemed to caress the perfect cheekbones to which it clung. Her name was Eliara. Schmendrick spoke her name several times on being introduced, and said very little else for some while.

"Forgive my distress and dishevelment, I pray you." Her voice was thick with weeping, but still soft and appealing. "You come at an ill time—the only visitor we three sit expecting is the one whom I would rather die than welcome through my door. Indeed—" and she shook her lovely head, as though in wonder—"your unfortunate fate may have brought you here to be my undertaker and gravedigger all in one." Her grandparents broke into tears again, but she went on harshly. "For I swear, on the instant that *that man* takes my hand, that moment will the dagger in my other hand find my heart." She reached into a fold of her dress and showed it to Schmendrick: thin and sharp as her laughter, with a single red stone in the hilt. "I know exactly where the heart hides behind my ribs. It will not escape me."

Schmendrick gaped back and forth from her to the old people. It was the grandmother who answered his wordless question. "The Lord Buccleuch. She took his fancy a scant month ago, outside the church he built and never attends, and he made proposal to her there and then . . . such a proposal . . ."

Misery stopped her speech then, and the grandfather took up the tale. "When she refused him before all the town, he first thought it charming, for no one had ever told him *no* in his life. It took him near the month to understand that she meant what

173

she said. Now he has let the town know that he will be coming tonight for the woman who humiliated him so. Buccleuch settles his scores, always."

The girl Eliara laughed again. "I hope only that he stands close enough that my blood spatters that black doublet he is so proud of. That would be *my* score."

Schmendrick found words somewhere in his throat. "Please, I beg you ... surely there must be some other way ..."

"There is none." The grandmother's voice was a desert. "We have known the Lord Buccleuch far longer than she. I would kill her myself before I let him put his hand on her."

The pride and confidence with which Schmendrick had set out from Nikos's door, and which had abandoned him in the public house at the moment when he reached for his purse, had been slowly returning, wary as a once-trapped fox, while he walked the road from farms to fairs, to farms again. He said, "Wait. Listen to me," speaking not so much to the girl Eliara as to her sea-colored eyes. "*Listen . . .*" and somehow there was no one in the little room but the two of them. She did not answer him, but waited.

Schmendrick said, "*Listen,*" for a third time. He said, "I am a wizard. To me, your Lord Buccleuch is an ant, a stinkbug, a dungbeetle. I have a dozen dark worlds from which to summon my servants, and if the least of them should set about your Buccleuch at my command ..." He snapped his fingers once, and the girl tensed in startlement, as though she had expected fire to leap from the tips. Slightly embarrassed, he shrugged his shoulders and crooked a corner of his mouth, just as he remembered Nikos doing. "Leave your Buccleuch to me. It may not be pleasant, but I can promise you that it will be ... entertaining."

The casual assurance in his voice rang hollow as they heard

the approaching hoofbeats. Eliara was instantly on her feet, as was her grandfather, moving in front of his wife with a hand on her shoulder. He was holding a basting spit at the ready, for all Eliara motioned to him to set it down. But Schmendrick, in his turn, gestured the three of them to calmness, said courteously, "By your leave," and walked boldly to the door to open it. No one else spoke a word.

The night had turned cold, as it often did in that country, however warm the days; but the moon had risen, making candles of the chain mail worn by the dozen men approaching the house. Their leader wore no armor of any sort, but for the hardness of his face and the implacable rigidity with which he held himself. Schmendrick thought him older than himself and Eliara together, but there was steel and stone in him still.

Drawing rein before the door, he said, "Whoever you may be, I have come for your mistress. Send her out to me." His voice had the sound of boot heels in it.

Schmendrick smiled at him, and said quietly, "Go home."

The Lord Buccleuch did not seem to have heard him. "Tell her that I will burn this rathole over her head if she is not up behind me in two minutes' time."

"I do not wish it said that I gave you no warning," Schmendrick said. "Go home, lord."

The hard old man's gray eyes seemed to take him in for the first time. The Lord Buccleuch said, "And I have already given you warning enough." The sword made only a small whisper clearing the scabbard, but what Schmendrick said was even softer. Buccleuch's sword blade turned to glittering ice for a moment, then melted and ran down his arm as he stared at the hilt in his hand.

Schmendrick took a deep breath, wishing that Nikos could be there to observe his triumph: that particular skill had taken him almost three years to master. Then the Lord Buccleuch uttered a choked curse, hurled the sword hilt away, raked his spurred heels savagely along his horse's sides, and charged straight for him. The gray eyes were very wide.

There was no time for thought, no time for skill, however dearly acquired. Schmendrick heard himself shouting as he sprang aside, but he did not recognize the words, nor the voice in which he cried them. All he knew at the time was that he had never spoken them aloud before, and that they tasted like gunpowder and brickdust as they blew through his mouth.

What answered him limped slowly out of the night, all but shapeless, chuckling muddily. It smelled like wet dead leaves; and the slow sound that its great blurred body made as it moved at the horsemen and their master was like the sound dead leaves would make if they had a reason. It had the round ears of a bear, but no eyes that Schmendrick could see. It did not seem to need eyes.

One of the Lord Buccleuch's men-at-arms cried out in fear, and, unordered, loosed off an arrow at the bear-creature. The bolt struck its target squarely in what would have been the belly on a human, and passed through altogether, coming to rest in a rain barrel. The creature took no notice of the attempt, but the bowman did. He uttered a skin-freezing shriek and bolted, followed by every one of the riders, all streaming back the way they had come, blundering for the shelter of the shadowy trees on either hand. Only the Lord Buccleuch remained, in opposition to the clearly expressed desires of his own horse. Weaponless, white-faced, wicked, brave, asking no more quarter than he would have given, he looked from Schmendrick to the thing Schmendrick had summoned; then back to Schmendrick again; then beyond him to the girl Eliara in the doorway. All the while, he spoke no word.

Schmendrick said, "I am Schmendrick the Magician. These people are under my protection. You will not come near them ever again."

He could say that now; he felt the right to say it moving within him, determined to be born, feeling its time. The bear-creature grinned a wet grin, and moved steadily closer to the Lord Buccleuch. Schmendrick spoke firmly, saying, "No need, no need, good servant. Our friend has understood." The creature extended a paw like a clawed spade, as imploringly as any beggar. The Lord Buccleuch's horse was trembling so violently that the old man came near to being thrown; but he held it in position by sheer force of will, the impossibly taut cords of his face and neck threatening to slice up through his skin. He had bitten deeply into his lower lip, and his mouth was bleeding badly.

"No," Schmendrick said again. "No." In the prescribed formal manner, he said. "I give you leave to depart in peace." He spoke the prescribed words and made the prescribed series of gestures, exactly as he had seen Nikos do any number of times when discharging spirits or demons from duties accomplished. "With my respect and gratitude . . . *begone.*"

The bear-creature reached out again. The gesture this second time was almost a caressing one; it took Schmendrick a terrible fraction of a second to realize what was happening. The paws that Schmendrick had taken for smoke and mist, menacing but flesh-less, snatched the Lord Buccleuch out of his saddle, then held him up in the air and began to fold him, bending him this way and that with surprising care and delicacy, like a child turning a flat sheet of paper into a boat or a bird. Schmendrick heard the sound of it, even under the screaming of the Lord Buccleuch's horse.

The creature was not a dexterous or artistic folder, but it tried. What fell from the spade-paws when it was done was as crumbled as a dead leaf, and blew away quickly and silently in the gentle night breeze. There was nothing left on the ground.

The only thing that kept Schmendrick's legs from buckling completely was his awareness of the three terrified faces in the doorway behind him. He repeated the spell he had just spoken, taking numbly obsessive care with the accent and pronunciation. The bear-creature remained disturbingly present, still grinning.

"I *order* you to depart," Schmendrick declared. "In the name of Gallaric . . . Aubryn . . . *Nikos*! In the name of the great Nikos, depart at once!"

The bear-creature's grin seemed to grow slightly wider. Schmendrick tried every other dismissal spell he had ever heard Nikos use, whether permitted or forbidden to him by his master, but he might as well have been reciting recipes or nursery rhymes. His summoning's attention appeared to be focused on Eliara and her grandparents; indeed, the creature had now begun limping toward the house, ignoring him entirely. It had begun making a low sound to itself.

There was no magic; there was no least trace of the power that had swept through him for a single shattering instant and abandoned him again, leaving him bereft of everything but cheapjack sleights and tricks to amuse peasants' children, and the bitter certainty that this was all he had ever been meant for. Suddenly close to laughter, he heard himself think or say somewhere, "No wonder Nikos never took any fee for my apprenticeship. He knew . . ."

But behind him were the faces, the three to whom he had sworn protection: the strangers foolish enough to believe in him. Schmendrick backed and backed, keeping his back to the door, and the bear-creature looming blindly over him, like a storm about to break, he snatched off the strange, many-pointed cap that Nikos had given him and threw it down on the ground, as though drawing a borderline between them. He spread his arms as wide as he could and shouted out of a splintering throat, "You will pass no further! Hear me—I am Schmendrick! Schmendrick the Magician!"

The bear-creature stopped in its shambling tracks. It peered eyelessly down at him, and he felt the seeing, felt himself—his *self*—being handled, weighed, and winnowed by something that could not exist except when called upon by wizards. In a smaller voice, almost a whisper, he repeated, "I am Schmendrick. I am."

The bear-creature began to laugh.

It was a dreadful laughter, the more so because of the astonishing joy in it, as though a being constructed of darkness, hopeful of nothing but continued darkness, had suddenly discovered ridiculousness: stumbled upon the wondrous absurdity of the humans who bid and banished it as they chose, and thereby imagined themselves its mighty superiors. The creature was still laughing as it faded gradually into the night—Schmendrick would have sworn that it actually bent over and slapped its nonexistent thighs, and that the laughter continued to carom around the sky for some moments after it had vanished completely.

Schmendrick picked up his hat. He took longer than he needed brushing and smoothing it, knowing that if he turned he would see three faces grateful to the point of near-worship, urging him into their home for praise and celebration. But he lifted his hat to them without turning, and set off along the dark road he had come. Someone behind him—*Eliara?*—called his name, but he walked on until, when he did turn, he could no longer see the lights of the little house where she lived with her grandparents. Tonight, for the first time in some while, he would sleep by the roadside under his blue cloak, with his many-pointed hat for a pillow.

And serve you right, wizardlet.

GREAT-GRANDMOTHER IN THE CELLAR

Beyond the fact that this story takes place in the world of The Innkeeper's Song, *which I sneak back to every chance I get, I can't tell you much about it. After the fact, when I think about it, the tale might have a slight connection to a Robert Frost dialogue-poem, in which a mother and son are recounting a scary tale to a stranger, having to do with a skeleton in their cellar, which tries periodically to find its way upstairs to avenge itself on the husband who killed it. I read that poem long ago, in my parents' living room, and I couldn't quote it today—but that's the only tie I can think of. Like every other story in this book, I told it to myself as I was going along.*

✂

I thought he had killed her.

Old people forget things, I know that—my father can't ever remember where he set down his pen a minute ago—but if I forget, at the end of *my* life, every other thing that ever happened to me, I will still be clutched by the moment when I gazed down at my beautiful, beautiful, sweet-natured idiot sister and heard the whining laughter of Borbos, the witch-boy she loved, pattering in my head. I *knew* he had killed her.

Then I saw her breast rising and falling—so slowly!—and I saw her nostrils fluttering slightly with each breath, and I knew that he had only thrown her into the witch-sleep that mimics the last sleep closely enough to deceive Death Herself.

Borbos stepped from the shadows and laughed at me.

"*Now* tell your father," he said. "Go to him and tell him that Jashani will lie so until the sight of my face—and only my face—awakens her. And that face she will never see until he agrees that we two may wed. Is this message clear enough for your stone skull, Da'mas? Shall I repeat it, just to be sure?"

I rushed at him, but he put up a hand and the floor of my sister's chamber seemed to turn to oiled water under my feet. I went over on my back, flailing foolishly at the innocent air, and Borbos laughed again. If *shukris* could laugh, they would sound like Borbos.

He was gone then, in that way he had of coming and going, which Jashani thought was so dashing and mysterious, but which seemed to me fit only for sneak thieves and housebreakers. I knelt there alone, staring helplessly at the person I loved most in the world, and whom I fully intended to strangle when—oh, it had to be *when!*—she woke up. With no words, no explanations, no apologies. She'd know.

In the ordinary way of things, she's far brighter and wiser and simply *better* than I, Jashani. My tutors all disapproved and despaired of me early on, with good reason; but before she could walk, they seemed almost to expect my sister to perform her own *branlewei* coming-of-age ceremony, and prepare both the ritual sacrifice *and* the meal afterward. It would drive me wild with jealousy—especially when Father would demand to know, one more time, why I couldn't be as studious and accomplished as Jashani—if she weren't so ridiculously decent and kind that there's not a thing you can do except love her. I sometimes go out into the barn and scream with frustration, to tell you the truth . . . and then she comes running to see if I'm hurt or ill. At twenty-one, she's two and a half years older than I, and she has never once let Father beat me, even when the punishment was so richly deserved that I'd have beaten me if I were in his place.

And right then I'd have beaten *her*, if it weren't breaking my heart to see her prisoned in sleep unless we let the witch-boy have her.

It is the one thing we ever quarrel about, Jashani's taste in men. Let me but mention that this or that current suitor has a cruel mouth, and all Chun will hear her shouting at me that the poor boy can't be blamed for a silly feature—and should I bring a friend by, just for the evening, who happens to describe the poor boy's method of breaking horses . . . well, that will only make things worse. If I tell her that the whole town knows that the fellow serenading her in the grape arbor is the father of two children by a barmaid, and another baby by a farm girl, Jashani will fly at me, claiming that he was a naive victim of their seductive beguilements. Put her in a room with ninety-nine perfect choices and one heartless scoundrel, and she will choose the villain every time. This prediction may very well be the one thing Father and I ever agree on, come to consider.

But *Borbos* . . .

Unlike most of the boys and men Jashani ever brought home to try out at dinner, I had known Borbos all my life, and Father had known the family since his own youth. Borbos came from a long line of witches of one sort and another, most of them quite respectable, as witches go, and likely as embarrassed by Borbos as Father was by me. He'd grown up easily the handsomest young buck in Chun, straight and sleek, with long, angled eyes the color of river water, skin and hair the envy of every girl I knew, and an air about him to entwine hearts much less foolish than my sister's. I could name names.

And with all that came a soul as perfectly pitiless as when we were all little and he was setting cats afire with a twiddle of two fingers, or withering someone's fields or haystacks with a look, just for the fun of it. He took great care that none of our parents ever caught him at his play, so that it didn't matter what I told them—and in the same way, even then, he made sure never to let Jashani see the truth of him. He knew what he wanted, even then, just as she never wanted to believe evil of anyone.

And here was the end of it: me standing by my poor, silly sister's bed, begging her to wake up, over and over, though I knew she never would—not until Father and I . . .

No.

Not ever.

If neither of us could stop it, I knew someone who would.

Father was away from home, making arrangements with vintners almost as far north as the Durli Hills and as far south as Kalagira, where the enchantresses live, to buy our grapes for their wine. He would be back when he was back, and meanwhile there was no way to reach him, nor any time to spare. The decision was mine to make, whatever he might think of it afterward. Of our two servants, Catuzan, the housekeeper, had finished her work and gone home, and Nanda, the cook, was at market. Apart from Jashani, I was alone in our big old house.

Except for Great-Grandmother.

I never knew her; neither had Jashani. Father had, in his youth, but he spoke of her very little, and that little only with the windows shuttered and the curtains drawn. When I asked hopefully whether Great-Grandmother had been a witch, his answer was a headshake and a definite *no*—but when Jashani said, "Was she a demon?" Father was silent for some while. Finally, he said, "No, not really. Not exactly." And that was all we ever got out of him about Great-Grandmother.

But I knew something Jashani didn't know. Once, when I was small, I had overheard Father speaking with his brother Uskameldry, who was also in the wine-grape trade, about a particular merchant in Coraic who had so successfully cornered the market in that area that no vintner would even look at our family's grapes, whether red or black or blue. Uncle Uska had joked, loudly enough for me to hear at my play, that maybe they ought to go down to the cellar and wake up Great-Grandmother again. Father didn't laugh, but hushed him so fast that the silence caught my ear as much as the talk before it.

Our cellar is deep and dark, and the great wine casks cast bulky shadows when you light a candle. Jashani and I and our friends used to try to scare each other when we played together there, but she and I knew the place too well ever to be really frightened. Now I stood on the stair, thinking crazily that Jashani and Great-Grandmother were both asleep, maybe if you woke one, you might rouse the other . . . something like that, anyway. So after a while, I lit one of the wrist-thick candles Father kept under the hinged top step, and I started down.

Our house is the oldest and largest on this side of the village. There have been alterations over the years—most of them while Mother was alive—but the cellar never changes. Why should it? There are always the casks, and the tables and racks along the walls, for Father's filters and preservatives and other tools to test the grapes for perfect ripeness; and always the same comfortable smell of damp earth, the same boards stacked to one side, to walk on should the cellar flood, and the same shadows, familiar as bedtime toys. But there was no sign of anyone's ancestor, and no place where one could possibly be hiding, not once you were standing on the earthen floor, peering into the shadows.

Then I saw the place that wasn't a shadow, in the far-right

corner of the cellar, near the drainpipe. I don't remember any of us noticing it as children—it would have been easy to miss, being only slightly darker than the rest of the floor—but when I walked warily over to it and tapped it with my foot, it felt denser and finer-packed than any other area. There were a couple of spades leaning against the wall farther along. I took one and, feeling strangely hypnotized, started to dig.

The deeper I probed, the harder the digging got, and the more convinced I became that the earth had been deliberately pounded hard and tight, as though to hold something down. Not hard enough: whatever was here, it was coming up now. A kind of fever took hold of me, and I flung spadeful after spadeful aside, going at it like a rock-*targ* ripping out a poor badger's den. I broke my nails, and I flung my sweated shirt away, and I dug.

I didn't hear my father the first time, although he was shouting at me from the stair. "What are you doing?" I went on digging, and he bellowed loud enough to make the racks rattle, *"Da'mas, what are you doing?"*

I did not turn. I was braced for the jar of the spade on wood, or possibly metal—a coffin either way—but the sound that came up when I finally did hit something had me instantly throwing the instrument away and dropping down to half-sit, half-kneel on the edge of the oblong hole I'd worried out of the earth. Reaching, groping, my hand came up gripping a splintered bone.

Great-Grandmother! I flung myself face-down, clawing with both hands now, frantic, hysterical, not knowing what I was doing. Fingerbones . . . something that might have been a knee, an elbow . . . *a skull*—no, just the top of a skull . . . I don't think I was quite sane when I heard the voice.

"Grandson, stop . . . stop, before you really do addle my poor old *bones. Stop!"* It was a slow voice, with a cold, cold rustle in it: it sounded like the wind over loose stones.

I stopped. I sat up, and so did she.

Then Father—home early, due to some small war blocking his road—was beside me, as silent as I, but with an unfriendly hand gripping the back of my neck. Great-Grandmother wasn't missing any bones, thank Dran and Tani, our household gods, who are twins. The skull wasn't hers, nor the fingers, nor any of the other loose bones; she was definitely whole, sitting with her fleshless legs bent under her, from the knees, and her own skull clearing the top of my pit to study me out of yellowish-white empty eye sockets. She said, "The others are your Great-Aunt Keshwara. I was lonely."

I looked at Father for the first time. He was sweating himself, pale and swaying. I realized that his hand on my neck was largely to keep me from trembling, and to hold himself upright. "You should not have done this," he said. He was almost whispering. "Oh, you should never have done this." Then, louder, as he let go of me, "Great-Grandmother."

"Do not scold the boy, Rushak," the stone rustle rebuked him. "It has been long and long since I saw anything but dirt, smelled anything but mold. The scent of fear tells me that I am back with my family. Sit up straight, young Da'mas. Look at me."

I sat as properly as I could on the edge of a grave. Great-Grandmother peered closely at me, her own skull weaving slightly from side to side, like a snake's head. She said, "Why have you awakened me?"

"He's a fool," Father said. "He made a mistake, he didn't know . . ." Great-Grandmother looked at him, and he stopped talking. She repeated the question to me.

How I faced those eyeless, browless voids and spoke to those cold, slabby chaps, I can't tell you—or myself—today. But I said my sister's name—"Jashani"—and after that it got easier. I said, "Borbos, the witch-boy—he's made her sleep, and she won't wake up until we give in and say he can marry her. And she'd be better off dead."

"What?" Father said. "How—"

Great-Grandmother interrupted, "Does she know that?"

"No," I said. "But she will. She thinks he loves her, but he doesn't love anybody."

"He loves my money, right enough," Father said bitterly. "He loves my house. He loves my business."

The eye sockets never turned from me. I said, "She doesn't know about these things . . . about men. She's just *good*."

"Witch-boy . . ." The rusty murmur was all but inaudible in the skeletal throat. "Ah . . . the Tresard family. The youngest."

Father and I gaped at her, momentarily united by astonishment. Father asked, "How did you. . . ?" Then he said, "You were already . . ." I thanked him silently for being the one to look a fool.

Great-Grandmother said simply—and, it might have been, a little smugly—"I listen. What else have I to do in that hole?" Then she said, "Well, I must see the girl. Show me."

So my great-grandmother stepped out of her grave and followed my father and me upstairs, clattering with each step like an armload of dishes, yet held firmly together somehow by the recollection of muscles, the stark memory of tendons and sinews. Neither of us liked to get too close to her, which she seemed to understand, for she stayed well to the rear of our uncanny procession. Which was ridiculous, and I knew it then, and I was ashamed of it then as well. She was family, after all.

In Jashani's chamber, Great-Grandmother stood looking down at the bed for a long time, without speaking. Finally, she said softly, almost to herself, "Skilled . . . I never knew a Tresard with such . . ." She did not finish.

"Can you heal her?" The words burst out of me as though I hadn't spoken in years, which was how I felt. "She's never hurt a soul, she wouldn't know how—she's foolish and sweet, except she's *very* smart, it's just that she can't imagine that anyone would ever wish her harm. *Please*, Great-Grandmother, make her wake up! I'll do anything!"

I will be grateful to my dying day that Jashani couldn't hear a word of all that nonsense.

Great-Grandmother didn't take her empty eyes from my sister as I babbled on; nor did she seem to hear a word of the babble. I'm not sure how long she stood there by the bed, though I do recall that she reached out once to stroke Jashani's hair very lightly, as though those cold, fleshless fingers were seeing, tasting . . .

Then she stepped back, so abruptly that some bones clicked against other bones, and she said, "I must have a body."

Again, Father and I stared stupidly at her. Great-Grandmother said impatiently, "Do you imagine that I can face your witch-boy like this? One of you—either one—must allow me the use of his body. Otherwise, don't waste my time." She glowered into each of our pale faces in turn, never losing or altering the dreadful grin of the long-dead.

Father took a long breath and opened his mouth to volunteer, but I beat him to it, actually stepping a bit forward to nudge him aside. I said, "What must I do?"

Great-Grandmother bent her head close, and I stared right into that eternal smile. "Nothing, boy. You need do nothing but stand so . . . just so . . ."

I cannot tell you what it was like. And if I could, I wouldn't. You might ask Father, who's a much better witness to the whole affair than I, for all that, in a way, I *was* the whole affair. I do know from him that Great-Grandmother's bones did not clatter untidily to the floor when her spirit—soul, essence, life-force, *tyak* (as people say in the south)—passed into me. According to Father, they simply vanished into the silver mist that poured and poured into me, as I stood there with my arms out, dumb as a dressmaker's dummy. The one reasonably reliable report I can relay is that it wasn't cold, as you might expect, but warm on my skin, and—of all things—almost *sweet* on my lips, though I kept my mouth tightly shut. Being invaded—no, let's use the honest word, *possessed*—by your great-grandmother is bad enough, but to *swallow* her? And have it taste like apples, like *fasteen*, like cake? I didn't think about it then, and I'm not thinking about it now. Then, all that mattered was my feeling of being crowded to the farthest side of my head, and *hearing* Great-Grandmother inside me saying, dryly but soothingly, "Well done, Da'mas— well done, indeed. Slowly, now . . . move slowly until you grow accustomed to my presence. I will not hurt you, I promise, and I will not stay long. Slowly . . ."

Sooner or later, when he judged our anguish greatest, Borbos would return to repeat his demand. Father and Great-Grandmother-in-me took it in turns to guard Jashani's chamber through the rest of that day, the night, and all of the following day. When it was Father's turn, Great-Grandmother would march my body out of the room and the house, down the carriageway, into our orchards and arbors; then back to scout the margins again, before finally allowing me to replace Father at that bedside where no quilt was ever rumpled, no pillow on the floor. In all of this, I never lost myself in her. I always knew who I was, even when she was manipulating my mouth and the words that came out of it; even when she was lifting my hands or snapping my head too forcefully from side to side, apparently thrilled by the strength of the motion.

"He will be expecting resistance," she pointed out to us, in my voice. "Nothing he cannot wipe away with a snap of his fingers, but enough to make you feel that you did the best you could for Jashani before you yielded her to him. Now put that thing *down!*" she lectured Father, who was carrying a sword that he knew would be useless against Borbos, but had clung to anyway, for pure comfort.

Father bristled. "How are we to fight him at all, even with you guiding Da'mas's hand? Borbos could appear right now, that way he does, and what would you do? I'll put this old sword away if you give me a spell, a charm, to replace it." He was tired and sulky, and terribly, terribly frightened.

I heard my throat answer him calmly and remotely, "When your witch-boy turns up, all you will be required to do is to stand out of my way." After that, Great-Grandmother did not allow another word out of me for some considerable while.

Father had not done well from his first sight of Jashani apparently lifeless in her bed. The fact that she was breathing steadily, that her skin remained warm to the touch, and that she looked as innocently beautiful as ever, despite not having eaten or drunk for several days, cheered him not at all. He himself, on the other hand, seemed to be withering before my eyes: unsleeping, hardly speaking, hardly comprehending what was said to him. Now he put down his sword as commanded and sat motionless by Jashani's bed, slumped forward with his hands clasped between his knees. A dog could not have been more constant, or more silent.

And still Borbos did not come to claim his triumph . . . did not come, and did not come, letting our grief and fear build to heights of nearly unbearable tension. Even Great-Grandmother seemed to feel it, pacing the house in my body, which she treated like her own tireless bones that needed no relief, though I urgently did. Surrounded by her ancient mind, nevertheless I could never truly read it, not as she could pick through my thoughts when she chose, at times amusing herself by embarrassing me. Yet she moved me strangely once when she said aloud, as we were crouched one night in the apple orchard, studying the carriageway, white in the moon, "I envy even your discomfiture. Bones cannot blush."

"They never need to," I said, after realizing that she was waiting for my response. "Sometimes I think I spend my whole life being mortified about one thing or another. Wake up, start apologizing for everything to everybody, just on the chance I've offended them." Emboldened, I ventured further. "You might not think so, but I have had moments of wishing I were dead. I really have."

Great-Grandmother was silent in my head for so long that I was afraid that I might have affronted *her* for a second time. Then she said, slowly and tonelessly, "You would not like it. I will find it hard to go back." And there was something in the way she said those last words that made pins lick along my forearms.

"What *will* you do when Borbos comes?" I asked her. "Father says you're not a witch, but he never would say exactly *what* you were. I don't understand how you can deal with someone like Borbos if you're not a witch."

The reply came so swiftly and fiercely that I actually cringed away from it in my own skull. "I am your great-grandmother, boy. If that is not all you need to know, then you must make do as you can." So saying, she rose and stalked us out of the orchard, back toward the house, with me dragged along disconsolately, half-certain that she might never bother talking to me again.

My favorite location in the house has—naturally enough—always been a place where I wasn't ever supposed to be: astride a gable just narrow enough for me to pretend that I was riding a great black stallion to glory or a sea-green *mordroi* dragon to adventure. I cannot count the number of times I was beaten, even by Mother, for risking my life up there, and I know very well how foolish it is to continue doing it whenever I get the chance. But this time it was Great-Grandmother taking the risk, not me, so it plainly wasn't my fault; and, in any case, what could I have done about it?

So there you are, and there you have us in the night, Great-Grandmother and I, with the moon our only light, except for the window of Jashani's chamber below and to my left, where Father kept his lonely vigil. I was certainly not about to speak until Great-Grandmother did; and for some while she sat in silence, seemingly content to scan the white road for a slim, swaggering figure who would almost surely not come for my sister that way. I ground my teeth at the thought.

Presently Great-Grandmother said quietly, almost dreamily, "I was not a good woman in my life. I was born with a certain gift for . . . mischief, let us say . . . and I sharpened it and honed it, until what I did with it became, if not as totally evil as Borbos Tresard's deeds from his birth, still cruel and malicious enough that many have never forgiven me to this day. Do you know how I died, young Da'mas?"

"I don't even know how you lived," I answered her. "I don't know anything about you."

Great-Grandmother said, "Your mother killed me. She stabbed me, and I died. And she was right to do it."

I could not take in what she had said. I felt the words as she spoke them, but they meant nothing. Great-Grandmother went on. "Like your sister, your mother had poor taste in men. She was young, I was old, why should she listen to me? If I am no witch, whatever it is that I am had grown strong with the years. I drove each of her suitors away, by one means or another. It was not hard—a little pointed misfortune and they cleared off quickly, all but the serious ones. I killed two of those, one in a storm, one in a cow pen." A grainy chuckle. "Your mother was not at all pleased with me."

"She knew what you were doing? She knew it was you?"

"Oh, yes, how not?" The chuckle again. "I was not trying to cover my tracks—I was much given to showing off in those days. But then your father came along, and I did what I could to indicate to your mother that she must choose this one. There was a man in her life already, you understand—most unsuitable, she would have regretted it in a month. The cow-pen one, that was." A sigh, somehow turning into a childish giggle, and ending in a grunt. "You would have thought she might be a little pleased this time."

"Was that why she. . . ?" I could not actually say it. I felt Great-Grandmother's smile in my spine.

"Your mother was not a killer—merely mindless with anger for perhaps five seconds. A twitch to the left or right, and she would have missed . . . ah, well, it was a fate long overdue. I have never blamed her."

It was becoming increasingly difficult to distinguish my thoughts—even my memories—from hers. Now I remembered hearing Uncle Uska talking to Father about waking Great-Grandmother again, and being silenced immediately. I knew that she had heard them as well, listening underground in the dark, no soil dense enough to stop her ears.

I asked, "Have you ever come back before? To help the family, like now?"

The slow sigh echoed through our shared body. Great-Grandmother replied only, "I was always a fitful sleeper." Abruptly she rose, balancing more easily on the gable than I ever did when I was captaining my body, and we went on with our patrol, watching for Borbos. And that was another night on which Borbos did not come.

When he did appear at last, he caught us—even Great-Grandmother, I *think*—completely by surprise. In the first place, he came by day, after all our wearying midnight rounds; in the second, he turned up not in Jashani's chamber, nor in the yard or any of the fields where we had kept guard, but in the great kitchen, where old Nanda had reigned as long as I could remember. He was seated comfortably at her worn worktable, silky and dashing, charming her with tales of his journeys and exploits, while she toasted her special *chamshi* sandwiches for him. She usually needs a day's notice and a good deal of begging before she'll make *chamshi* for anybody.

He looked up when Great-Grandmother walked my body into the kitchen, greeting us first with, "Well, if it isn't Thunderwit, my brother-to-be. How are those frozen brains keeping?" Then he stopped, peered closely at me, and began to smile in a different way. "I didn't realize you had . . . company. Do we know each other, old lady?"

I could feel Great-Grandmother studying him out of my eyes, and it frightened me more than he did. She said, "I know your family. Even in the dirt, I knew you when you were very young, and just as evil as you are now. Give me back my great-granddaughter and go your way."

Borbos laughed. It was one of his best features, that warm,

195

delightful chuckle. "And if I don't? You will destroy me? Enchant me? Forgive me if I don't find that likely. Try, and your Jashani slumbers decoratively for all eternity." The laugh had broken glass in it the second time.

I ached to get my hands on him—useless as it would have been—but Great-Grandmother remained in control. All she said, quite quietly, was, "I want it understood that I did warn you."

Whatever Borbos heard in her voice, he was up and out of his seat on the instant. No fiery whiplash, no crash of cold, magical thunder—only a scream from Nanda as the chair fell silently to ashes. She rushed out of the kitchen, calling for Father, while Borbos regarded us thoughtfully from where he leaned against the cookstove. He said, "Well, my goodness," and twisted his fingers against each other in seeming anxiety. Then he said a word I didn't catch, and every knife, fork, maul, spit, slicer, corer, scissors, and bone saw in Nanda's kitchen rose up out of her utensil drawers and came flying off the wall, straight for Great-Grandmother . . . straight for me . . . for us.

But Great-Grandmother put up my hand—exactly as Borbos himself had done when I charged him on first seeing Jashani spellbound—and everything flashing toward us halted in the air, hanging there like edged and pointed currants in a fruitcake. Then Great-Grandmother spoke—the words had edges, too; I could feel them cutting my mouth—and all Nanda's implements backed politely into their accustomed places. Great-Grandmother said chidingly, "Really."

But Borbos was gone, vanished as I had seen him do in Jashani's chamber, his laughter still audible. I took the stairs two and three at a time, Great-Grandmother not wanting to chance my inexperienced body coming and going magically.

Besides, we knew where he was going, and that he would be waiting for us there.

He was playing with Father. I don't like thinking about that: Father lunging and swinging clumsily with his sword, crying hopelessly, desperate to come to grips with this taunting shadow that kept dissolving out of his reach, then instantly reappearing, almost close enough to touch and punish. And Jashani . . . Jashani so still, so still . . .

Borbos turned as we burst in, and a piece of the chamber ceiling fell straight down, bruising my left shoulder as Great-Grandmother sprang me out of the way. In her turn, she made my tongue say *this*, and my two hands do *that*, and Borbos was strangling in air, on the other side of the chamber, while my hands clenched on nothing and gripped and twisted, tighter and tighter . . . but he got a word out, in spite of me, and broke free to crouch by Jashani's bed, panting like an animal.

There was no jauntiness about him now, no mocking gaiety. "You are no witch. I would know. What *are* you?"

I wanted to go over and comfort Father, hold him and make certain that he was unhurt, but Great-Grandmother had her own plans. She said, "I am a member of this family, and I have come to get my great-granddaughter back from you. Release her, and I have no quarrel with you, no further interest at all. Do it now, Borbos Tresard."

For answer, Borbos looked shyly down at the floor, shuffled his feet like an embarrassed schoolboy, and muttered something that might indeed have been an apology for bad behavior in the classroom. But at the first sound of it, Great-Grandmother leaped forward and dragged Father away from the bed, as the floor began to crack open down the middle and the bed to slide steadily toward the widening crevasse. Father cried out in horror.

I wanted to scream; but Great-Grandmother pointed with the forefingers and ring fingers of both my hands at the opening, and what she shouted hurt my mouth. Took out a back tooth, too, though I didn't notice at the time. I was too busy watching Borbos's spell reverse itself, as the flying kitchenware had done. The hole in the floor closed up as quickly as it had opened, and Jashani's bed slid back to where it had been, more or less, with her never once stirring. Father limped dazedly over to her and began to straighten her coverlet.

For a second time, Borbos Tresard said, "Well, my goodness." He shook his head slightly, whether in admiration or because he was trying to clear it, I can't say. He said, "I do believe you are my master. Or mistress, as you will. But it won't help, you know. She still will not wake to any spell, except to see my face, and my terms are what they always were—a welcome into the heart of this truly remarkable family. Nothing more, and nothing less." He beamed joyously at us, and if I had never understood why so many women fell so helplessly in love with him, I surely came to understand it then. "How much longer can you stay in the poor ox, anyway, before you raddle him through like the death fever you are? Another day? A week? So much as a month? My face can wait, Mother—but somehow I don't believe you can. I really don't believe so."

The bedchamber was so quiet that I thought I heard not only my own heart beating but also Jashani's, strong but so slow, and a skittery, too-rapid pulse that I first thought must be Father's, before I understood that it belonged to Borbos. Great-Grandmother said musingly, "Patience is an overrated virtue."

And then I also understood why so many people fear the dead.

I felt her leaving me. I can't describe it any better than I've been able to say what it was like to have her in me. All I'm going to say about her departure is that it left me suddenly stumbling forward, as though a prop I was leaning on had been pulled away. But it wasn't my body that felt abandoned, I know that. I think it was my spirit, but I can't be sure.

Great-Grandmother stood there as I had first seen her. Lightning was flashing in her empty eye sockets, and the pitiless grin of her naked skull branded itself across my sight. With one great heron-stride of her naked shanks, she was on Borbos, reaching out—reaching out . . .

I don't want to tell about this.

She took his face. She reached out with her bones, and she took his face, and he screamed. There was no blood, nothing like that, but suddenly there was a shifting smudge, almost like smoke, where his face had been . . . and there it was, somehow *pasted* on her, merged with the bone, so that it looked *real*, not like a mask, even on the skull of a skeleton. Even with the lightning behind her borrowed eyes.

Borbos went on screaming, floundering blindly in the bedchamber, stumbling into walls and falling down, meowing and snuffling hideously; but Great-Grandmother clacked and clattered to Jashani's bedside and peered down at her for a long moment before she spoke. "Love," she said softly. "Jashani. My heart, awaken. Awaken for me." The voice was Borbos's voice.

And Jashani opened her eyes and said his name.

Father was instantly there, holding her hands, stroking her face, crying with joy. I didn't know what those easy words meant until then. Great-Grandmother turned away and walked across the room to Borbos. He must have sensed her standing before him, because he stopped making that terrible snuffling sound. She said, "Here. I only used it for a little," and she gave him back his face.

I didn't really see it happen. I was with my father and my sister, listening to her say my name.

When I felt Great-Grandmother's fleshless hand on my shoulder, I kissed Jashani's forehead and stood up. I looked over at Borbos, still crouched in a corner, his hands pressed tightly against his face, as though he were holding it on. Great-Grandmother touched Father's shoulder with her other hand and said, impassively, "Take him home. Afterward."

After you bury me again, she meant. She held on to my shoulder as we walked downstairs together, and I felt a strange tension in the cold clasp that made me more nervous than I already was. Would she simply lie down in her cellar grave, waiting for me to spade the earth back over her and pat it down with the blade? I thought of those other bones I'd first seen in the grave, and I shivered, and her grip tightened just a bit.

We faced each other over the empty grave. I couldn't read her expression any more than I ever could, but the lightning was no longer playing in her eye sockets. She said, "You are a good boy. Your company pleases me."

I started to say, "If my company is the price of Jashani . . . I am ready." I *think* my voice was not trembling very much, but I don't know, because I never got the chance to finish. Both of our heads turned at a sudden scurry of footsteps, and we saw Borbos Tresard charging at us across the cellar. Head down, eyes white, flailing hands empty of weapons, nevertheless his entire outline was crackling with the fire-magic of utter, insane fury. He was howling as he came.

I automatically stepped into his way—too numb with fear to be afraid, if you can understand that—but Great-Grandmother put me aside and stood waiting, short but terrible, holding out her stick-thin arms. Like a child rushing to greet his mother coming home, Borbos Tresard leaped into those arms, and they closed around him. The impact caught Great-Grandmother off-balance; the two of them tumbled into the grave together, struggling as they fell. I heard bones go, but would not gamble they were hers.

I picked up a spade, uncertain what I meant to do with it, staring down at the tumult in the earth as though it were something happening a long way off, and long ago. Then Father was beside me with the other spade, frantically shoving *everything*—dirt and odd scraps of wood and twigs and even old wine corks from the cellar floor—into the grave, shoveling and kicking and pushing with his arms almost at the same time. By and by I recovered enough to assist him, and when the hole was filled, we both jumped up and down on the pile, packing it all down as tightly as it would go. The risen surface wasn't quite level with the floor when we were done, but it would settle in time.

I had to say it. I said, "He's down there under our feet, still alive, choking on dirt, with her holding him fast forever. Keeping her company." Father did not answer, but only leaned on his spade, with dirty sweat running out of his hair and down his cheek. I think that was the first time I noticed that he was an inch or so shorter than I. "I feel sorry for him. A little."

"Not I," Father said flatly. "I'd bury him deeper, if we had more earth."

"Then you would be burying Great-Grandmother deeper, too," I said.

"Yes." Father's face was paper-white, the skin looking thin with every kind of exhaustion. "Help me move these barrels."

UNDERBRIDGE

"The Fremont Bridge," as it's called in Seattle, where I lived for a year before spending five years on Bainbridge Island, is actually under the Aurora Bridge . . . but the Troll of this story is quite real, and something of a landmark. It was sculpted by four local artists, stands 18 feet high, and weighs some 13,000 pounds. It's clutching a genuine Volkswagen in one paw (its one eye is a hubcap); and while tourists are encouraged to climb on it and have their pictures taken, I've always found it unnerving. (Though I liked the Fremont area a lot when I lived within walking distance on Queen Anne Hill—how could you not warm to a locality that stages a nude bicycle race every year?) As for the gypsy-professor's tragic professional crisis . . . well, I taught novel-writing and screenwriting at the University of Washington for two quarters, which isn't a long time, but it was long enough to teach me why I am not a professor.

❧

The Seattle position came through just in time.

It was a near thing, even for Richardson. As an untenured professor of children's literature, he was bitterly used to cutting it close, but now, with nothing in the wings to follow his MSSU gig but Jake Riskin's offer to sub remedial English in the Joplin high schools, life was officially the bleakest Richardson could remember. Easy enough to blink through grad school dreaming of life as a Matthew Arnoldesque scholar-gypsy; harder to slog through decades of futureless jobs in second-rank college towns, never being offered the cozy sinecure he had once assumed inevitable. What about professional respect and privileges? What about medical insurance, teaching assistants, preferred parking? What about *sabbaticals?*

Rescue found him shopping in the West 7th Street Save-A-Lot. His cell phone rang, and wondrously, instead of Jake pushing for a decision, the call was from a secretary at the University of Washington English Department. Would he, she wondered, be free to take over classes for a professor who had just been awarded a sizable grant to spend eighteen months at Cambridge, producing a study of the life and works of Joan Aiken?

He said yes, of course, then took a brief time settling the details, which were neither many nor complicated. At no time did he show the slightest degree of unprofessional emotion. But after he snapped his phone shut, he stood very still and whispered "*Saved . . .*" to himself, and when he left the store there were red baby potatoes ($2.40 a pound!) in his bag instead of 34-cent russets.

Most especially was he grateful at being able to take over the Queen Anne Hill apartment of the traveling professor. It was snug—the man lived alone, except for an old cat, whom Richardson, who disliked cats, had dourly agreed to care for— but also well-appointed, including cable television, washer and dryer, microwave and dishwasher, a handsome fireplace and a one-car garage, with a cord of split wood for the winter neatly stacked at the far end. The rent was manageable, as was the drive to the UW; and his classes were surprisingly enjoyable, containing as they did a fair number of students who actually wanted to be there. Richardson could have done decidedly worse, and most often had.

He had been welcomed to the school with impersonal warmth by the chairman of the English department, who was younger than Richardson and looked it. The chairman's name was Philip Austin Watkins IV, but he preferred to be called "Aussie," though he had never been to Australia. He assured Richardson earnestly on their first meeting, "I want you to know, I'm really happy to have you on board, and I'll do everything I can to get you extended here if possible. That's a promise." Richardson, who knew much better at fifty-one than to believe this, believed.

His students generally seemed to like him—at least they paid attention, worked hard on their assignments, didn't mock his serious manner, and often brought up intelligent questions about Milne and Greene, Erich Kästner, Hugh Lofting, Astrid Lindgren, or his own beloved E. Nesbit. But they never took him into their confidence, even during his office hours: never wept or broke down, confessing anxieties or sins or dreams (which would have terrified him), never came to him merely to visit. Nor did he make any significant connections with his fellows on the faculty. He knew well enough that he made friends with difficulty, and wasn't good at keeping them, being naturally formal in his style and uncomfortable in his body, so that he appeared to be forever leaning away from people even when he was making an earnest effort to be close to them. With women, his lifelong awkwardness became worse in the terminally friendly Seattle atmosphere. Once, younger, he had wished to be different; now he no longer believed it possible.

The legendary rain of the Pacific Northwest was not an issue; if anything, he discovered that he enjoyed it. Having studied the data on Seattle climate carefully, once he knew he was going there, he understood that many areas of both coasts get notably more rain, in terms of inches, and endure distinctly colder winters. And the year-round greenness and lack of air pollution more than made up for the mildew, as far as Richardson was concerned. Damp or not, it beat Joplin. Or Hobbs, New Mexico. Or Enterprise, Alabama.

What the greenness did *not* make up for was the near-perpetual overcast. Seattle's sky was dazzlingly, exaltingly, shockingly blue when it chose to be so; but there was a reason that the city consumed more than its share of vitamin D, and was the first marketplace for various full-spectrum light bulbs. Seattle introduced Richardson to an entirely new understanding of the word *overcast*, sometimes going two months and more without seeing either clear skies or an honest raindrop. He had not been prepared for this.

Many things that shrink from sunlight gain power in fog and murk. Richardson began to find himself reluctant enough to leave the atmosphere of the UW campus that he often stayed on after work, attending lectures that bored him, going to showings of films he didn't understand—even once dropping in on a faculty meeting, though this was not required of him. The main subject under discussion was the urgent need to replace a particular TA, who for six years had been covering most of the undergraduate classes of professors far too occupied with important matters to deal with actual students. Another year would have required granting him a tenure-track assistant professorship, which was, of course, out of the question. Sitting uncomfortably in the back, saying nothing, Richardson felt he was somehow attending his own autopsy.

And when Richardson finally went home in darkness to the warm, comfortable apartment that was not his own, and the company of the sour-smelling old gray cat, he frequently went out again to walk aimlessly on steep, silent Queen Anne Hill and beyond, watching the lights go out in window after window. If rain did not fall, he might well wander until three or four in the morning, as he had never before done in his life.

But it was in daylight that Richardson first saw the Troll.

He had walked across the blue and orange drawbridge at the foot of Queen Anne Hill into Fremont, which had become a favorite weekend ramble of his, though the quirky, rakish little pocket always made him nervous and wistful at the same time. He wished he were the sort of person who could fit comfortably into a neighborhood that could proclaim itself "The Center of the Universe," hold a nude bicycle parade as part of a solstice celebration, and put up signs advising visitors to throw their watches away. He would have liked to be able to imagine living in Fremont.

Richardson had read about the Fremont Bridge Troll online while preparing to leave Joplin. He knew that it was not actually located under the Fremont Bridge, but under the north end of the nearby Aurora Avenue Bridge; and that the Troll was made of concrete, had been created by a team of four artists, weighed four thousand pounds, was more than eighteen feet high, had one staring eye made of an automobile hubcap, and was crushing a cement-spattered Volkswagen Beetle in its left hand. As beloved a tourist photo-op as the Space Needle, it had the inestimable further advantages of being free, unique, and something no lover of children's books could ignore.

It took Richardson a while to come face to face with the Troll, because the day was blue and brisk, and the families were out in force, shoving up to the statue to take pictures, posing small children and puzzled-looking babies within the Troll's embrace, or actually placing them on its shoulder. Richardson made no effort to approach until the crowd had thinned to a few teenagers with cell-phone cameras; then he went close enough to see his distorted reflection in the battered aluminum eye. He said nothing, but stayed there until a couple of the teenagers pushed past him to be photographed kissing and snuggling in the shadow of the Troll. Then he went on home.

Two weeks later, driven by increasing insomnia, he crossed the Fremont Bridge again and eventually found himself facing the glowering concrete monster where it crouched in its streetside cave. Alone in darkness, with no fond throng to warm and humanize it, the hubcap eye now seemed to be sizing him up as a tender improvement on a VW Beetle. *Grendel*, Richardson thought, *this is what Grendel looked like*. Aloud, he said, "Hello. Off for the night?"

The Troll made no answer. Richardson went a few steps closer, fascinated by the expression and personality it was possible to impose on two tons of concrete. He asked it, "Do you ever get tired of tourists gaping at you every day? *I* would." For some reason, he wanted the Troll to know that he was a sympathetic, understanding person. He said, "My name's Richardson."

A roupy old voice behind him said, "Don't you get too close. He's mean."

Richardson turned to see a black rain slicker which appeared to be almost entirely inhabited by a huge gray beard. The hood of the slicker was pulled close around the old man's face, so that only the beard and a pair of bright, bloodshot gray eyes were visible as he squatted on the sidewalk that approached the underpass, with four shopping bags arranged around him. Richardson took them at first for the man's worldly possessions; only later, back in the apartment, did he recall glimpsing a long Italian salami, a wine bottle, and a French baguette in one of them.

The old man coughed—a long, rattling, machine-gun burst—then growled, "I'd back off a little ways, was I you. He gets mean at night."

Richardson played along with the joke. "Oh, I don't know. He put up so nicely with all those tourists today."

"Daytime," the old man grunted. "Sun goes down, he gets around . . ." He belched mightily, leaned back against the guardrail, and closed his eyes.

"Well," Richardson said, chuckling to keep the conversation reasonable. "Well, but you're here, taking a nap right within his grasp. You're not afraid of him."

The old man did not open his eyes. "I got on his good side a long time ago. Go away, man. You don't want to be here." The last words grumbled into a snore.

Richardson stood looking back and forth at the Troll and the old man in the black rain slicker, whose snoring mouth hung open, a red-black wound in the vast gray beard. Finally, he said politely to the Troll, "You have curious friends," and walked quickly away. The old man never stirred as Richardson passed him.

He had no trouble sleeping that night, but he did dream of the Troll. They were talking quite earnestly, under the bridge, but he remembered not even a fragment of their conversation, only that the Troll was wearing a Smokey Bear hat and kept biting pieces off the Volkswagen, chewing them like gum and spitting them out. In the dream, Richardson accepted this as perfectly normal: the flavor probably didn't last very long.

He didn't go back to see the Troll at night for a month. Once or twice in the daytime, yes, but he found such visits unsatisfying. During daylight hours, the tourist buses were constantly stopping, and families were likely to push baby carriages close between the Troll's hands for photographs. The familiarity, the chattering gaiety, was almost offensive to him, as though the people were savages out of bad movies, and the Troll their trapped and stoic prisoner.

He never saw the old man there. Presumably he was off doing whatever homeless people did during the day, even those who bought French baguettes with their beggings.

Richardson's own routine was as drearily predictable as ever. Over the years, he had become intensely aware of the arc of each passing contract, from eager launch through trembling zenith to the unavoidable day when he packed his battered Subaru and drove off to whatever job might come next. He was now at the halfway point of his stay at the UW: each time he opened his office door was one twisting turn closer to the last, each paycheck a countdown, in reverse, to the end of his temporary security. Richardson's students and colleagues saw no change in his tone or behavior—he was most careful about that—but in his own ears, he heard a gently rising scream.

His silent night walks began to fill with imagined conversations. Some of these were with his parents, both long deceased but still reproving. Others were with distantly remembered college acquaintances, or with characters out of his favorite books. But the ones that Richardson enjoyed most were his one-sided exchanges with the Troll, whose vast, unresponsive silence Richardson found endlessly encouraging. As he wandered through the darkness, hands uncharacteristically in his hip pockets, he found he could speak to the Troll as though they had been friends long enough that there was no point in hiding anything from one another. He had never known that sort of friendship.

"I am never going to be anything more than I am already,"

he said to the Troll-haunted air. "Forget the fellowships and grants, never mind the articles in *The New Yorker, Smithsonian, Harper's*—never mind the Modern Language Association, PEN . . . None of it is ever going to happen, Troll. I know this. My life is exactly like yours—set in stone and meaningless."

Without realizing it, or ever putting it into words, Richardson came to think of the concrete Troll as his only real friend in Seattle, just as he began resenting the old man in the rain slicker for his privileged position on the Troll's "good side," and himself for his own futility. In the middle of one class—a lecture on the period political references hidden within Lewis Carroll's underappreciated *Sylvie and Bruno*—Richardson heard his own voice abruptly say, "To hell with *that!*" He had to stop and look around the hall for a moment, puzzling his students, before he realized that he hadn't actually said the words out loud.

On the damp and moonless night that Richardson finally returned to the end of the Aurora Avenue Bridge, the old man wasn't there. Neither was the Troll. Only the concrete-slathered Volkswagen was still in place, its curved roof and sides indented where the Troll's great fingers had previously rested.

Sun goes down, he gets around . . . Richardson remembered what he had assumed was a joke, and shook his head sharply. He felt the urge to run away, as if the *absence* of the Troll somehow constituted an almost cellular rebuke to his carefully manicured sense of the rational.

Richardson heard the sound then, distant yet, but numbingly clear: the long, dragging scrape of stone over asphalt. He turned and walked a little way to look east, toward Fremont Street—

saw the hunched shadow rising into view—turned again, and bolted back across the bridge, the one leading him to Queen Anne Hill, a door he could close and lock, and a smelly gray cat wailing angrily over an empty food dish. He sat up the rest of the night, watching the QVC channel for company, seeing nothing. Near dawn he fell asleep on the living-room couch, with the television set still selling Select Comfort beds and amethyst jewelry.

In the morning, before he went to the university, he drove down into Fremont, double-parking at 36th and Winslow to make sure of what he already knew. The Troll was back in its place with no smallest deviation from its four creators' positioning, and no indication that it had ever moved at all. Even its grip on the old VW was displayed exactly as it had been, crushing finger for finger, bulging knuckle for knuckle, splayed right-hand fingers digging at the earth for purchase.

Richardson had a headache. He stepped graciously aside for children already swarming up to pose with the Troll for their parents, hurried back to his car, and drove away. His usual parking space was taken when he got to the UW, and finding another made him late to class.

For more than two weeks Richardson not only avoided the Aurora Bridge, but stayed out of Fremont altogether. Even so, whether by day or night, strolling the campus, shopping in the University District, or walking a silent waterfront street under the Viaduct, he would often stand very still, listening for the slow, terribly slow, grinding of concrete feet somewhere near. The fact that he could not quite hear it did not make it go away.

Eventually, out of a kind of wintry lassitude, he began drifting down Fourth Avenue North again, at first no farther than the drawbridge, whose raisings and lowerings he found oddly soothing. He seemed to be at a curious remove from himself during that time, watching himself watching the boats waiting to pass the bridge, watching the rain on the water.

When he finally did cross the bridge, however, he did so without hesitation, and on the hunt.

"Fuck off," Cut'n-Shoot said. "Just fuck off and go away and leave me alone."

"Not a chance."

"I have to get *ready*. I have to *be* there."

"Then *tell* me. All you have to do is tell me!"

Richardson had found the bearded old man asleep—noisily asleep, his throat a sporadic bullroarer—under a tree in the Gas Works Park, near the shore of Lake Union. He was still wearing the same clothes and black rain slicker, now with the hood down, and there was an empty bottle of orange Schnapps clutched in his filthy hand. Bits of greasy *foie gras* speckled his whiskers like dirty snow. When glaring him awake didn't work, Richardson had moved on to kicking the cracked leather soles of the man's old boots, which did.

It also got him a deep bruise on his forearm, from blocking an angrily thrown Schnapps bottle. Their subsequent conversation had been unproductive. So far, the only useful thing he had uncovered was that the old man called himself "Cut'n-Shoot," after the small town in Texas where he'd been born. That was the end of anything significant, aside from the man's obvious agitation and impatience as evening darkened toward night.

"Goddamn you, somebody gets hurt it's going to be *all your fault*! Let me go!" Cut'n-Shoot's bellow was broken by a coughing spasm that almost brought him to his knees. He leaned forward, spitting and dribbling, hands braced on his thighs.

"I'm not stopping you," Richardson said. "I just want answers. I know you weren't making that up, about the Troll moving at night. I've seen it."

"Yah?" Cut'n-Shoot hawked up one last monster wad. "So what? Price of fishcakes. Ain't *your* job."

"I'm a professor of children's literature—a *full* professor"— for some reason he felt compelled to lie to the old man—"at the University of Washington. I could quote you troll stories from here to next September. And one thing I knew for certain—until I met *you*—was that they don't exist."

Cut'n-Shoot glared at him out of one rheumy eye, the other one closed and twitching. "You think you know trolls?" He snorted. "Goddamn useless punk . . . you don't know shit."

"Show me."

The old man stared hard for a moment more, then smiled, revealing a sprinkling of brown teeth. It was not a friendly expression. "Might be I will, then. Maybe teach you a lesson. But we're gonna pick up some things first, and you're buyin'. Come on."

Cut'n-Shoot led him a little over three-quarters of a mile from the park, along Northlake Way, under the high overpass of the Aurora Avenue Bridge and the low one at Fourth Avenue, then right on Evanston. Richardson tried asking more questions, but got nothing but growls and snorts for his trouble. Best to save his breath, anyway—he was surprised at how fast the old man could move in a syncopated crab-scuttle that favored his right leg and made the oil slicker snap like a geisha's fan. At the corner of 34th Street, Cut'n-Shoot ignored the parallel white stripes of the crosswalk and angled straight across the street to the doors of the Fremont PCC. He strode through them like Alexander entering a conquered city.

The bag clerk nearest the entry waved as they came in. "Hey, Cut! Little late tonight."

Cut'n-Shoot didn't pause, cocking one thumb back over his shoulder at Richardson as he swept up a plastic shopping basket and continued deeper into the store. "Not my fault. Professor here's got the rag on."

When they finally left—having rung up $213.62 of luxury items on Richardson's MasterCard, including multiple cuts of Eel River organic beef and a $55 bottle of 2006 Cadence Camerata Cabernet Sauvignon—it was a docile, baffled Richardson, grocery bags in hand, who trudged after the old man down the mostly empty neighborhood streets. Cut'n-Shoot had made his selections with the demanding eye of a lifelong connoisseur, assessing things on some qualitative scale of measurement Richardson couldn't begin to comprehend. That he and his wallet were being taken advantage of was self-evident; but the inborn curiosity that had first led him to books as a child, that insatiable need to get to the end of each new unfolding story, was now completely engaged. Rambling concrete trolls weren't the only mystery in Fremont.

Cut'n-Shoot led him east along 34th Street to where Troll Avenue started, a narrow road rising between the grand columns that supported the Aurora Avenue Bridge. High on the bridge itself, cars hissed by like ghosts; while down on the ground, it was quiet as the sea-bottom, and the sparse lights from lakeside boats and local apartment buildings only served to make the path up to the Troll darker than Richardson liked.

"Stupid ratfucks throw a big party up there every October," Cut'n-Shoot said. "Call it 'Trolloween.' *People*. Batshit stupid."

"Well, Fremont's that kind of place," Richardson responded. "I mean, the Solstice Parade, Oktoberfest—the crazy rocket with 'Freedom to Be Peculiar' written on it in Latin—"

"Don't care about all that crap. Just wish they wouldn't rile *him* so much. Job's hard enough as it is."

"And what job would that be, exactly, anyway?"

"You'll see."

At the top of the road, the bridge merged with the hillside, forming the space that held the Troll, with stairs running up the hill on either side. Tonight the Troll looked exactly as it had the first time he saw it. It was impossible to imagine this crudely hewn mound of ferroconcrete in motion, even knowing what he knew. Cut'n-Shoot made him put the grocery bags on the ground at the base of the eastern stair, then gestured brusquely for him to stand aside. When he did, the old man got down heavily on one knee—not the right one, Richardson noticed—and started searching through them.

"That's the thing, see. People never know what they're doing. Best place to sleep in town and they had to go fuck everything up."

"It's concrete and wire and rebar," Richardson responded. "I read about it. They had a contest back in 1990—this design won. There used to be a time capsule with Elvis memorabilia in the car, for Christ's sake. It's not *real*."

"Sure, sure. Like a troll cares what it's made of, starting out. Hah. That ain't the point. Point is, they did *too good a job*."

Cut'n-Shoot struggled to his feet, unbalanced by the pair of brown packages he was holding—two large roasts, in their taped-up butcher wrapping. "Here," he said, holding out one of them to Richardson. "Get this shit off. He won't be able to smell 'em through the paper."

"You *feed* him?"

"Told you I was on his good side, didn't I?"

Grinning fiercely through his beard now, the old man marched straight to the hulking stone brute and slapped the bloody roast down on the ground in front of it. "There!" he said, "First snack of the night. Better than your usual, too, and don't you know it! *Ummm-mmm*, that's gonna be good." He looked back at Richardson just as a car passed, its headlights making the Troll's hubcap eye seem to flicker and spin. "Well, come on—you wanted this, didn't you? Just do like me, make it friendly."

Richardson was holding the larger unwrapped roast in front of him like a doily, pinching the thick slab of meat between the thumb and forefinger of each hand. It was slippery, and the blood dripping from it made him queasy. As he stepped forward with the offering, an old Norse poem suddenly came to him, the earliest relevant reference his magpie mind could dredge up. "*They call me Troll*," he recited. "*Gnawer of the Moon, Giant of the Gale-blasts, Curse of the rain-hall . . .*"

Cut'n-Shoot looked at him approvingly, nodding him on.

"*Companion of the Sibyl, Nightroaming hag, Swallower of the loaf of heaven. What is a Troll but that?*"

Richardson laid his roast down gently beside Cut'n-Shoot's, took a deep breath, and backed away without looking up, not knowing as he did so whether this obeisance was for the Troll's benefit, Cut'n-Shoot's, or his own.

The old man's grating chuckle came to him. "That's the good side, all right. That's the way, that's the way." Richardson looked up. Cut'n-Shoot had pushed back the hood of his rain slicker, and was scratching his head through hair like furnace ashes. "But he likes *lively* a sight better. You get the chance, you remember."

"Nothing's happening," Richardson started to say—and then something was.

One by one the fingers of the Troll's right hand were coming free of the ground. Richardson realized that the whole forearm was lifting up, twisting from the elbow, dust and dirt sifting off as it rose. The giant hand turned with the motion, dead-gray fingers coming together with a sound of cracking bricks. Then—like a child grabbing for jacks before the ball comes down, and just as fast—the Troll's hand swept up the two roasts in one great swinging motion and carried them to its suddenly open mouth. The ponderous jaw moved up and down three times before it settled back into place, and Richardson tried to imagine what could possibly be going on inside. A moment later, the Troll's hand and arm returned to their original position, fingers wriggling their way back into the soil and once more becoming motionless.

There was no moon, and no more cars went by, but the hubcap continued to twinkle with a brightly chilling malice, and even—so it seemed to Richardson—to wink. He was still staring at the Troll when Cut'n-Shoot finally clapped his palms together with satisfaction.

"Well! Old sumbitch settled *right* down. Think he liked that fancy talk. Know any more?"

"Sure."

"My lucky day," the old man said. "Now lemme show you what the wine's for."

Richardson woke the next morning hungover, stiff-backed, and with a runny nose. He was late to class again; and that evening, when he returned to Fremont, he brought lambchops.

❊ ❊ ❊

From then on, he never came to the bridge without bringing some tribute for the Troll. Most often it came in the form of slabs of raw meat; though now and again, this being Seattle, he would present the statue with a whole salmon, usually purchased down at the ferry dock from a fisherman's wife. Once—only once—he tried offering a bag of fresh crab cakes, but Cut'n-Shoot informed him tersely, "Don't give him none of that touristy shit," and made him go back to the Fremont PCC for an entire Diestel Family turkey.

Richardson also read to the Troll most evenings, working his way up from obvious fare to selections from the *Bland Tomtar och Troll* series, voiced dramatically in his best stab at phonetic Swedish. He had no idea whether the Troll understood, but the expressions on his own face as he dealt with the unfamiliar orthography made Cut'n-Shoot howl.

It didn't always go easily. By day, the Troll was changeless, an eternally crude concrete figure with one dull aluminum eye, a vacantly malevolent expression, and bad hair. At night, its temperament was as unpredictably irritable as a wasp's. Richardson began to measure his visits on a scale marked in feet, yards, and furlongs, assessing the difference between *this* Tuesday and *that* Saturday by precisely how far the Troll stirred from its den. In that way he came to understand—as Cut'n-Shoot never bothered to explain—that the old man's task wasn't to feed the Troll at all, but rather to distract it, to confuse it, to short-circuit its unfocused instinct to go off unimpeded about its trollish business, whatever that might be. Food was a means to that end; as, now, was Richardson's cheerfully garbled Swedish. Even so, there were nights when it would not yield, and lumbered half a mile or more before they could tempt and coax it—like two Pekingese herding a mastiff—back under the bridge. On those nights, nothing would do but "the lively," usually in the form of a writhing rat or pigeon. Cut'n-Shoot never told Richardson how—or with what—he caught them.

The months passed, and the weather turned relatively mild and notably dry. On campus this was generally spoken of as a function of global warming, and greeted with definite anxiety. Richardson paid little attention to climate crises, having his own worries. His temporary tenure at the university was coming to an end with the summer quarter, and thoughts of the department chair's vague early promises moved in his heart like schooling fish: instead of calling up job listings and sending out inquiries he found himself manufacturing excuses to go by Aussie's office, or sit near him in the faculty dining hall, hoping that mere proximity might make the man offer him work he couldn't possibly ask for.

He also began to drink, at first in pretended sociability with Cut'n-Shoot, but later with the devotion of a convert. It was not an area in which he had any sort of previous expertise. He could neither tell good champagne from bad, nor upper-shelf vodka from potato-peel swill; only that in each case the latter was distinctly cheaper. It all invariably left him with a hammering headache the next morning, which seemed to be how you could tell you were doing it right.

Having no one to drink with in comfort and understanding, he came to spend the early part of many evenings drinking with the gray cat, for whom he had conceived an increasing dislike. Not only did it smell bad; it had taken to urinating on the floor outside its box and knocking down the clothes hamper to tear and scratch at Richardson's dirty clothes. Richardson, who had never hated an animal in his life, no more than he had ever loved one, brooded increasingly and extensively about the gray cat.

Nothing would probably have come of this growing fixation, had he not already been drunk on the evening he discovered that the cat had peed in his only pair of carpet slippers. Having noticed a pet-transport cage in one of the closets, he pounced on the unwary animal and forced it into the cage, threw on his coat, and stalked down the hill toward Fremont, muttering in counterpoint to the cat's furious wails, as the cage banged against the side of his left knee, "Lively. Right, lively it is. Lively it bloody is."

Cut'n-Shoot said nothing when Richardson set the cage down facing the Troll, shouted "Lively!" and walked quickly away, paying no heed to the cat's redoubled howling. He did look back once, but cage and bridge were both out of sight by then.

In the morning, between the expected headache and the forgotten pre-finals lecture summarizing works intended for children from A.D. 1000 to 1850, he remembered the cat only as he was locking the apartment door. There was no time to check on the cage just then; but all day long, he could concentrate on almost nothing else. Along with trying to invent something to tell the cat's owner, he became obsessed with the notion that the Humane Society would be waiting for him at the bridge with a charge of felony animal abuse, and quite possibly littering.

That evening he found the remains of the empty cage between two of the Troll's huge fingers. The door had been ripped clean away, as had most of the front of the cage, and the rest of it had been pounded almost shapeless, as though by a hammer, or a great fist. There was fur.

Richardson just made it to the bushes before he was very

sick. It took him a long time to empty his stomach, and he was shaking and coughing when he was done, barely able to stand erect. His throat and mouth tasted of chewed tinfoil.

When he finally forced himself to turn back toward the statue, he saw Cut'n-Shoot grinning derisively at him from the shadow of the bridge. "One thing when I do it, another when you do, hah?"

"You could have stopped it. You had other food there. I saw it. You could have let the cat out of that thing, let it go." His stomach contracted, and he thought he was going to be sick again, but there was nothing left to vomit.

"Waste not, want not," Cut'n-Shoot chuckled. "'Sides, now you really *do* know trolls."

With a mean cunning that he would not have suspected himself of possessing, Richardson designed an advertisement for a lost gray cat—even including the name he had never once called it— had a hundred copies Xeroxed, and mounted them in sheltered places up and down Queen Anne Hill. Thus, when the owner returned from that enviable, *enviable* sabbatical in England, he would see that Richardson had done everything possible to track down his unfortunately vanished cat. *Would have died soon anyway, old and incontinent as it was. He surely wouldn't have wanted the poor thing peeing all over his nice condo.*

The next morning, he went to a pet shop in the Wallingford district and bought two carrier cages, the first identical to the one he had found in the apartment. The second was a bit larger, since one never knew. With the latter in his hand, he continued his nightly routine, the only differences being that his rounds were now somewhat more purposeful, and that with purpose came a reduction in his drinking. He often whistled as he walked, which was unusual for him.

It astonished him to realize how many animals—strays and otherwise—were running loose on the streets of Seattle. Cats and the smaller dogs were the easiest to capture, though he felt a certain amount of guilt over the ones that came trustingly to his leather-gloved hands. But he learned that people make pets out of the most unlikely animals: he caught escaped ferrets on two or three occasions, lab rats and mice with surprising frequency, and once even a tame crow with clipped wings. He was going to set the crow free—it had a vocabulary of several words, and a way of cocking its head to consider him . . . but then he thought that its inability to fly would make it easy prey for any cat, and changed his mind.

He did go through cages rather often; there was no way to avoid that, given the Troll's impetuous manner of opening them.

Feeding the Troll distracted him only somewhat from his terror of impending joblessness. It was now much too late to expect reprieve: all the best positions at even the worst colleges and universities had long since been snapped up without his ever applying, the community colleges were full, and thanks to Seattle's highly educated population, there were thirty people ahead of him in line for any on-call substituting, even assuming someone would have the human decency to come down ill. Meanwhile the ever-smiling Aussie had turned evasive Trappist. Richardson stopped sliding by his door.

He had no idea that he was going mad with fear, frustration, and weariness. Most people don't; and most—frightened academic gypsies included—go on functioning fairly well. He remained faithful to his classes and his office hours; and if he was more terse with his students, and often more sharp-tongued, still he fulfilled the function for which he was yet being paid as conscientiously as he knew how, because he still loved it. And love will keep you reasonably sane for a long time.

Then came the bright and breezy day when word began circulating through the department—a whisper only, at first, the merest of hints—that the Tenured Prodigal was not coming home.

At 9:30 P.M. a resurrected Richardson was thinking furiously as he knocked back half a bottle of Scotch and picked at his Indian takeout. This late in the game it would surely be impossible for Aussie to fill the Prodigal's slot; he would *have* to extend Richardson now. And if God could create concrete Trolls that moved and miracles as plain as this one, why, He might yet manage a way to make this change permanent.

Richardson had no plans to go out, not even to round up a stray dog or cat (which had been growing more difficult in recent weeks, as Queen Anne residents had been keeping closer track of their pets, blaming coyotes for the recent disappearances). Considering what to say to Aussie in the morning was paramount. But eventually he could not bear to sit still, and found his legs carrying him to Fremont after all. Something special was clearly called for, a little libation to luck, so at the PCC he bought more of the Eel River beef for the Troll, and for himself and Cut'n-Shoot a half-gallon of a unique coconut-and-molasses ice cream he had found nowhere else.

He left the grocery grinning, turned left—and saw, a block up 34th Street, walking away, Dr. Philip Austin Watkins IV.

The Scotch proved stronger than good judgment. "Aussie!" he shouted. Then louder: "Aussie!" Bag swinging wildly, he began to run.

✄ ✄ ✄

The department head had dined out late with friends, imbibing one too many himself as the evening wore on. "You've never been screwed until you've been screwed by the British," he'd said, and meant it. Thank heavens he'd had foresight enough to lay contingency plans.

It took him a moment to realize that his name was being called, and a troubling moment more when he turned around to recognize who it was. His apprehension should perhaps have lasted longer: instead of a simple greeting, followed by meaningless chat, Richardson slammed full tilt into the issue of the job opening. "Aussie, I heard about Brubaker. And you promised. You *did* promise."

"I promised to do everything I could to help you," Aussie countered. "And I did, but obviously it wasn't enough. I'm sorry."

"You can't leave the slot open, and it's too late—"

"Mr. Richardson. You knew you were a fill-in, just as I knew from the beginning that the Aiken grant was a recruiting hook in disguise. If the fish had bitten later, I might have had to keep you on. As it happens, he did it while my own preferred replacement was still sitting by the phone at Kansas State, waiting for my call, exactly where he's been since I first talked to him last April. The *slot*, as you call it, is already filled."

"Oh." Without thought, Richardson removed the frozen half-gallon of coconut-and-molasses ice cream from his grocery bag and smashed Aussie in the head with it just as hard as he could. The man was insensible when he hit the ground, but not dead. Richardson was particularly glad of that.

"That was satisfactory," Richardson said aloud, as though he were judging a presentation in class. He heard his voice echoing in his head, which interested him. Looking around quickly and seeing no one close enough to notice what he was doing, or to interfere with it, Richardson got Aussie—who was not a small person—on his feet, hooked an arm around his waist, and draped one of the chairman's arms around his own neck, saying loudly and frequently, "*Told* you, Aussie, you can't say I didn't tell you. *Sip* the Calvados, I said, don't *guzzle* it. Ah, come on, Aussie, *help* me a little bit here."

Ordinarily, the walk to the Aurora Bridge would have taken Richardson a few minutes at most; dragging the unconscious Aussie, it took months, and by the time he came near the Troll's overpass he was panting and sweating heavily. "The last lively!" he called out in a louder, different voice. "Here you *go*! Compliments of the chef."

A hoarse, frantic voice behind him demanded, "What you doing? What the *hell* you doing?" Richardson let go of Aussie and turned to see Cut'n-Shoot gaping at him, his bleared eyes as wild as those of a horse in a burning barn. "What the hell you think you doing?"

"Tidying up," Richardson said. His voice sounded as faraway as the old man's, and the echoes in his head were growing louder.

"You dumb shit," Cut'n-Shoot whispered. He was plainly sober, if he hadn't been a moment before, and wishing he weren't. "You crazy dumb shit, you fucking killed him."

Richardson looked briefly down, shaking his head. "Oh, let's hope not. He's twitched a couple of times."

Cut'n-Shoot was neither listening to him nor looking directly at him. "I'm out of here, I ain't in this mess. I'm calling the cops."

Richardson did not take the statement seriously. "Oh, please. Can you stand there and tell me our friend's always lived on warm puppies? Nothing like this has ever, ever happened before?"

"Not like this, not never like this." Cut'n-Shoot was beginning to back away, looking small and cold, hugging himself. "I got to call the cops. See if he got a cell phone or something."

"Ah, no cops," Richardson said. He was fascinated by his own detachment, by his strange lightheartedness in the midst of what he knew ought to be a nightmare. He took hold of Cut'n-Shoot's black slicker, which felt like slimy tissue paper in his hand. "You have *got* to get yourself a new raincoat," he told the old man sternly. "Promise me you'll get a new coat this winter." Cut'n-Shoot stared blankly at him, and Richardson shook him hard. *"Promise,* damn it!"

Richardson heard the long scraping rumble before he could turn, still keeping his grip on the struggling, babbling Cut'n-Shoot. The Troll was moving, emerging from its lair under the bridge, the disproportionate length of its body giving the effect of a great worm, even a dragon. In the open, it braced itself on its knuckles for some moments, like a gorilla, before rising to its full height. The hubcap eye was alight as Richardson had never seen it: a whipping forest-fire red-orange that had nothing to do with the thin, wan crescent on the horizon. He thought, madly and absurdly, not of Grendel, but of the Cyclops Polyphemus.

The Troll crouched hugely over Aussie, prodding him experimentally with the same hand that perpetually crushed the Volkswagen. The man moaned softly, and Richardson said as the Troll looked up, "See? Lively."

For the first time in Richardson's memory the Troll made a sound. It was neither a growl nor a snarl, nor were there any more words in it than there were words in Richardson to describe it. Long ago he had spent three-quarters of a year teaching at a branch of the University of Alaska, and what he most remembered about that strange land was the *sense* of the pack ice breaking up in the spring, much too distant for him to have heard it, or even felt the vibration in his bones; but like everyone else, he, foreigner or not, knew absolutely that it was happening. So it was with the sound that reached him now: not from the Troll's mouth or throat or monstrous body, but from its entire preposterous existence.

"Saying grace?" Richardson asked. The Troll made the sound again and his head descended, jaws opening wider than Richardson had ever seen. Cut'n-Shoot screamed, and kept on screaming. Richardson kept a tight grip on him, but the old man's utter panic set the echoes roaring in Richardson's head. He said, "*Quit* it—come *on*, relax, enjoy a little dinner theater," but one of Cut'n-Shoot's flailing arms caught him hard enough on a cheekbone that his eyes watered and went out of focus for a moment. "*Ow*," he said, and then, "Okay, then. Okay."

Very little of Aussie was still visible. Richardson took a firmer hold of Cut'n-Shoot, lifted him partly off the ground, and half-hurled, half-shoved him at the Troll. The old man actually tripped over a concrete forearm; he fell directly against the Troll's chest, snuggling grotesquely. He opened his mouth to scream again, but nothing came out.

"How about a taste of the guardian?" Richardson demanded. He hardly recognized his own voice: it was loud and frayed, and hurt him coming out. "How about a piece of the one who's always there to make sure you behave? Wouldn't that be nice, after all this time?"

When the Troll's mouth opened over Cut'n-Shoot, Richardson began to laugh in delighted hysteria. Not only did the great gray jaws seem to hinge at the back, exactly like a waffle iron, but they matched perfectly, hammer and anvil, when the mouth slammed shut.

After the jaws finally stopped moving, the Troll stretched toward the sky again, and Richardson realized that it was somehow different now—taller and straighter, its rough edges softening, sinking into themselves, becoming more fluid. Becoming more *real*. It stared down at Richardson, and made a different sound this time.

Like a troll cares what it's made of, starting out, he thought, and somehow the echoes in his head and Cut'n-Shoot's crazy laughter were one and the same.

"Well shit," he said. "That meal sure agreed with you."

He was just turning to run when the thing's hand, no longer concrete but just as hard, just as vast and heavy, fell on his shoulder, breaking it. Richardson was shrieking as the Troll lifted him into the air, tucked him clumsily under one arm, and began squeezing back into the lair under the Aurora Bridge. Crumpled against the monster's side—clothing shredded, skin lacerated, his ribs going—Richardson heard the tolling of an impossible heart.

THE VERY NASTY AQUARIUM

This one began as an intriguing title, with absolutely no story to go with it. It went through several rewrites, to the point where I actually gave up on it, and more or less forgot about it for some while. But I was always quite fond of my retired-English-teacher heroines and intrigued by West Indian folklore, and the legend of the duppy: wholly evil, but somehow pitiably human as well. If you're interested in tracing its literary roots, you might look up "Where Do You Live, Queen Esther?" a masterful short story by my old friend and mentor Avram Davidson. Or any other story of Avram's, come to that.

❋

Once there was an old lady named Mrs. Lopsided whose nephew gave her an aquarium for her birthday.

He was a nice boy, and he thought it would give her something to look at when she was alone. He brought the aquarium over himself and spent a whole afternoon setting it up, with just the right gravel and peat base for aquatic plants, and just the right filters and hoses and purifiers, and a little figure of a diver opening a treasure chest on the bottom. Then he brought her little plastic bags full of guppies and angelfish and neon tetras, and snails to keep the aquarium clean, and he taught Mrs. Lopsided how to feed them all, and even what medicine to put into the water if any of the fish looked sickly. When he was through, she had the finest aquarium in the whole neighborhood.

Mrs. Lopsided loved her aquarium, and she took very good care of it. She began to spend more and more of her time looking for other fish to live in it, and other decorations to amuse the fish. She even bought a beautiful plastic mermaid, which not only swam gracefully over the Diver and his treasure, but also helped the snails and the tiny catfish to keep the sides of the aquarium free of algae. And as she grew more confident, she added another filter, in the shape of a sea-green castle, so that the water remained as clear as the glass, and the glass stayed as transparent as a perfect spring dawn. There had never been such an aquarium, Mrs. Lopsided was quite convinced.

She had always been a solitary sort of woman: perfectly content with her own company, finding her pleasure in work— she was a retired elementary-school teacher—and after that in reading and in watching baseball games on television. But nothing had ever filled her days as rewardingly as her tranquil obsession with her new aquarium. She could sit for hours in her living room, watching the brilliantly glowing little fish flowing to and fro like clouds, while the Mermaid seemed to be teasing and flirting with the Diver, playing with the lacy streams of bubbles flowing upward from his treasure chest and the sea-green castle. She even made up stories about their relationship, characterizing the Diver as shy and taciturn, unable to express his feelings for the Mermaid, whom Mrs. Lopsided imagined as innocently romantic, hoping daily that he would pluck up the courage to speak. Her courtship of her own husband had been quite similar, and she wished the Mermaid well.

But one day she made a terrible mistake.

Although one of her new delights was to wander through pet stores, looking for decorations that might suit her dear aquarium, as time went by she bought fewer and fewer of such things. She had a natural sense of balance and proportion, and she knew instinctively when to leave well enough alone. Now and then, she might add another swordtail or golden barb, or a plant that caught her eye, but in general the browsing was its own pleasure. She named her fish, usually after characters in historical novels (she was especially fond of Dorothy Dunnett); and when one of her guppies or mollies gave birth to live young, she named them too. There are a lot of names in Dorothy Dunnett.

But she had never meant to buy the Pirate. The shopkeeper even tried to talk her out of it. It was not a pet shop, but something closer to an unintentional-antique store, whose front window had drawn her with its array of old sheet music, single-sided phonograph records, wind-up toys, Captain Marvel lunchboxes, Uncle Wiggily books, dolls and board games out of her own childhood, an Erector set—the model with the electric motor—a box of magic tricks, a cardboard walkie-talkie kit labeled *Made In Occupied Japan* . . .

. . . and the Pirate. He sat brooding in a far corner of the shop window, staring far away—as Mrs. Lopsided imagined then—in search of his ocean, his ship, his black flag, his great sea battles. When the shopkeeper, clearly reluctant to do so, lifted him out of the window for Mrs. Lopsided's inspection, she saw that he was only a little larger than her Mermaid, but clad in such detailed finery that he brought to mind an old poem her pupils had always loved, about a pirate who

"*. . . was wicked as wicked could be,*
but oh, he was perfectly gorgeous to see . . ."

Her Pirate—for so he became on the instant—wore a plumed, broadbrimmed black hat, a frilled and puff-sleeved white shirt under a slashed red coat trimmed in gold, baggy trousers just this side of pantaloons, and thigh-high black boots. He had a splendidly waxed and curled mustache over a thin red mouth, a tattoo of a blood-dripping dagger on his left wrist, and no eyepatch but a crooked scar running from the corner of his right eye across his brow. A cutlass swung at his hip; a dirk and a bell-mouthed pistol were shoved into the scarlet sash at his waist; and the hilt of a very small dagger peeped from one boot. The expression in his hand-painted eyes was shadowy and cold.

"I got him in an estate sale," the shopkeeper told Mrs. Lopsided. "I don't know why I took him. He gives me the creeps, always has. I'd leave him be, myself."

"Well, I think he looks grand," Mrs. Lopsided replied. "I think there's an elegance about him—something dashing and debonair. Do you think he'd do well in an aquarium?"

"Oh, *he'd* do all right," the shopkeeper said sourly. "*He'd* do fine—he's hardwood, solid on his feet, and if that paint job's lasted as long as it has, old as he is, it's won't be fading anytime soon." He cleared his throat and did fussy things with his hands. "It's everything else in the aquarium I'm not too sure about, if you take my meaning. Like I said, he just gives me the creeps."

"In that case," Mrs. Lopsided said, "I'd be happy to take him off your hands." The shopkeeper charged her almost nothing for the Pirate; and as she was leaving the little store with her package, she saw his face in the gilt-framed mirror beside the door. He was sweating with relief, and wiping his forehead.

"Well, I don't care," Mrs. Lopsided told the Pirate as she made her way home. "I'm sure you'll feel right at home in my aquarium, and make friends with everybody the very first thing. Just be gentlemanly to the Mermaid, because she's young and dreamy. She's never seen anyone like you before. Besides, she's already spoken for, in a way."

When she unwrapped the Pirate at her kitchen table and studied him for some while, she began to feel, if not exactly doubts, certain nameless anxieties. It was his eyes that troubled her, more than anything. Whatever angle she studied them from, however much she reminded herself that they were nothing more than dark dots daubed in with the tip of a camel's-hair brush . . . all the same, there was something in them that made her a bit uncomfortable when she imagined them looking upon the Diver's treasure chest. Could she ever trust those eyes to be kind to the Mermaid?

But finally she said aloud, "Well, that's just the way pirates look, they can't help it," and she picked up the Pirate again, marched into the living room, and without any ado deposited him in her aquarium, toward the rear of the tank, next to the sea-green castle. Surprisingly light in her hands, he proved as solidly balanced as the shopkeeper had said: he rocked only once or twice as Mrs. Lopsided set him in place on the gravel, and he came to rest facing the Diver, whose own expression, behind his helmet mask, seemed to have become watchful and uneasy. But the Mermaid immediately swam down to investigate, and a cloud of guppies swarmed around the new figure until they got bored and went away. The catfish kept their distance, but the two golden barbs circled and circled the figure, unable to decide what they thought of it. They never did.

As for the Pirate, he stood where Mrs. Lopsided had set him, his cold dark eyes still staring far beyond the glass walls of his new world. The fish grew used to him quickly, and ignored him thereafter; the Diver never took his eyes off him for long, and seemed to guard his treasure chest even more warily than before. But the Mermaid, plainly fascinated by his rakish appearance, kept sporting with him, as she had with the Diver, pretending to knock his plumed hat off with her tail and letting her long golden hair drift across his face whenever she swam by him. But the Pirate paid no mind to her, nor to anything else.

For a time, his presence made no difference in the aquarium, nor to Mrs. Lopsided, dreamily watching in the darkness of her living room as the fish rippled across her vision and the Mermaid danced her private dance with the bubbles from the treasure chest. Whatever tender fancies the Pirate's sudden arrival may have set astir in her dainty plastic head, he showed no apparent interest in any of them, or in anything else that went on under his dark gaze. Mrs. Lopsided herself quite often forgot that he was there, except when she cleaned the filter of the sea-green castle, or patiently untangled the air hose that the Mermaid had once again wrapped around the topmost turret, where she liked to linger to spy on the Pirate. And so the aquarium and its creator alike went along serenely together.

But one morning, when Mrs. Lopsided came cheerfully into her living room to turn on the aquarium light and feed her fish, she noticed a curious dark tone to the water: more of a shadow than a tone or a tinge. Nothing else had changed, and after a time she persuaded herself that the only difference was in her old eyes, and dismissed the matter altogether. The fish themselves seemed as healthy as ever; the Diver and the Mermaid went about their business unconcerned; and, as the water continued to darken—very, very slightly—over the mornings that followed, so did she.

Then a new transformation came about which did alarm Mrs. Lopsided, and which she could not pretend not to see. The expression on the Pirate's face had changed notably: from brooding, as she had always liked to imagine, over his lost estate in the world, now he was very nearly smiling, as though welcoming someone—or something—whose approach he alone could perceive. Further, there was a new pale light in one of the upper windows of the sea-green castle, which she had never observed before that day. The Mermaid had noticed it too, and no longer swooped and darted about that favorite turret of hers, but now avoided that corner of the tank altogether, though she still cast wistful glances at the Pirate from time to time. Behind the mesh of his mask, the Diver—or so it seemed to Mrs. Lopsided—appeared to be watching over her as much as over his treasure.

As the days passed, and the water of her aquarium grew steadily darker, despite everything she did to keep it clear— as the Pirate's expression grew more evilly eager, and the ugly light in the sea-green castle's window brightened with it—as the Mermaid cringed farther into her far corner, and the fish more and more took refuge in shadows and under limp, rotting plant leaves—Mrs. Lopsided realized more and more that she should have heeded the shopkeeper's warning, and that it was her duty to take action immediately. Elementary school teachers always recognize such moments of decision.

Her first solution was the simplest: to undo her mistake and remove the Pirate from the aquarium. That proved much easier said than done, however, for when she took hold of him, his feet remained as stubbornly embedded in the gravel as though he had grown roots down below the tank itself, and something like an electric shock jarred its way up her arm and numbed it for half an hour. This, of course, frightened Mrs. Lopsided, but it seriously annoyed her as well; and when her arm had recovered enough for her to pick up a pair of kitchen tongs that she used mainly for taking muffins and other small pastries out of the oven, she unceremoniously gripped the Pirate around his scarlet sash and tugged as though she were pulling a tooth. He never moved an inch.

"Very well, then," Mrs. Lopsided said to the Pirate. "*Very well.*" Those same words had set generations of unruly schoolchildren scrambling back to their desks, but they were utterly ineffectual against a painted pirate. Not only did he refuse to budge, but the useless tongs vibrated in her hands, as though with his contemptuous laughter. She finally let go and sank down on the living-room couch, realizing that she was trembling with fear. This outraged her more than anything the Pirate had yet done.

"I am *not* a helpless old woman," she said aloud. "I will *not* be terrified by a silly little piece of wood." She poured herself a glass of sherry, a good hour earlier than she was accustomed, and sat thinking as calmly as she could, while her fish, usually so placid, flurried this way and that in the dark water that even the aquarium lamp hardly penetrated anymore. Then she rose, went briskly to the telephone, and called Bettyann Bascomb.

Mrs. Bascomb was Mrs. Lopsided's oldest friend: a widow and a former teacher like herself, long retired to what she called "a geezerplex" in a nearby community. They met for lunch and a movie every other week, and went to concerts together, when they could agree on the program, Mrs. Lopsided favoring the Romantic composers, and Mrs. Bascomb the Baroque. Mrs. Bascomb looked a good deal like a muffin herself, being small and round and brown; but she had traveled widely, frequently to very odd corners of the world, and was still likely on occasion to disappear for a month or so at a time, and to return with tales and memories that might have seemed outlandish to anyone who didn't know Mrs. Bascomb. She had taught junior high school English, and feared nothing.

Now, listening to Mrs. Lopsided's account of the Pirate's effect on her once-peaceful aquarium, she made soft, thoughtful growls and murmurs of attention, as she always did when she was genuinely interested; but she never interrupted until her friend had finished her story. Then she said, "Well. Weezie—" Mrs. Lopsided's given name was Louise; no one except Mrs. Bascomb ever called her Weezie—"the first thing we do is we go back to that store where you bought your pirate. I can think of a mess of questions I'd like to ask that shopkeeper, and I have a feeling we'd better ask them in a hurry. We'll do it tomorrow—it'll give me an excuse to call off lunch with my niece and her husband. A possessed aquarium has got to be a major improvement on that man."

When Mrs. Bascomb called for her friend the next morning, she studied the Pirate and the aquarium silently for some while before she nodded and said softly, almost inaudibly, "Uh-huh." Mrs. Lopsided had no car, so Mrs. Bascomb drove as she directed to the odd little store that now had in its window a tin music box in which, when wound up, figures of Li'l Abner and his friends played "She'll Be Comin' 'Round The Mountain." Mrs. Bascomb almost bought it on the spot, but settled on the magic tricks instead.

The shopkeeper greeted Mrs. Lopsided with a certain wariness, reminding her immediately that he gave no refunds on any purchase, for any reason. He hardly wanted to deal with Mrs. Bascomb at all, from the moment she asked him, "Where in Jamaica did you buy that pirate? Kingston? Ocho Rios? Don't tell me Montego Bay—you wouldn't find anything like that in Montego Bay. Spanish Town?"

"I didn't find it in Jamaica at all," the shopkeeper wailed, giving ground steadily as Mrs. Bascomb advanced on him. "The

estate, the people selling off—*they'd* lived in Jamaica, a long
time, I don't know where they got a lot of the stuff they had. All
I know about the pirate, he's real old—hundred, hundred fifty,
around there—"

"What wood?" Mrs. Bascomb demanded. The shopkeeper
blinked at her. "What sort of wood was he carved from? You *must*
have some record, some provenance. Come *on*, man!"

Mrs. Lopsided looked on in some astonishment, never having
seen her old friend so intensely aggressive. The poor shopkeeper
told them to wait and almost ran to a filing cabinet in the rear
of the store, returning shortly with a detailed list of the items
included in the estate sale. Mrs. Lopsided's Pirate was near
the bottom of the list, along with the cookbooks and costume
jewelry. "*Duval Estate: figure, five and one-half inches, buccaneer,
carved silk-cotton wood; age, place of origin indeterminate . . .*"

Now it was Mrs. Bascomb who backed away, saying very
softly, as though to herself, "Oh dear . . . Oh dear . . ." She took
Mrs. Lopsided's arm without another word, and drew her out of
the store, still whispering, "Oh dear . . ." Even her lips seemed to
have lost all color.

Outside, on the sidewalk, she seemed to regain at least some
of her normal vivacity. She answered no questions, however, but
said only, "Weezie, I need a bar. I don't think we're in sherry
anymore." They found a pub nearby, and Mrs. Bascomb had
two fast Bloody Marys, each with a shot on the side, while Mrs.
Lopsided ordered a Singapore Sling, which was her notion
of depravity, besides being the only mixed drink she ever
remembered. Then she folded her hands on the little table and
simply waited for Mrs. Bascomb to speak. It was a long wait,
but Mrs. Lopsided was a patient woman.

"Silk-cotton," Mrs. Bascomb said finally, flatly and mystifyingly.

She waved to the bartender for another Bloody Mary, this time without the extra shot. "Weezie, did you ever see a silk-cotton tree?"

Mrs. Lopsided shook her head. "I never even heard of such a thing, until now."

"Oh, they're enormous things," Mrs. Bascomb told her. "Two hundred feet high, ten feet around, sometimes more than that. Great big buttresses grow out of them, near the base, they help hold the tree up. They grow all over the tropics—Africa, India, Southeast Asia, even Australia. And the Caribbean." She paused. "And Jamaica. That's where I saw them, in Jamaica."

"And the Pirate's made of silk-cotton wood," Mrs. Lopsided said. "When he read that, that's when you started looking so scared."

"The trouble is, I know just enough to be scared," Mrs. Bascomb replied, "but not enough to be much use." She sipped her third drink thoughtfully, instead of gulping it down. "Weezie, there are places where nobody would dare to cut down a silk-cotton tree, let alone carve a human figure out of one. Other areas, yes, people make dugout canoes from the trunk, they sell the kapok, the cottony fibers from the fruit, to stuff pillows and life-jackets with—things like that. But what matters about those trees . . ." She hesitated again, and then reached across the table to take both of Mrs. Lopsided's hands. "It's the duppies, Weezie. Duppies live under silk-cotton trees."

It was not the word that frightened Mrs. Lopsided, but the intensity of Mrs. Bascomb's grip, and the look in her eyes. "Just what *is* a duppy?"

"A duppy is a spirit," Mrs. Bascomb said. "A restless spirit—a bad spirit. People in the Caribbean believe that everyone has two souls, not one—a good soul and an evil one, the sum of all the

239

bad things you ever did in your life. When you die, your good soul goes up to heaven to be judged by God, but your evil earthly soul stays with the body, in the coffin, for three days, And if your family doesn't take certain measures, sometimes that bad soul escapes, and then it becomes a duppy. They live in the caves that those buttresses make under the trees, and they can take human shape—and other shapes, too—and they can haunt things. Possess them."

Mrs. Lopsided hugged herself and shivered, though the bar was warm and humid. "And you think that's what's . . . *wrong* with my Pirate?"

"Jamaica was the heart of piracy in the old times," Mrs. Bascomb said. "Seventeenth, eighteenth centuries, Port Royal and Kingston really belonged to English and French privateers, preying on Spanish shipping. And when treaties were signed and deals were made, and that sort of thing played out, a lot of the privateers just went freelance and started sticking up everybody. Blackbeard, Bartholomew Roberts, Edward Vane, Calico Jack Rackham, Ben Avery, Jack Duval, Henry Morgan—Morgan wound up the *governor* of Jamaica, for lord's sake . . . Women, too—Anne Bonney, Mary Read, Grace O'Malley—"

"How do you *know* all this?" Mrs. Lopsided marveled. "I mean, I know you've been everywhere, but I didn't think they taught about piracy in middle school."

Her friend shrugged dismissively. "A lot of the pirates were escaped slaves, you know. They must have brought their West African traditions with them—including duppies." She frowned, considering. "I'd be willing to bet that your figurine was carved very specifically from a silk-cotton tree limb in the image of some real pirate like Edward Vane or Ben Avery." Mrs. Bascomb took a deep breath, and put her hand on Mrs.

Lopsided's hands. "And I'd bet there's been a duppy haunting it from the first day."

Mrs. Lopsided, to her own amazement, found herself signaling for another Singapore Sling. "But how would that happen? How could a duppy possess a little wooden statue?"

"Death," Mrs. Bascomb answered. "With duppies, it starts and ends with death." She was silent long enough for Mrs. Lopsided's second drink to arrive; then she said slowly, "Usually, when a pirate buried a treasure—and they did, just like in the movies—he'd have a mate along to help him dig. Afterward, when they were done . . ." She shrugged again. "There'd only be one living person who knew where the treasure was . . . and one duppy, who would haunt it and protect it forever. I'd guess something like that happened with your pirate."

They sat staring at each other for some time. Then Mrs. Lopsided said, very quietly, "I have to go home now."

Mrs. Bascomb considered the glasses on the table and said, "We'll split a cab, I'll come back for my car tomorrow."

When the cab dropped Mrs. Lopsided off at her house, Mrs. Bascomb admonished her, "You call me if there's anything nasty happening around that aquarium. *Anything.*" Mrs. Lopsided had to assure her she would three times before the cab pulled away.

The front door of the house opened directly into the living room. She walked in slowly, reminding herself that, even if everything Mrs. Bascomb had told her was true, still she had no reason to be afraid—there was no way an evil spirit trapped in a five-and-a-half-inch figurine could harm her. Nevertheless, she found herself edging warily around the room, unable to raise her eyes from the patterned carpet until she was near the door that led to her kitchen. Only then did she force herself to stand still and look straight at the aquarium.

The water in the tank had darkened further in her absence: her fish glinted only sporadically through it, on and off like fireflies. The fluorescent lamp had had gone out; and yet the aquarium itself appeared to be glowing brilliantly, because the Pirate's face was burning in the shadowy water. He had not moved from where she had placed him, but he was smiling a long, thin smile, and his hungry painted eyes saw her for the first time. Mrs. Lopsided neither screamed nor fainted; she only made a sound too small for her to hear, and backed against the wall.

There were lights flickering in all the windows of the sea-green castle now: blue as veins, pale yellow as old teeth. Mrs. Lopsided looked urgently for the Mermaid, and could not find her at first. She finally made her out in the dimness, huddling as close as she could to the Diver, who could do nothing for her comfort but stare back at her over the lid of his open treasure chest. All the same, Mrs. Lopsided was glad—and somehow comforted herself—to see them together.

"I'll be over right away," Mrs. Bascomb said on the phone. "I'll spend the night."

"No, I'll be all right," Mrs. Lopsided answered, only a little shakily. "I really will be, Bettyann. I was thinking, maybe I ought to empty the tank—you know, put all the fish in jars and vases and such for the night, and just drain the whole thing. And I could put the Mermaid and the Diver somewhere safe, and do *something* about the castle—"

Mrs. Bascomb informed her quite firmly that this would not be a good idea. "It's the duppy we've got to get rid of, Weezie, not the water. I'm reading up on it online, right now, and I'm sure I'll have some good ideas tomorrow. Don't be scared—just try to get some sleep, okay?"

As they were about to hang up, she added, "Wear some red

underwear, with elastic in the legs. Black's good too, if you don't have red, but red's really better. Remember about the elastic." Mrs. Lopsided—bewildered but committed—promised.

Mrs. Lopsided spent an understandably restless night in her second-floor bedroom, which had seemed a reassuring distance from the Pirate and the sea-green castle. But when she fell asleep, she dreamed that the duppy itself had stepped out of the aquarium and was striding up the stairs to her, growing as it came, grinning flames and smelling like stagnant water, its skin as rubbery as a dead frog's. She woke with a small scream, and spent the rest of the night shivering in a chair by the window, praying, not for mercy or deliverance, but simply for dawn.

Mrs. Bascomb came early, as she had promised, and insisted that they two make breakfast for themselves before even talking about the aquarium, let alone dealing with it. So she made banana pancakes, which was a specialty of hers, and Mrs. Lopsided squeezed oranges, fried bacon, and brewed Mexican hot chocolate, since that was what *she* did best. They ate in the kitchen and discussed poetry, relatives, the last movie they had seen together, and Mrs. Bascomb's most recent journey to Madagascar. Only then, after a certain silence, did they put the dishes and utensils in the sink, and enter the living room.

In the murky water, all that was clear to the two old ladies were the Pirate's fierce, fiery grin and the blazing windows of the sea-green castle. The Mermaid was plainly struggling to reach the Diver—but the water itself seemed to be holding her back. The Pirate seemed to be looking directly at Mrs. Lopsided, leering into her trembling soul; unconsciously, she shrank away behind Mrs. Bascomb. "My little fish," she said sadly.

The guppies, swordtails, barbs, and tetras were altogether invisible now; the Diver could be traced only by the column of bubbles still stubbornly streaming upward from his treasure chest. Mrs. Bascomb's reply was short, and seemingly irrelevant. "Did you remember about the underwear?"

Mrs. Lopsided blushed slightly. "I found one red pair. James bought them for my birthday. They're a little tight now."

Mrs. Bascomb grinned wickedly at her. "I always did like that man of yours. Elastic?"

"On the sides. Why is that important?"

"Supposed to keep the duppy from possessing you. My cousin Cedric's married to a Jamaican woman, and that's what she told me, very specifically. And they're never bothered by duppies, so there you are. I figured, what could it hurt?"

But Mrs. Lopsided was still back at an earlier word. "Possess? I thought you said duppies just possessed things like—well—statues. Inanimate things, objects." She was looking anxiously at Mrs. Bascomb for reassurance. "Are *you* wearing red underwear?"

"Black," Mrs. Bascomb admitted, uncharacteristically diffident. "Herman always had a sort of thing for black silk." She turned from the aquarium to take Mrs. Lopsided's hand. "Remember, Weezie, a duppy is altogether evil—it's what they're made of, what they're meant for, what they do. And if Cousin Cedric's wife is right, they *can* possess people sometimes, and this one would be a lot happier in the body of a nice old schoolteacher lady than being trapped forever in a useless little figurine in a tank." She patted her friend's hand comfortingly. "But you've got your special red underwear on, so that's not going to happen. Now, where's my reticule?"

Reaching into her deceptively capacious handbag—which Mrs. Lopsided had known to contain anything from a three-course French meal, to a shortwave radio, to a small dog—she brought out nothing more dramatic than a salt shaker. "Give him the works," she directed. "Duppies hate salt—imagine you're seasoning that great black bean soup I'm always asking you to fix. Or the biggest margarita in the whole world, whichever. Let him have it!"

So Mrs. Lopsided held the salt shaker over the aquarium, and shook it until her wrist ached and she had to give it back to Mrs. Bascomb. "Is anything supposed to happen right away?" she asked wonderingly. "Maybe it takes a little time."

But Mrs. Bascomb was already shaking her head. "Nope, these things work or they don't work. I guess that Jamaican lady didn't know everything. Lord, I hope I remembered to bring the coffee beans."

She had, in an ordinary sealed freezer bag. Opening this, she shook out a dozen small beans, arranging them in a semicircle within sight of the Pirate. "Duppies can't count," she explained. "Sometimes you can keep them out of a place by putting down a bunch of identical objects at the door. Sand's the best, a whole pile of sand, because they'll try to count every grain, and they mostly give up and go away. But I do think—" she suddenly clutched Mrs. Lopsided's arm—"I do think we've got his attention . . ."

A faint, almost unnoticeable line, like an overlooked slip of the paintbrush, had appeared between the Pirate's sardonic brows. It affected his expression not at all, but it was *there*, where both women agreed that it had not been before. Nothing else had changed, however, and the aquarium remained as dark and sinister as ever. Mrs. Bascomb shook her head and clicked her tongue, seeming no whit discouraged. "Not to worry—I promise you, we're just getting started."

"It's all my fault," Mrs. Lopsided said. For all her friend's cheerfulness, she was feeling increasingly miserable and despairing. "If

I hadn't put him in the aquarium—if I'd never seen him at all, never walked past that shop—"

"Now you hush," Mrs. Bascomb scolded her. "That is just exactly what duppies love to hear, that kind of talk. None of that *if I hadn't, if I weren't, if I'd known*, if you please." She rummaged in her bag again and produced a small bottle of white rum with what Mrs. Lopsided guessed was a picture of Henry Morgan on it. Holding it out to her, Mrs. Bascomb ordered her to take a mouthful. "Don't swallow, mind—just hold it and do what I do. I've got the directions—watch me now, Weezie."

Filling her own mouth with the rum, she leaned over the aquarium and sprayed it, with a child's spluttering glee, directly over the Pirate, being careful to save a little for the sea-green castle. Mrs. Lopsided joined her, and the two of them, reloading as necessary, emptied the bottle into the aquarium, mouthful by mouthful, as Mrs. Bascomb directed. She tried to explain the paradox to Mrs. Lopsided: on the one hand, duppies loved good Jamaican rum, and would eagerly go out of their way to get it. "Other hand, rum that's been in contact with something as intimate as a human being's mouth . . . not so good. They're afraid of it—somehow it actually hurts them, the way holy water's supposed to hurt vampires." There was a certain dry emphasis on the word *supposed*.

The sea-green castle showed no least effect from having been so thoroughly showered with Captain Morgan's Best, but the Pirate was another matter. He stared into Mrs. Lopsided's face, as he had done before, and she saw his expression alter from contemptuous arrogance to something momentarily close to alarm. Then he moved.

All her strength, and a good pair of kitchen tongs, had not sufficed to move him half an inch: but now his feet came lightly up out of Mrs. Lopsided's peat-and-gravel bed, so patiently smoothed over every day with her tiny rake, and he took a single long stride toward the sea-green castle. Then he wheeled and sidestepped . . . sidestepped again, moving in the murk as though in air . . . and slipped smoothly into the courtly paces of what Mrs. Lopsided realized would have been some sort of quadrille, a gliding formal dance translated to the heaving, bloody deck of a pirate ship. At first his steps were stiff-legged and wooden; but as the two women looked on, they quickened into a jig that became a hornpipe, with something in it of a sword-dance's savagery. The Pirate never took his painted eyes from hers, and Mrs. Lopsided could not look away. Even though she felt him climbing the link between them, just as he would have scrambled up a ratline, as avidly seeking escape from his wooden body as from the aquarium, she could not look away.

Then, beside her, Mrs. Bascomb said, "He's not very good, is he?" The connection snapped abruptly, almost physically, so that Mrs. Lopsided actually lurched forward, bumping her forehead lightly on the aquarium's rim. But her friend was quite right: the Pirate's dance was, in fact, no more than polished repetition of a few stock steps and turns, nothing that a ploughboy, or Mrs. Lopsided herself, could not have mastered in an afternoon. She wondered aloud, in answer, "Do you suppose he might be modeled on a real person? One of the family who sold him, the Duvals?"

Mrs. Bascomb turned to stare at her with a kind of astonishment that Mrs. Lopsided had never seen on her friend's face before. She snapped her fingers sharply; but instead of speaking her response, she softly sang a few bars of an old song:

> "At seventeen with Blackbeard,
> she'd a hand in every haul,

And all men took her for a man,
but Dancing Jack Duval . . ."

Mrs. Lopsided's eyes widened, and Mrs. Bascomb nodded vigorously, slapping her hands together. "I think that's whom you've got there, Weezie. I think that's Dancing Jack himself."

"I don't know that song," Mrs. Lopsided said hesitantly. "I know who Blackbeard was, but I've never heard of Jack Duval. And who is the song about?"

"Mary Read," Mrs. Bascomb answered. "She was a lady pirate, early eighteenth century, and she dressed as a man and passed for one, and nobody knew the truth except her friend Anne Bonney. And Jack Duval." She sang another stanza:

"Now Jack Duval had one wall eye
and a pale and greasy jowl.
He never struck an honest blow
if he could deal a foul.
His pleasure was in corners,
and the dark was all his creed—
but women love the strangest rogues
and so did Mary Read . . ."

While she sang, Mrs. Lopsided gazed at the Pirate in greater fascination than ever before.

Abruptly, as they stared, neither one speaking, the open window of the sea-green castle burst open with a silent bang, and a tentacle the color of the Pirate's scarlet sash came plunging and battering its way through the frame. Mrs. Lopsided, who maintained and concealed a secret fondness for the low-budget horror films of her youth, numbly expected the bulbous head of a giant octopus to follow, and then realized, first, that instead of sucker discs, this tentacle was studded with claws like crocodiles' teeth; and, second, that whatever was inside the sea-green castle was plainly too big to emerge through the window. But the tentacle was lashing so hard against the castle walls that the entire plastic façade must surely shatter in another moment, to admit . . . what? Even Mrs. Bascomb, for all her knowledge and experience, could not have said.

"We must stay calm, Weezie," she kept repeating firmly, trying her best to suit performance to injunction. "We must not panic—when you are panicky, you can't think, and that is just what the duppy wants. Keep *calm*, Weezie.

"Bettyann, stop saying that! I *am* panicky, I *am* about to start screaming, and I don't care *what* the duppy thinks. Let it have the aquarium—let it have the whole room, the whole house, I'm done, it's too much, I'm too frightened, I *can't* think, I don't *want* to think! Come away, Bettyann, *please!*" She pulled frantically on her friend's arm.

But Mrs. Bascomb remained firm. "Weezie, listen to me! If he gets out of that Pirate, out of the tank, we're in real trouble then. Because he *will* come after you, he *will* possess you, and there won't be anything I can do to help you. We have to stop him here, but you have to be brave—do you understand me? You *mustn't* let him see you're afraid."

"If he can't see *that*, he's the stupidest duppy ever hatched," Mrs. Lopsided whimpered. "And I'm the stupidest human being." Now she was almost crying. "Oh, Bettyann, I've made such an awful mistake, but I didn't know! I didn't know about duppies, or cotton-silk trees, or anything—I just thought a pirate would look nice, because of the treasure chest being there already, and the Mermaid, and him being so handsome . . ." The last words were swallowed by tears.

"Hush, hush, lovey, hush," Mrs. Bascomb comforted her. "There's one thing yet we haven't tried. I can't say it'll work—I've never seen it done—but if it does, no duppy will ever come near your house again. Courage now, because I need you to help me. Are you ready, Weezie?"

"No," Mrs. Lopsided sniffled. "No, I'm *not* ready, and I won't ever be." But she wiped her eyes, took a quick swallow of the white rum, coughed, choked, gasped, and said, "All right. I'm ready."

The Pirate moved again. This time they saw him.

He lifted his right foot and took a long, sliding step toward the sea-green castle. The scarlet tentacle seemed to go mad at this, redoubling its whipping, pounding attack on every inch of the wall it could reach. The castle's front swayed violently without yielding; but through a new crack, Mrs. Lopsided saw a great pale eye roiled like a stormy sea with eager hatred. She felt Mrs. Bascomb taking her hand, carefully cupping the fingers, and then pouring a fine, dark-smelling powder into her palm. In her ear came the whisper, "Mangrove tree bark. The mangrove is the sworn enemy of the silk-cotton tree—they fight for the same place in the world, and they have hated each other since the world began. You must fight for your home, your soul, in just the same way. When I count to three, pour the mangrove bark into the aquarium, as close to *him* as you can manage . . . One . . . two . . . Now, Weezie!"

Mrs. Lopsided opened her hand and hurled the mangrove-bark powder as hard as she could into the aquarium, so that it floated down directly over the Pirate, except for the small amount that drifted into the bubble stream that marked the Diver's treasure. Out of the corner of her eye, she saw Mrs. Bascomb launching her handful of the powder straight at the sea-green castle and its dreadful tenant—or was it perhaps a prisoner, after all? She couldn't care either way: in that moment, a frightening rage of her own rose in her, and she cried out loudly, "Go away! Go away—*shoo!*" as she would have shouted at a strange cat in her garden. "*Shoo!*"

And with those words—perhaps even because of them; she never knew—her aquarium swallowed her up.

Between one second and the next . . . one word and the next . . . between the first and second *o*'s of *shoo* . . . the aquarium become the world all around her. Dazedly she realized that she was *in* the water, but somehow not *of* it: she was quite dry, breathing as normally as any of her little fish, as they came and went in the gloom like shooting stars, flashing brilliantly across her vision and gone again. Mrs. Bascomb seemed a long way from her, facing the sea-green castle with her brown fists clenched at her sides, shouting something that Mrs. Lopsided could not quite hear over the thundering of the clawed scarlet tentacle against the castle wall. There was another sound, too: a kind of thin, mewing laughter that Mrs. Lopsided had always feared in the winter wind for its triumphant despair. *It's all hopeless, every bit of it, everything you ever wished or dreamed or did. Lie down, lie down, lie down . . .*

It was coming from the Pirate, grown far taller than she, as had the sea-green castle, and advancing on her in a stiff-legged wooden march that became more fleshly and human with every step he took. His smile mimicked the curl of his mustache, as it in turn seemed to copy the twists and ringlets of that winter laughter. The sword—decidedly no longer wooden—was partway out of its sheath as he toyed with the hilt, and Mrs. Lopsided knew that he meant to kill her, not possess her; that her death was to be the flavoring of his freedom. Yet she was not at all afraid, but faced him with a young woman's near-eagerness: feeling, as young people do, that whatever happened next was bound to be interesting. She could not remember being this curious, this happy.

The Mermaid flashed out of the murk, almost knocking the Pirate off his feet as she swept past him, not pausing there but heading directly for the sea-green castle, and a window yet a fraction too small to permit the escape of a tentacled beast, but just right for a sea creature defending her home and touched with mangrove-tree powder. A kind of awful, unendurable squealing, like that of a pig sensing slaughter, greeted her before she was nearly through the window, and the battle was joined.

In the same moment, the Diver stood up from his stooped position, slammed his barely-visible treasure chest shut, shoved his helmet more securely down on his head, and caught the Pirate around the neck with a loop of his air hose. He tossed it like a cowboy roping a steer, and it brought the Pirate down on his back, thrashing furiously. The Diver uttered a war cry no less fierce for being inaudible, and leaped on him.

The aquarium was growing steadily larger, as Mrs. Lopsided could tell by how far away her fish gleamed, huddling in a far-distant corner. As far as she could tell, she remained in proportion to her surroundings, but everything had slowed down for her, as so often happens to people caught in a crisis, even one taking place in a fish tank. She became abruptly aware that she had lost sight of Mrs. Bascomb and hurried forward, as best she might, to find her. The dark, fetid water was less impenetrable than it had seemed from above, and she was able to guide herself by the tumult of the combat between the Mermaid and whatever was raging behind the battered walls of the sea-green castle. The Pirate was plainly growing weaker in his struggle with the Diver as the clash in the sea-green castle grew more and more desperate. The lights in the castle's windows went violently on and off, and at times the Mermaid was visible, struggling against the tentacle sometimes enlacing her waist or her tail, sometimes her throat, while the Pirate and the Diver tumbled over and over in the churned-up bed of the aquarium of which Mrs. Lopsided had been so proud.

But her concern was all for Bettyann Bascomb. She finally caught sight of her, just as the wall of the sea-green castle split and came down, hurling the Mermaid almost across the aquarium, and hiding Mrs. Bascomb in the swirl of stone and dirt and plants jarred loose in the crash, as Mrs. Lopsided herself felt torn away from any roots, any footing she had ever known in the world. Yet she stumbled on, so completely focused on her friend that she almost ignored—not quite, but almost—the great creature surging over the wreckage directly toward her. It was not making the pig-sound now, but came at her in utter silence, and all its eyes were horridly blue.

In trying, and failing, to describe it afterward to her nephew—the only person, other than Mrs. Bascomb, with whom she ever discussed what she had seen from both inside and outside her own aquarium—she said, "It kept *shifting*, changing its outline, like one of those children you can't ever get to sit still, but it was somewhere between a bear and a . . . a squid, or an octopus. Only an octopus with fur—or something *like* fur—or a squid that could get up on its hind legs, if it had hind legs, which it did. Short ones." But the description came nowhere near what she had seen; nowhere near what shadowed her sleep that same night, and for many nights thereafter, and caught her each time. And even when, in the dreams, she learned not to see it whole, not to admit its entire presence, there were always the blue eyes.

But at the time she all but ignored the creature, being thoroughly occupied with pulling Mrs. Bascomb out from under the splintered corner of the wall that had pinned her, half-conscious and helpless, down in a hollow left by scattered gravel and torn-up bubble-leaf lace plants. Only when she had her friend on her feet—dazed still, but unhurt—did she pay much mind to the nightmare looming above her. There would be time for terror any minute now, but not quite yet.

Nearby, to Mrs. Lopsided's astonishment—and, clearly, the tentacled beast's—the Pirate lay sprawled, strangled with the Diver's air hose: a harmless figurine once more, never again to counterfeit being. The bear/squid/furry octopus stood over it for some time before it turned toward the two old women, blazing with avid rage, yearning at them like a lover. Mrs. Bascomb said thickly, "That's the duppy."

"I don't understand." Mrs. Lopsided was suddenly very tired. "I thought the Pirate . . ."

"I told you, duppies are shapeshifters. This one let a little bit of itself go into the Pirate, so that it could go wherever the Pirate went and grow again—like transplanting a cutting. But the mangrove-bark powder made him weaker than he should have been, and strengthened the Diver and the Mermaid." She looked around in growing awareness and alarm. "Weezie, where *is* your Mermaid?"

"I don't know," Mrs. Lopsided whispered. "I don't know."

The stillness in the aquarium was like the silence after the fall of a huge tree, or the uttering of something everyone knows to be absolutely unforgivable. The water had not lightened in the least, but somehow the fall of the sea-green castle made it seem as though it had. The duppy faced the women, growling softly now as it gradually took on the form of the lifeless Pirate. As in Mrs. Lopsided's dream, it stretched up to twice and three times her height, its smile filling with fire, its eyes turning the exact shade of the fouled water. It started toward them, and Mrs. Lopsided and Mrs. Bascomb, without looking at each other, unconsciously reached for each other's hands.

The Mermaid shot between them, breaking out of the cloud of fish that had covered her approach. Swift and silver and deadly as a barracuda, she swooped low to sweep the statue-Pirate's sword from his belt, then to wheel and half-somersault, with the aid of her powerful tail, and fire the weapon underhanded directly at the duppy's chest. It sank in almost to the hilt, and the Pirate-duppy looked, in rapid succession, surprised, contemptuous, outraged, vaguely alarmed, and dead. It was dissolving like a jellyfish in the sun by the time it hit the bottom of the tank, and was long gone by the time the water had truly cleared, revealing the Diver back at his open chest and the Mermaid floating serenely above him. And two old ladies were standing side by side in Mrs. Lopsided's living room, and they were still holding hands, very tightly.

Neither Mrs. Lopsided nor Mrs. Bascomb was ever certain whether the wooden sword briefly turned real had truly made an end of the duppy. Mrs. Lopsided, being by nature optimistic, ventured the opinion that the wicked spirit had either been annihilated completely, or else driven back to shelter and brood among the roots of the silk-cotton tree that had given it birth. Mrs. Bascomb, wiser in the ways of such beings, warned her frequently—as we are told concerning matter itself—that evil could neither be created nor destroyed, and that the safest precaution for her would be to burn both the Mermaid and the Diver immediately and sink the ashes in the sea, since it would have been entirely within the duppy's powers to take refuge in either of her two plastic defenders. "He may not have done that—he may not have had time—but he went *somewhere*, and why take chances? Get rid of them, Weezie. I know how you feel about them, but you must do this."

But that step Mrs. Lopsided could not take, the Diver and

the Mermaid remaining sacrosanct and untouchable in her view. "They protected me, they came to my rescue when you and I were helpless, and what kind of gratitude would I be showing if I turned my back on them now? I can't do it, Bettyann. I could never do such a thing."

And there the matter rests to this day. Mrs. Bascomb still retains her suspicions, as long as it has been, and still maintains a good supply of the mangrove-bark powder that, as she believes, gave true, though brief, life and the courage of their loyalty to the Mermaid and the Diver, who have never moved again. She is even likely to stop by unannounced now and then, just to inspect the condition of the aquarium—now more tranquil and soothing to eye and heart than ever—although she admits that she has never found the least hint of a trace of a misgiving to warn Mrs. Lopsided about. Mrs. Lopsided, for her part, teases her about her continuing wariness, and makes tea.

But a rather curious change has occurred, though neither of them talk about it very much, if at all. Whether it can be set down to her long and intense exposure to the duppy itself, or to her much longer association with Mrs. Bascomb, Mrs. Lopsided appears to have developed a new taste for adventure. She travels a good deal now—sometimes in company with her old friend, rather more often on her own—and there is a tilt to her white head and a slow twinkle in her eye that was not there before. In the Azores—or was it in the Maldives?—she bought a captain's cap that she wears on every occasion, even to the symphony. It is undoubtedly becoming, and Mrs. Bascomb generally approves. Generally.

Music, When Soft Voices Die

I've never been great at choosing titles. Why the opening line from Shelley's posthumously published poem chose itself for this story, I honestly can't say. For that matter, I can't say why I agreed to write it at all, to be included in a steampunk collection, when I still don't fully understand what "steampunk" means. I've never yet read any of William Gibson's work (my loss, decidedly), and the only thing I'm sure of—pretty sure—is that if, at a fantasy convention, I see people dressed more or less like the Red Baron, in a mix of mismatched costumes—top hats and bicycle chains, monocles and World War I pilots' gear, engineers' overalls laced and overlaced by military medals and parts from 19th-century typewriters—they're most likely steampunkers. My story is set in the time just after a fictional Anglo-Turkish war; the names of my English characters are taken from a row of Chicago mailboxes (one of which belongs to a friend of mine); and, in candor, the more I look at this one—not having reread it after publication—the more relieved I am that at least I didn't disgrace myself. I'll settle for that.

There were four of them living in the gabled rooming house with two chimneys on Geraldine Row, on the east side of Russell Square. This would have been perhaps six years after the Ottoman War, and quite shortly following the wedding of Queen Victoria's youngest daughter, Princess Maude Charlotte Mary, to Prince Selim Ali, who eventually became Sultan Selim IV. The marriage was not a happy one.

The four men's names were Vordran, Scheuch, Griffith, and Angelos. They were not friends.

Scheuch and Vordran might have been thought to have something in common, since Scheuch was a bank clerk, while Vordran, eldest of the four, worked in a Bishopsgate law firm. But Vordran was not a clerk, nor ever would be, no more than he would ever be a barrister or a solicitor. He was merely a copyist and, since he took shorthand, an occasional secretary. Once, when jolly young Scheuch had the bad form to invite him to join him for tea, Vordran ticked him off sharply before the other two, saying coldly, in his slight, unplaceable accent, "I am a jumped-up office boy, and I will be treated so or left in peace. Do not ever dare to condescend to me again." Scheuch kept his distance from then on.

Angelos was a second-year medical student at Christ's Hospital, himself quite sensible of the fact that names such as his—further, his mother was Jewish—were rarely admitted to study at the ancient institution. Even younger than Scheuch, he appeared a much more serious soul, but on further acquaintance one discovered that his interests and fancies ranged from pigeon-racing to hot-air ballooning (very much in vogue since the Turkish bombing of London), to the newly recognized science of galvanic phrenology, by means of which one could unfailingly identify a future Mozart or a mass-murderer-to-be through analyzing the electrical resistance in different portions of the skull, neck bones, and clavicles. He played the banjo, but never past eight o'clock, or before ten.

Griffith had been at Balliol. That was very nearly all one was allowed to know about Griffith, besides the fact that he was a waiter at Simpson's-in-the-Strand. His term at university had apparently been interrupted by his enlistment in the war, of which he was justifiably very proud; but why he never returned to Oxford after the Pact of Trieste remained a mystery. What was *not* mysterious about him was the fact that, where Vordran was undeniably brittle and prickly, Griffith was, quite simply, arrogant to the point of being unbearable. Everything in his life— and, consequently, every person as well—was viewed through the prism of his lost world, and found wanting. He seemed less a proper snob than a kind of wretched exile, but this understanding made him no more likable, or even tolerable; the others came to speak to him as little as they could, except when encountered entering or leaving the house, or meeting on the stair. Griffith appeared more than satisfied with this arrangement.

The rooming house was managed by a smiling, swarthy man named Emanetoglu, whose brother actually owned it, as well as two other buildings across the river. Mr. Emanetoglu manifested himself promptly at 8 A.M. on the fifteenth of every month, to collect the rent, and to drift into corners and corridors like smoke, commenting diffidently on the condition of paint, wallpaper, and bathroom floorboards. Impossible to dislike— except by Griffith, who referred to him as "Glue Pot," when he was not calling him "The Wog"—he had, nevertheless, the rainy air of an apologetic ghost, as much trapped in the house by fate as they by finances. On the rare occasion that any roomer was briefly late with a rent payment, he was patient, but oddly sorrowful, as though the lapse were somehow his own fault.

"You shouldn't call him that, you know," Scheuch chided Griffith once. "He's a decent enough chap, Turk or no."

"I hate seeing them strutting around so, that's all." Griffith bit down hard on the stem of the briar pipe he had lately taken to affecting. "Never used to see a one of them west of Greek Street. Now they're all over London, got themselves the Ritz, got themselves Lord's, got themselves Marks and Sparks, got themselves a bloody princess, they'll shove a white man off the sidewalk if he don't look slippy about it. You'd think they'd won the bloody war—and by God, I think that's what *they* think. But they *didn't* win the bloody war!"

Vordran spoke up then, in the way he had that always made him sound as though he were talking to himself. "Didn't they, then? They fought us to a standstill. We bled ourselves dry, for no reason that I could ever see, and now they own half the Empire. We were fools."

"Feel that way, you ought to go and enlist for a Turk," Griffith mumbled as he stalked away.

It was during the late summer and early fall of 18__ that Angelos became obsessed with the study of what he called "etheric telegraphy." His top-floor room—inconvenient to reach, but immensely practical for his pigeons—quickly became a hotbed of strange small sounds, and he began increasingly to ask Scheuch for assistance in dealing with certain mathematical issues. "There's this chap named Faraday, and another one named Maxwell, and there's a Yank *dentist*, if you'll believe it, with some outlandish name like Mahlon Loomis, and all of them rattling on about electromagnetism, etheric force, amperes, communal fields . . . I don't half know what three-quarters of that gibberish means, but I have to know. Can't say why, I just *do*." Scheuch, who was by nature an amiable, accommodating man, did his best to oblige.

Knowing Angelos better than either Griffith or Vordran ever bothered to know anyone, Scheuch expected this new passion to burn itself out by Boxing Day, at the very latest. But time passed, and snow fell; and, if anything, Angelos's fervor only grew more intense. He spoke to Scheuch of partial differential equations, of spark-gap transmission and a thing called a *coherer*, apparently as indescribable as a state of grace. He returned late from work with packages from shops Scheuch had never heard of, crammed with wire coils, hand-cranks, and strangely shaped glass bottles, along with magnets—endless magnets of every form and size. He went frequently without sleep; and Scheuch, who left for work at the same time as he, often saw him stumbling downstairs, his eyes plainly fogged and his step unsteady. He would not have been at all surprised to see Angelos brusquely dismissed from Christ's for habitual drunkenness, but somehow he continued to be well regarded by his instructors, and to keep his marks at least at a respectable level. The tattered oilcloth leftovers from the last experimental balloon gathered dust in a far corner, in company with the banjo. The pigeons disappeared.

"I cannot even say what it is that he is aiming for," Scheuch told Griffith, on one of the days when the latter was in a mood to be comparatively genial with a non-public-school man. "He speaks constantly of ethereal waves of some sort—of induction, conduction . . . even of being able to affect physical objects in another room, another *country*. I'd set him down as a pure crackpot, except that he's such a *plausible* chap, if you know what I mean. One could almost believe . . ." He shrugged helplessly and raised his eyebrows.

"We had a fellow like that up at Balliol," Griffith reflected. "Rum cove from the first. Other chaps kept bullpups, ratters— he kept a monkey, called it his *associate*. Never could find a roommate because of that beast. Always experimenting, night and day—chemistry, I suppose, from the smell, or maybe that was the monkey. Killed in the war, poor chap. Him, not the monkey. Can't say what became of the monkey."

"Different sort, Angelos," Scheuch replied. "Not defending him or anything, just saying he's not exactly round the bend. Eccentric, absolutely, but not . . . I don't know—not *potty*, not like that. Eccentric."

Griffith, his interest lost well before Scheuch had finished speaking, raised an eyebrow himself and said, "Jew."

That winter was a hard one, even for London. The Russell Square rooming house, like most such, lacked any form of central heating, and all four men suffered to one degree or another from colds and chilblains. The world-famous London fog, which was not a proper fog at all, settled over the city, leaving a coal-oil film over everything; the Thames froze over, and a few starving wolves invaded from the countryside, as none had been known to do since prewar days. The men trudged to their various occupations through the dirty snow, or—in Vordran's case—waited with hats pulled tightly down for one of the new streetcars, which might, in postwar London, be steam- or battery-driven on one day, then pulled by teams of men or horses the next. Simpson's suffered a notable falling-off in custom, enough that Griffith was on involuntary furlough an extra day out of the week; while the bank where Scheuch was employed frequently went whole days without a single client coming in from the street. The city closed down, as though under a filthy potlid; and—with the same legendary stoicism through which they had endured the Turkish siege—Londoners simply waited for the winter to end.

But in Russell Square, Angelos remained the single cheerful soul. ("Well he might be," Griffith sneered, "as many frozen paupers as he and his grisly crew must be slicing up these days.") The young man still worked a full day at Christ's Hospital, then made his way home to spend half the night making odd, frequently disquieting noises with his homebuilt machines for which Scheuch had no names. Most often he slouched into Scheuch's rooms to slap down a scribbled-over clutch of foolscap, grumbling, "Bloody Faraday, bloody Hughes, bloody diamagnetism, makes no bloody *sense!*" and appealing for assistance with a new batch of equations. "If you could just cast an eye over these, I swear I'll not trouble you again. *Bloody* Faraday!"

Scheuch aided as best a country day school education and a certain natural bent for mathematics allowed him to do, thus becoming the closest thing Angelos possessed to a colleague, without in the least comprehending exactly what the other could possibly be driving toward. As he commented warily to Vordran, "It's a good bit like playing blindman's buff, where your eyes are covered and you're spun around until you can't tell where you're facing, or which way anything is. I don't know what on earth the man has in mind."

Much to his surprise, the older man answered him slowly and thoughtfully, saying, "Well, many of the people he quotes to you share an interest in wireless communication. Who knows—he may yet have you talking to people in Africa or China, this time next year. If you know anyone there, that is to say," and he made the little half-hiccough sound that qualified as a chuckle with Vordran.

Scheuch gave a weary shrug, spreading his hands, as he found himself doing more and more when asked about Angelos's behavior. "That could be what he's after, for all of me—as much time as I've spent with the fellow, I confess I haven't the least idea." Turning away, he added, "I do sometimes fancy I hear voices in his rooms, you know. Through the door, when I'm passing."

"Voices?" Vordran had a longer attention span than Griffith. "What sort of voices?"

"*Pieces* of voices," Scheuch answered vaguely. "Snatches, phrases . . . probably not voices at all, just Angelos talking to himself, the way he does." Vordran stood looking after him for some while, rubbing his chin.

The winter passed. The snow melted, leaving the city gutters running with soiled water; hawthorn and horse chestnut trees began to bloom in Victoria Park, and bluebells cautiously replaced the snowdrops of Highgate. The women of London began to be seen in the filmy headscarves and baggy iridescent pantaloons that had become the highest style since Princess Maude had worn them to a state dinner in Prince Selim Ali's honor. Griffith was fully employed at Simpson's once more, while the Bishopsgate firm where Vordran would never be a clerk bustled with new clients suing their families. Scheuch spent most days at the bank on his feet, jovial and patient as ever as he handled other people's money and tended the firm's shining brass calculators. London— at least the London they three knew—was London again.

And Angelos, one pleasant Sunday afternoon, invited them all to tea in his rooms.

Scheuch, being the only one who had spent any length of time there, was far less taken aback than Vordran or Griffith by the cheery chaos of the sitting room, which—like Angelos's bedroom and the small alcove which served him as a closet—did double duty as laboratory and storage space. Tea was brewed over the fireplace, identical to the hearths they all had, and served at a large round table that had once been a chandler's cable spool. Vordran sat in the one reasonably sturdy armchair, Scheuch on the precarious settee. Griffith stood.

Angelos began slowly, uncharacteristically hesitant, plainly feeling for words. "I believe I have something interesting to tell you. To show you, rather—and it is entirely likely that you three will be the only chaps I ever *do* show it to. It's not something I can exactly take down to the Patent Office, as you'll see." He started to add something else, but halted, and only repeated lamely, "As you'll see."

Vordran cleared his throat, "May I make the occasion perhaps a bit easier for you? I've already suggested to Scheuch here that you are probably attempting to create some form of long-distance communication, such as others are seeking in France and Germany, and—I believe—America. Am I correct?"

"Well," Angelos said. "Yes. I mean . . . well, yes and no. *Yes*, that was how I started out—*yes*, that's what I got caught up in like Faraday and Maxwell and those fellows. I mean, imagine being able to push a button, turn a knob, and immediately be speaking to someone on the other side of the world. Of *course*, I was . . . oh, I'm sorry—more tea, anyone? Biscuit?"

No one wanted either, for excellent reasons. Angelos continued. "But something else happened . . . yes, something rather else. I can't quite explain it yet, even to myself, so I'll just have to show you. If you'll give me a moment."

He hurried into his bedroom and returned quickly with an armload of assorted wires, a fragile-appearing copper disc in a linen wrapper, and a pair of metal frames. One of these had a spindle that was plainly meant for the disc, and a hand-crank to turn it; the other featured a small dial and a needle like that of a compass, mounted on a pivot and surrounded by a tightly-wound copper coil. "In any case," he said, "whatever I was after, electricity was my main problem from the start—can't do anything without electricity, can you? Had to produce it myself, since I couldn't afford any sort of voltaic battery, so I did what I could, stealing my betters' ideas. You mount the disc on the generator—so—and connect your galvanometer—that's what this thing is, measures the current, you see—and then you crank the, ah, crank, and there you are. Child's play—" he grinned shyly—"speaking as a child."

He gripped the hand-crank lightly, but did not turn it. "Mind you, it's really not very efficient, for what it does. You get

265

counterflow in certain areas, and there's a lot of energy wasted heating up the disc itself. But I've mounted a couple of magnets on the disc, as you see, and that does seem to settle things down a bit. I'm still tinkering with it—it's all hit or miss, really." He spread his arms in a mock-dramatic attitude. "All my own work, as those screever chaps who draw on the pavement say. And that's how *I* spent my Christmas hols."

Griffith's Oxford drawl cut across the younger man's enthusiasm like a shark's fin in a bathtub. "Perfectly charming, Angelos, utterly captivating, but people are producing electricity left and right everywhere you turn. Can't throw a brick these days, can you, without hitting someone's new toy, someone's *ee*-lectro-whatsit, though what it'll all come to in the end, I'm sure I can't say. What makes *your* toy—ah—unique, distinctive? If I may ask?"

For a moment, it seemed to Scheuch that Angelos might actually cry, not so much at Griffith's words as at his tone, which deliberately, precisely, and finally implied the insuperable distance between a Balliol College man (if not a graduate) and a Jewish medical student who would never quite lose his East End accent. Then Angelos said quietly, "Right. Quite right. Yes. I'll show you."

He reached into his coat pocket and removed a common stethoscope, of the sort that first-years at Christ's Hospital aspired earnestly toward and wore like a badge of honor after its awarding. "Really a perfect machine, when you think about it," he remarked, fondling it like a cherished pet. "I don't imagine anyone'll ever improve on old Cammann, I really don't. No moving parts—nothing to break down—and no sound made by the human body has the least chance of escaping it. Seemed to me that it might work just as well when it came to . . . voices."

"Voices." Scheuch looked around at the other two men. "There, *told* you I thought I heard voices."

"You have excellent hearing," Angelos said. "Better than mine. It took me some while before I began to make sense of what I thought might even be mice, rustling in the corners late at night. Then I considered whether or not it might be static electricity of some sort, given the nature of my experiments. Finally . . . well. Judge for yourselves."

He fitted the round end of the stethoscope into a clip on the generator frame, settling it carefully. "Had to fix this with soft solder, took me forever. I'm obviously not a dab hand at this type of thing . . . *there*, now the galvanometer . . . *and* off we go." He began, slowly and rhythmically, to turn the crank.

"You don't have to rotate it all that fast, that's the remarkable thing. You just have to keep it going steadily, evenly. It takes a bit of a while—maybe some sort of charge has to build up. Something *like* a charge. I don't really know. You'll see."

Griffith had been whistling thinly and idly as Angelos went on, toying with his watch and paying little attention to the demonstration. Scheuch and Vordran, however, were watching intently, with Vordran appearing especially rapt, as though he were staring at something beyond the rickety generator and its equally flimsy attachments. To Scheuch, the slow whir of the revolving disc became almost hypnotic, somewhat like the pulse of a sewing-machine treadle. The air in the room was close and warm, and he felt himself swaying forward on Angelos's old settee.

Vordran said, "What am I hearing?"

Even Griffith looked at him. Angelos said nothing, but only kept on rotating the copper disc. Vordran's voice rose, the terror in it making his accent markedly more pronounced. "What am I hearing? Who is that speaking? *Who is that speaking?*"

The galvanometer needle was jerking on the dial, and Scheuch saw a few small sparks spitting off the edge of the disc, but he heard no voice beyond Vordran's. It seemed to him that Angelos was turning the generator crank slightly faster than before, but the increased speed made no apparent difference to anyone but Vordran. He was out of the armchair, gaping fearfully in every direction. "Don't you hear? Does no one *hear?*" He took a step toward Angelos, raising his arms as though he meant to bring both clenched fists down on the generator. "You *must* be hearing!"

Angelos quickly stopped cranking the generator, holding up his hands with the palms out. "No one's here, it's all right, I promise you. No one's speaking, not now." He reached out to pat Vordran on the arm, a bit timorously. "Really, there's no one."

Vordran stood still, shaking his head heavily, like an exhausted animal. He said, "Not now. But there was. I heard. There *were* voices, more than one. None of you heard?"

Scheuch said, "No, nothing, I'm sorry," and could not have said why he had apologized. Vordran continued to stare at Angelos. "*You*—you yourself—you heard nothing?" Angelos did not respond.

To everyone's astonishment, it was Griffith who suddenly said, "I did." Vordran wheeled to look at him in disbelief, and Scheuch jumped to his feet without realizing that he had done so. Only Angelos's expression remained unchanged.

Griffith had the air of someone who had been shaken out of deep slumber, roughly and without warning. He said dazedly, "How did you do that?"

"What did you hear?" Angelos's voice was clear, and without any particular inflection, but it seemed to Scheuch at the time—though he was never sure afterward—that the medical student was smiling faintly. "Tell me exactly what you heard, Griffith."

The Oxford man was plainly struggling to retain control of the tone that mattered most to him. Putting the words one after another, like a blind man finding his way down a strange street, he said hoarsely, "There were two of them. I couldn't understand the woman . . . very faint, you know—rather think she was speaking French, some such." Vordran nodded. Griffith said, "But the man . . . the man was speaking English, no doubt of it." After a moment, he added, somewhat more himself, "His speech had a distinct Midlands accent."

The room was completely silent. All that could be heard was Vordran's breathing, slow as falling blood. Scheuch said finally, "Old chap, Angelos, I really think you ought to clarify things a bit. Elucidate—I believe that's the word. What the *devil* is going on here?"

Angelos sighed. "I don't know."

"Not good enough," Scheuch said, feeling himself flushing in embarrassment. "Really not."

"How are you making those voices?" Vordran demanded. "Where are they coming from?"

"I don't *know*, God's my witness!" Angelos raised his voice for the first time. "I'd tell you if I knew!" He was alternately twisting his fingers together and hugging himself. "I don't bloody *know*!"

Griffith said, surprisingly calmly, "You must have some notion, surely. Are they coming through your electro-thing? Those— what do you call them?—ah, *wave* things?"

Angelos opened his mouth and then shut it again. He stood silent, regarding the three of them with the air, not so much of an animal brought to bay, but that of a lost child in darkening woods. He said, "I think I can bring them in a trifle louder."

Vordran said, "No," but Angelos was already beside the generator, turning the hand-crank notably harder than he had done previously. He used both hands at first; then, as the copper disc picked up speed, he freed his left hand to lift the stethoscope and held the end out toward Scheuch, who took hold of it gingerly. Angelos gestured to him to fit the little rubber earpieces to his head.

At first Scheuch heard nothing beyond the hiss of the disc and an occasional tiny sputter of fluctuating electricity. Then, very slowly, a word, two words, at a time . . . a woman. This one, unlike the woman Griffith had heard, was plainly speaking in English, but Scheuch could make nothing coherent of what she was saying. ". . . Carrots . . . the minister . . . Martin . . . coal chute . . . Martin . . ." Her voice dissolved into crackle and buzz, and Scheuch looked up to meet Angelos's inquiring gaze with his own wide eyes. He said, "I heard. Not quite sure what, but yes, I did hear . . ." In spite of himself, he let his voice trail away.

"Give it to me," Vordran said. All but snatching the stethoscope from Scheuch's hands, he clamped the earpieces on his head, which, being larger than Scheuch's, required angry, hurried readjustment. Angelos kept the generator turning steadily—the galvanometer needle hardly stirred from its near-center point—and Vordran listened with his jaw sagging and his eyes utterly unfocused. Abruptly he tore the stethoscope from his head and hurled it back at Angelos, shouting, "It is a trick, it has to be! This has nothing to do with your electricity, not a thing!" Yet the sound of his words was not so much angry, Scheuch thought, as somehow bereft.

Angelos stopped the generator for a second time. He said softly, "I wish it were a trick. Oh, you don't know how much I wish it were." The three others stared at him. Angelos said, "What did you hear?"

Vordran shook his head. "Not important. What is important

is how you made me hear it. The rest of this—" he waved a dismissive, if slightly trembling hand—"is nonsense. Tricks, like those American spiritualists. Table-rapping. *Fraudulent*, my good sir!" But his eyes were, astonishingly, bright with tears.

Angelos was a long time responding; or at least it seemed so to Scheuch. When he finally spoke, his rigidly calm voice twanged in a way that Scheuch could not recall ever hearing from him. He said, "Whatever it is, Vordran, it's not fraudulent. I think I wish it were."

He glanced around the room at them all, his eyes squirrel-quick, squirrel-anxious, never quite meeting anyone else's eyes fully. "You're right about one thing. I did start out rather larking about with wireless telegraphy, just out of curiosity, wanting to see if an ordinary chap like me could do it. It's been pretty well established since the Maxwell equations that electromagnetism travels in waves, and I started by seeing whether I could tap into those waves some way and use them to conduct voices, actual human voices, you know. No experience, no training, no proper equipment—and, of course, no laboratory assistants, except for good old Scheuch there." He patted Scheuch's arm, adding, "Eternally obliged, old man."

"Don't mention it," Scheuch mumbled. "Glad to be of service." Then, louder, "But if you aren't making them, those voices—"

"Tricks," Vordran said again, louder than before.

"—and if they aren't here, some way, in your rooms—"

"They aren't—" Angelos started to reply, but he caught himself noticeably, and Scheuch pressed on.

"Then, as Griffith just asked, are they speaking through your generator, through your stethoscope, or . . . or *what*? Whose voices *are* they? Where are they coming from? And stop saying you don't know—you must have *some* notion!" He turned to

Vordran on his right, then to Griffith. "I think I speak for all of us when I say we're not leaving until you tell us a bit more."

Vordran nodded. Griffith said grimly, "Quite a bit more." He coughed, longer than he needed to, and then asked, "What about—ah—ghosts? We had a ghost up at Balliol. Old scout, don't you know—spent his whole life cleaning after students, didn't have anywhere else to go after he died. Quite true. Saw him myself."

Angelos did not answer. He began disassembling the generator and its attachments, putting the copper disc carefully back in its linen pocket, folding the stethoscope away. Scheuch put a hand on his wrist. "That can wait, don't you think, Angelos? Talk to us."

Angelos clasped his hands together behind his back, rocking slightly from foot to foot as he spoke. "All I can tell you with any degree of certainty is that they are real voices of real persons. That I do believe, however absurd it may seem to anyone else. I also suspect—I'm not sure of this, mind you—that they are somehow being carried to us on electromagnetic radio waves, as Maxwell calls them." He wet his dry lips, took a long, slow breath. "But what I have also come to believe—" a very small chuckle, nearly inaudible—"which might very well get me stuck away in Northampton, is that *all* voices, every word ever spoken or sung or shouted, everything screamed or whispered . . . it's all still here, all around us, whether we can hear it or not. The ghosts of voices, if you like, Griffith. The radio waves pick them up—they attach themselves in some way I don't understand. I can't say what the range is, or how far back in time the voices go—"

"Oh, by all means, go all the way with it," Griffith jeered. "Do let us know when you listen in on Adam and Eve."

Angelos shrugged. "You've heard what you've heard. Myself,

I've caught medieval church Latin, I'd swear to that, and a few bits and scraps of English that didn't sound as though they'd been spoken in this century—or the last one, either. I've heard a woman who seemed to be scolding a child, and a man crying and cursing some faithless friend as though his heart would break. German, that last." He rubbed the back of his bent neck, wincing wearily. "There's no pattern to it, there doesn't seem to be any predominance of language or nationality—it's a wilderness of voices, that's all I can tell you. If any of you can explain it to me any better, I should certainly appreciate it."

The room was silent. Angelos began to gather up the teacups and uneaten biscuits. Griffith left without speaking. Scheuch said, "Well, then, cheery-bye," and followed him out. Vordran, however, stood in the doorway for a long moment before he turned and said, "This is a bad idea, Angelos."

Angelos blinked in apparent puzzlement. "Idea? It's not an *idea* at all, Vordran, it's barely an experiment. I'm only listening, as best I can—listening to people talking as I might overhear them in the street, at the next table in a restaurant. Eavesdropping, if you like. Nothing more structured or scientific than that."

"Eavesdropping," Vordran repeated. "Yes. And you do remember what they say about eavesdroppers, Angelos?"

Angelos's long sigh was dramatically elaborate. "Why, no, Vordran, I *don't* remember what they say about eavesdroppers. Do enlighten me."

"That sooner or later they hear something they don't like at all. Sooner or later." Vordran was gone.

Ramadan came early that year, the moon giving its blessing on the eleventh of August. For all the country's postwar fascination with everything Turkish, the month-long holiday had not yet made its way onto the calendar of the United Kingdom; but

Griffith groused daily about the fact that Simpson's-in-the-Strand, fabled home of good English roast beef and saddle of mutton, always carved at your table, was now offering kebabs and hummus, along with *kofte, doner, kokorec, borek,* and *gozleme.* "Not to mention their bloody sweets—rot your teeth just *looking* at them. I promise you, I'd quit the damnation job in two shakes, if there were something else going fit for a white man." But Mr. Emanetoglu, coming for the month's rent, also brought delicacies from his family's celebration, and at least three of his four roomers consumed all their share, without ever learning the dishes' names.

When he climbed, panting slightly, to Angelos's top-floor rooms, he shook his head in wonder, as he always did, saying, "My goodness, how do you ever find what things you need?" And Angelos, as always, made his usual joking response. "Oh, I never do, Mr. E. Instead, I find wonderful things I didn't know I needed. Remarkable, the way that happens."

"Well and good," Mr. Emanetoglu customarily replied, "so long as you can pretend you are not looking for the rent, so that you can find it for me." And they laughed together, loudly enough to annoy Vordran, who lived on the floor below.

But on this occasion, Mr. Emanetoglu felt himself curiously oppressed by the air of Angelos's rooms. Or perhaps neither *oppressed* nor *air* was the correct word: the effect on him, rather, was of being somehow overcrowded, pushed in upon, whether by clutter, which had never particularly disturbed him before, or by Angelos's obvious distraction and poorly concealed disquiet. He was not even offered a cup of tea, a drink which Mr. Emanetoglu was determined to like, however long it took him. He asked hesitantly, "Is all well with you, Mr. Angelos? You are not perhaps troubled in some way?"

Angelos, fishing hastily in his purse for the monthly payment, reassured him that all could not be better, calling him "old man" in the process, not once but twice. Mr. Emanetoglu pondered this development as he pattered down the stair. *Old man . . .* there was an expression that meant something to the English: an admission to a certain closeness, if any dark-skinned foreigner could ever be said to be close to an Englishman. Mr. Emanetoglu knew himself to be a naïve soul, quite often feeling out of place in this bewildering country, but he was not a fool.

"I know how many of them see every Turk as that dog Griffith does," he said that night at dinner in Haringey, where he lived with his elder brother Ismail, his sister-in-law Ceylan, and their three young sons. "I hear them on the street when they think I do not understand—I know very well what they say, how bitter and spiteful they still are about the War, how many of them would wish us all drowned in the Strait of Marmora, if they did not more and more need our money. But there are some, like Mr. Angelos . . ." He sighed, his smile more than half mocking his own words. "I don't know—what should I say? *Old man . . .* I am sure that is more significant than being invited to tea."

"I am ready to believe anything of the English," Ismail said flatly. "They are a mad people, and completely untrustworthy. If they were otherwise, there would not have been a war. It may be *old man* to your face, but it will be *nigger* behind your back. I would put no stock in their words, not ever."

"Perhaps not." Mr. Emanetoglu sighed again. "Perhaps."

But he said nothing of what he had almost felt, almost sensed, in Angelos's rooms, partly because he could find no words in Turkish or English to describe his impression, partly because he knew that his brother regarded him—quite kindly—as a well-intentioned blunderer at the best of times. All the same, hurrying

275

to one or another of Ismail's properties, he often found himself going out of his way to pass the tall old house in Russell Square, often lingering in the street for no purpose that he could have explained either to Ismail or to Angelos—or, for that matter, to the helmeted policemen who came along more than once to stare and sniff and harry him elsewhere.

He did talk about it, a little, to his youngest nephew, Ekrem, who was five years old, because he talked to Ekrem a good deal, as he had done almost since the boy's birth. Being a practical child for his age, Ekrem asked him, "Why don't you ask the *hodja?*" meaning the venerable healer who lived two streets over from the Emanetoglus' home. The *hodja* always kept sweets for children in the pouches at his waist, and Ekrem had great faith in him.

"What could I ask him?" Mr. Emanetoglu demanded. "What could I tell him? That I think something is wrong in that house, when I don't even know whether that really is what I think? The *hodja* would laugh at me, as he should."

"Well, he would give you candy, anyway," Ekrem insisted stubbornly. "The *hodja* is nice."

Angelos was becoming increasingly withdrawn, seeing less and less of his housemates, who, by and large, appeared plainly relieved to have a polite excuse to avoid him. Griffith, of all people, occasionally came seeking him at Christ's, stepping as haughtily as a cat between hurrying lecturers, prankish students, and charity patients moaning in their own filth, waiting to be seen. Inconvenienced and irritated, Angelos would nevertheless give him a brief account of his latest experiments, and Griffith would stalk away again, apparently unwilling to be seen by social equals asking for information. Griffith was a notably catlike person in a number of ways.

Dispensing early with the stethoscope, Angelos had managed

to set granules of common charcoal between two metal plates to create what he called "a carbon button," serving as an improvised amplifier when connected to his hand-cranked generator. The fragmented whispers, mumbles, and cries came crowding in, the vast majority of them in languages that Angelos could barely distinguish from each other, let alone translate, or even guess at. The rare English voices were hardly any easier to understand: very few came in university accents, but rather from all points and ancestors of the Empire. On the occasions when he actually sought Angelos out in his rooms, Griffith himself sometimes became as intrigued by a recognizable Lancashire or Cornish inflection as though he were coming home at last to Balliol. To Angelos, he commented, "D'you know, even the Wog—old Glue Pot—even he's starting to sound human after a bit of this gabble. Remarkable, rather."

Only Scheuch continued to spend any considerable time in Angelos's rooms, frequently—as Angelos was forced to admit—to the project's benefit. He proved to have the most discerning hearing of all four men, often catching phrases completely opaque to Angelos himself, and learning to react to tones rather than guessing at literal meaning. Crouching as close to the "carbon button" as he could, he would mutter, "Couldn't make out a bloody word, but there's a sweet voice she's got . . ." and, later, "What're *they* all on about, then? Sounds like my mum's whole family on Christmas morning . . . That chap's an idiot. You don't have to understand an idiot to know he's an idiot . . . Oh, *that* poor bugger's in trouble—that one's in awful trouble, poor soul—you can hear it. I wish . . ."

He always made his comments in the present tense, without exception. When Angelos pointed out to him that if his theory was correct, the chances were that almost every voice he was hearing—if not, indeed, every single one—was of someone long dead, Scheuch answered simply, "I know that, old fellow. But I *can't* know that, if you follow me. Just can't, that's all." Angelos never raised the matter again.

Vordran did come once, quite late at night, to ask directly when Angelos opened the door, "Do you ever hear the same voice twice? Do you ever recognize a voice you might have heard before?"

Angelos frowned. "What could the odds be? It would be like recognizing the same fish in a school that swam past you—lord, even an hour ago. Vordran, it's as I told you, we could be sweeping up the remains of every word that's ever been uttered—perhaps only in England, only in London, perhaps only within a few square miles of this house. And even so . . ."

"And even so . . ." Vordran nodded. "I understand. London is very old. I was only wondering." He stood looking down at Angelos for a moment. "I am impressed, Angelos. You have taught yourself a great deal in a short time." He paused, frowning. "Do you find the voices louder than they were?"

"Louder?" Angelos shook his head. "I don't think so. A bit more intelligible, yes—that's the carbon button—but louder? I only wish they were."

"Perhaps you do not. Remember what I told you about eavesdroppers." Vordran paused, seemingly waiting for an answer, or a further question. He got neither and left.

Yet as spring aged into a patchy, dusty London summer, one at least, of all the numberless voices, was indeed growing clearer in Angelos's rooms, and steadily more familiar as well, if no louder. It was a woman's voice, though low enough in timbre that Angelos at first took it for the sobs of a man in soul-strangling anguish. He could never determine its language or nationality, no matter how carefully he listened, nor how piercingly pleading the voice became. Never swelling in volume, it did not pass on like the others, but only continued to wail in soft desperation: a cry like wind over stone at first, though later it took on the sound of a torture victim long beyond screaming for mercy, broken and barely whining with each turn of the rack. At other times, it— *she*—sounded as though she were making love with a demon, which terrified Angelos and made him squeeze his eyes shut until they hurt. There were words in it then, but none he knew.

No one heard it beyond his rooms, at first. There were times when he was certain that the little homemade amplifier could not possibly contain the terrible crying; that it existed only in his riven head. He shut down the generator altogether, sometimes for days, but the voice continued whimpering in the walls of his rooms when he tried forlornly to sleep, and followed him pitilessly when he dragged himself to lectures at Christ's Hospital. It came to grieve, finally, through his entire life, and he wept nightly for the horror it witnessed at the same time that he cursed it and prayed for it to leave him alone. He grew to believe beyond question that he was going mad, and had a lawyer draw up papers to make certain that he was to be delivered to Bensham Asylum, and not to Devon Pauper. He made copies for each of his housemates and slipped them under their doors.

When they in their turn at last began, one at a time, to hear the lone voice in its own context—whether or not Angelos had the generator running—each reacted as differently as might have been expected. Griffith denied fiercely that anything unusual was happening at all, while Vordran admitted to the voice, but blamed Angelos's foolhardy experiments for waking some ghost or spirit long resident in the old rooming house. Only Scheuch considered the situation more or less as it was: the four of them bound, whether as victims, prey, or helpless bystanders, to the endless imploring sorrow of a single human being from another time and—in all likelihood—another country. No less frightened than the others, he determined consciously to drown himself in the voice, to listen to it to the point of numb boredom, inoculating himself against its eternal misery. The technique had proven remarkably effective against the mean arrogance of his bank's manager; he saw no reason why it should not aid him in this situation. Scheuch was not a highly imaginative man, but he paid attention to what worked.

With his keen hearing, he was the one who first noticed that the voice was beginning to be audible in Russell Square. He thought at first that he might be imagining it; but when Vordran commented on it, and Angelos's increased pallor and sleeplessness gave silent assent, Scheuch conducted his own research, carefully pacing out the exact range of the voice—which increased, block by block, every week or thereabouts—and also making note of the local residents' awareness of the sound, or lack of it. Some seemed as yet unaffected, but many were beginning to look as though, like himself, they had taken to spending their nights with their heads buried under several pillows. Scheuch found it cheaper than gin and laudanum, though no more effective.

It was at this point, on the fifteenth of August—a Saturday morning—that Mr. Emanetoglu came to collect the rent.

The small, dark man turned, as always, at the northeast corner of the square, passed the Cabmen's Shelter, walked another block—and then abruptly froze where he stood, raising his head and cocking it sideways, like an attentive bird, or a hound on point. After a moment, he began to run, which was not something Mr. Emanetoglu did at all often, and children laughed at his clumsy gait as they scattered out of his way. Reaching the house on Geraldine Row, he first knocked, then rang, as was his invariable custom, no matter his current urgency. When no one responded, he waited no longer, but let himself in, thrusting the door open so violently that it rebounded from the wall and banged shut behind him. He took the long stair two steps at a time, like a young man hastening to his beloved. He was talking loudly to himself in Turkish, and his normally serene brown eyes were wide and wild.

Griffith's room being just off the first-floor landing, it was the one that Mr. Emanetoglu burst into without announcing himself, demanding as the door slammed open, "What have you done? What has *happened* here?"

Griffith was not asleep. Griffith did not appear to have ever been asleep. He was sitting on the edge of the bed, with his head in his hands, and he did not immediately look up at Mr. Emanetoglu's furious question. He muttered at last, "Ah, hello there, old Glue Pot—pull up a chair." He raised his head, blinking. "Is it that time already? Half a second, then—"

"Never mind the rental fee!" Mr. Emanetoglu shouted at him. "What have you *done*, you foolish man?" He actually took Griffith by both slumped shoulders, as though to shake him into sense, and then released him and stepped back, making every effort to calm himself.

"Who did this?" he asked. "If it was not you, who then? Answer me!" He realized that he was sweating through his good linen suit, which he always wore on rent-collecting day. "Who is this who is responsible? Which man?" He was vain of his proficiency in English, but knew that when he was hurried or upset, the impossible grammar tended to set gleeful traps for him. "Who? Which?"

Griffith shrugged. "Angelos . . . yes, why not Angelos? Bloody

Jew, you know, Angelos . . ." His head lolled forward. Mr. Emanetoglu pushed him back on his bed and went up the stair at a run.

Angelos met him at the top, waiting with his arms folded resignedly across his chest. He looked very nearly skeletal, and even nearer to complete collapse than Griffith, but he held himself with a stubborn, painful dignity. He said, "Mr. Emanetoglu, I'm going to have to ask you for one or two days' grace on the rent. No more than two, I assure you."

"Never mind the bloody rent!" Mr. Emanetoglu would go to his grave—he was certain of it—never truly comprehending the significance and usage of that single English word, but he employed it at every sensed opportunity, hoping that if it should fit into the conversation, so perhaps would he. "What has occurred here, Mr. Angelos? Tell me precisely what you and your friends—" for Scheuch and Vordran had come trudging up the stair behind him—"have done to my brother's nice house?" He was outraged to realize that he was close to weeping.

Angelos's voice was wearily conciliatory, without being at all defensive. "Mr. Emanetoglu, this is my fault entirely. I have been experimenting at random to learn whether it might be possible for people, say, in Turkey to speak directly to people here in England—and instead, I began to hear voices right in my rooms—"

"Voices of spirits who haunt my brother's house?" Mr. Emanetoglu broke in furiously. "No, it is you four, you yourselves, who are haunted—whatever ghosts or demons may be in this house, you surely brought them with you! I could feel it, hear it, *smell* it on the street outside!" He checked himself, turning— as he never failed to do in such crises—to the calming words of his personal guru, the great Sufi Muhammad al-Ghazali, who never failed to comfort him by reminding him that it was wisdom always to consider and to doubt. *"Doubt is the scholar's dear friend, and self-doubt the dearest . . ."* Therefore, taking several deep breaths before he spoke again, he said quietly, "It is an old house, this, and I know from my own experience that some old houses can in some way retain the . . . the shadows of those who once lived there. Is that what happened, Mr. Angelos? Did you and your . . . *experiments* awaken Ismail's house?"

Angelos shook his head, which seemed to take an enormous effort from him. "That is not what happened, Mr. Emanetoglu. I dismantled my generator more than two weeks ago—" a crooked half smile at the silent surprise of the others—"without informing these gentlemen, since it was my decision alone to make. Yet we all still keep hearing the voices of people who cannot have lived here, people who can have had nothing to do with this house, this time—perhaps even with London itself. I cannot tell you anything more useful than that. I would if I could. I can only beg your forgiveness, and say that we will do all we can to make things right again."

Mr. Emanetoglu looked slowly around at Scheuch and Vordran, seeing Griffith crossing the landing to join them. Each was obviously as fatigued as Angelos, exhausted down to his bones, and to the soul beyond. He said, "You are all hearing the . . . these voices, then?"

Griffith and Vordran nodded without answering. Scheuch said, "Mine, last night . . . mine was a child, I could tell that much. I think it was being killed. It went on and on." He began to cry, weakly, without making a sound.

Angelos looked at Mr. Emanetoglu, but did not speak. Mr. Emanetoglu said heavily, "I see. Yes, I do see. And I do not know what to do about all this, no more than you do." He paused, lowering his head almost to his chest, and then raising it again. He said, "I will not be collecting the rent today. Tomorrow, at two o'clock—will that suit all present?"

Everyone nodded without replying. Mr. Emanetoglu said, as brightly as he could, "Well, then—ta, all?" He could never keep the slang phrase—so jauntily British, so important—from coming out slightly questioning, but he did his best. Then all four men said, as he could not remember them ever saying to him together, "Ta, Mr. Emanetoglu."

He went on home then, to the little courtyard in Haringey, greeted Ceylan—Ismail being in the neighborhood coffee shop with his best friends, as was his custom on Saturday—and waited for Ekrem to come home from playing football in the street with older boys, who always trampled him, but never made him cry. When he could, Mr. Emanetoglu helped Ekrem clean off the worst of the game before his mother noticed the blood and the bruises. Mr. Emanetoglu worried sometimes about the fact that he considered his five-year-old nephew his own best friend; but then he would remind himself that in only a few years the boy would have no time for him. Which would undoubtedly be as it should—Mr. Emanetoglu knew that.

When Ekrem did arrive, Mr. Emanetoglu took him aside as soon as Ceylan had scolded and released him and asked him earnestly, "Nephew, would you say that the *hodja* would know how to deal with ghosts? Think carefully before you answer."

Superfluous advice: Ekrem always thought things through with great precision. He replied, "How many ghosts, Uncle?"

Mr. Emanetoglu had no idea, and said so. "Maybe a lot— maybe only one. I suppose we had better assume there would be a good many."

Ekrem shook his head decidedly. "Then no. Not for a lot of

ghosts, not the *hodja*. I am sorry." He read the disappointment in his uncle's face and brightened suddenly. "But the *hodja* has a *hodja* himself, did you know that? I think the old *hodja* would know all about ghosts."

"The *hodja's hodja*?" Mr. Emanetoglu felt as though he had not laughed in years. Ekrem himself laughed delightedly at his amusement, very proud of himself for causing it. Mr. Emanetoglu said, "Tell me, boy, where does the old *hodja* live, then?"

"I will take you there right away." Ekrem scratched his head solemnly. "You know, Uncle, maybe it would be a good idea for you to bring them both to see the ghosts. Two *hodjas* . . . they could surely fight all the ghosts in London, couldn't they?" He spread his arms as wide as he could. "All the ghosts in *England!*"

"I will be happy if they can help me get rid of all the spirits in your father's house. One or a thousand, however many there may be." Mr. Emanetoglu patted his nephew's shoulder. "Thank you, Ekrem. I knew you would find a way."

So it came about that Mr. Emanetoglu, dressed, not in English clothing, but in his finest summer *mintan* and *salvar* trousers, was standing on the doorstep of the Geraldine Row house at two o'clock the next afternoon. Behind him, folded hands hidden in the sleeves of their long robes, stood two bearded old men, one notably older and taller than the other. The second man, on the other hand, was notably plumper, and still had a scattering of black in his chest-long gray beard, while the first man's beard was closer trimmed, and as white as his hair. Both *hodjas* had an air of scholarly command about them, but each wore it lightly, as though they had no reason to parade overweening knowledge or virtue. They were looking, not at the front door, nor at Mr. Emanetoglu, but at each other, their hands already weaving empty cat's cradles in the air, as though they were trying to capture the soft, wild grieving that all three men had heard all the way up the street. Mr. Emanetoglu wanted badly to cover his ears with his own hands, but in the presence of the *hodjas* he dared not.

The old men bowed to Griffith, who opened the door at Mr. Emanetoglu's knock, without speaking. Mr. Emanetoglu said politely, "God save the Queen and Princess Maude. I am honored to present *Hodja* Abbas—" indicating the older man— "and *Hodja* Cenghiz." He added something poetically insulting in Turkish and walked calmly past Griffith, followed by the two old men.

Angelos was coming down the stair to greet him, followed by his two other housemates, each looking that much more worn than the day before. Mr. Emanetoglu introduced the *hodjas* to them all.

Angelos bowed himself, as only Scheuch beside him did, saying, "I am most pleased to meet you both," and, to Mr. Emanetoglu, "Do they speak any English?"

Mr. Emanetoglu replied, "They understand quite well, but speak poorly. I shall translate as necessary." He watched the old men moving in the vestibule, heard them whispering to each other, saw them raising their heads, just as he had done—only a day ago?—flaring their nostrils to sample the lightning taste of the air. *Hodja* Abbas turned to look straight at him, and Mr. Emanetoglu felt himself cringe inside, like a schoolboy who knows an answer is wrong even as he gives it. *Little Ekrem would never feel like that, but I do. What is the good of being grown?*

Hodja Abbas spoke in Turkish, and Angelos looked questioningly at Mr. Emanetoglu. "Was he speaking to me?"

Mr. Emanetoglu nodded. "He wishes to know whether you have had any training in the philosophy of magic. Magic of any sort—even English." He could not keep from smiling at the expression on Angelos's face—nor on the ancient shaman's stern countenance either. "I am of the opinion that *Hodja* Abbas does not think very much of English magic."

Angelos almost laughed, but looked over at the tall old Turk and muffled the sound into something like a sneeze. "Tell him *no*—tell him I've no training at all, except in medicine, and not much of that. We English haven't studied magic since Merlin, tell him. We believe in machinery, just like the Germans. Tell him that."

Mr. Emanetoglu translated, plainly with a certain trepidation. *Hodja* Abbas's lean face lost all color; even his dark eyes seemed to pale. He began to speak very fast, his normally deep voice rising in pitch until the words clattered and rang against each other like swords. Mr. Emanetoglu had trouble keeping up with the right English words, but he did his best.

"He says that you are a magician born . . . and the biggest fool he has ever met. He says that he would kill you here and now and bury you under a lime tree, to protect the world from your—forgive me, Mr. Angelos—from your stupidity—" Angelos was not the only one who had noticed the curved dagger in the old man's belt—"if it were not that since he went to Mecca, he has sworn never again to take a life."

"Decent of the old boy," Griffith snickered wearily "Bet he's left a few flourishing lime trees behind him in his time. Along with assorted wives and *babas*." But the words lacked his usual scornful snap, and he sank down on the stair, leaning his head against the balustrade.

Hodja Abbas appeared to have finished his tirade, but then he burst out again in a further spittle-embroidered rant, which Mr. Emanetoglu did not bother to pretend he was not censoring as he went along. "He says he wants to see your rooms, the place where you do your . . . stupid work. He thinks he knows what you have . . . ah, where you have gone wrong, and there is a chance that he and *Hodja* Cenghiz may be able to help. But he must see where you . . . did it." He looked wretchedly apologetic when he finished, saying, "I am sorry, Mr. Angelos. He is a very old man."

Angelos laughed outright, but it took the remaining strength in his body, and he actually lurched against Mr. Emanetoglu. He said, "Old and tactless he may well be—and downright vulgar, that too—but of course he's absolutely right. But I do wish he'd tell me exactly what it is I'm supposed to have done, so I can apologize for it. Please ask him that, when he calms down a bit."

Mr. Emanetoglu did ask, but *Hodja* Abbas refused to comment further outside of Angelos's rooms. So they climbed the long stair, Englishmen and Turkish sages crowded together, and *Hodja* Abbas strode in the lead. *Hodja* Cenghiz, who had not yet said a word during the entire visit, and who clearly had bellows to mend, toiled in the rear, breathing hard and distinctly wheezing. Scheuch fell back beside him, impulsively offering the small old man his arm. But *Hodja* Cenghiz smiled, showing a full set of brown teeth, and said gently, "I thank you, no. It is good for fat old men to sweat in the middle of children. I shall survive."

"I didn't know you spoke English." Scheuch was frantically going back over his behavior toward both old Turks. "I'm sure I would have—I don't know—paid more attention, if I'd known."

"Yes," said *Hodja* Cenghiz. "I am sure you would have."

The stairway funneled the monstrously suffering voice—as Scheuch had long since come to think of it—making it sound louder than he knew it was. He said as much to *Hodja* Cenghiz, who responded simply, "It is loud enough." Pausing momentarily on the stair to catch his breath, he added, "Loud enough to shake the sun loose in the sky. I sometimes wonder why this has never happened." Scheuch did not know how to respond.

At the top floor, prowling in Angelos's rooms, *Hodja* Abbas moved impatiently from instrument to instrument, device to homemade device, muttering to himself as a curious counterpoint to the haunting, horrible wailing that rose and fell and rose, and never went away. Mr. Emanetoglu, embarrassed but determined, stayed on his heels, translating a jeweled chaplet of Turkish obscenities as *Hodja* Abbas cursed several generations of Angelos's ancestors backward and forward for bringing such an imbecile to birth. Angelos himself, not knowing the language, and being more exhausted than even he recognized, only smiled feebly and made sounds that he was certain were words. It was Mr. Emanetoglu who finally plucked up enough courage to demand of the *hodja*, "What has he done, after all? What crime have his experiments committed?"

The two old men looked at each other for a long moment before *Hodja* Abbas spoke again—this time, surprisingly in hoarse, limited, but comprehensible English. "Sorrow . . . Heart of Sorrow . . . he have prowoke—awake—no . . ." He shook his head irritably, groping for the right word. "*Touch.* He have *touch* in deep, deep place, world place. The Sorrowheart. We call." He turned toward *Hodja* Cenghiz for confirmation.

Griffith, having seated himself in the one armchair when Angelos opened his rooms, had promptly fallen asleep, mouth open and his hands futilely covering both ears, since the voice was always more pervasive here, though no stronger. *Hodja* Cenghiz said, "What you are hearing—what Mr. Angelos has reached, roused, by accident—is the grief at the center, the heart of the world. It is just as old as human beings, to the minute, and it is always a woman's voice. We Turks call it *Sorrowheart*—other

times, other languages, some other name. But always a woman."
He bowed to Angelos, slightly but unmistakably. "How Mr.
Angelos reached it, touched it with his little electrical researches,
I have no idea—only a very few of our poets have ever done that
before. Most of them went mad." He sighed and shrugged. "I
sincerely congratulate you, Mr. Angelos."

In the silence, Scheuch's sharp ears heard Angelos's laughter
begin, impossibly deep in his belly, well before it ever billowed
into daylight. It was not loud laughter, nor did it last very long;
but it woke Griffith, and caused even *Hodja* Abbas to take a
step backward and regard him with the same anxiety—though
less of it—as Mr. Emanetoglu. Angelos said at last, "So. Let me
understand. We here, we will all continue to hear these voices?"
The two *hodjas* looked at each other, and then back to him,
without answering. Angelos asked, "Forever?"

Vordran echoed him. "Forever? For the rest of our lives?"

Hodja Cenghiz answered him slowly, "Not all the voices. Only
the one. And not all of you: only for him." Angelos stared back
at him, not laughing now, his tired eyes as blank as walls. *Hodja*
Cenghiz said, "The other voices, they are a different matter—
whoever they were, they will pass on ahead, causing no trouble,
only showing us the way we will go in our turn. *Hodja* Abbas can
make certain that no one living in this house, now or in future,
will any longer hear or listen to them. That we can promise in
good faith." Angelos nodded.

Scheuch looked away from both Angelos and the *hodjas*,
wrapping his arms around his own shoulders. Griffith started to
speak, and then stopped. Mr. Emanetoglu could not take his eyes
from Angelos. To his own considerable surprise, his heart hurt
for the Englishman in that moment, as it would have hurt for
Ekrem. *Hodja* Cenghiz continued, "But *that* voice—the voice of

the Sorrowheart—that voice your friend will never stop hearing. It is not just, for he surely meant no harm. But Allah's justice is not ours." *Hodja* Cenghiz cleared his throat. "For what it is worth, which is nothing, I am sad for you, Mr. Angelos."

Griffith was already dozing off again, and Vordran's eyes had turned as unfocused as when he first listened to Angelos's stethoscope. Scheuch seemed to be the only person reacting to the reality of what Angelos had just been told. He said loudly, "I say, you can't do that! Set that voice trailing him everywhere— haunting him forever! Who do you chaps think you are, anyway?"

Neither *Hodja* Abbas nor *Hodja* Cenghiz even bothered to look at him, so Mr. Emanetoglu plucked up his courage and intervened, saying sternly and earnestly, "Mr. Scheuch, these gentlemen are scholars, healers—even what you would call magistrates, when necessary. Surely you must be at peace with their judgment."

"No, I mustn't be at bloody peace with a damned thing," Scheuch mocked him. "And you're a bloody hypocrite for saying so, Emanetoggle." He had never gotten closer than that to the proper pronunciation. "You heard him say it—it's not *right*, and you all buggering know it! Like Job in the bloody Bible, and I never understood that story either, if you want to know. How you can stand there and say *be at peace.* . . ?"

He was very tired, and he ran out of words and rage at more or less the same time. Mr. Emanetoglu, looking on, heartsick, saw Vordran puzzled and irritated, and Griffith not entirely among those present. Angelos, of them all, remained as strangely calm as though he were opening a letter that promised to be interesting. He said, "Well. Don't exactly see myself staying on in Geraldine Row, I suppose."

Hodja Cenghiz coughed and cleared his throat. "Mr.

Angelos, I am afraid that you cannot really stay anywhere, not for long. The Sorrowheart, the deepest pain of the world, has chosen to speak to you, and wherever you go, it will follow— wherever you rest, those near you will hear its voice and feel its grief. It will spread like a marsh under a poorly drained road, growing steadily deeper and wider, and sucking everything— everything—down into it on every side." His own voice was very nearly imploring. "Do you understand, Mr. Angelos? Please, do you understand me now?"

"I understand you." Angelos rocked on his heels and ran a hand through his hair. *Such ordinary gestures,* Mr. Emanetoglu marveled dazedly, *for someone who has just had his life shattered, undeservedly. Could I behave so, I wonder?* Angelos said, "Well, if you will excuse me, I'll need, as the phrase has it, to get my affairs in order. I can be gone by tomorrow night." Mr. Emanetoglu saw nothing but affable flatness in his expression.

The *hodjas* consulted, the elder stooping like a hawk to mutter in the younger man's ear. *Hodja* Cenghiz said, "*Hodja* Abbas will speak to the other voices in the house and tell them to be silent. It will take some little while."

"By all means. Fumigate the baseboards to your hearts' content." Angelos bowed formally to the two old men. "I will be at Christ's, seeing whether I can possibly pry some of my fees out of their grasp, since I will clearly not be attending classes this term." He turned to Mr. Emanetoglu, holding out an envelope. "My usual payment."

Mr. Emanetoglu accepted it, shaking his head miserably. "It will be too much by half. You will not have been here the whole month." Their eyes met, and Mr. Emanetoglu whispered, "I am sorry—I am so sorry. I should never have brought them here."

Angelos patted his arm. "You did the best thing for everyone, sir. Even, it may well be, for me. After all, I was never much of a medical student, and I have always wanted to travel. And there will certainly always be company—" he chuckled suddenly— "and voices may be answered, spoken to as well as heard. Imagine . . . *imagine*, if I should actually strike up a conversation with the sorrowing heart of the world." He touched Mr. Emanetoglu's arm a second time. "Perhaps that is what I'm supposed to do, old man. Who knows?"

Behind them, *Hodja* Abbas paced back and forth in what had been Angelos's rooms, talking to himself—as it seemed—in ponderous, rolling Turkish. *Hodja* Cenghiz followed him, step by step, writing down the words he recited on the strips of gilded paper they had brought with them from Haringey. Folding the strips according to a precise pattern, he then inserted them into various cracks in the floor and in the molding. Mr. Emanetoglu, watching, thought, *Nothing exists for us Turks unless it is written down. Even our magic has to be in writing.* He turned to say this over his shoulder, but Angelos had already left.

The night was cold and still when Angelos finally returned, well after the *hodjas* and Mr. Emanetoglu were gone, and Scheuch, Vordran, and Griffith long abed. The only voice he heard was the one he knew, the one that continued and continued: wordlessly, incomprehensibly, pounding itself through his skull like a blazing nail. He stood and listened for a long while, before he finally said aloud, "We will be friends, you and I. There's plenty of time for us to understand one another." He went to bed then and slept, if not well and deeply, at least without dreams.

Oddly, it was Griffith who was the most help in packing his belongings the next day. Scheuch, being as burly as a navvy, carried most of his bags and boxes to the hired wagon waiting in the street; but Griffith actually quarreled with him for the privilege. He appeared on the edge of telling Angelos the full story behind his failure to return to Oxford after the war, but they were interrupted by Vordran's farewell, which was awkwardly emotional and vaguely accusatory at the same time. Angelos never did learn the truth of Griffith's Balliol days, but he rather suspected that there had been a monkey involved.

Scheuch never said goodbye. He simply shook hands with Angelos, handed him the original envelope Angelos had given Mr. Emanetoglu the day before—it contained the same cheque, as well, and a short message from the Turk—growled, "I believe you know where I live," and walked away. Angelos got up beside the driver, said to someone the driver could not see, "If you don't care for the new digs, we won't be there long," and the cart rumbled away out of Russell Square

None of his former housemates ever saw Angelos again. Mr. Emanetoglu's brother Ismail quickly found a tenant to replace him, and he jogged along as well with the others as Angelos ever had. Scheuch eventually married and went to work in a Bristol branch of his London bank, while Vordran was eventually and unwillingly pensioned off from the Bishopsgate law firm where he was never a clerk. Griffith moved back to Oxford, went mad so genteelly that no one recognized it for quite some while, and ended his days in Bensham, as Angelos had feared for himself. Russell Square no longer played host to constant shadowy voices seeping down Geraldine Row—most especially not that *one* which had set children and their cowering parents running futilely indoors with their hands over their ears. There were, over time, legends of similar occurrences in Bayswater, Clerkenwell, and Holborn; but each of those faded with the passing months and years of the new century, as happened even with that awful business up in Durham, so there you are.

Olfert Dapper's Day

In the summer of 1962, my artist friend Phil Sigunick and I (we have known each other for more than seventy years now) shared a cabin on a hill in Cheshire, Massachusetts. Phil would be gone most of the day, painting in the woods, while I, after a couple of misfires, started a story about a unicorn who is—or thinks *she is—the last of her kind. One afternoon, out of curiosity, I hopped on my motorscooter and drove to the nearest library within easy reach, in Pittsfield. But all I could find there by way of research into the legend was a mention that one Dr. Olfert Dapper had seen a wild unicorn in the Maine woods in 1673. It wasn't presented as a rumor, but as a flat statement of fact; so I simply made it part of the dedication to* The Last Unicorn. *There having been no Internet available in 1962 (and Odell Shepard's classic work* The Lore of the Unicorn *being out of print at the time), it took me until just a few years ago to find out the historical truth about Dr. Dapper. He lived mostly in Utrecht, in Holland, in the mid-17th century, and he wrote learned, greatly detailed books about places he'd never been—such as Japan, India, Africa, and the New World. The books sold quite well; and, as far as I know, he never had to leave town in a hurry and take ship for a wretched little colony called "No Popery" to hide from his sins back in Utrecht.* But just suppose . . .

⁂

Dr. Olfert Dapper had never attended any medical school: neither in Amsterdam, where he was born, nor in Utrecht, where he had first begun employing the title *Doctor Medicinae* after two years of occasional attendance at the university. Nor, in candor, had he ever visited India, China, Persia, or Africa, about all of which lands he had nevertheless published voluminously detailed and well-received books. A placid, sedentary, somewhat portly man by nature, he had seen no reason to disturb a peaceful existence by crossing undependable oceans, conducting tedious expeditions, or otherwise placing the said existence at risk of discomfort or termination. Much better to write out of a fecund imagination, an even more bountiful fantasy life, and the rich sense of survival that had served him so well for nearly forty-five years. He was, take him for all in all, a pleasant soul who had always trusted in the trust of others, and who had, until quite recently, never found that faith misplaced.

Unfortunately, his confidence in the gullibility of country bumpkins from Eck en Wiel had lately been badly shaken when one bumpkin turned out to be related—who could have known?—to a seriously powerful member of the States-General capable of recognizing a very slightly fraudulent land contract when he saw one. On the whole, as a presumed man of medicine, Dr. Dapper recommended travel to himself: travel for reasons of health and longevity, travel to destinations which seemed a good deal less important than the swiftness of his departure. The beadle, summons under his arm, was knocking on Dr. Dapper's front door as that good entrepreneur slipped out the back way, his quickly packed valise firm in his grip.

But the beadle, a practiced hand in such matters, had thoughtfully stationed two large men halfway down the muddy alley that led from Olfert Dapper's rear door to the street. Both men carried heavy bludgeons, which twitched very slightly as they waited, like the tails of stalking cats. Dr. Dapper never hesitated at the sight of them, but walked slowly forward, one hand held up in a sign of hopeless surrender, which his shamed-spaniel expression mirrored. The other arm hung limply at his side, as though he had forgotten the battered valise dangling at the end of it. The two bullies grinned at each other, anticipating quick remuneration from their employer and an early night at Fat Mina's on the Zuilenstraat. They even glanced momentarily over Dr. Dapper's shoulder, calling their triumph to the beadle as he lumbered through the open back door. This was a mistake.

Olfert Dapper disapproved of running on both general and practical principles, but in a real sense his entire life had been made up of exceptions to rules. He was almost on the beadle's men when his forlorn shuffle turned into a sprinter's burst from the blocks. He swatted one half-raised club away with his valise, simultaneously kicked the second man reprehensibly low, and lunged between them to race away down the alley. The beadle shouted to him to come back, but Dr. Dapper could not believe that he was truly serious.

He was briefly impressed with his own turn of speed, since he had not had to flee physical attack since his earliest youth. Unfortunately, he had not bargained for his pursuers' endurance and determination. Hulking they were, and stupid they undoubtedly were; but they saw Fat Mina's slipping away, and they came pounding tirelessly after a plump middle-aged man. He could not lose them. His breath was coming hard now, and he began to be afraid.

At one time—fifteen minutes ago, perhaps—Olfert Dapper had known very nearly every grand street and unpaved lane or alleyway in Utrecht, as well as each dwelling, tavern, shop front, or business of every possible degree of legitimacy and possible usefulness. Now they blurred and ran thickly together like spilled paint before his eyes as he wheezed by, and the only clear impression he had of any of them was that no door swung open for him, and not a single soul ran out to his aid. But it was not in his nature to feel wounded or abandoned; he was too busy hoping that he would at least not disgrace himself by throwing up when the beadle's men ran him to earth. He was a proud man, in his way.

But then a diligence rumbled around an approaching corner, with the driver's tip of his tall hat signifying that the small coach was unoccupied and available for hire. Dr. Dapper wrenched the door open, scrambled inside, and sprawled out over the seat while the diligence was still moving. It was some while before he was able to sit up and breathe without pain; consequently, he never had the chance to wave blithely back at his frustrated pursuers, as he would have preferred to do. But their furious shouts carried to his ears for a surprisingly long time, so he did have that satisfaction.

The diligence, after some intense negotiation, took him by a circuitous route to the great—and hearteningly anonymous— seaport of Rotterdam. Coachman and passenger had developed a companionable rapport during the journey; and Dr. Dapper's driver, on arriving at their destination, recommended an inn, counseled against certain others, and suggested that a man as much in demand as Dr. Dapper appeared to be might be well-advised to consider the harbor at his first opportunity. "You can't go back to Utrecht. Not for a year, maybe two years, maybe never. Rotterdam's no place for you, either—your little chums'll track you here, sooner or later. And there's too many of your sort here already." His eyes grew unfocused, and seemed momentarily to change color. "Me, I'd be looking at the ships."

Dr. Dapper, for all the writing he had done about traveling to strange foreign lands, had, in fact, never been aboard anything larger than a duckpond raft, and that as a child. Wandering slowly along the waterfront the next day, and the days after, studying the schooners, frigates, merchantmen, whalers, and fishing boats—all so imposing at their quays, so small when he looked out at the rain-gray water beyond—he felt strangely lonely, and very far from all he understood. He looked in the windows of chandlers' shops, recognizing almost nothing he saw there; he heard songs he had never heard in his life; he cautiously sampled fruits and shellfish he did not recognize from barrows manned by peddlers clad in bright colors, who spoke no language he knew; he sidestepped invitations from girls who needed no language. But most of all, he smelled the sea.

A burly, one-eyed captain with a Frisian accent eventually agreed to ferry him across the Atlantic to make, like so many other passengers, a fresh start in the New World. The fare was remitted on Dr. Dapper's agreement to serve as ship's physician, even surgeon, if this should prove necessary. The voyage, fortunately, turned out to be a remarkably tranquil one, except for Dr. Dapper's stomach, which had loudly announced its distaste for a life on the rolling deep before the ship had even cast off in Rotterdam harbor. For the next seven weeks, he was his own best patient—and, fortunately for all concerned, very nearly the only one. He did, in mid-Atlantic, have to coax the ship's cat down from the rigging, into which it had been deposited and abandoned by a malicious sailor. Dr. Dapper, who liked cats, tripped the sailor overboard not long afterward. The ship lost half a day's progress coming about to pick the man up, and the captain was quite cross.

Dr. Dapper disembarked in the Americas at Falmouth, on the northeastern coast, and spent a weary, anxious week trying to decide where to go from there. Back to Utrecht would have been his most fervent choice: never having ventured beyond the Netherlands, except in his excellent imagination, he had no difficulty picturing himself being murdered by any of the raw-faced, raw-voiced people thronging the muddy streets and unspeakable inns, or being torn to pieces by wild animals, or being tortured at the stake by Red Indians. But Utrecht remained out of the question, and staying in Falmouth was just as frightening, since he had no faith that the men he had offended would let three thousand miles of ocean keep their hands from his collar: for all he knew, the next sail on the horizon might convey his continued pursuit. Despite the lure of Falmouth's many ingenuous gulls, veritable canvases for an artist like himself, there was nothing to do but bury himself for as long as necessary in the forests and backlands of this so-called New World. The hunt would surely cool down, sooner or later . . . surely.

Supply wagons, fur traders' pack mules, *voyageurs'* canoes, and his own blistered feet eventually delivered Olfert Dapper into the Territory of Sagadahock, that province of Britain located east of the Kennebec River in the vaguely delineated colony of Maine. The French had their own name for the region, *Acadia*, and their own long-standing claims of ownership, but in the village of No Popery, Dr. Dapper encountered few French, all of them Huguenot refugees. The local settlers were mainly recusants from the Roman-leaning reign of Charles II—English Puritans, Dutch Calvinists, and Salzburger Lutherans, plus a sprinkling of Anabaptists and a few Jews. Surrounding the village were largely ignored populations of Micmac, Abenaki, Passamaquoddy, and Penobscot Indians, most of them good-humored and rather bewildered. Dr. Dapper rather took to the Abenaki. He found their peaceful dispositions and placidly bleak view of the universe comfortingly akin to his own.

For the rest, he liked neither his fellow colonists—whom he judged ignorant, unsophisticated, mostly illiterate, and generally too poor and unimaginative to be worth the effort of swindling—nor his enforced frontier existence. The houses of No Popery were, without exception, constructed of rough-timber, their roofs either thatched or bearing a fine crop of grass, for better insulation, their chimneys built from clay-covered logs, their windows not even of horn but mere oiled paper. Sanitary arrangements were worse than anything he had endured aboard ship, and the climate was, as he wrote in his journal,

> ". . . insalubrious in the extreme, being pitilessly hot and miserably cold by turns, and plagued in all seasons by wicked varieties of insect life such as never we encountered in the Netherlands. Nor is this all, for there are wolves larger than the European sort, whose main prey is a kind of monstrous deer known to the Indians as a moose, and there is also a creature like an unspotted leopard, and great bears too, and not a soul with whom one can exchange ideas in a civilized manner. In truth, they are welcome to their Sagadahock, the lot of them, and it to them, and I am surely the most wretched Hollander that ever was. Worst of all, by acclamation they have made me their physician, and apothecary as well, as it was on the ship . . ."

Coming from as small and topographically tidy a country as Holland, with its gray, sea-menaced flatness and its cathedral skies, he was overwhelmed in both senses of the word by this New World. Everything was too big, monstrously big—trees, animals, rivers, and bellowing waterfalls, even the very seasons themselves, storm and snow and April alike—while the shocking splendor of the changing leaves, the wildflowers, the vast, foggy hills, the dark, virgin, sweet-smelling earth made him want to hide. *I would be better in prison. I have no business here.*

There are a limited number of crises and emergencies for which a ship's doctor, however counterfeit, needs to be prepared. Fractured limbs, scurvy, drunkenness, various souvenirs of Venus, even treatment after a disciplinary flogging—these can be anticipated and prepared for, even by a reasonably experienced impostor, with, in general, no worse damage left in his wake than might be expected from a genuine doctor. But in an isolated settlement of assorted dissenters, fanatics, and castaways, stranded in a completely strange land, with neither impressive-looking implements nor reasonably harmless medications at hand (though the local Abenaki were sometimes whimsically helpful here), Olfert Dapper was most often the only resort of people who had fallen down cliffs, abruptly removed hands or legs while cutting firewood, contracted a disease of which he knew neither the name, the cause, nor the treatment, or come off second-best in some encounter with a bear or a panther. Even had he actually possessed a medical degree, it would likely have proved worse than useless, faced with the dangers and mysteries of Sagadahock. He felt almost as sorry for his patients as he did for himself.

"Wretched Hollander" or no, paradoxically, he was held in higher respect in No Popery than he ever had been in his homeland.

Until recently, he had been acceptably successful in his various questionable enterprises, if *successful* can be defined as *getting away with it.* Not a day of his life had been spent in prison, physical labor, or repentance: a situation that felt far more natural to him than holiness to a saint, since sainthood involves constant struggle and failure, and struggle again. If he had not had a single true friend, there had been few true enemies—or, at least, none who knew where he lived—and it can honestly be said that he had borne ill will toward no man living. Nor woman, either, if it came to that; except perhaps for one Margot Zeldenthuis, who had long since vanished from his life, along with the forty-nine guilders under his pillow. Yet he sighed more often than he cursed when he thought of soft-footed Margot. Like his victims, Olfert Dapper had always had a streak of romance in his nature . . . just less than they.

In No Popery, to his horror, he was *needed*. There was no one else in the village who could do what he did, even if he could do little. Gaining trust had always been his living; more than that, it had been his gift, his art, his entire existence, and his purpose for existence. Trust bestowed, trust gratefully volunteered, was another matter entirely, and Dr. Dapper would have been the first to admit that, if there had been anyone in his new life to admit it to. His patients—who, for the most part, paid him in venison, wild turkeys, rabbits, vegetables from their small gardens, and labor around the tiny house they had built for him—remained admiring and utterly loyal, whether or not his medications, all invented out of thin blue air, were successful. Socially, he ranked with the minister, a grim, lantern-jawed soul named Giles Kirtley, lean as a winter wolf; slightly ahead of Matthew Prouty, the schoolmaster; and he was a frequent guest at far more well-provided tables than was even Nathaniel Markham, the wealthiest farmer of No Popery, who had real clapboards covering the raw frame of his house, and real glass in his windows. These, according to the lights of the village, were successful men: Dr. Olfert Dapper was *celebrated*.

But the nearest thing he had to a friend, or even a drinking companion, had strong liquor not been harshly forbidden in No Popery, was an Abenaki Indian named—as near as he could ever translate it for Dr. Dapper—Rain Coming, who dwelled with his tribe in a birchbark village some three or four miles away. He was short, square-built, and ageless, his skin the texture of granite and the color of a worn old coin, and he actually spoke only a little more English than the handful of Abenaki words that Dr. Dapper had awkwardly acquired. Yet somehow they were comfortable in one another's company, and could spend unlikely amounts of time together in complete silence. The Indian's herb lore, proffered in brief grunts and gestures, had resulted in more than one miraculous-appearing cure, for which Dr. Dapper received the credit. In return, he did his best to teach Rain Coming how to cheat at cards. That enterprise failed, due primarily to the other's complete lack of the competitive instinct; or, rather (at least, so Dr. Dapper always felt), to Rain Coming's serene certainty that whatever the game, he had already triumphed simply by taking part, and there was nothing further to say. Dr. Dapper would have given a good deal to possess such inborn assurance.

Rigorously honest with himself, if with no other, Dr. Dapper never blamed Mistress Remorse Kirtley, the minister's thin, whispering wife, for luring him into temptation. While she was hardly the most attractive woman of his extensive experience, marriage to the good Reverend having bleached most of the color and spirit out of her, curiously she aroused Olfert Dapper's occasional sympathy as well as his lust, which was not something that had happened to him before. Her husband suffered frequently from what Dr. Dapper pronounced to be "dyspeptic lassitude," but which even a middle-aged Dutch cardsharp could recognize as a stomach exhausted by constant and indiscriminate overeating. He treated these regular complaints with various decoctions of dandelion, mint, wormwood, and yarrow, and spent much time in the kitchen with the grateful, attentive Mistress Kirtley, carefully explicating these remedies to her. In this manner, they became well-acquainted, though Dr. Dapper was careful never to presume on the warming relationship. The first commandment of his chosen profession, passed down through every age of mankind, remained, as it still remains, *"Thou shalt let them come to you . . ."*

The days passed, and the seasons passed: the hottest summer Olfert Dapper had ever endured crisping into the most dazzlingly delightful autumn by far, then hardening into a winter as merciless as any he had known in the Netherlands—more so, indeed, for the complete lack of civilized refuge, such as a lively coffee shop or a cheerful bordello. Dr. Dapper spent those endless months most often in bed, or huddled at his fireside with a quilt over his shoulders, his feet in a bucket of heated snow water, and his mind lost in memories of a Utrecht pub, drinking spiced *jenever* with Margot Zeldenthuis. Would she remember him, after all this time? More to the point, would that Eck en Viel idiot recognize him on the street, and could his States-General cousin, or whatever he was, still be holding a grudge? How much longer must he remain exiled in this fearful, barbaric place? He thought of the canals of Utrecht, and of the sharp wind over the Rhone, and for the first time since coming ashore felt no slightest trace of hope.

Spring slipped up imperceptibly, its timorous inroads into the iron cold like the forays of the turning tide just beginning to nibble at a child's invulnerable sand fortress. Dr. Dapper was yet suffering from chilblains when Rain Coming, whom he had not seen for a good month—and whom he rather suspected actually hibernated during the worst of the winter—came to tell him that the ice was two days from breaking on the Kennebec, and that the first rains, a day after, would almost immediately produce the various wild herbs Dr. Dapper had grudgingly begun to depend on for his improvised medicines. They set out together on the first nearly-warm day in April, with a pale, watery sun overhead and a small breeze honing its edge on the back of Dr. Dapper's neck.

They walked for a long time, in and out of pine groves, crossing muddy meadows, up and down the slopes of thickly wooded valleys and ravines. Their path seemed aimless, almost without direction, but periodically Rain Coming would halt and nod toward a few tiny petals in the shadow of a tree, or a fungus growing on that same tree; a single mushroom poking its brown head out of a patch of damp grass; a few queer-looking leaves, invariably hanging somewhere out of reach. And Olfert Dapper would dutifully climb and stretch, tug and twist and pluck, sometimes digging with both hands to fetch some plant up by its roots, and then drop his find carefully into the sack he carried at his waist, and trudge on beside the Abenaki. The sack grew heavier.

It was nearly twilight, with a half-moon already rising, when Rain Coming finally grunted in satisfaction, and they turned back toward No Popery. Weary as he was, Dr. Dapper was anxious to move quickly, knowing that the great wildcats whose broad footprints he had seen several times—"catamounts," the villagers called them—hunted mainly at dusk and dawn. He also knew that the black bears of the region were just waking now from their winter sleep, most often hungry and irritable. He walked increasingly close beside Rain Coming as the sky darkened, even bumping against him from time to time.

When his companion halted abruptly, and he heard, directly ahead, the sound of a large body moving in a thicket, then glimpsed the shadow in the moonlight, Dr. Dapper froze where he stood and refused to go farther. Rain Coming's nods and earnest gestures of reassurance made no difference, so the Abenaki finally shrugged—something Dr. Dapper had never seen him or any Indian do before—and walked calmly on, quickly vanishing into the same thicket. He did not look back.

The threat of abandonment changed Dr. Dapper's mind for him, and he hurried to catch up with Rain Coming. The Abenaki had halted again at the far edge of the clearing, staring toward a rough, stony meadow slanting slightly uphill. They had come that way, and Dr. Dapper remembered glimpsing deer there, and stumbling over two or three burrows of the badger-like diggers the colonists called "land-beavers." But now there was nothing at all to be seen in the meadow . . .

. . . except something that should not have been.

Dr. Dapper did not write of it for a long time, for reasons that he never could explain to himself. When he did come to describe what he saw that spring night, remembering his fear that he might have been hallucinating out of weariness, he wrote:

> "*. . . by moonlight its coat is a kind of golden-gray, the very color of the moon itself. It seems a sturdy-built creature, though rather small—I cannot imagine it bearing a person of my stature for any distance. The hoofs are indeed cloven, as Pliny attests, though he is much in error regarding nearly every other aspect of the beast. The tail is lionlike, the mane as long as that of the wild ponies of the English moors— though less thick and shaggy—and the celebrated*

*horn above its eyes would seem disproportionate in
length and evident mass to the musculature of its
rather slender neck. Yet so is the unicorn made."*

Dr. Dapper cried out at the sight, a loss of self-control quite
outside his usual humours. The unicorn wheeled on the instant,
its horn fiery as a new scar in the moonlight—and then it was
gone, leaving no footprints behind on the wet and muddy hillside
. . . leaving nothing but the wondering glory in Dr. Dapper's eyes.

Rain Coming looked at Dr. Dapper without speaking, and
Dr. Dapper looked back at him. There was no need to speak
on either side: what had been seen, even for the single crystal
moment, was greater than accusation, beyond apology. They
walked on back to the village of No Popery together, bound in
an understanding far greater than when they had set out that
morning, so long ago.

What Rain Coming thought of their encounter, Dr. Dapper
never knew, nor expected to know. Indeed, when he asked
his friend whether the Abenaki tongue even had a word for
unicorn, Rain Coming pretended not to comprehend, and grew
plainly irritated when the matter was pressed further. He came
less often to the village in those later days, and was even less
conversational when he did. He seemed to Dr. Dapper almost
to have set his body aside to follow in his puzzled heart whatever
that moment on the meadow had meant to him. A good—if
uneasy—Netherlandish Calvinist, Dr. Dapper mused at times
over the question of whether Indians could become saints.

Dr. Dapper missed his friend, but Rain Coming's place had
largely been taken by a conflagration of yearning to see the
unicorn again. He spoke to no one about it—certainly not to
the Reverend Kirtley, who would have immediately denounced

his vision as a sending from hell. Nor did Dr. Dapper consider taking Prouty, the schoolmaster, into his confidence, for the man was even more fearfully rigid than the Reverend, who at least had his unshakable faith to bolster him; while Prouty, Dr. Dapper suspected, needed only the least suggestion that the universe was not as he had been taught—such as the existence of unicorns—to push him quite over the edge of reason, likely into Quakerism, or something worse. Dr. Dapper had enough on his conscience, such as it was, without the added responsibility for destroying Master Prouty's trembling foundations.

It does say something to his good, surely, to the influence that the simple life and simple values of No Popery had had on him—or perhaps it was only the silent, mysterious reproach of Rain Coming—that it never occurred to Dr. Dapper that there could be immense profit in the possession of a live unicorn, or even the hide, hair, and horn of a dead one. He merely wanted to see it again; and he knew without questioning, as one sometimes knows these things, that he never would be allowed to see it alone. It had clearly never been meant for him in the first place, but rather for his wise and strangely innocent companion, for Rain Coming of the Abenaki. *Whom do I know in this savage land who is wise and innocent in that same way, who deserves to see what I by chance saw? With all their talk of Jesus, and all their damned endless praying, there must be someone!*

And it was at that moment, in the spring, that Remorse Kirtley came to him, as he had known she would.

It was not an occasion of sin that brought her, but the perfectly legitimate pretext of her husband's rebellious stomach quarreling with his eight-course dinner, as it and he were habituated to do. If Dr. Dapper could possibly attend on him. . . ?

Remorse Kirtley was not a beauty, but her eyes were the deep, sweet brown of a sunflower heart, and her mouth, close to, was not nearly as thin and prim and small as it appeared most of the time. Indeed, she was definitely standing closer to him than was at all proper for a good Puritan wife, and it was with a real and regretful effort that Dr. Dapper banished temptation and agreed to accompany her once more to the Reverend's bedside. A thought had occurred to him, gazing into those sunflower eyes.

While the infusion of wild grasses that he had learned would not only soothe the Reverend's much put-upon intestines but send him off to sleep as well was steeping, he told the minister, "That, I fear, was the last of the herbal medicines that I have gathered with my heathen friend of the Abenaki. Tomorrow, or the next day, I must go forth again to replenish my supply, and I would ask that you give your wife leave to accompany me. These plants grow close to the ground, and my eyes are not what they were."

Reverend Kirtley was a fool, but not quite the fool he seemed. Having long since reassured himself of his wife's holy unattractiveness, his main objection to her passing an afternoon in Dr. Dapper's company concerned not what she might do, but that she might be thought to be doing it. "It would give the impression of unseemliness," he protested, "of impropriety. Surely another—a child, perhaps, to avoid false appearances. . . ?"

Olfert Dapper shrugged plaintively, if such a thing were possible. "The little ones can so rarely identify what I seek," he pointed out, "while their elders know, but cannot see. Mistress Remorse would be the perfect choice, as—ah—intimately acquainted with your intestinal needs as she is, and with the exact admixture and administration of my medicinal agents. Still, if you would prefer that I employ a stranger, which would require at least some inescapable discussion—"

What had worked in Amsterdam and Utrecht worked just as

flawlessly in the Territory of Sagadahock. The Reverend hastily disavowed any such suggestion, assuring Dr. Dapper that he might borrow his good wife's assistance on whatever day suited him best, for all the world as though he were granting him the use of a favored spade or horse. Dr. Dapper suggested the following Monday, and Reverend Kirtley agreed eagerly. Mistress Remorse Kirtley's opinion was not solicited, which did not seem to distress her at all.

She was waiting, dressed as roughly and soberly as any farm laborer, when Dr. Dapper came to the minister's house at dawn on that Monday morning. They spoke little on setting off, making use of a route that kept them largely out of sight of anyone who might be working his fields early or slipping home from some wrongful enjoyment with a view to avoiding the village constable's eye. Mistress Kirtley was hardly the equal of Rain Coming in espying a half-hidden leaf in a patch of nettles, or a few wild berries among the weeds reclaiming a long-abandoned garden; but she did well enough, and she kept easy pace with Dr. Dapper, her stride suggesting longer legs than he had permitted himself to imagine. Once or twice, when he glanced sideways to see her lifting her pale face, eyes almost closed, to the warming sun, she would turn and show him a very small smile, such as he had never seen on her mouth before. He fancied that perhaps no one else ever had.

She appeared not to notice that Dr. Dapper was slowly, subtly bending their search in a wide curve back toward the little meadow where a greater wonder even than her smile had come upon him. But when they sat down together upon the ground just beyond the clearing—considerably drier now than then—to eat the midday meal she had prepared of dried meat, cheese, barley bread, and mild ale, Mistress Kirtley looked straight across the lunch into Dr. Dapper's eyes and said quietly, "I know this place. There are none of your herbs growing here."

"That is true, ma'am," Dr. Dapper replied, for he always knew when lying would not serve him. It was a skill that set him apart from most other practitioners of his silken art.

"Then why did you bring me here?" Mistress Kirtley neither raised her voice nor showed any sign of alarm. She might have been asking the question out of casual politeness, had it not been for the slightest dilation of her eyes.

"Because there is something I greatly wish you to see." Dr. Dapper nodded calmly toward the meal laid out on a kerchief between them. "Do enjoy, as I am enjoying it, the repast you have so clearly gone to a deal of trouble to prepare for us—and wait meanwhile. Only wait a little, dear Mistress Kirtley."

In fact, for all the assurance in his tone, he had no notion whether the unicorn would appear at all. He knew it had been no phantasm, no trick of the moon or of his mind—one look at Rain Coming's reaction to the vision had told him that—but whether or not it would return to the meadow, whether or not a certain legend might prove true . . . all that was pure gamble, and Olfert Dapper in his soul was as pure a gambler as had ever lived in Old World or New, in Utrecht or No Popery. He washed his meat and cheese down with his ale and smiled at Mistress Kirtley, and she smiled back at him. And they waited together.

But the day was warm, the ale excellent, and the early gnats' almost inaudible buzzing became a kind of lullaby for Dr. Dapper. He never admitted that he had been asleep when the unicorn came; but it was Remorse Kirtley's soft gasp that roused him, and he saw her on her feet with both hands pressed to her mouth and her dark Dutch-style cap fallen to the ground. He had never seen her rich brown hair loose before.

The unicorn was standing in the center of the meadow, facing her, plainly considering her, as surely as she was taking its truth into herself. By moonlight, it had seemed more delicately made, almost fragile; today, it appeared not only larger than he remembered, but quite possibly dangerous, with the sun glinting on the long spiral horn. Dr. Dapper, rising slowly to his feet, noticed for the first time the small curl of beard beneath its lower jaw, such as he had given to his depiction of a lion in his book on Africa. Did that mean the creature was male? Was it a sign of maturity? These and other questions tumbled roundabout through his mind, for Dr. Dapper had always possessed the passionate curiosity of the true scientist in his inmost nature. He had, however, always been careful not to let it get out of hand.

Remorse Kirtley held out both of her open hands to the unicorn. It tossed its head once, like a horse, but did not whinny or nicker—indeed, Dr. Dapper had never heard it make a sound. It paced slowly toward the woman, its horn pointing at her heart. She did not flinch, but sank slowly into a sitting position, her legs folding under her as gracefully as those of the unicorn's as it lowered its head into her lap. The horn lay across her thighs.

Dr. Dapper could see her face now. It wore the dazed, foolishly transcendent expression he had seen and scorned in so many of the paintings of his homeland: Mary receiving the Annunciation, saints ravished by the converse of angels, holy hermits gazing up enraptured at golden clouds aswarm with cherubim . . . every one looking as gloriously vacant as Remorse Kirtley looked now. Dr. Dapper envied her, and made notes for another book.

He could not tell whether the unicorn was actually asleep. Remorse Kirtley stroked its neck and played timidly with the white feathers of its mane—she never touched the horn—but the unicorn's eyes remained closed, and its slow breathing never altered. Dr. Dapper thought, in a vague and distant way, *this is the moment when the knights rush out from cover and spring on it, as it rouses a moment too late. I know what I should do, if I were a braver man, and a worse one.* The unicorn smelled to him like new bread, and like new candles, and, strangely, like cool old wells in shadowy gardens.

How long the unicorn slept in Remorse Kirtley's lap, Dr. Dapper never knew. He stood where he was, while the sun moved and the ragged grass whispered, and the tiny insects danced in the sunlight. The unicorn's sides breathed in and out, like those of any other drowsing animal, and now and then it twitched its lion-tufted tail to brush away a fly. And Remorse Kirtley sat utterly motionless, her eyes fixed, as Dr. Dapper imagined, on the world the unicorn had come from. Now and then she turned her head toward him, but he knew that she never saw him at all.

Then, in time, the unicorn rose, and looked in Remorse Kirtley's face, and brushed its horn over her hair, and went away.

Neither Mistress Kirtley nor Dr. Dapper moved for a long while afterward, not until she stood up in her turn and went to him, and he put his arms around her. They remained so, with nothing sinful or adulterous in their embrace; but by and by she asked him in a small voice, "How did you know?"

"I did *not* know," Olfert Dapper answered her candidly. "I guessed only."

"That the wife of the Reverend Giles Kirtley might yet be a virgin? A clever guess, wise Doctor." She leaned closer, pressing breasts not as childish as he had imagined against him. "And one deserving of some return, surely?" The sunflower eyes were soft and tender.

Strangely, it was Dr. Dapper who held back in that moment, actually putting away from himself the woman whose mysteries had tantalized his dreams all that winter. "Good mistress," he heard himself saying, to his own considerable amazement, "should we do this, you will—thou wilt—forfeit thy chance ever again to see a unicorn—to hold a unicorn in thy lap. I am not such a scoundrel as to wish to deprive thee of such a blessing." He was horrified by the sound of his own earnest pomposity, the more so because it was uttered with truly good intent. *Some of us were not born for the generous gesture.*

But Remorse Kirtley laughed at him, and stretched her arms stiffly out on his shoulders, so as to hold his head firmly while she looked into his eyes. "One unicorn in a lifetime is a miracle beyond anyone's deserving, virgin or no. More than one . . . no, no, Doctor, that is for another life than mine." She kissed him then, with a force that would likely have knocked him down had she not still been holding him upright. Still gripping his eyes with her own, she said, with as much gravity as he had spoken to her, "The unicorn set me free, can you understand me? Freed me from the world I have always been taught, and always believed, was the only world for a Christian soul. While I sat there and held him, he came into me—how else should I put it, dear Doctor?—he came into me and showed me the magic beyond poor, crabbed No Popery, the beauty beyond the sour singsong God of my worship. And for that I will forever be more grateful to thee than anyone else is ever likely to be, my scoundrelly friend."

She kissed him again, and then she stood back from him a little and slowly began to unlace her drab dark bodice, never taking her eyes from his. She said, "Now it is for thee to complete my liberation. Help me here . . ."

And he did help her, his usually deft fingers as clumsy as those of an ignorant youth, and they did indeed cleave together, and were one flesh, as the Bible recommends and approves.

Later, drowsy in the dappled shade, his herb-gathering bag pillowing both of their heads, he said, "It grieves me yet that you tossed away so lightly your chance to ever again call a unicorn. Truly, I never brought you here for that—" which was only half a lie—"but because I wanted to see the creature a second time. I cannot help feeling at fault."

Propped on one elbow, her own eyes heavy, she made severe reply. "I tossed nothing away—and certainly never for you, vain man, but for myself. What I have lost, I gave away freely. Even the God of No Popery would understand that difference. The unicorn understood."

Whereupon, and without explanation, Remorse Kirtley began to cry. Deciding for perhaps the hundredth time in his life that he knew nothing about women, Dr. Dapper let her tears dry on his chest and throat; and somewhere in the middle of that, they were one flesh once again, and she was giggling like a girl about something she wouldn't share. When he asked, she only laughed harder, her hair a twisting whip across his face, and he became fascinated then by other things, like the little pink mole between her shoulder blades, a miniature *fleur-de-lys* that he suspected the Reverend Kirtley had never seen.

They walked back side by side, just as they had set out; but when Dr. Dapper reached to take her hand, like any village swain, Mistress Kirtley shook her head and pulled away. Hair invisible again under the Dutch cap, bodice laced to near-constriction, long brown dress respectably free of any telltale grass stains, she had reassumed the role of meek Puritan goodwife, playing it with the passionate attention to detail of the actress she had spent her life becoming. Even when she glanced sideways at him and smiled just a trifle, it was not the smile of Remorse Kirtley. Dr. Dapper knew that smile well.

They parted at the outskirts of the village: he to his mortar and pestle and improvised scales, she to tend her husband, and to prepare a full dinner after a full day. When, at Reverend Kirtley's next visceral complaint, Dr. Dapper hurried to him with his potions already prepared, there was never the smallest suggestion that anything ignoble might have passed between anyone and anyone else; nor did Mistress Kirtley do more than nod attentively at her family physician's instructions and notate them without quite looking at him. Dr. Dapper stayed longer than he might have, constantly attempting surreptitiously to catch her eye, but he had no luck.

News of the colonists' various homelands came infrequently at the best of times—and not at all during the winter months—and was delivered haphazardly, most often by traveling peddlers, tinkers, and circuit-riding preachers who chanced through No Popery. Olfert Dapper had received no messages at all from the Netherlands since his arrival, and had almost resigned himself, not only to the probability of spending at least another year in this drearily savage New World, but also to the worse horror of realizing that he was gradually adapting to his life here. He liked and respected the Abenaki of his acquaintance, and he very nearly liked two or three of the settlers, and he was even developing a certain taste for succotash.

Oh, whatever might be waiting for him back in Utrecht, he had to get out of this place!

Mistress Remorse Kirtley went on about her business as a dutiful No Popery wife, cooking and gardening and praying and keeping a proper house, never allowing herself to be alone in Dr. Dapper's company for more than the few minutes it might take him to hand her his newest medication for her husband's ever-truculent stomach and instruct her in its application. She kept her eyes cast down at all times, her hair completely covered, and her modest bearing an example for all Puritan women. Dr. Dapper, thinking about it, could never say whether he actually loved her—love, as it is generally used, being an emotion as honestly foreign to him as the Turkish language, or the finer points of infralapsarianism. Neither could he call it plain sinful lust anymore: it was, perhaps, that, having glimpsed the mysterious heart of the minister's wife, he simply wanted to see it again, more than he had ever wanted to see the unicorn a second time. It has been mentioned that Olfert Dapper had more than a little of the romantic in his nature.

He went on occasion, when he had the time free (his fraudulent medical practice having gradually approached the genuine), to the meadow where he and Remorse Kirtley and the unicorn had once been together. He had no expectation of finding either one of them there, but it comforted him strangely to stand exactly where he had watched in numbed wonder as the unicorn lowered its head into her lap; and where, a world afterward, he had helped her unlace her bodice, while she never took her eyes from his.

Once he encountered his old Abenaki companion Rain Coming standing in the same place, his black eyes watching everything, yet seeing nothing that Olfert Dapper could see. They greeted each other briefly and soberly, and Dr. Dapper said gently, after a while, "It will never come here again. I cannot say how I know that, but I do."

Rain Coming nodded a very little. He said only two words. "She come."

Dr. Dapper stared at him. "*She?* Whom do you . . . do you mean Mistress Kirtley?" A squirrel observing them from a branch abruptly dashed away at the sound of his voice.

The Abenaki met his eyes calmly, taking a long time before he answered. "When you go home. She come then."

"When I go home . . ." A sudden immense sadness filled Dr. Dapper's chest, and the words came out almost in a whisper, in contrast to his earlier cry. He said, "But I may never go home, my friend. There are some very angry people waiting there for me, and they might even put me in prison. *Prison*." He repeated the word, emphasizing it carefully, knowing that the Abenaki, like the other Algonquian tribes in general, had no real equivalent for such a word, such a concept. He said again, "I do not know whether I will ever go home."

"You go home soon." Rain Coming's own voice was slow and certain. "She come to Abenaki when you go."

"Why then?" Olfert Dapper demanded. "There is no connection between us anymore—we barely speak, except about her husband's medicines. Why would she run off to your people when I am gone?"

But Rain Coming himself was gone, in that particularly disturbing way of being gone that he had, which the Reverend Kirtley always said plainly showed the infernal origins of all his folk. Dr. Dapper stared into the silent woods after him for a time, and then wandered back to No Popery.

He knew that the Abenaki had taken in runaways and exiles from the various Sagadahock colonies; and he knew further that the Algonquians had no God-given laws concerning the properly submissive status of women. An Abenaki, Micmac, or Passamaquoddy woman might, in his undeniably limited experience, look away from a man, or past him, or through him, but never down at the ground. A woman of spirit and resource, such as Mistress Remorse Kirtley had shown herself to be, might well rise higher in Indian society than would ever be possible for her in Puritan surroundings. He wondered less how Rain Coming had learned of her decision than whether she herself knew of it yet.

The weather was warm still, but close to turning—after more than a year in Maine, even Dr. Dapper could tell this by the changes in the birds' behavior and the taste of the dawn wind— when he was roused from an evening doze by a rapping at his door. Peering through a crack in the wall which no amount of caulking would ever patch for long, he recognized, to his astonishment and immediate anxiety, the Reverend Kirtley. The minister had never once been to visit him at home, and their occasional conversations in church usually involved either the state of Dr. Dapper's immortal soul or Reverend Kirtley's highly mortal stomach. *Could he know? Could someone have . . . could she have confessed all?* The question was heightened by the fact that the Reverend was carrying a musket. It was a very large musket, with a mouth like a tulip.

But Olfert Dapper had not gained the rank and respect that he enjoyed in his mendacious art without learning (always with the exception of Margot Zeldenthuis) when to put his faith in a woman's eyes. His panic left him as swiftly as it had come, and he opened the door to welcome Giles Kirtley.

The minister entered with an oddly furtive air, looking over his shoulder as though he were the one well-acquainted with thief-takers and persons bearing heavy sticks and unreasonable grudges. Offered the one good chair, he leaned his musket gingerly against the wall, accepted a mug of somewhat dubious *jenever*—a thing Dr. Dapper could never remember having seen him do—and began the conversation by saying abruptly, as though the fact had just come to his attention, "Brother Dapper, you're a Dutchman."

Dr, Dapper raised his eyebrows and spread his hands. "I cannot deny it, sir."

"Ah." Reverend Kirtley cleared his throat several times. "Perhaps that is why I find it easier to confide in you, even though we have not been—ah—close? Warm? Intimate. . . ?" His voice wandered away into the random corners where his glance had gone.

"My loss, certainly," Dr. Dapper said graciously. "What can I do for you, Reverend?"

"My wife . . ." Reverend Kirtley stood up, turned in a constricted circle, like a bear tied for baiting, and sat down again. "My good wife has been kidnapped. Stolen away. By those red savages. *Savages*, man!"

Caught completely by surprise, Dr. Dapper could only blink and stare. "By the Abenaki? Kidnapped?"

"What else? *Who* else? There are tracks—obvious, unmistakable! They dragged her away in the night, poor creature, before she could utter a cry. Even now it may be too late to prevent . . ." He bent almost double in his chair, covering his eyes. The position was not unlike the one he usually screwed himself into when his stomach was demanding its due.

"*Prevent*," Dr. Dapper said, and then, "Oh. *Oh*. Well, we must certainly rouse the village, Reverend. If you take the houses east of Bear Creek, I will take all the west side—"

"No!" The Reverend Kirtley seized both of Dr. Dapper's wrists in his big-knuckled hands. "I could not bear it if . . . if the worst were known to . . . to . . ."

"To all your congregation," Dr. Dapper finished for him, more respectfully than he felt. "Your following of the faithful. Yes, of course, I understand. We will begin our search tomorrow, at first light—"

"Tonight! We dare not wait!" The Reverend was on his feet again, reaching for his musket.

But Dr. Dapper shook his head firmly, and did not rise. "There are wolves out there, and catamounts—I heard one scream close by, yesternight. We can do nothing in darkness but run ourselves into worse danger than she may be in, trying to rescue her. I will go with you at first light, as I said."

And with that the minister had to be content, though as he left Olfert Dapper's house, he added, "Remember to bring your gun."

To which Dr. Dapper responded, "I have no gun. I do have an excellent belaying pin from the ship that brought me to these shores. But no gun."

"I will have one for you," Reverend Kirtley assured him grimly.

And so saying, he plunged out into the night, leaving Olfert Dapper sleepless until sunrise.

When they met at the empty church, Reverend Kirtley indeed handed Dr. Dapper a loaded musket. It felt so heavy and cold in his hand that he almost dropped it. He protested that he had never handled such a weapon before and was likely to be more of a menace to any companion than to the supposed kidnappers of Mistress Kirtley. The Reverend replied only, "The hand of the Almighty will be on the trigger at the appointed time. You need have no fear."

But Dr. Dapper had a great deal of fear turning his own belly to a solid block of ice as they set forth, following the tracks—unmistakable, as the Reverend Kirtley had said—of Mistress Kirtley's small, clumsily-shod feet to the point, just out of sight of No Popery village, where they crossed a set of moccasined footprints and went on in company with her companion . . . or her abductor. Mistress Kirtley's prints were closer together now, showing only the balls of her feet, which could have meant she was either running or being dragged along. There was no doubt of the Reverend's opinion: his normally ruddy face was iron-pale, except for the blood-drops standing out on his bitten lips. He swung his musket from side to side, like a scythe, as they walked on; and from time to time, he sighted along it at random targets, grinding his teeth and grinning a wolf-grin. Olfert Dapper feared for everyone.

At one point, the Reverend studied him sharply—not quite swinging the musket around—and said, "You have a certain sympathy for the savages, or I am mistaken." It was not a question.

Cautiously Dr. Dapper replied, keeping his tone carefully inexpressive, "I find them a not uninteresting people, and well worth studying." As casually as he could, he edged around to the far side of the minister.

"Children of Satan," Reverend Kirtley spat. "Whatever unspeakable, demon-born humiliation they have visited upon my wife, I will take her back *as* my lawful wife, with no shame ever on my part. But I shall kill every one of them, and I shall burn their filthy lodges to the ground, and plow the earth with salt afterward. This I swear." He halted for a moment to glare fiercely at Dr. Dapper. "You have heard my oath before God."

"Yes," Olfert Dapper answered quietly. "I have heard you."

The tracks of Mistress Kirtley and her presumed captor grew more difficult to follow as the ground hardened and the undergrowth became thicker. Whenever possible, Dr. Dapper did his best to scuff out a print with his foot, or to mislead the grim Reverend; but the path to the Abenaki village was known to all the inhabitants of No Popery, and by now the minister had no need of a trail to lead him where he was convinced his wife must have been taken. It would take only a sight of Mistress Remorse Kirtley to unleash a massacre; and Dr.

Dapper, born during the Eighty Years' War, knew something about massacres. In frantic silence, he rummaged through the stratagems and devious contrivances of a lifetime, but utterly in vain. He marched by the side of a man planning murder and could think of no way to stop him.

So despondent had he become that he never noticed the first cloven hoofmarks—neither the delicate prints of a white-tail deer, nor the dinner-plate tracks of a moose—joining those of the moccasins and work-booted feet. When he did finally become aware of them, at the point where they began to veer from the familiar path, heading together up a low, mossy rise of ground that bore all three prints clearly, he pointed them out to the minister, feeling the first twitch of a scheme in his belly as he did so. "Behold, Reverend!" he cried, as dramatically as he knew how. "Whatever can you make of these uncanny slots?"

Giles Kirtley halted, leaning on his musket and shaking his head very slowly as he pondered the sudden new tracks. The cloven prints were generally in the middle of the path, with Mistress Kirtley's close on the left side and those of the unknown Indian farther off on the right. The Reverend was muttering, almost inaudibly, "I like this not . . . and yet it cannot, cannot . . ." At one point, he bent to the ground to sniff at the hoofmarks, then raised his head, murmuring, as though he were alone, "No . . . I will not believe . . . No. No . . ."

Dr. Dapper followed, deliberately hanging a little way behind, to give the impression of growing reluctance at such ominous signs. The Reverend did not look back for him, but kept advancing, step by heavy step, staring only at the earth, the musket loose in one hand; he might have forgotten completely that he was holding it at all. Olfert Dapper's legs were beginning to trouble him, but he labored on, uncertain of everything except for the one hope that had blossomed in him, like a small bright coal to blow on in the night of great fear. *Remember—remember always—they must come to you, they must deceive themselves.*

Nearing the top of the rise, the Reverend Kirtley abruptly paused in his slow advance, pointing at the ground. "See, the savage's tracks have vanished!" he declared, glowering directly at Dr. Dapper for the first time since they had begun their climb. "What can this mean?"

Bless me, God of Liars . . .

Hesitantly, almost mumbling himself, casting the fear he felt in another, more purposeful shape, Dr. Dapper gestured at the cloven marks and said, very quietly, "He walketh about like a roaring lion, seeking whom he may devour."

For a wonder, the minister did not immediately catch the reference. Then he did, and his face turned a sickly, feverish red, and then absolutely colorless once again. He whispered, "I felt . . . in my heart I felt the Lord's warning, the Lord's merciless pity . . . but I put my fears away. . . ." He took a sudden fierce step forward and gripped Dr. Dapper by the collar, his strength a monster's strength in that moment. Aloud, he cried, "But I smelled no brimstone when I stooped to the tracks! No brimstone—no hellish fumes at all! How do you explain *that*, physicker?"

Careful, careful . . . "If I remember the Holy Word correctly . . . which, doubtless, I do not—" Dr. Dapper smiled and ducked his head in embarrassment—"there is a mention of the Evil One having power to assume a pleasing appearance. May that not extend to—ah—scent, as well as looks? May not even the stink of Hell be at Satan's command, after all?"

The Reverend Kirtley shook his entire body like a tormented bear. "No, I cannot believe—I *refuse* to believe that the Devil

could possibly touch . . . that she could be . . ." He did not finish
the phrase, but hung his head for a long moment.

"I read my Testament in Dutch," Dr. Dapper said with pious
humility, "which surely cannot match the mighty language of
your King James Version—but does it not say that Satan hath
no power over a pure heart?" He paused, mentally counting off
seconds, before he pressed home. "How few of us can claim such
a condition, when the full balance of sin is told?"

*Forgive me, my maligned Mistress Remorse. Speak up for an
errant Hollander in that other New World, when the time comes.*

When the minister lifted his head again, Dr. Dapper felt a
sudden qualm at the thought that he might glimpse tears in
the wolf-eyes. But they were just as dry as before, and just as
ruthlessly resolute. The Reverend Kirtley said only, "Follow on."

As they continued their slow advance toward the hilltop, Dr.
Dapper heard the minister arguing endlessly with himself in a
droning undertone. "But if the Devil took the savage on the spot,
for what infernal purpose drag her along . . . why keep her alive,
except as bait for the righteous—what purpose, what *purpose?*"
Dr. Dapper noticed that the tracks of Mistress Kirtley's work-
shoes had become fainter on the moss, while the cloven hoofs
had cut steadily deeper into the soil, as though Satan had been
stamping or even dancing in triumph at his catch. The Reverend
Kirtley must have felt the same, for he groaned aloud, studying
one such passage of signs, but then added aloud, "But she fought
him, as we all must fight the Devil—the very earth itself bears
witness to her battle. My poor sinful wife . . ." He was holding
the musket in both hands again, across his chest.

At the top of the rise Mistress Kirtley's footprints vanished
abruptly and completely into a bewildering swirl of the cloven
marks. On witnessing this dreaded conformation of his fears,

the minister uttered a single great raw cry and fell to his knees, clasping his hands and wailing hoarsely, "Oh, my poor Remorse— her faith was not strong enough to save her! She struggled against her woman's weakness, but the Evil One snatched her up—he devoured her like a roaring lion! My poor lost child!" He was tearing at his long gray hair with one hand, at his shirt with the other, and blood followed his fingernails.

Dr. Dapper said nothing, but fell to studying the confused marks in the earth. He had known them from the first for the unicorn's prints—the Devil having, as everyone in Holland knew, one human foot and one clumsy, betraying cow-hoof— but his only explanation for the disappearance of Mistress Kirtley's tracks was that she must have mounted the unicorn, virgin or no, and ridden it . . . *where?* The trail was so confused that the hoofprints seemed to lead away in every direction from the hilltop, as though the unicorn itself had been the one dancing in celebration of their reunion.

Something lying on the ground caught the corner of his eye, and he knelt himself in a gesture of absent-minded piety to pick it up, putting his musket down first as he did so. Almost invisible against the trampled moss, it proved to be a bit of the dark lace of Remorse Kirtley's bodice, cleanly severed, though by what he could not guess. He slipped it into the wallet at his belt without passing it to the Reverend. *Mine.*

Reverend Kirtley was rocking to and fro on his knees, moaning unintelligibly to himself, as Olfert Dapper had known old Amsterdam Jews to do on the death of a parent or child. He crouched down beside him and placed a tentative hand on the broad, unyielding shoulder. Speaking instinctively in the intimate case, for only the second time in this country, he said, "Thou must be brave. Thou must pray for her and be brave."

The Reverend Kirtley's head whipped around to glare at him so fast that Dr. Dapper almost fell over backward. "Pray for one so lost to virtue as to fall into Satan's claws? Nay, to rail against the verdict of God is to risk damnation oneself, and I'll none of it." The minister's hoarse voice was painful to hear. "The judgments of the Lord are forever righteous," he said, and his eyes were not at all mad, but murderously sane.

"Surely," Olfert Dapper said, nodding fervently, though his own words came out in a choked whisper. "Surely, amen." He thought, *If I get out of this place alive, I will never leave the Netherlands again. I will never leave Utrecht again. I will never leave my house.*

As though he had caught the unspoken words, the Reverend Kirtley rose slowly to his feet, and all his attention was on Olfert Dapper. The musket did not swing to point directly at him, but neither was it pointing as much away from him as he would have preferred. The Reverend said, "It is necessary that you leave No Popery this very day. I lament to say it, but I can brook no dispute." The toneless words sounded like millstones grinding into motion.

"Today? Why today? What makes me . . . why am I suddenly become so unwelcome between one minute and the next?" But he already knew, which lent a certain hollowness to his protestations. *Of course. Hoist by your own petard, clever Dapper.*

"You have seen what you have seen, and it is vain to pretend that you fail to understand its import. The Evil One has taken my wife for his own—been *permitted* to take her, because she was clearly the weaker vessel of—" to his credit, he did falter here—"of our household. Unworthy as I am, I remain the head of this greater household of No Popery, and it would not be advisable to have it known . . ." He made a slight helpless gesture with his hands, without finishing the sentence.

Considering that his passionate desire to leave Maine, Sagadahock, and this entire miserable outpost of ignorance and fear dated from his first day in No Popery, Dr. Dapper was astonished at the flare of genuine anger which possessed him at the minister's words. He was close to losing English in his rage. "You for your wife care nothing, hypocrite you—only for your standing in this place, this . . . this—" and here he did use a Netherlandish word—"that you call a village. Your wife is with the Duyvil better off than she was with you—"

At which point the Reverend Kirtley swung his musket viciously across Dr. Dapper's face, knocking him down. He stared up into the bell-mouth of the musket and the minister's strangely composed, almost expressionless visage. The Reverend Kirtley said, "I grieve to have had to injure you, my friend, but I could not permit you to continue abusing me in such a fashion." He cocked his head to study Dr. Dapper's face, clucking softly to himself. "I see your mouth is bleeding—I pray you, by your leave—" He reached out to wipe the blood away with the edge of a sleeve.

Dr. Dapper struck his hand away, which was not behavior he would ever have advised to anyone facing a madman armed with a musket and the favor of God. He rose shakily to his feet and said, quietly but clearly, "No wonder your wife ran off with Heer Duyvil. Who would not?"

The musket came up sharply, but the Reverend Kirtley neither shot him nor struck him again. Equally calmly, he responded, "You see, obviously, why you must leave us, and leave directly." It was not a question. The Reverend said, "One such public declaration, even a mere rumor, born—as they always are—of a mere private thought . . . and confusion is come upon poor No Popery. You are a doctor—you understand about contagion. Confusion leads inevitably to chaos, Sir, and chaos is the portal to Hell, as utter, unshakable faith is the threshold and fortress of Heaven. I cannot imagine, good Dutch Calvinist as you are, that you would gainsay me on that point."

Dr. Dapper did not reply, but looked away, trying to focus on the maze of footprints surrounding them. His head was still ringing from the blow, and when he shook it to clear his vision, his neck hurt. But it seemed clear at least that Remorse Kirtley had indeed ridden off on the unicorn, with Rain Coming—as he was somehow certain it must have been—mounted as well. Olfert Dapper imagined him with one hand tangled gently in the unicorn's mane, his black eyes alight with the lost brilliance of long-dead stars. In his sly, sidestepping, faithless heart, Dr. Dapper whispered, "Go well. Yes."

The Reverend Kirtley said briskly, "Isaac da Silva will be leaving at dawn." Dr. Dapper knew the cross-grained old Portuguese peddler as sour company, but honorable enough in his trade. "He will carry you to where the Penobscot becomes navigable—from there, you should have no difficulty finding transportation downcoast to Falmouth, and a ship to take you wherever suits your fortune. Tonight, when you assemble such belongings as you may care to take with you—" he shrugged, and very nearly smiled—"I would consider it a kindness if you would leave behind some of your most excellent stomach medicaments. I have never known their like for immediate relief."

"It would be my honor," Dr. Dapper replied. "But if it should come to my attention that you have blamed the Abenaki people for your wife's disappearance, or that they have been harmed in any way—"

The Reverend Kirtley nodded gravely. "You have my word."

They walked back to the village of No Popery in silence, and parted there. The minister went home to a house that no longer held Mistress Remorse Kirtley; and Olfert Dapper applied a bit of last winter's bear grease to his torn lip, then began to pack the few things he would bother to take along on his journey to whatever might await him in Holland. Prison, perhaps, perhaps Margot Zeldenthuis . . . Olfert Dapper had always recognized those moments when it was best to leave his fate to whims beyond his own.

It was a longer night's work than it should have been, considering how little he actually meant to take along. A handful of dried herbs . . . a small, extremely sharp knife . . . a jar of wild grape preserve (payment for setting and splinting a child's broken arm) . . . a couple of grotesquely abscessed molars . . . his pinewood mortar and pestle, the shallow bowl still containing a dusting of crushed tansy, the flower's camphorlike aroma lingering . . . a fragment of dark lace, carrying its own aroma . . . each of these was charged with a memory of this ridiculous, terrifying, terrifyingly beautiful new world that had unicorns in it. He was leaving with far more than he had brought.

When he was done, he sat on the front step—the only step, in fact—of his little house, built by his neighbors, and waited in the still-warm night for the grumble of Isaac da Silva's wagon wheels, which always sounded to him like the peddler's wearily complaining voice. Exhausted as he was, he had no expectation of sleep: the day had been too draining for that, and he felt as though he might never sleep again. All the same, his eyelids did drift closed from time to time—though never for long, to judge by the moon—and so it was that Rain Coming seemed to materialize out of nothing before him, as silent, as profoundly still, and as indubitably *present* as ever. Dr. Dapper did not rise to greet the Indian, but smiled, although it hurt his mouth. He said, "I will miss you."

He thought that Rain Coming nodded slightly, but he might have been wrong. He asked, "Is she with your people?" When that did elicit a nod, Dr. Dapper chided the Abenaki mildly, saying, "You see, you had it backward. She has come to you first, and I am only leaving now. It was you she went away with?"

Rain Coming definitely nodded this time. Olfert Dapper asked, "Will she be well with you?"

"Little time," Rain Coming responded. "Long time . . ." He shrugged and shook his head slightly. He said, "Sometime. Somewhere." He made a gesture with both hands, as though he were pushing away the horizon.

"You mean that she has long journeys yet ahead of her?" Rain Coming did not reply. Dr. Dapper said slowly, "I am sad for her. Tell her that I wish . . ." But he had no idea what he would wish for Remorse Kirtley, and so he simply said, "Keep her safe while she is with you—and tell her that I will never forget her. Please tell her that."

"For you," the Abenaki said. He reached into the deerskin pouch that hung ever at his waist and produced, crumpled and slightly frayed on one side, the small Dutch-style cap that Olfert Dapper had never seen Mistress Kirtley without, except on the one occasion. He accepted it hesitantly, his throat suddenly too dry to thank Rain Coming for bringing the gift. He could only manage to nod himself, bending his head over the cap for a brief moment. There was no smell of her. He had hoped there would be.

Rain Coming had turned away before Dr. Dapper heard da Silva's wagon coming. He said, "The unicorn. I still do not know your word for it, but I know you have one." The Abenaki paused, but did not turn again. Dr. Dapper asked, "Did she . . . did you both ride it? I have imagined so."

Rain Coming looked back at him then, but said nothing. The peddler's wagon sounded closer; he tried not to think about what the ungreased axles would sound like during the long ride ahead. Raising his voice, he said, "I saw it twice, and I had no right, I know that. I should never . . . did it . . . I mean, the creature—did it . . . do you think. . . ?" But he did not know what he meant to ask about the unicorn, any more than he knew what he wanted Remorse Kirtley's life to be, and so he never finished the question.

The night was dark yet, but a cock crowed sleepily in Schoolmaster Prouty's coop, and the bulk of Isaac da Silva's wagon was now visible as it neared Dr. Dapper's house. He rose to bring out his belongings, but realized as he did so that Rain Coming was still looking fully at him, and that the Abenaki's eyes had changed, becoming as they had been when they two had sight of the unicorn for the first time. Rain Coming's eyes were wide and young, brilliantly young as Dr. Dapper had never seen them, and so painfully clear that he could not look directly into them for long. Rain Coming said softly, "No more," and there was no sorrow or loss in his voice, but only an aching joy. "Never come back," he said again, almost singing it. "Never no more. Gone away."

Then he was gone too, and Isaac da Silva was demanding that Dr. Dapper get himself and his scraps of rubbish into the wagon immediately, if he thought he was going to stand there and let his fine horse get chilled.

Olfert Dapper rode all that first day facing backward, turning a woman's dowdy Dutch cap over and over between his hands. But the next morning, he placed Mistress Remorse Kirtley's cap carefully into his pocket, and, sitting up beside the peddler, he set his face toward the sea.

ABOUT THE AUTHOR

Peter Soyer Beagle is the internationally bestselling and much-beloved author of numerous classic fantasy novels and collections, including *The Last Unicorn, Tamsin, The Line Between, Sleight of Hand, Summerlong,* and *In Calabria.* He is the editor of *The Secret History of Fantasy* and the co-editor of *The Urban Fantasy Anthology.*

Born in Manhattan and raised in the Bronx, Beagle began to receive attention for his artistic ability even before he received a scholarship to the University of Pittsburgh. Exceeding his early promise, he published his first novel, *A Fine & Private Place,* at nineteen, while still completing his degree in creative writing. Beagle's follow-up, *The Last Unicorn,* is widely considered one of the great works of fantasy. It has been made into a feature-length animated film, a stage play, and a graphic novel.

Beagle went on to publish an extensive body of acclaimed works of fiction and nonfiction. He has written widely for both stage and screen, including the screenplay adaptations for *The Last Unicorn* and the animated film of *The Lord of the Rings* and the well-known "Sarek" episode of *Star Trek.*

As one of the fantasy genre's most-lauded authors, Beagle is the recipient of the Hugo, Nebula, Mythopoeic, and Locus awards as well as the Grand Prix de l'Imaginaire. He has also been honored with the World Fantasy Life Achievement Award and the Inkpot Award from the Comic-Con convention, given for major contributions to fantasy and science fiction.

Beagle lives in Richmond, California, where he is working on too many projects to even begin to name.